THE
HONG KONG
GAMBIT

A PLOT TO BUY THAILAND

A Novel

PHILLIP CHURCH

Fulton Books
Meadville, PA

Published by Fulton Books 2022

ISBN 978-1-63985-114-0 (paperback)
ISBN 978-1-63985-115-7 (digital)

Printed in the United States of America

Dedicated to Rampueng

ACKNOWLEDGMENTS
AND DISCLAIMER

I am deeply grateful to all those who helped me research and write *The Hong Kong Gambit*. Retired navy pilot Michael Rimmington was generous with his time and patient with his explanations of how to fly and land a passenger plane in trouble. Fellow University of Chicago Thai alumni willingly shared their knowledge about Thailand's financial world. Members of the Thai media, notably from the English-language *Bangkok Post*, helped me understand the country's sex industry, and academicians at Thailand's Chulalongkorn University interpreted the subtle nature of Confucian capitalism and the intricate workings of the Thai economy. I owe an especially deep thanks to Rampueng Phoeksoeugn, who introduced me to the Thai fishing village that in the story became Ban Khao, and who helped me learn from its members and elders about the challenges they faced from the modernizing world around them.

For helping me assemble on paper a story that is hopefully engaging and readable, I thank fellow writers Judy Politzer, Eileen Curtis, and Esther MacLively and reviewers Grace Fox, Roger and Gail Doughty, Billy Souders, Robert Dakan, and Joanne Fields.

Finally and most importantly, I thank Connie, my wife, for the tireless hours she gave to editing drafts and to being there when I needed to talk about the novel's characters and tease out the story they were compelling me to write.

While *The Hong Kong Gambit* is a fictional tale built around actual events, I take full responsibility for any errors of fact upon which it is based.

AUTHOR'S NOTE

Chaos theory. It's an esoteric branch of the sciences and mathematics that attempts to model relationships between outwardly random and independent events. Frequently cited in descriptions of chaos theory is the challenge of quantifying the impact of a butterfly flapping its wings in the forests of an African country, say Cameroon, and weather conditions in, say, northern California. The advent of supercomputers has greatly enhanced theoreticians' capacity to handle millions of variables and calculations to formulate connections between disparate occurrences such as these with the goal of identifying order in chaos.

Events in the geopolitical and financial worlds also lend themselves to the application of chaos theory. This author, however, is not aware of much application to date of chaos theory in the political and economic sciences. That's a shame. Global financial markets offer many opportunities for the curious to explore possible relationships between seemingly independent occurrences. *The Hong Kong Gambit* responds to one such opportunity. It draws a fictional but plausible line between two outwardly random and unrelated recent events in the international arena.

The first was the turnover of the British island protectorate of Hong Kong to mainland Chinese administration on July 1, 1997. The second event, following less than two days later, was the collapse of Thailand's national currency, the *baht*, with severe recessionary ripple effects throughout East Asia, from Japan to Indonesia. These two events were covered in international news media as if they were separate and distinct. But were they?

One explanatory variable that a supercomputer might pick up is the Chinese "triads," the organized crime syndicates, which operated with relative impunity from Hong Kong during the period of British colonial administration until they found themselves in need of a new country base of operations once Hong Kong came under the less permissive control of Mainland China. A potential new home for the syndicates? Open and welcoming Thailand.

The existence of the Chinese crime syndicates would not seem to be of much consequence to US investors. However, sporadic reporting from the region hints that Chinese syndicates operating out of Hong Kong had for years been cloaking the comingling of their illicit revenues from gambling and sex trafficking with American dollars flowing into Hong Kong real estate and other investment schemes. All the while Wall Street financial managers saw Hong Kong as a high-performing emerging market opportunity for clients seeking to diversify their investment portfolios with international holdings.

The Hong Kong Gambit places the reader in the middle of contemporary concerns about how global economic growth has too often benefitted the few at the expense of the many, all in the guise of the assertion that a rising tide raises all boats. That's true only if those boats don't have holes—political corruption, government ineptitude, public ignorance—in them, as is the more likely scenario in parts of the world like Asia. Add to that a region where corporate operations are more opaque and financial market oversight less rigorous than in the United States, then conditions exist for illicit gain often at the expense of those least equipped to defend themselves.

Those were the conditions prevailing in the late 1990s when, as *The Hong Kong Gambit* tells, the butterfly is a young Thai village girl raped and forced into prostitution; the impact is collapse of the Thai *baht* and financial turmoil throughout East Asia. Remote connections, yes. Fictional circumstances, certainly. Impossible outcome? Let the reader be the judge.

CHAPTER 1

Paul Ellis broke stride to pause at the Hong Kong International Airport terminal's large glass windows that looked out at the Air Siam jetliner parked at his gate. The plane sat shrouded in a rising mist from a passing nighttime summer storm that had dampened the warm tarmac. Ground crews rushed to load the last of the passengers' luggage as overhead spotlights pierced the mist. The scene produced an eerie halo effect around the plane that made Paul shudder.

HKIA, a major Asian air transport hub, was congested during the daylight hours, but at Air Siam's Flight 224 scheduled 1:00 a.m. departure time, most of the concourses and gateways were deserted and quiet. This meant few air traffic delays to tarnish the small regional airline's nearly perfect on-time departure and arrival record. Most important for the airline's owner, Air Siam's early morning departure slot allowed discreet boarding of its passengers. A scheduled early dawn arrival at Bangkok's Don Mueang airport three hours later enabled Air Siam to disembark its passengers with equal anonymity.

The passenger flight manifest on this day in late July 1997 was typical for Air Siam, though somewhat unique among Asian airlines. First class was sparsely filled, mostly with a few Asian business conventioneers headed to meetings and recreation in Thailand. The only non-Asians listed on the first-class passenger manifest were the last-minute book-ings of three Americans.

The coach class passenger list revealed the uniqueness of Air Siam flights. The manifest showed nearly 150 names, Thai names, and after each the notations: "Occupation: Domestic Worker" and "Status: Deportee." These coach-class passen-gers had been boarded through a separate gangway before the first-class passengers began arriving at the gate.

Paul found his way down the jetway and into the belly of the plane. He slumped down into his seat, drained and exhausted. His two traveling companions, Dan and Ben, had already arrived and collapsed into theirs. The three had just endured a long fifteen-hour polar route flight between Washington Dulles and Hong Kong International. Turbulent air during much of the flight made sleeping impossible in their tight coach class seats.

The United Airlines flight attendants had done all they could to make the rough flight tolerable, but some passen-gers had fared worse than others. Ben couldn't keep anything down and had to bolt frequently for the nearest toilet to calm his agitated stomach. *Well,* Paul thought, *thank goodness for Ben that he had been sitting next to me, not Dan, a seasoned former navy fighter pilot. Ben would've gotten no sympathy from Dan.*

To make matters worse, a messy mid-summer weather front had delayed their US departure, so the three Americans missed their scheduled Bangkok connection in Hong Kong. Air Siam, it turned out, was a timely alternative. On this final leg of their trip they at least could feel more comfortable in more spacious seats in the sparsely populated first-class sec-tion of the plane. Paul sat in the window seat next to Dan on the aisle. Ben sat by himself in the aisle seat directly in front of them.

Only Dan, the most fastidious of the group, had enough interest to explore the plane's main cabin. His inquisitive nature forced him to take in his temporary surroundings even in his sleep-deprived state. Despite efforts of the Air Siam flight attendants to keep him in his seat with a predeparture drink, Dan maneuvered past them into the coach cabin, declaring he was looking for an American magazine to read. A few minutes later he returned and plopped down in his seat, smiling broadly.

"Why are you so goddamned happy?" groused Ben. "Did you get a quickie from a flight attendant while you were back there?"

"Nope. But see for yourself," Dan taunted. "The scenery is quite attractive in coach class."

"Not on your life. I'm going nowhere." Ben spoke loud enough for Dan and Paul, as well as the passenger across the aisle, to hear him clearly.

The passenger across the aisle, a short, gaunt young Asian man, had been the last to board before the cabin doors were closed. He had come up the aisle, boarding pass in hand, and stared directly down at Ben. "This my seat!" he declared.

Indeed, Ben had chosen a vacant aisle seat in the empty row in front of his two friends instead of the one assigned him directly across the aisle from them. He could see no difference in the two aisle seats; he told Paul and Dan as they settled in.

"Take mine over there, if it's all the same to you," Ben said to the Asian man and pointed across the aisle. "We're traveling together." He inclined his head toward his friends behind him.

"It is not all same to me," said the young man. "You are in my seat. I want to sit there."

Ben displayed no desire to move his short stalky body until they landed in Bangkok.

"Look, there's two dozen empty first-class seats. Be my guest. Take any one of them!" Ben's voice was nearly drained now of any tone of civility.

The young Asian was not to be put off. He appealed to the approaching flight attendant who appeared more concerned about getting all the passengers seated for takeoff. Her gentle intercessions on behalf of the passenger were futile. Ben was not moving. The standoff continued until the pilot announced they could not depart until all passengers were seated. Outwardly resigned, the young man dropped into the aisle seat across from Ben, fastened his seat belt, and transferred his glare from the flight attendant back to Ben.

From his seat behind Ben, Dan took in this minor altercation with a snicker and whispered between the seatbacks. "Way to stand up, er, sit down to that five-foot weenie, tiger!"

Ben snorted and gripped his armrests.

Without further incident, Air Siam lifted off and set its course across the South China Sea toward Bangkok. At the controls were two Aussie pilots and their Thai flight engineer. Since its inaugural flight six years earlier in 1991, Air Siam had a special agreement with Qantas Airlines for the lease and operation of the Australian carrier's older equipment. With the agreement came maintenance and piloting services and use of the Qantas overseas terminal facilities at off-peak times. In all, from its Bangkok home base, Air Siam ran biweekly flights to Seoul, Tokyo, Manila, and Hong Kong in the north and to Singapore, Sydney, and Brisbane in the south, along with a handful of domestic flights within Thailand.

These arrangements served Air Siam's owner well. Aussie pilots were dependable and the retired Qantas hand-me-down jetliners cheap but airworthy. The small Thai air transport firm had carved out a small market niche of East and South Asia routes that held little interest to Thai Airways, the much larger national airline. Air Siam's flights were bush league in the highly competitive East Asian air transport market. Air Siam's owner was not concerned that his airline failed to make a profit. The airline was part of the owner's much larger Thai business conglomerate to which the small regional airline contributed much more than passenger and cargo revenue.

Once they were in the air and leveling off at cruising altitude, Dan broke the silence. "Well, thanks for getting us back on track, Paul. Let's hope this is the end of our travel problems."

Dan had by far the most flying experience and endurance among them. Paul knew that. He saw, though, that Dan was not going to let him off easy when his planning and execution fell short. "Christ! I got us upgraded to first class on this leg. Doesn't that count for something?"

Paul had meticulously planned and prepared for this outing, an Asian golf and deep-sea fishing trip for himself and his friends. The original concept was his, and he had promoted it vigorously. The three, all early retirees from government service, had established a bond over nearly five years now, since they discovered their common interests. Together they formed their Early Out Club and invited a few other fellow retiree friends to join them for summer biking trips and winter ski outings or afternoon poker lunches. The three became the core of the club's members.

Paul often wondered what held the three of them together. They were an odd mixture who shared little in common besides being turned loose early from government careers. Paul was the one showing the most signs of middle age though he kept his lanky body in good shape with regular golfing and jogging. He was the only one, he recognized, with a wife and kids, two college-age daughters, at home. Dan was tall and lanky, a handsome guy, widowed but still a good catch for any woman who could succeed breaking through his aloofness to relationships.

Paul saw in Ben almost a polar opposite of Dan. His short, paunchy, unkempt appearance belied the clever CIA snoop he had been until he took early retirement and never looked back. A family man he was not. By the time Ben moved in next door to Paul and his family with his most recent wife, he had been through at least four unsuccessful marriages, as each woman came to realize that he was as much a roamer as a romantic. Ben loved the thrill of the chase when it came to dating, but once successful, he quickly lost interest and admitted to Paul that he felt stifled by any commitment expected of him.

Perhaps it was the very fact that the three of them had so little in common that they felt more relaxed together. No competition to top each other's career accomplishments. Rather, by sharing life's stories they each found they could vicariously live a different life through the other's experiences.

It was Paul who suggested that for their next big outing together they tackle a more far-afield adventure—a couple of weeks away from it all in exotic lands. Paul's companions warmed to the idea slowly and only after imposing a series of conditions. No destinations where they might run into ladies' garden clubs! No budget cruises with septuagenarians. It has gotta have adventure; it has gotta be suave.

Paul felt pretty streetwise internationally as a retired commercial attaché, who served most of his career working in US embassies abroad. He had not revisited Thailand since he was posted there early in his diplomatic career, and it did not take much research to come up with a list of the appealing options the country had to offer. Some of the best golf courses, some of the best deep-sea fishing, not to mention plenty of expat bars with stimulating go-go girl entertainment.

"It's on the other side of the world," Ben had been the first to point out. Like their military colleagues and career diplomats, Central Intelligence Agency employees enjoy the option of early retirement. Ben had opted for his early out from the agency after serving a bit more than two decades buried in the bowels of its headquarters building in Langley, Virginia, where he worked as a translator and analyst of Mainland Chinese media and communications. Ben was seeking a life's change, a second journey, as his CIA retirement seminar coach had called it, but after more than a year since leaving the agency, he had yet to find that second calling.

"A downer in getting there, yes," Paul confessed, "but airline connections are pretty manageable." Paul put together the program, and as expected, it was he, Dan, and Ben who had finally rallied around it. Most of their other Early Out Club retirees had wives who weren't willing to give their husbands such loose reins as a two-week trip to Thailand. Well, so much the better. A threesome made for a solid and supportive group on the golf course during the day or touring the bars at night. Enough so that they could convince themselves that they would take care of each other and keep themselves out of serious trouble.

Both Paul and Dan had done enough diplomatic and military flying to know that long hauls can turn out differently than planned. Flexibility needed to be built in. So when they found themselves arriving late into Hong Kong and missing their onward connection, Paul stepped in to get them out of their fix. He turned for help to the United

Airlines Hong Kong agent, who at first offered to lodge the threesome for the night at a downtown Hong Kong hotel and schedule them on the next day's connecting flight. The offer appeared attractive. Some rest, a shower, and a change of clothes seemed most agreeable, particularly for Ben, who had barfed up half his innards during the Pacific crossing.

Then an alternative arose. The United agent's computer showed space available on another flight scheduled to leave shortly for Bangkok. There was just enough time for the group and their luggage to make the connection. Moreover, she could book them all in first class at no added cost. No hour-long trip into Hong Kong or the hassle of a departure the next day.

Paul jumped at the offer. It meant they could still salvage an otherwise lost day of their vacation. They could get back on schedule, sleep it off when they arrived, and have the traveling behind them. First class would be a balm for an otherwise rocky start of what they had looked to as an exotic getaway. Ben held out for the overnight stay, but Paul mustered support from Dan, and together they convinced Ben to tough it out. They all were numb from lack of sleep at this point, anyhow. Why not see it through and get it over? Before Ben had a chance to say another word, they darted down the largely vacant concourse of Hong Kong's glass-encased international terminal to the isolated gate where the Air Siam flight was in its final boarding stage.

An hour into the flight, Paul and Dan were awake and hungry enough for the warm meal offered them by the cabin attendant. As expected, Ben declined. Even the smell of food was more than Ben's stomach could tolerate. No sooner did the meals appear than Ben hastily unbuckled himself from the seat and headed toward the toilet in the front of the cabin.

What unfolded in the next moments made Paul feel every bit as ill. As soon as Ben closed the toilet compartment door behind him, Paul and Dan saw the young Asian slink from his seat across the aisle and slip quickly into Ben's. "Oh god!" Dan muttered. "Are we going to have an East-West confrontation all the way to Bangkok?" Then they both looked on as the Asian crouched down on the floor and groped under the seat where Ben had been sitting. In the next instant the young man moved swiftly toward the front of the plane. Paul caught sight of a gun in his hand. "He had a gun planted under that seat!" Paul whispered to Dan. "That's why he made such a fuss over seats."

"He's headed to the cockpit," Dan interrupted in a matter-of-fact tone, but Paul saw in his face a look of foreboding.

Several moments passed before they heard muffled thuds in rapid succession from the front of the plane. Then, silence. A look of terror on the airline attendant's face as the young Asian stood behind her with a gun pointed at her neck drove home to Paul what was happening. In the next moment the young Asian shoved the flight attendant forward into an empty seat and directed the semiautomatic pistol at the first-class passengers seated in front of him.

"This plane is now under command of the Chinese Peoples' Liberation Army! We are taking control of the plane to rescue all the passengers and show the communist and capitalist pigs we will not tolerate human slavery!" he shouted. His voice was tense, and his eyes followed the aim of the pistol in his hand as he swept it from left to right and back across the breadth of seats in the Cabin. "You will fasten yourselves in seats. Put hands behind heads. Not to move. Do it now!"

Ben opened the toilet door at the sound of the commotion to see the weapon pointed at his head.

"You want what the pilots got? Go ahead. It no matter to me!" said the hijacker.

"Why you little—"

"Ben, can it! We've got a loony on board," Dan whispered. "Do what the nice man says!" he added in a more audible voice. Ben complied and hustled back to his seat.

Paul watched as the hijacker used his free hand to take the flight attendants' cabin phone from its wall mount and talk over the plane's loudspeakers in Chinese.

"He's calling for his pals on the flight," Ben translated in a low whisper.

"He's not alone? There are others?" asked Paul.

"Apparently so," said Ben.

A long silence followed before the hijacker repeated his message over the plane's speaker system. Still, no one came forward. No one spoke.

Several more minutes of anguished silence followed.

Then Paul began to feel it, the sensation of the plane slipping away from beneath him. They were in a descent, gradual, yes, but headed down.

The hijacker must have felt it too. Again, this time in a more frantic tone, he cried out into the cabin phone. Ben interpreted. "He's pleading for his partners to come forward, to pilot the plane." Still there was no movement from anywhere in the plane. The sinking motion became more pronounced, and wails from both passenger sections filled the plane.

Paul sat motionless with his hands clasped behind his head. His elbows rubbed against Dan's next to him. Awareness of the moment began to take hold of him. The plane was on a pilotless descent toward the open expanse of ocean below. In moments it would all be over. Shit! Why was it ending this way? What a royal screwup! Probably nothing would ever be found of them. His premature death he could reluctantly accept. But not this kind of ending for his friends! He had gotten them into this situation. And now they were along for the same fatal final ride.

As the plane continued to pitch forward, Paul saw the young hijacker's features melt from nervous resolve into beseeching denial. The young man slouched back against the cabin bulkhead, the weight of his weapon appearing to overwhelm his arm and pull it slowly downward. Then, in an instant of renewed energy, the hand and arm appeared to take on a detached life of their own, raising the weapon swiftly to the man's temple.

Paul winced as he heard the sickening thud of the weapon and saw blood and gore explode from the hijacker's head across the bulkhead as his lifeless body slumped to the floor.

CHAPTER 2

Dan Spencer had been thinking far ahead of his two companions the instant he heard the muffled shots from the cockpit. In the following moments when the hijacker held them at gunpoint, Dan's mind raced over scenarios of what might have taken place. The one he kept coming back to was the one he feared most. Both captains and the flight engineer dead or incapacitated. The plane was pilotless.

Dan's twenty years as a navy pilot and then a brief boring stint flying buses—commercial jetliners—had taught him to read flying sensations his travel companions could not have recognized. The repeated subtle adjustments of the plane's ailerons indicated to him that the plane had been placed on autopilot, the altitude and course preset by the pilots. Good, as long as it lasted. But now the sensation of the plane's descent indicated forward pressure on the controls. Had one of the pilots slumped forward onto the yoke?

Light pressure wouldn't affect the autopilot. The course and altitude would remain unchanged. But if the pressure increased, as Dan feared it had, then the autopilot would obediently defer to whomever, alive or dead, was at the controls. That would explain the plane's current accelerating descent, placing it in a power dive.

Dan remembered the pilots announcing the plane's planned 35,000-foot cruising altitude. He calculated that with no letup on the throttle, the plane was diving at close to

250 knots; from that altitude and current angle of descent, they'd hit the water in less than five minutes.

As the hijacker's body hit the floor, Dan sent his dinner tray flying and leaped from his seat. He shouted at Paul as he rushed up the aisle. "Follow me. Now!"

Nearing the cockpit, he slowed his steps just long enough to reach down and grab the revolver from the hijacker's limp hand. Dead, most likely, he imagined, but his navy training taught him not to play the probabilities. Besides, if by chance there were other hijackers on board, Dan now had a weapon with whatever unspent ammo remained.

By the time Dan passed the hijacker's body, the plane's angle of descent was so steep it propelled him forward faster than he could run. Catching himself against the cabin door, he leveraged it open and lurched into the cramped cockpit.

The cockpit layout looked familiar, but the scene before him did not. Dan had been certified and checked out on a passenger jet like Air Siam's Boeing 707 early in his commercial flying days. Knowing the flight controls well, he instinctively drilled in on the flight-deck gauges and their readings.

His eyes went first to the plane's altimeter that read just over 25,000 feet, down substantially already from their cruising altitude. The altimeter needle continued winding down at a constant pace. Dan recognized from his many hours of flying that only a few minutes remained before the plane would hit the ocean.

He saw that a struggle had ensued, and both the pilot and copilot appeared to have taken bullets to their heads. The flight engineer as well. The copilot apparently had been shot in the head after getting up from his seat. He had fallen in the narrow space between the pilots' seats. The pilot lay slumped over the control yoke, pushing it forward, and as

Dan suspected, his body weight was overriding the autopilot's altitude-hold and putting the plane into a descent.

Dan slipped into the empty copilot's seat and pulled back all four engine throttles, a move that would save him precious seconds by slowing the speed of the descent. Knowing that in a 707, both the pilot's and copilot's control yokes were connected to the same set of cables, Dan pulled back with all his strength on the copilot's yoke to raise the nose of the plane. All the while, he had to fight the force of the dead pilot's body for control of the plane.

"Paul!" Dan shouted. "We've got to get the pilot's body off the yoke. Take off your belt, put it around the pilot's neck, leverage yourself against the seat, and pull his body back!"

Easier said than done, Dan recognized. As he attempted to ease up the nose of the descending jetliner, the pull of gravity intensified on both of them. He could see Paul struggle against the sensation of everything getting heavier, just like a roller coaster hitting the bottom of a drop and heading up. As the plane slowly pitched up, the weight of the dead pilot's body dropped to normal. Even so, it was clear Paul was mustering everything he had to pull the pilot's body off the controls. Finally, Paul gave Dan a thumbs-up.

"Good! Now fasten your belt around the seatback to secure his body. That will keep his body in place for the rest of the flight."

Paul's work was done for the moment, but Dan's was not. While the nose started to come up, Dan knew that he had slowed the dive but had not yet ended the plane's fall. The momentum of descent still exceeded the upward lift forces on the plane's wings. The altimeter continued to unwind as they dropped below ten thousand feet…eight thousand feet…six thousand feet…five thousand feet…four thousand feet.

From being almost seven miles high, the plane now had less than a mile of air separating it from the ocean. At three thousand feet, Dan had no recourse but to apply more elevator and increase engine thrust to make the plane fight more against its descent. Not too much upward pull on the wings of the descending plane, Dan was aware, or it could pull the wings off the aircraft. His focus now was dampening the impact of hitting the water by raising the nose and landing tail first. The plane complained with audible shuddering and buffeting. Then at 1,500 feet, the shuddering subsided, the downward momentum dissipated, and the unwinding altimeter needle came to a halt. Dan gradually applied more power to accelerate the plane into level flight.

Moonlight reflecting off the white caps of the ocean waves just below them gave Dan the sensation of landing lights on a ghostlike runway. For a long moment he remained motionless and frozen to the controls. *Not yet, boss,* he thought to himself. *I'm not ready to go out yet!* Slowly, as if he had just executed a normal takeoff, like the ones he'd done hundreds of times as a navy pilot, he pushed forward on the throttles and increased power to all four engines. As he did, he let up a bit more on the yoke to increase airspeed, boost lift, and coax the plane back up to cruising altitude. It was then that he began to shake and to sweat. The reality of what he had accomplished finally fought its way into his consciousness.

Things in the cockpit were hardly back to normal, but for the moment, the plane was flying safely. Paul's voice brought Dan back to the moment. "Ben! Help me out here. Grab the copilot's legs and help me pull him into the galley. We've got to get him and the flight engineer out of the way. Check to see if you can detect any signs of life. I'll check the pilot. They both look pretty bad, pretty bloody. I don't have much hope."

"No signs of life," Ben reported as he bent over the copilot's body, then the flight engineer.

"The pilot neither," added Paul.

Dan looked up at Paul and Ben from the copilot's seat. "The plane's flying stable now. But we have a lot to do to get us back on course and on the ground somewhere friendly."

That last task was a particular concern to Dan. He had no desire to put the plane down where he and his pals would undergo interrogations by countries that had issues with the United States, particularly China and Vietnam, both of them along their route to Thailand. They had to get back on course and catch up on time or else they might get intercepted by fighter aircraft from those not-so-friendly countries investigating why they were where they were.

"Ben, I need you in the flight engineer's seat. You're going to read some instruments and gauges for me. Are you up to that?"

Ben nodded, now oblivious to the stomach discomfort he'd felt only minutes earlier. Settling into the flight engineer's swivel seat, he took in the array of gauges and the radar screen indicating their course and direction.

"Paul," Dan continued, "find one of the flight attendants! One that speaks English as well as Thai and Chinese if that's possible. You and the flight attendant need to calm the passengers. Have the flight attendant announce that the plane is back on course after some severe turbulence and headed to Thailand as scheduled. I suspect you will not find any more troublemakers on the flight, but if you do, alert me somehow. I could give you the hijacker's weapon just in case, but that could spook the passengers and crew even more. Are you okay with that?"

"Sure," said Paul. "You just fly the plane. We'll try to calm the cabin crew and passengers."

Ben wasn't so sure. "Shouldn't we call for help? Shouldn't we let any nearby air traffic control know our situation?"

"No, Ben!" Dan's voice was firm. "Well, yes! Yes, we should. By international protocols this is a Mayday situation we're in. But I am not sure there are any real friends nearby to help us. And there are a lot of not-so-friendly 'friends' who'd love to help us down on their terms. I don't want to alert them. Not with an emergency call for help right now. I guess we're well within two hundred miles of the Chinese coast. China claims its national waters extend out two hundred miles from its shores, not a twenty-mile limit like the US. We need to scramble back up to our cruise altitude and reset our course to Bangkok before we're noticed by anybody's radar. And that's gonna take a few minutes."

Dan remembered that the pilots said they'd need to divert from their regular route to fly around a weather front along the Southeast Asian coast but that it would not delay them too much past their scheduled 5:00 a.m. arrival time in Bangkok.

"With the storm the pilots reported at takeoff from Hong Kong, we should have been routed south and then west over Vietnam into Thailand. I don't look to be a guest of either the Vietnamese or Chinese governments right now. And I don't think you and Ben want that either. Both China and Vietnam will be alerted by any Mayday call, and if they get curious, they might scramble their fighters to escort us to one of their landing fields. We don't need that kind of help."

Dan looked at both Ben and Paul. They were both visibly trembling. *The reality of what they just went through is beginning to settle in,* Dan thought. *I've got to help calm them a bit.*

"At the moment we're flying safe. But we still don't know what exactly is going on here. If I can get us back on course without raising suspicions along the way, Bangkok is still the best place to land. We have an embassy there. We have at least some diplomatic protection. But that won't be the case if we land in China or Vietnam!"

"No disagreement there!" Ben was only too aware that as a CIA employee who had been tracking communist Chinese movements for the past twenty years, he would be an interesting subject to interrogate. "How soon are we expected to report our position again?"

"About now, I would calculate. But first we need to determine what our position is." Dan looked up at Ben. "At some point the pilots were to turn west at a right angle and fly directly into Don Mueang, the two sides of a right triangle if you can picture it. Can you read me our position coordinates on the left lower corner of the radar screen and confim our compass heading from the digital radar readout? We've been in the air for about two hours. We should be getting close to the point where the pilots planned to turn west to Thailand."

"Give me a minute." Ben found the flight engineer's clipboard and jotted down the plane's latitude and longitude readings and its compass course heading without a problem and passed them to Dan. The plane most likely had begun to drift off its intended course soon after the hijacking and while Dan was wrestling with the controls to halt its descent, restore level flight, and regain altitude. From his compass reading and from the coordinates that Ben handed him, Dan could see that the jetliner had strayed too far off course to the west and was approaching the Chinese air defense identification zone, its ADIZ. They most likely would be unobserved until they got into radar range and crossed into the mainland Chinese ADIZ. Dan began a slow rollout to the left and set a course southeast, away from the Chinese mainland and toward the position south of where the plane should have been before the attempted hijacking began.

Dan knew that the only thing that would cause alarm with local air traffic control systems was if the aircraft failed to call in at its designated reporting points. He was also aware that this was a coalition of the willing, and he could cheat and report a position even though that wasn't really where he indicated them to be. But he needed to get back on course before they were detected.

Too late! The plane's radio suddenly came alive. "Please identify yourself!" declared the disembodied voice in broken English over the cockpit speaker.

Dan took a deep breath and responded, "We are flight AS 224 out of Hong Kong destination Don Mueang, Thailand, on a course of two hundred degrees southwest. Deviation from flight plan made to avoid a weather system in route." Dan waited in silence for more than a minute, not sure what to expect as a reply.

Finally, he was relieved to hear the caller confirm his message by repeating it back with no further comments or questions. "That was close! Let's just hope that whatever surveillance the flight is under from the mainland is being handled by a junior officer assigned to the early morning hours while his superiors are asleep."

On the cockpit wall close to Dan's right arm hung the copilot's clipboard with a well-worn Jeppesen flight book of air navigation charts attached. The top chart covered the area where the plane was flying before the attempted hijacking. He paged ahead. The copilot had systematically organized the charts to cover their weather-diverted route all the way to Bangkok. Indeed, they were flying within two hundred miles or so off the coast of the Chinese Hainan Island right now. Dan read the route to himself, each intersection with its random but always five-letter name: "EPDOS, ENBOK, DOSOT, MESOX, and then AirNav PUCAT VOR into Bangkok."

Now, he thought, *which one of these is the next mandatory reporting point and how do we get back on course?*

Then Dan realized he had one more communications option open to him that could come in handy. Their flight would not only be monitored by mainland China but also by his former friends and buddies, the US Pacific Command. Most likely an E-2C Hawkeye airborne early warning aircraft, like he'd flown during the last few years of his navy career, was up there somewhere, perhaps not so far away. They'd be monitoring 24-7 whatever was in the air around them. All military aircraft monitored a common civilian frequency that they could use to communicate with commercial traffic. All commercial aircraft were also equipped with that same radio frequency to allow communication with military flights if required or to signal military aircraft that the plane was not hostile. Dan knew the frequency by heart and keyed it into the radio.

Again, he had to assume that this open frequency might also be monitored by hostiles as well as friendlies. His communication needed to sound as if AS 224 was a routine international flight while at the same time indicating that it was anything but routine. Dan took a deep breath and adjusted the plane's radio to the common US joint military-commercial frequency. "Any fleet command flyboys up tonight? A former E-2C driver needs some help. Anybody in the neighborhood?" Thirty seconds of silence followed.

Then, "We read you," came the disembodied reply in perfect English.

"Our position is 18 degrees, 41 minutes north and 105 degrees, 15 minutes east along Hainan coast. Destination

Don Mueang. Advising of possible interdiction. In need of possible assist." Dan was trying to be circumspect while at the same time communicating a sense of urgency in his message.

"Continue your course to return to international airspace," was the quick reply. "We will attempt to pick you up on radar. Will advise if you have any company headed your way."

Dan maneuvered the plane onto a slight southeastern course and away from mainland China. "Ben!" he shouted. "Monitor the radar screens in front of you. Tell me what you see. You're looking for any moving blips that might show up. If you see any, check to see if any appear to be approaching the center of the screen. That's us!"

From the cockpit window, all Dan could see was solid blackness. There were no clouds now to reflect the moonlight. He was flying totally on instruments.

Several minutes passed, and then the radio came alive again. "Air Siam two-two-four, we have you located. You are a foreign commercial carrier. Please confirm!"

"Affirmative," Dan replied instantly. "Air Siam is a Thai national airline. But it is now under command of a former E-2C jockey. We've had some issues up here with one of the passengers. The regular pilots are incapacitated. Do you read me?"

"We read you, brother! We also have two bogies closing in on you at about four o'clock. Up from Haiku base on Hainan, Island. Do you need assist?"

"Affirmative," replied Dan.

"Roger. It's been a slow night. Time to party. We'll vector a couple friendlies your way to escort you back into international airspace. You need to get there ASAP!"

ASAP? As soon as possible! thought Dan. But it couldn't be soon enough, he worried. "Ben, what do you see?"

"Couple of blips in the lower righthand corner of the screen. Outer corner…but moving toward the center of the screen. Just as you said. What's it mean?"

"It means we will have company soon. In a few minutes we should have a visual from the copilot's side window. We've been off our flight plan route, below assigned altitude, and in Chinese airspace. It appears the Chinese have scrambled a couple of planes to investigate. They could force us to land if they suspect things are not normal aboard. Unlikely they want to precipitate an international incident by forcing down a commercial airliner from a friendly Asian neighbor. But I have no idea what they might know about what's been happening here."

Paul came into the cockpit to update Dan. "Things have quieted down in both passenger sections. The flight attendants are as relieved as the passengers that we are getting back on course to Thailand. Everyone seems to accept our explanation."

Dan smiled for the first time and put the plane back on autopilot while he worked to determine their precise position. He anticipated that the Don Mueang airport control tower would be expecting them to radio in their flight progress when they crossed a preset air intersection. He did not need to be physically at that intersection; over international waters, there was no way anyone could tell he was not, except for his American E-2C Hawkeye friends who were tracking him on radar. But failing to report the correct intersection coordinates would certainly raise concerns for Don Mueang Control and could also alert other nearby airport traffic control systems that all was not routine.

The plane's deviation from Air Siam's scheduled route and assigned altitude during the attempted hijacking had already been enough to alert the Chinese air defense system.

And there they were off his right wing now: two MIG fighters with large red stars on the tails and fuselages.

A large jetliner is relatively slow and stable, and a good fighter pilot can easily maneuver close enough to peer into the plane's cockpit. At night, the lights from the cockpit would illuminate the flight crew. When flying carrier-based fighters, Dan could look into the cockpits of the KC-135 strato-tankers after midair refueling and exchange visible salutes. Now he sensed the pilots off his right wing were similarly looking him up and down as well. He looked over at the dead pilot seated next to him. He hoped the scene in the cockpit looked innocent enough in the dim night light. Several eternally long minutes passed with the Chinese MIGs cruising along beside them. Then two US Navy F-18 Hornets came into view, and the Chinese fighter jets disengaged and peeled off toward the mainland.

Back on course, the last hour of the flight was uneventful. Once Dan confirmed that they were in Thai airspace, he declared a Mayday emergency to Don Mueang flight control. He kept the specifics of the hijacking brief. He'd have time after they landed to explain everything in detail. The flight recorders would've also captured much of the cockpit conversations. Dan focused on following Don Mueang flight control instructions for a straight-in approach and landing, asking only that immediate medical help be available once they were on the ground.

Right on schedule, as if everything had gone routinely, AS 224 touched down at Bangkok's Don Muong International Airport. Dan followed Don Mueang ground control instructions to taxi to a far corner of the airfield near the Thai Air Force hangars and away from the commercial transport terminal.

When the plane came to a stop, Dan sat with his eyes closed and his hands still locked onto the yoke. He knew that ahead of all of them was a long, sleepless day of questioning by Thai authorities about what took place aboard AS 224. No sleep until the Thai interrogations would be over!

Dan looked over at the dead pilot in the seat across from him. He swore to himself that after they were cleared by authorities and rested from a good night's sleep, he'd be on the next available plane back to the United States. He'd already experienced enough excitement from this Early Out Club adventure. He was ready to return home. ASAP!

CHAPTER 3

Inspector Sittichai sat in the lead car of several vehicles that maneuvered like a serpentine funeral procession, headlights on, toward the jetliner that sat isolated at the far end of the Don Mueang International Airport parking apron. It was still early morning. Before these civilian or diplomatic vehicles had been allowed to approach, the Thai military had already surrounded, boarded, and searched the plane, then stationed guards, weapons at the ready, over the still-seated passengers and American "flight crew." Led by the international intelligence wing of the Thai national police, the vehicles' occupants included forensic and investigative specialists as well as representatives from the US and Australian embassies and Air Siam's security and management staff.

As head of the Thai National Police International Intelligence Service team assigned to investigate an attempted hijacking, Inspector Sittichai led the others up the access stairs and into the jetliner. The bloody scene on board forewarned him of a long intense investigation ahead.

From the moment when he was awakened by a predawn call from headquarters, Sittichai had gone over in his head the initial steps he would take and moved quickly to start the process. Of the five fellow Thai investigating officers he could mobilize on short notice that day, he assigned two to interview the three Americans and the other three to the rest of the passengers in the first-class cabin. The coach class passengers, almost all young Thai girls, would be interviewed by his junior officers. No special language capabilities beyond the junior officers' native Thai were required.

"I want the airport VIP lounge sealed off from the public for the day to use in taking passengers' statements," Sittichai instructed airport personnel from his phone on his way to Don Mueang. "I want all interviews conducted before any of the passengers is allowed to depart the airport area. And I want a statement from each passenger individually and out of the hearing of the others." He agreed that an official representative from their respective country embassies could be present if the passengers chose, but he insisted that person would be prohibited from intervening in any way during his team's questioning.

Sittichai was looking for patterns in the witnesses' statements as well as any special facts that might corroborate each individual's story or contradictions that would force him to dig deeper into what had happened aboard the Air Siam flight. He expected that collecting statements would take most of the day, and he imagined the passengers were already quite exhausted. Still, he wanted as much information as possible before time and sleep would begin to erode their memories.

It was late afternoon before Sittichai's team of investigators finished their questioning, and the passengers were sent off under police escort to a nearby hotel for a needed rest. Sittichai instructed his uniformed police to isolate the passengers from the press and prohibited incoming and outgoing phone communications from their hotel rooms unless he first approved them.

"We most certainly want you to communicate with your families back home that you have arrived safely in Thailand," Sittichai explained when challenged by the American passengers for why they were being kept incommunicado. "It is still the early hours of the morning in America. Best to contact your families during the day their time. That will give you some time to rest and recover from the events of your trip."

More importantly, Sittichai wanted time to review the passengers' statements and confer with his investigative team before the local and foreign press and media began tracking down information from the passengers' friends and relatives to construct their own interpretations of events. Even before the plane had landed, Sittichai had obtained a faxed copy of the passenger manifest from Air Siam's Hong Kong dispatcher and had contacted the embassies of each of the non-Thai nationalities on board with a request for background checks. Sittichai was confident of a quick response with information about the Americans from the US embassy authorities, a matter of a day at best. He was equally convinced that the other legations would drag their feet. Still, he wanted the benefit of those reports before he had to face the press himself.

Sittichai had only a small window of time during which he was relatively free to collect and assess information on events surrounding the attempted hijacking. He knew that the airline's owner would follow his investigation closely. Air Siam was a small airline but with a big role in the owner's business empire as Sittichai and several of his colleagues were aware. An incident such as the attempted hijacking, no matter how random it appeared to be on the surface, could well have a deeper backstory and expose forces at play beyond those of a delusional hijacker. The airline's owner would certainly work to control any negative press to come out of the investigation.

Sittichai was also painfully aware of the political delicacy of the situation, of the damage that a poorly reported event could do to the nation's lucrative tourism industry. The attempted hijacking could scare off future passengers concerned about Air Siam's security measures. That could have ripple effects impacting foreigners' trust of the much larger Thai Airways, Thailand's flagship airline, as well. Foreign travelers, he knew, made little distinction between airline companies and were only concerned with the security of air travel and destinations. Because international tourism was such a big revenue earner for the country, few in his government wanted to disrupt it. International travelers had to feel confident that new precautions would be put in place to thwart any such future hijacking attempts on all airlines operating in and out of Thailand.

The most politically convenient conclusion for Sittichai to reach in his investigation was the outwardly obvious one: a deranged hijacker attempts to take over control of a commercial jetliner but is overpowered by passengers who by good fortune had the piloting skills to land the plane safely. Pilots and hijacker dead. Plane and passengers saved. The Thai Prime Minister's office would issue condolences to the Australian government and families of the pilots. Air Siam would commit to improving security and tightening the screening of its passengers. Case closed. End of story. That scenario was one that Sittichai worried that his politically sensitive superiors would be pressured to adopt.

All the more troubling because Sittichai found early reports by the American passengers somewhat disquieting. The three consistently indicated that the hijacker had retrieved a weapon from under the seat originally assigned him on the plane. If true, that suggested there was at least one conspirator involved in planting the weapon. It also meant he faced the daunting task of investigating the airline's ground crews and those servicing the plane in both Bangkok and Hong Kong. Sittichai would ask his Hong Kong counterparts to look into the hijacker's background and interrogate members of the dissident group of which he claimed to be a part.

Hijacking a jetliner put any dissident group in an entirely different league from those groups which simply organized demonstrations and protests against social injustices they perceived. A hijacking would give the group considerable immediate attention but would be a tremendous liability in conducting civil disobedience in the long run. Their movements would be watched much more closely, their leadership periodically locked up to destabilize their efforts. For those reasons, not many dissident groups chose to go the path of becoming international pariahs unless convinced there were big gains to be made for their efforts.

Sittichai mused that lately mainline China, the Peoples Republic of China, the PRC, was showing itself to be more tolerant in its efforts to access Western markets and win foreign investments. In addition, the July 1, 1997, date for the British turnover of Hong Kong to mainland China was just two weeks away. Many Hong Kong-based businesses were positioning themselves for the changes in administration that would result. Sittichai was aware that the ripple effects of the return of Hong Kong to China were already beginning to arrive in Thailand, where money, not always clean money, was looking for a new safe haven after PRC takeover. Could the attempted hijacking be tied in any way to changes about to take place in the Hong Kong political scene?

Then there was the airline's owner, a very powerful and wealthy Thai businessman of Chinese descent. He had friends, but he also had detractors in both Thailand and Hong Kong. It troubled Sittichai to think that anyone would go to the extreme of crashing a plane and killing all aboard to get to Air Siam's owner. The inspector would need a great deal of support to allow him the freedom to pursue such a conspiracy theory. There were people who would attempt to thwart his efforts at every turn.

Sittichai also did not want any supposed conspirators to know that the Thai investigative police were exploring such a possibility. A gun planted on the plane was something that he would like to keep from the press. To conduct an international conspiracy investigation would require additional time, contacts, and resources, all of which he must justify to his superiors. And as soon as he shared the information that formed the basis for his request, word would get out and likely alert the persons behind the conspiracy that they were under investigation. The Thai police force was too porous for an investigative process to work any other way. So back in his office that afternoon, Sittichai began to send out discreet inquiries to his network of international police counterparts in Hong Kong.

On his way home in the early evening, Sittichai went to the Americans' hotel to find them at dinner with a consular officer from the American embassy. He introduced himself again to the Americans then to the consular officer and asked their permission to join them at their table.

"You heroes have caused quite a stir on the evening news here in Thailand," Sittichai heard the consular officer say. "Overpowering a hijacker and landing a pilotless plane safely is not an everyday event."

"The hijacker blew his brains out with no help from us. We did little more than try to save our own asses!" Speaking was the former American navy pilot who had landed the plane at Don Mueang early that morning. Sittichai understood the implications of the navy pilot's words even if the American consular officer did not.

"Whatever!" said the young consular officer. "The point is you performed a commendable deed for a key Thai business leader. His name is Patthana, and his son, Thanakit, has spoken twice with me already. Thanakit has asked me each time how you are doing and how he might express his appreciation for what you did. He has also offered to—"

"I'll settle for a return ticket home. By bus, if necessary! It'll be a cold day in hell before I try another silly trip halfway around the world with these guys!" It was the short stocky American whom Sittichai knew to be the former CIA agent who had interrupted.

Sittichai saw the US consular officer attempt a smile and join in the laughter as well but then regain his composure and assume a more serious posture. "I've been informed by the Royal Thai Government that there are some procedures, some investigative requirements, that will keep you all here in Thailand for a few days," the consular officer continued. "You did have plans to vacation while you were here, didn't you? We are trying to arrange with the Thai authorities so you can go ahead and do just that. With the agreement, of course, that you will make yourselves available when necessary to cooperate with their investigation."

"Shit! I'm sure my golf handicap has gone all to hell from what has happened in the last twenty-four hours. How many more strokes off my handicap are you guys willing to give me for this nightmare of a trip?" It was the heavyset American again, prodding his companions.

"Shut up, Ben!" said the ex-navy pilot. "Don't think for one minute that you are the only one still shaking right now."

The inspector took the opportunity to inject himself into the conversation. "I confess that the American consular officer is correct. We would most sincerely appreciate your cooperation here in Thailand over the next few days as we investigate events further. We will need to visit with you again to corroborate what we learn." Sittichai saw that he now had the attention of everyone around the table. "Please be aware that we consider each of you to be friendly witnesses in this investigation. The Royal Thai Government promises that you will not incur any expense or inconvenience while you are in our country."

Sittichai said no more but remained at the table observing the Americans as they discussed needs and concerns with their consular officer. The American, Ben, needed a prescription filled for stomach medicine. The taller, gaunt American, Paul, whom Sittichai learned was the organizer of the group, asked the consular officer if he could locate and give a message to an embassy Thai employee with whom he had worked when he was stationed in the country as American commercial attaché. The ex-navy pilot, Dan, had fallen silent and pensive, perhaps aware that he, more than the others, would be the center of the investigation.

Finally, the consular officer spoke, "Khun Patthana, the airline's owner, has insisted that the American heroes be VIP guests at his golf and beach resort just outside Bangkok on Thailand's east coast. He will send a car and driver around in the morning to pick you up. That is, if Inspector Sittichai approves."

Sittichai was surprised by the offer. He knew that housing his key witnesses an hour outside Bangkok at a private resort would make his information gathering logistically more challenging. At the same time, his office would no longer need to budget for the American's meals and lodging expenses while he held them in Thailand. A trade-off, Sittichai recognized. He sighed. Such is the reality of law enforcement in Thailand. He would cope with this reality as he had with others in the past.

"Of course!" Sittichai responded. "The Americans have been through quite a bit and have done Thailand a service with their bravery and quick thinking. I agree they should be made as comfortable as possible while they are here in our country."

"Good," responded the consular officer. "I will contact Khun Patthana immediately."

Sittichai excused himself from the table and left. There would be a load of work for him and his investigative team in the morning, and it had been a long day for all of them. They all needed rest. All the members he had selected for his investigative team were bilingual in English and Thai. They had learned English and received US government-sponsored training in international law enforcement at police training academies in the United States under grants provided by US embassy-sponsored exchange programs. So it now fell to them to render each American witness's depositions into readable English for the Americans to review and sign and then to have those statements translated into Thai for their superiors to read and digest. Copies would be requested not only by his own superiors but also by investigative branches of the Thai military and the Thai prime minister's office given the international nature of the incident. Then there would be several rounds of meetings, first to assess what the witnesses' statements contained and then to agree on what face would be put on the incident in reporting to the media.

The next hurdle would be equally critical. Sittichai would need the budget and staff to pursue leads provided by the witnesses and by the evidence he collected. That required cooperation from foreign intelligence services in Hong Kong and elsewhere, most likely the United States. Yes, Sittichai wanted to see those background reports even on the American heroes. The Hong Kong intelligence services would certainly be looking into the incident as well since the hijacker had boarded the plane there.

But the willingness of other intelligence services to share information would depend on what information Thailand could bring to the table in return. And for that Sittichai needed to make his case to headquarters that, at the very least, he be relieved of other pending assignments to dedicate himself exclusively to the hijacking investigation until it was completed and that he be given control over a sufficient budget and staff to complete the task as promptly as possible.

If, as Sittichai feared, the Thai government wished to suppress the whole conspiracy theory and report the attempted hijacking as an isolated act of a single deranged political fanatic, getting the resources and staff he needed would not be easy. He sighed at the thought of what lay ahead.

He would have only limited say in the selection of the team with whom he would have to work on a broader conspiracy investigation. Any time, money, and staff he was given would come with strings attached. His investigators would be selected under pressure from military and ministry officials who had an interest in having one of their people involved so that they would have channels to whatever new information was uncovered. Some of them might have little interest in having findings from a broader investigation become part of the official record or be revealed in the press. If he uncovered anything too sensitive in the judgement of his superiors, he could find himself suddenly reassigned to other casework.

Still, Sittichai had been a survivor within the Thai law enforcement community during his nearly thirty-year career. He was aware that the early morning call he received had come because of his reputation for integrity during sensitive investigations he had conducted in the past. If he could count on launching this investigation down the right path, with a little discretion he could achieve some degree of independence and autonomy over the process. Police investigations in Thailand were so porous with inside informers. With tact he could feed out information that allowed him to move forward to the next step without contradicting the official story of events that the Thai government wanted the public to hear.

Sittichai was certain of only one thing at this point. The investigation that lay ahead was different from the many crime investigations that had surfaced and been allowed by his superiors to languish because one very rich Thai business leader was a little too clumsy in his pursuit of power but wealthy enough to reward those authorities willing to look the other way.

So perhaps it was best to have the Americans sequestered away from public view at Patthana's beach resort. They perhaps held keys to developments behind the hijacking about which they might not even be aware. The Americans had already unwittingly shed a ray of light on the darker side of Thai political and economic power by landing a plane with an unusual passenger manifest that would have gone unnoticed had there not been an attempted hijacking. It was not often that Sittichai had such an opportunity to peer into those unseemly depths and attempt to discern the faces and motives of those operating there.

The fact that it was Patthana, one of Thailand's wealthiest and most politically connected business leaders, did not dissuade Sittichai from this investigation. Rather, he was drawn to one more chance at caging the man who had been so elusive in past investigations. It had been a long day for him and every bone of his diminutive body ached. Still, he was animated by the belief there was something about the events surrounding Air Siam flight 224 that might expose his nemesis. He had to believe. Being so close to retirement, there would not be many more opportunities open to him.

CHAPTER 4

Moon Li stood at the window of his mansion office looking across Kowloon Harbor at the jagged Hong Kong cityscape. The rising morning sun reflected off the tops of the city's office skyscrapers giving them the appearance of pearly teeth. He used to take joy in watching the light of the rising sun gradually move down the buildings' sides in those brief early morning moments; it was like a dragon's mouth yawning widely as it greeted the new day.

But today, Moon Li's face was expressionless and his mind indifferent to the morning spectacle before him. He shifted his eyes downward to catch the movement of his hillside mansion's electric iron gates as they responded to his touch of a button on his desk and dutifully swung open to let a black limousine enter the secluded courtyard below. The vehicle carried special emissaries whom he had been instructed to receive.

Word had already reached Moon Li about events aboard Air Siam's Hong Kong to Bangkok flight the night before. An attempted hijacking had been averted, though at the cost of the lives of the pilots. His sources also informed him that the hijacker was dead, apparently by his own hand, and that due to efforts on the part of an American commercial pilot who was a passenger on the flight, the plane had landed safely. Before informing his boss, the Syndicate Chairman, Moon Li had quickly checked to verify this news through other

Bangkok sources who informed him that an investigation was already underway but that the Thai police and media at the moment were treating the incident as the act of a lone deranged political radical.

So Moon Li was prepared for the early morning call informing him he was summoned by the Chairman. Moon Li expected no less. He had always prided himself as a good judge of character and traded heavily on that skill, which earned him the honor of being the Syndicate's most senior field lieutenant. Accurate judging of his boss's moods and motivations had kept him in that slot, while many of the others around him sooner or later had misstepped and had been eliminated.

Moon Li could read the Chairman's temperament now. He would be furious and exasperated by the failure of his plan. He would not care to know why it went wrong. He would hold Moon Li responsible for that. The Chairman would want to know what Moon Li was prepared to do next.

Moon Li had made mistakes before and accepted his scolding but had always been able to bring the Chairman around with the persuasiveness of his argument not to lose sight of the bigger goals they sought. He was convinced he could hold out with his boss again this time.

He had been up most of the night going over what he would discuss with the Chairman. Despite his lack of sleep, Moon Li was invigorated and waiting with anticipation for the chance to sit down with the Chairman and work out the next move in their plan to relocate their base of operations from Hong Kong to Thailand.

He could convincingly argue that the hijacker had conducted himself precisely as he, Moon Li, had predicted, right down to taking his own life as well as those of the pilots. Young radical dissidents are most often driven by both their political passions and personal egos, and he had harnessed both in the aspiring People's Liberation Front leader he had recruited. Boys with impractical dreams, all too coddled and complacent by their middle-class upbringings, normally don't have the guts to carry through with the ambitious social and economic reforms they espouse. And they were so naive as well. Could none of the PLF dissidents fathom that they were manipulated by both the mainland Chinese communists and the Hong Kong syndicates for their respective purposes?

The PLF followers were harmless in their political tactics but radicalized enough in the dogma they embraced that the communist Chinese government could use their existence as a pretext to subdue dissident movements in general. Allow a few radical groups to spawn, monitor their movements, and then when they strike, use retaliation to bring into line all dissenters, moderate and radical. The failed Tiananmen Square protests eight summers earlier in 1989 were a classic example of how the spillover of PLF protesting could provide Beijing with the opportunity to corral and control its detractors.

And for the Hong Kong Syndicate, the PLF served an equally useful purpose. Its leaders couldn't operate without funds and were not above partnering with the Syndicate to raise money. And money meant influence. The Syndicate shared with the PLF a strong loathing of the repressive mainland Chinese communist regime. Both were disenfranchised and marginalized organizations which could find common cause, even if they had dramatically different objectives. And now they shared the common intent of seeking out safer grounds to pursue those disparate interests. Once mainland China regained administrative control over Hong Kong, neither the PLF nor the Syndicate would be able to operate as freely as before. Both looked to a relatively benign Thailand as a welcoming new port in the political, social, and economic storms that were again engulfing East Asia.

Moon Li's hijacking plan was by far the biggest effort in which the Syndicate had played its PLF card. Hong Kong was just two weeks away from the July 1, 1997, date for termination of Britain's ninety-nine-year lease for administration of the territory. Both Britain and the People's Republic of China were anxious for the transition to take place smoothly, without incident. Mainland China was particularly concerned to show investors that Hong Kong not only would continue to conduct business as usual but that mainland China would be as welcoming as the British to Western money and technology.

"Was there any better time for the PLF to make a powerful political statement?" Moon Li proposed to the movement's leadership. "Beijing hates embarrassment, especially in the West at a time when it is trying to clean up its international image and become a major trading nation. You have a unique opportunity to call attention to the oppressed minorities throughout Asia at the very time the Chinese Communist regime is moving to project itself as a responsible trading partner. You can put the Beijing leadership on notice that they cannot continue to ignore the PLF's demands."

Moon Li saw that the PLF leadership was divided over planning a major show of power. Senior PLF leadership considered the plan too risky and too bloody, perhaps alienating support of the Western sympathizers they also were courting.

The PLF's younger Turks were more aggressive, more impatient, hungrier for action and power. "We're dissatisfied with our leaders' vacillation over how to pressure Beijing," they had confided to Moon Li. "The communist leadership each day is solidifying ties with Western nations as part of its program of staged authoritarian capitalism. We fear that there would be even greater reluctance by the West to criticize Beijing when it continues to suppress minorities and crack down on dissent. We need to act now, at the time when China is assuming administrative control over Hong Kong to reveal how badly minorities are treated."

"I agree you need to act very soon," Moon Li had replied. "And you must act boldly before you lose the sanctuary of Hong Kong, where the British administration has exercised benign tolerance toward your efforts to advocate for political and economic rights of Chinese women and ethnic minorities. As Hong Kong administrators, the British have pretty much left you alone. The PLF will lose all that when Hong Kong reverts to mainland Chinese control. You need a new base of operations now and international support to help you obtain it."

Moon Li began secretly courting one of the PLF aspiring leaders, cultivating his dissatisfaction with the marginal roles he had been assigned in the movement and his envy of the movement's current leaders. To PLF senior leadership, the young man was unpredictable and a potential liability to the group. To Moon Li he was an ideal candidate for manipulation. It did not take long to discern the young man's restless yearning to demonstrate his worth.

Like a tiger first separates its prey from the herd before pulling it down, Moon Li had met secretly with the young man and planted his plot within the young man's head so it was as if he himself had conceived it. "In one major strike," Moon Li had convinced the young man, "you can advance the PLF cause a hundredfold and propel yourself into the group's leadership. I can arrange the support you need to pull it off."

Just as Moon Li had anticipated, the young man had carried out his part of the plan perfectly, right down to the point where Moon Li knew the young man would discover his betrayal and take his own life. And had it not been for a quirk of fate beyond Moon Li's control, the young man would have been the instrument of Moon Li's plot, taking down the plane and Patthana, one of Thailand's most powerful businessmen, with it. It was the happenstance occurrence of a passenger with piloting experience on board that saved the plane and Patthana from the fates that Moon Li had intended.

Moon Li listened to the footsteps as they grew louder on the tile steps leading from the courtyard up to his office suite. The Chairman had sent three of his most loyal and trusted henchmen to fetch him, a sign of respect Moon Li recognized. It put him at ease. The Chairman understood what Moon Li had nearly accomplished. And Moon Li had already formulated new plans to complete their mission. Any repercussions from the Air Siam hijacking attempt could be contained. Aside from the Chairman, only Moon Li knew of their scheme to seize control of Patthana's conglomerate, Heron Holdings, and use it as a front to build a new base of syndicate operations in Thailand. The original plan was so simple that it called for no involvement other than that of the hijacker, who now was dead and no threat to their plans. Planting the hijacker's weapon on the Air Siam flight was done with total anonymity through the Syndicate's network of agents within the airline company. Moon Li knew those agents also would be eliminated very shortly, ending that trail of the hijacking investigation.

Moon Li turned from the window at the sound of a soft knock on the door. "Come in!" he said.

Jimmy Lin's henchmen entered the room and bowed with deferential respect to both Moon Li's seniority in both age and rank. Moon Li motioned them to chairs in front of his large carved teak desk. They approached but remained standing.

"We ask your indulgence, sir," said the elder of the three visitors. "The Chairman wishes you to—"

Moon Li cut him off with a wave of his hand. "I understand. There are important matters for the Chairman to attend to today. I will not be the cause of any delay. I am ready now to go with you."

The staccato sounds of their footfalls on the tiled steps mingled together as they descended through the circular catacomb-like inner stairwell. As they emerged into the still heavily shadowed courtyard where the car awaited them, Moon Li looked back at the crimson-colored blossoms that hung from the bougainvillea vines clinging to the mansion's walls. He would miss this residence when they relocated to Thailand.

They reached the car, and Moon Li waited for the younger man to open the rear passenger side door for him to enter. He was startled when the young man stood looking at him without moving. Then from behind, Moon Li heard the elder of Jimmy's men speak. "The Chairman wishes you to ride back here," he said.

Moon Li recognized each of the two very similar sounds he heard next. The sounds came in rapid succession, the sound of a trunk latch being released and the sound of a pistol being cocked, but he could not distinguish one from the other. It would not matter, though. They were the last sounds that Moon Li would ever hear.

*****

Huan Lin, "Jimmy," picked up the phone and listened to the caller's voice. Then, without speaking in reply, he slowly lowered the receiver back into its cradle. A moment passed during which there was no change at all in the blank expression frozen on his face. Then gradually a grim smile formed, and he slumped back into his high leather chair for an uncharacteristic instant of unguarded relaxation.

Release at last, he thought. Permanent for Moon Li, temporary for himself he feared. Moon Li had been a good and loyal syndicate field lieutenant and an unrelenting fighter when challenged. Jimmy knew Moon Li's loyalty had been strong, that he would have fallen on his own sword if instructed.

The unusual twist of fate that had spoiled their plans meant that all links between the Syndicate and the airline hijacking had to be erased. Not that Moon Li would ever betray his boss. Still, Jimmy could no longer afford the risk of any association with Moon Li.

So he gave the order but instructed that Moon Li's life must end with no warning, no anguish. His good friend must go quickly and be spared all unnecessary pain. That was not typical of the way Jimmy normally operated with those he removed. He most often chose to make a much harsher display of their demise to send a signal to enforce discipline within the Syndicate ranks and to strike fear among his rivals. But a quick, unsuspecting end for Moon Li was something Jimmy felt he owed his loyal friend.

Now Jimmy had to wait and learn the repercussions of the failed attempt to bring his Bangkok-based Thai associate, Patthana, to his knees and gain control over his business empire. There would be an investigation, with some repercussions felt in Hong Kong. Because it was an international incident, both Thai and Hong Kong investigators would be

snooping into his business affairs with the airline and with
Heron Holdings. He most likely would need to contend with
an Interpol criminal investigation as well. From his sources he
would gain a sense of whether involvement of the Syndicate
was among the investigators' theories. Jimmy was convinced
that all Syndicate operations were sufficiently opaque as to
provide investigators with no leads to follow whatever their
theories might be about him. But Heron Holdings sought to
be perceived as a legitimate organization and transparent in its
operations. Interpol investigators might just find a back door
through Heron Holdings to the Syndicate through some of
his transactions with the corporation's airline. Should he be
found out, the Syndicate's entire fortune would be in jeop-
ardy and, with it, his own future.

Jimmy was facing the pressure of the clock. He feared
his Thai associates would immediately look for signs of his
hand in the plot even if they had no evidence to prove the
link. Jimmy was not worried that they would share their suspicions with the police or Interpol investigators. To do so
would call attention to their own extralegal undertakings.
No, that was not a concern. What did trouble Jimmy was
that now his Thai partners might move to fortify themselves
against him, and that would make his efforts much harder
in the time that remained for action. Already he was getting
daily warnings about financial stresses on the Thai economy.
Jimmy's Thai associates were aware of those reports as well
and were not nearly as patient as he.

"Well, Moon Li," Jimmy sighed. "It would have been
a beautiful plan if it had come out the way we hoped. Rest
in peace, my good friend! At least you can longer be hurt by
what may happen now."

CHAPTER 5

Paul gazed out the window of the stretch limousine that pulled through the gated entrance under the elaborate black wrought iron sign announcing, "Ban Khao Resort." With him in the chauffeured limo were his companions, Dan and Ben, and their host, Thanakit. Outside the gate on a pedestal stood a traditional small Thai spirit house marking where the road branched off and led down to the neighboring fishing village of Ban Khao. Paul cracked the limo's tinted window to let in the seductive scented aroma of the blossoming magnolia trees that flanked the one-kilometer road from the main highway to the resort facilities and Ban Khao village along the coast of the Sea of Siam.

"That's a welcome smell after hot and humid Bangkok! You can almost taste the Bangkok air it is so gritty," Paul declared.

"I like the peace and quiet," added Dan. "It is quite a change from the phalanx of TV cameras and reporters that surrounded us as we left the hotel. I'm not into the celebrity thing. I'm hoping there's a chance we'll have some quiet here."

"And some decent American food!" Ben added. "I wonder if they serve burgers and beer in the resort restaurant."

Thanakit, their host, replied to both of them. "You will not have the bother of news reporters here. We pride ourselves in assuring privacy to all our resort guests. And yes, your burgers and beer are on the clubhouse bar menu. We have many American guests here, particularly during your winter season in the US."

Paul's gaze shifted between the exterior views of Ban Khao Resort and Thanakit, who sat opposite him in the seat that backed up against the glass partition separating them from the driver. He observed Thanakit's face brighten noticeably with each whistle of amazement from his American guests as the luxurious layout of the resort facilities rolled into view. Along the golf course roughs and roadsides, gazelles grazed contentedly, undisturbed by the passing vehicle or the players on the fairways and greens. A high chain-link fence ran along the resort perimeter, but the outwardly contented wildlife acted more as if the enclosure served to keep the world out than to keep them in.

"Ten years ago, all this was rice paddy land," said Thanakit. "It produced about a ton of rice per hectare per year, worth maybe $200 for local farmers. Now some of those same farmers are earning that much in a week, working the greens and gardens around the resort. Or even more by carrying golf bags or serving tables for resort tourists." Thanakit's enthusiasm for his resort project was apparent to the Americans.

The limo ascended a road carved serpentine-like into a rocky promenade that at the top afforded panoramic views of the main resort complex in one direction and in the other a white coral sand beach and the deep blue Bay of Siam that stretched to the horizon. Along their descent toward the ocean, walled enclosures with their own gated entrances signaled the locations of private villas erected for the more affluent resort club members. Around the golf course fairways below at discrete distances from each other were scattered weekend bungalows. Facing the ocean, a multistory resort hotel rose above a sprawling outdoor swimming pool and adjacent patio restaurant. The adjoining clubhouse was the gateway to two eighteen-hole golf courses that branched out across the gently rolling hills of emerald green grass, punctuated by jungled roughs, lotus-adorned water hazards, and pure-white sand traps.

"We'll go first to the clubhouse for a drink while your bags are delivered to your rooms. We have reserved a private three-room villa for your stay with us," Thanakit said to get his guests' attention. "Then I will have your personal butler show you around the resort facilities. We provide electric carts for moving about, but it is easy to get lost at first among the resort roads and golf course pathways. A guided tour will help orient you."

The limo pulled to a stop under the clubhouse portico entirely canopied in drooping crimson bougainvillea. A gentle waterfall dominated the length of one wall, and its rushing sound muffled their footsteps as they made their way up the marble steps and through the giant carved teakwood doors that flanked the clubhouse entrance. The vaulted ceilings, sparkling tile floors, and enormous columns struck awe even in Ben, who very uncharacteristically removed his baseball hat and reverently held it to his chest. "Gawd!" he said in a failed effort to find more elegant words to express his amazement. "This place has got it all!"

Thanakit smiled and guided them to a table with a panoramic view of the golf course greens. "Ban Khao has begun to host several international golf tournaments. We can boast one of the most elegant and unique golf facilities in the world. Both our golf courses have won awards in global competitions with world-famous courses designed by famous former golf pros like Arnold Palmer and Trent Jones."

Thanakit continued as club waiters took their drink orders and quickly returned with a round of local Singha beers. "Ban Khao is making Thailand into a major international destination for golfers and trophy fishermen. Last year alone, Thailand received over a million tourists. About ten percent of those tourists come on golf and recreation vacations. Over the last five years, those numbers have been growing annually at double-digit rates. Thailand offers the best value for the recreational vacation dollar of any country worldwide."

Paul could see that Thanakit had launched into what sounded like a sales pitch for the resort. "We're aware. That's why we were coming to Thailand. I guess we're part of that tourist demographic you describe." He raised his glass, and his friends joined him in toasting their host.

Thanakit shared that Ban Khao Resort was his first major hospitality industry investment project after completing his MBA at Stanford University's Graduate School of Business five years earlier. "I researched global resort tourism while I was in business school in America. It appears to be a rapidly growing market. When I returned to Thailand, I assembled an investment package and convinced my father's company and some Chinese investors to put money behind it. Ban Khao Resort fits well within our company's transportation and construction businesses and is on its way to being one of our prime profit makers!"

Paul gazed around the club lounge and saw they were the only Americans there. "So from where does Ban Khao Resort draw its visitors?"

Thanakit continued as if he had expected the question. "At present our main markets are Japan, Korea, and Singapore. A growing number of visitors are coming from elsewhere in Asia as well, mostly Hong Kong and Taiwan, and a small number from Australia. Koreans are particularly into golf tourism right now. We are just beginning to advertise in the North American and European markets. We hope to expand Air Siam's routes to all those markets. Thai Airways, our national airline, is stiff competition, but we are going after destination packages that include airfare and resort vacation combinations. Heron Holdings has many friends in government and parliament, and our resort membership privileges are useful for persuading private investors and government regulators that we are worthy of their support." Thanakit added a sly wink with his last comment.

Thanakit's boasting did not escape Paul's notice. Dan also picked up on his words, and their eyes met in silent agreement to discuss the situation later. Was competition so cutthroat in Asia that companies might try to sabotage each other, even to the extent of downing an airliner? Did Patthana's enterprises have strong competitors, or had Thanakit and his father also engendered enemies while building their empire? Paul put himself to wondering.

Thanakit rose and prepared to leave. "Please enjoy your stay with us. Rest and get settled into your new surroundings this afternoon. My father invites you all to join him for dinner this evening. He wishes to thank you personally for what you have done. About six o' clock, at dusk. That should give you some time to rest and refresh yourselves this afternoon. All of our Ban Khao staff have been instructed to accord you full VIP attention. We have also arranged personal cell phones for each of you. The phones are in your villa rooms. They are connected through our main switchboard, and we have English-speaking receptionists who can help you place your local and international calls. I am sure you will want to stay in touch with your families back in the United States. Resort cars and drivers are at your service twenty-four hours a day should you wish to travel into Bangkok or elsewhere in Thailand during your stay with us."

Paul inquired again, "And how long do you expect the Thai government will require us to remain in the country? Do you have any idea how long the Thai authorities will take to complete their investigations?"

"I do not know what the Thai government requires of you. You are considered, as you say in your country, material witnesses to a rather serious international crime. The deaths of three pilots and an attempted hijacking. With no hijacker alive to interrogate, I expect the Thai authorities will need you to stay in the country through much of the initial crime investigation, for at least a full two weeks. But please understand. You are welcome at Ban Khao Resort for as long as you want to stay, as long as it takes to restore your golf handicaps, which I understand you are worried may have suffered a bit from recent events!"

Thanakit was attempting a smile now. "I would be most pleased if you stayed long enough even to shave a few more points off those handicaps. I will arrange for some private sessions, courtesy of the club, of course."

Dan replied as spokesman of the group, "Right now, we just welcome the quiet."

The welcoming smile that had graced Thanakit's face since he met them melted away for a moment. "You have performed an immensely valuable service to my father and to Heron Holdings. We are deeply in your debt. Indeed, we will assure you rest and quiet and, most important, the privacy you deserve." And with that Thanakit departed.

The three Americans were finally alone together for the first time in two days.

It was Dan who spoke first. "I'm frankly underwhelmed by all this hospitality being showered on us. It's excessive and a bit embarrassing. My ungracious take is that Air Siam's owner wants to cloister us here away from the press and the public."

Ben countered quickly, "Who's complaining? Not me!"

Dan glared at him. "That's quite a change, Ben. Just twenty-four hours earlier you were ready to catch the next flight back to the US and put all this behind you. We're here now, and I still need a few days to chill out before I board another flight anywhere. So yes, I can handle the pampering, even the cloistering. A few days without the press or those investigators on our backs is by far the better option."

Paul was more reflective. "I'm not so surprised by the hospitality, knowing the Thai culture from living here some twenty years ago. It is natural for Thais to want to return a favor. A lost jetliner with all its crew and passengers could be a pretty serious blow to any air transport company. Let's assume the plane had gone down in the South China Sea. Chances are Air Siam's fleet would be grounded until an investigation came up with some answers about how it happened, and Patthana could convince authorities he had put in place measures to assure it would not happen again. With its wings clipped for who knows how long, Air Siam would lose much of its business and revenues. When it was allowed to fly again, Air Siam would face pretty strong headwinds as it attempted to restore its client base."

"That assumes it can get insurance coverage and working capital to operate again," added Ben.

"You have a point," said Paul. "I wager Heron Holdings is sufficiently diverse to handle any short-term revenue loss, but it might have had to cede some of its control over the airline to its investors to get back in the air again."

They fell silent until Dan jumped into the conversation, "Would anyone be so ruthless as to intentionally crash a jet liner full of innocent passengers in order to wrest control of a small regional airline company from its owner? I find that hard to believe. But I can't reject that possibility as long as we lack an answer to the question of who planted a gun on the plane. And who was behind the hijacker?" They looked at each other blankly. "And how in the hell are we or anyone going to get answers to those questions?"

Always the spoiler, Ben jumped in. "Well, let's ask the big boss at dinner tonight. He owes us some explanations, doesn't he? It was his airline's lousy security practices that forced us to save our asses two nights ago!"

Paul was a bit surprised to hear himself defend a host they had yet to meet. "Well, Ben, maybe he does owe us. Certainly, opening his resort to us is a way of paying back, and yes, perhaps at the same time to discourage us as his guests from asking awkward questions. But we accepted his invitation, and we're his guests. In this culture, asking direct and sensitive questions of one's host is just not done. Certainly not at first meeting."

Ben quickly threw Paul's words back at him. "Attempting to hijack or crash a plane is something that normally is just not done either! We were asked some pretty damned direct questions by those Thai investigators. Did we know the hijacker? Or the airline's owner? Did we ever work for his company or its partners? Why were we on that particular flight?

"And the evidence! You, Dan, had to tell them they'd probably find your prints as well as the hijacker's on that gun. You, Paul, had to explain why your belt was around the neck of the dead pilot. And only the three of us could corroborate each other! We weren't being asked those questions because the investigators loved the owner or his airline or us. They were probing as if something was going on, and maybe we might be a part of it. Those investigators were not treating us as heroes or even witnesses, more like accomplices."

"Point taken, Ben!" Dan was now starting to get annoyed. "Stop sounding so damn conspiratorial! They're investigators! Everyone's a suspect at the outset of such an investigation, particularly when there are so few witnesses beyond us. None but us in the cockpit. The coach class was curtained off, and no one in that section saw anything. The first-class passengers besides us were all Asians. And not a one of them was willing to give more than his name and nationality. All refused to get involved as witnesses, the investigators told me when they were questioning us."

Paul was getting uncomfortable. "Enough! The room's filling up with the lunch crowd, and it's getting noisy and anything but private. Let's get out of here. I suggest we have a snack at our villa. We'll find some of that quiet and privacy there that Mr. Thanakit promised Dan."

*****

Back at their villa, the three Americans took advantage of the afternoon to rest and overcome the still lingering effects of twelve hours of jet lag and their travel saga. By evening they were refreshed. Paul was determined not to let time adjustments dull his capacity to take in their luxurious surroundings. He was sure Dan and Ben felt the same way. They gathered on the patio sitting in high-backed rattan peacock chairs at the edge of the villa's private swimming pool. Dan and Paul sipped Mai Tai cocktails and Ben threw back Singha beers that the resort's attentive young house girls replaced as soon as he set down an empty bottle.

At close to six o'clock, the Americans watched Thanakit's distinctive black Rolls-Royce limousine make its way along

Ban Khao's winding road toward their villa. As it passed the clubhouse and headed toward them, a second white stretch limo that was following it broke off and headed toward the Ban Khao Resort marina.

Thanakit's limo came to a stop under the villa's portico. He stepped out and made his way through the villa's spacious living area to the open-air patio where the Americans were sitting. He announced himself as the villa staff quickly exited the area, respectfully backing away from the room all the time with heads slightly bowed and hands held flat together in front of them, fingers pointing up almost in a praying position, as a demonstration of respect.

Thanakit greeted his guests with a western handshake, dispensing with the traditional Thai greeting. "My father has arrived and is anxious to receive you. We will dine tonight aboard the Blue Heron, my father's yacht. He wishes you to enjoy the sights of Ban Khao Resort from the water."

"Oh, boy!" Ben said with a clearly perceptible note of trepidation in his voice. "I'm not sure if I am a better dinner companion at sea than I am in the air. Perhaps I best stay here and have these lovely young villa ladies bring me a beer and a burger in the hot tub. That's about as much open water as I can handle right now!"

Thanakit chuckled. "We plan to anchor within the waters of Ban Khao Bay tonight, Mr. Ben Morgan. My father's yacht, the Blue Heron, is nearly as large as your villa and just about as stable, I assure you. The sea is so calm that I will be happy to make a wager that you will not become ill this evening."

Paul gave Ben a stern look. "Ben has made his point. We're all pleased to join you and your father for dinner."

A few minutes later they all exited from the limo dockside, and Thanakit led them up the gangway and onto the main deck of the 115-foot yacht. The crew cast off immediately, and the captain directed the boat out into the bay as Thanakit led them toward the rear deck, where a short, paunchy Asian in a white business suit and open-collar black silk shirt stood looking out toward the wake of the boat and the marina they had just departed. "Father," Thanakit spoke in English, "may I introduce—"

"Welcome!" Patthana turned quickly and cut off his son. He walked over to them and, in turn, took the right hand of each American in both of his, with a "Sawadee" greeting of welcome in halting but understandable English. "Please. Let us drink a toast to your arrival at Ban Khao! I instructed that the finest champagne be placed on board in your honor... but of course, if you have any other preference, any at all..."

"Champagne would be wonderful for all of us." Paul jumped in as spokesman for the group and to head off Ben, who appeared about to counter Patthana's offer with a request for another beer.

Conversation continued over dinner and ranged widely from resort amenities to recent political events in the United States. Paul was impressed with the range of knowledge about American lifestyles that Thanakit said he had acquired while attending business school in the United States. He also noticed how alike father and son were in stature and appearance. Paul also sensed, however, that in appearances was where father and son resemblances ended.

While they dined, Thanakit carried on about how he sought to improve Thai lives by investing in projects like Ban Khao Resort that would generate jobs and income for Thai workers and their families. He described his visions for similar projects elsewhere in the country where Heron Holdings was expanding its operations. "The children and youth like those from Ban Khao village next door to the resort are the future of Thailand, the next generation of consumers of Heron Holdings products and services," Thanakit pointed out to his dinner companions. "Improvement in their well-being will lead to our company's growth, to improvements in Heron Holdings bottom line."

Paul observed that rather than endorse his son's world outlook of business with a social conscience, Patthana directed their discussions more toward the importance of expanding the reach of Heron Holdings' business empire across as many sectors of the Thai economy as he could capture control. "First we must become a major player in the country's construction, transportation, and communications industries," Patthana countered his son's argument. "When there is enough money in the bank, then you can begin to look after the needs of the poor in any way you want. Thanakit has gained some important business skills from his time studying in your country. I expect him to put that training to work expanding Heron Holdings' operations and eventually take over the helm of the company from me. After he is in charge, he can have the luxury of helping Thailand's less fortunate. As many of the poor as he wants to help. Money should be no problem."

*****

"Beats airline food," Ben interjected when they approached the conclusion of their seven-course seafood and steak dinner aboard the Blue Heron.

Paul caught Patthana's confused expression. "Maybe the food on US planes, Ben. But you never gave Air Siam food service a chance." Paul's diplomatic effort to intercede for Ben and restore their host's composure opened the topic that until that moment all had skirted around.

Patthana spoke first. "I told Thanakit that I owe a huge debt to you for your brave actions in saving the plane and its passengers. I feel as if you were special messengers, guardians sent by Providence to protect not just those onboard Air Siam but Heron Holdings as well."

Patthana was beginning to warm up. "We are a proud and growing company. We take special pride in being among the pioneers of the Thai economic miracle."

Paul felt his gaze. "You, Mr. Paul Ellis, must know how much Thailand has prospered thanks to outside investors and to our open economy. In the last decade, no country in the Asia region has matched Thailand's rate of growth and no region in the world, not even North America, has matched East Asia's economic performance. I know you still call Thailand one of Asia's 'baby tigers' along with Indonesia and Singapore, not quite in the same league as Japan, South Korea, or Taiwan. But I tell you the teeth of those bigger Asian tigers are getting dull, and their claws are being clipped by rising labor costs. We baby tigers are growing up, our teeth and claws are sharper, and we are restless! Thailand has an abundant supply of cheap labor and a booming population of young workers. And we are putting that labor to work to sell you cheap quality clothing in America and good quality recreational experiences here in Thailand."

Paul sensed that Patthana had been briefed about his diplomatic service background as well as the backgrounds of Dan and Ben. So he was not surprised when Patthana chose to hone his "Buy Thailand" pep talk with him.

Patthana leaned over the table to within a foot of Paul. "Thailand has so much cheap labor here, that Heron Holdings exports some of it to other countries as well. Domestic workers to Japan, Hong Kong, and Korea, construction workers to the Middle East oil fields. Even Thai brides to Australia and America." Patthana smiled, but Paul noticed Thanakit shift uncomfortably in his chair. He knew that it was not for a Thai to inject himself uninvited into the discourse of one's elders. Still, Thanakit was westernized enough, Paul suspected, to know that the group would not be offended if he abandoned this Asian tradition. Paul sensed that Thanakit was silent not out of respect for his father but from disagreement.

"My father has helped bring the Thai economy and society into the modern global economy," Thanakit said finally. "What you see there along the coastline is a good example." Thanakit was pointing beyond the yacht's railing to the expansive shoreline of buildings and bungalows that made up Ban Khao Resort. "When first I came to Ban Khao as a young boy with my father some twenty years ago, I would go out into this bay like we are now but in one of the villager's small fishing boats. At that time the village made its living from growing rice and catching fish. There was no school, no medical clinic. No teacher or doctor. Not even a gravel road from the village to the highway and to the rest of the country.

"Today," Thanakit continued, "Ban Khao village is connected to the Thai economy by a road and by power and communication lines that Heron Holdings installed as part of the Royal Thai Government's programs to bring prosperity to every corner of the country. There are still many villages today like Ban Khao was twenty years ago. Heron Holdings is bringing similar improvements to many of them across Thailand.

"The Ban Khao village children now travel by bus to and from nearby schools on roads that Heron Holdings has constructed. And when they are old enough, they quickly find factory or construction jobs in nearby Rayong or Bangkok at one-hour distance. And as I told you earlier, there is work right here at the resort. Ban Khao village families can also continue their traditional fishing life but now without the drudgery of tending to rice paddies from morning till dusk. All Ban Khao villagers are now assured of an education, a job, and medical care for their families."

Paul reflected on the pastoral and bucolic setting across the bay as he listened to Thanakit and his father. He attempted to reconcile the seductive surroundings with the turmoil into which they were thrust at thirty thousand feet two days earlier. "It was quite a ride for us getting here, Khun Patthana. I can speak for all of us that your hospitality is most appreciated at the moment."

"Your unexpected trip aboard Air Siam was my father's good fortune," said Thanakit. "We are truly at your service."

The bright lights of the Ban Khao marina pierced the night like silver daggers as the Blue Heron returned them to the dock after their dinner cruise. Paul, Dan, and Ben thanked their hosts and boarded the waiting limo for the short drive back to their villa.

"Jezzus!" said Ben as the car carried them away from the dock. "I mean, is Thailand supposed to be a poor country or what? This Mr. Patthana could buy and sell the three of us ten times over even before he sat down to his lunch of fresh seafood and Kobe steak."

"No one said pockets of extreme wealth and poverty don't exist alongside each other," Paul replied. "In fact, how prosperous a country is measured better by looking at how extreme are the differences in income between the rich and the poor, than by comparing average income levels. Averages are deceiving. The Thai economy is growing fast, but it's also evident that the gap between the poor and the wealthy is still pretty wide. Until that gap is closed a bit, it's hard to convince me that any meaningful economic miracle is taking place here."

"Well, the rich in this country seem to be looking after the poor okay if Mr. Patthana is any example. As long as guys like him and his son are around, I guess the poor will make out all right."

"So it would appear," said Paul with a tone of skepticism in his voice.

CHAPTER 6

Patthana watched the limo with the Americans pull away from the dock. Then he signaled the Blue Heron captain to take him and his son, Thanakit, back out into Ban Khao Bay. He needed to talk to someone close whom he could trust to help him reason through recent events.

Patthana found his shipboard office to be the most conducive place for conducting his most private business ventures. Neither his palatial mansion at Ban Khao Resort nor his corporate penthouse director's office atop the forty-story Patthana Towers complex in Bangkok were as suitable for transacting substantive business deals and concluding sensitive contract negotiations as was the Blue Heron. At sea business could be conducted unfettered by the fear that others might be listening or watching, even remotely. All the amenities the yacht could offer guests were most conducive to executing his corporate strategy.

He smiled to himself. Many important decisions had been reached aboard the Blue Heron and many important agreements finalized. Heron Holdings often needed the help of influential Thai government administrators or parliamentary officials to secure lucrative contracts and business licenses. Taking Thai officials for a weekend ocean cruise, most often with female companionship he arranged, nearly always turned out to be a successful undertaking. Somehow, when out at sea in the Gulf of Siam and beyond the sight of land, Thai parliamentarians and bureaucrats seemed more disposed to bend their power and position his way. Such an outcome was much more difficult to achieve at Patthana Towers or Ban Khao Resort no matter how much liquor flowed or how beautiful were the women who entertained his guests.

"The Blue Heron is a cost liability that Heron Holdings cannot afford right now in its financially extended condition," his son, Thanakit, constantly argued since his return from business school studies in the United States.

"Yes," his father had agreed, "a thousand dollars a day to maintain and operate the Blue Heron is serious money. But I have recovered an entire year of those operating expenses in just one weekend trip with the right people on board. The Blue Heron has helped seal enough agreements to pay for itself for at least a decade into the future. With the ship's satellite uplinks and telecommunications, I can transfer funds electronically between any of my overseas bank accounts and those of my yachting guests."

For Patthana the matter at hand that evening was far darker in nature than any dealings in transport or construction contracts. He knew that the two men, father and son, held vastly different views on the future course that Heron Holdings should chart. He did not shy away from his son's criticism of how he ran the company nor from exploring the conflicting strategies that each of them held for future corporate undertakings. He welcomed their debates for the enlightenment they gave him. He had arranged for Thanakit's US business school education precisely because he wanted to bring modern business practices and planning to their firm.

But this was different. The survival of the Heron Holdings empire he built was in play. Before they returned to shore, Patthana recognized he and his son must agree on a plan to protect the company and build the mutual resolve to see it through. Patthana and Thanakit returned to the upper deck where they had just entertained their dinner guests. Patthana sat again at the head of the table, while Thanakit stood nearby leaning back on the stern railing facing his father.

"Do you believe—" Patthana started out.

"No. I do not believe it was just a politically motivated hijacking attempt by political dissidents, Father! Do you?"

Patthana tolerated his son's impetuous habit of interrupting his elder, though it still annoyed him, even when Thanakit confined his interruptions to their private conversations. It was his son's American business school education and what Thanakit called the Stanford Case Study method that conditioned Thanakit's interrogative responses, answering questions with a question. Patthana counted on his son's help in applying those skills to addressing the challenges facing a conglomerate that had now grown beyond Thailand's borders and beyond his own understanding of global trade and investment issues. He wanted to groom Thanakit to assume control of Heron Holdings and apply those international business skills he had acquired. An attempt at corporate sabotage was a compelling and timely life-or-death real-world case study right now. Patthana could tolerate his son's abrasive habits if they produced the strategy for corporate survival that he needed.

"Of course, I don't believe the official report of the hijacking attempt," Patthana continued. "The truth is somewhere else. We need to find it. A good place to start is what you believe from what you know." Patthana was willing for the moment to cede to his son the direction of their conversation.

"What I know at the moment is this. Heron Holdings is over its head financially, and if that plane had splashed down into the ocean, it would have produced financial waves great enough for us to feel it right here on this boat right now. Possibly we would face going under financially."

Thanakit spared no drama in his assessment. "You know that for some time now I have been studying Heron Holdings' balance sheets. This may be a good time to bring you up to date. Ever since the company went public, our share prices have nearly doubled annually on the Thai and Hong Kong stock exchanges. We have also had solid credit ratings that so far have made it possible to obtain significant loans from the Hong Kong banks. At the moment we are fortunate those banks are flush with cash and willing lenders. But we have heavily leveraged our investors' money in land purchases and construction projects. The Thai economy is strong. Most of the Asia region is showing skyrocketing and sustained growth, so investors are looking anywhere and everywhere to put their money to go along for the ride.

"However, Heron Holdings is a somewhat different story. Our revenue growth is not yet fast enough to cover rising operating costs after making debt service payments on our financial obligations. In fact, I am surprised that Heron Holdings has continued to be such an investment darling among the major Hong Kong financial houses.

"Now that we are a public company, our financial records are available to all our investors. They must know what kind of an investment risk Heron Holdings is right now. What explains their attraction? I don't know. But if that attraction wears off and they start pulling back their loans and liquidating their stock positions, we won't have the cash to cover those obligations. Right now we urgently need new investment cash to cover our debt servicing costs and underwrite our operations until they generate more revenue. If we default on covering our liabilities, our lenders and investors can take control of Heron Holdings away from us."

"You are both colorful and blunt," said the old man. "But a bit too dramatic, I fear. Over the years I have done exactly what you told me your business school training says I should have done. We have diversified to hedge our assets. Between your uncle in Hong Kong and me, we have gone from a startup land development and construction firm to a holding company that owns more than two hundred businesses across most sectors of the Thai economy—road building, air transportation, telecommunications, tourism facilities, and commercial real estate. We're now among the largest corporations in Thailand."

"We're also among the biggest corporate borrowers at the moment," Thanakit countered. "And with bigness comes vulnerability."

Patthana was well aware that his son worked daily to keep the conglomerate's creditors at bay. But a wry smile filled his face. "Yes, Heron Holdings is heavily leveraged. But our debtors have to love us. If we go down, so do most of them! They need us more than we need them."

"It's not all that pleasant a picture," Thanakit warned. "If any of the large commercial or government banks called in our loans, Heron Holdings would need to liquidate assets quickly. And many of those assets, particularly the buildings under construction across Bangkok right now, are still months and even years from generating enough revenue to cover mortgage fees let alone operating costs. In a liquidation they will fetch far less than the amount we borrowed against their completion. The avalanche of claims would force the company into bankruptcy. Without more cash revenue, we can't continue to operate by just buying favors for new contracts from Thai officials. Cash is not there right now to pay for such favors."

Patthana knew that moving Heron Holdings into the modern world of global competition was hard to do given the high cost structures of many of his corporate operations. What he needed was a ready source of cash to assure the political support for landing new contracts.

"Look at Ban Khao Resort," continued Thanakit. "We built a luxury facility that is mortgaged far beyond its market value and has yet to cover its annual operating expenses, not even counting the Blue Heron in the calculations. We hardly have enough income from Ban Khao Resort at the moment to bribe government officials to host lucrative international conventions and encourage Thai businesses to sponsor golf tournaments at our facility."

"You forget your uncle runs our Hong Kong operations and has always looked after us, son. So far he has helped us to underwrite or restructure any loans that have become due."

"Only if you and my uncle continue your sex trafficking and gambling operations uninterrupted, and that is the side of the business we agreed we want to close down."

Patthana did not want to go down that path with his son right then. He knew well that Thanakit found some of his business operations highly distasteful. He was aware that his son did not have much tolerance for any of the darker sides of Heron Holdings' business operations. Thanakit had determined early in his life that he would have nothing to do with the Chinese crime syndicates that ran the Asian drug, gambling, and prostitution networks in which his uncle and father were involved and which had provided the seed money that got Heron Holdings started. He was certain that if he were to have a son who would care for him in his old age and pray at his grave when he was gone, he would have to purge

Heron Holdings of its illegal operations and separate the firm from its unseemly origins. But distancing the firm from its illegal operations was a delicate and protracted process. And it had to be from a position of strength, not weakness.

Patthana wanted to focus their energies on the current crisis, the attempted airline hijacking and who was behind it. "Can we agree that there is someone behind the hijacking attempt who wants to do us harm? Do you care to speculate on who that might be?" It was a rhetorical question because he had already drawn his own conclusions. He watched his son attentively for a reaction. He observed the young man shift uncomfortably, standing erect now and no longer leaning on the deck railing.

"I have given some thought, Father, to who could have benefited from our Air Siam plane going into the ocean. You have told me about each of the earlier attempts on your life. Most of them amateurish and all of them bungled. You are still alive, but so are your enemies. If indeed the hijacking was an attempt to destroy you, it was much more sophisticated, much better planned than any earlier efforts. Whoever planned this probably had access to information about Heron Holdings' financial condition and was aware of the impact a plane crash would have on us. Let's suppose the Americans had not been on that flight and the plane had gone down. There are only a few who would stand to benefit. I think we can eliminate most. But we will never have the proof. We can only prepare ourselves for the next attempt. And I suspect there will be more." From where he sat, the old man watched his son talking at the ship's railing. Thanakit stood so that the expanse of Ban Khao's beach and coves spread out behind and on each side of him. In the light of the full moon, the scalloped white sand beaches appeared to sprout from Thanakit's shoulders like angels' wings. Light from the full moon caught the waves as they broke on the beach, adding a feathery appearance to his son's illusory wings. The sight of his son that way filled the old man with both awe and apprehension.

Patthana struggled to put the imagery behind him. "Tomorrow I will fly to Sydney. I want to extend my personal condolences to the families of the murdered pilots, to Qantas Airlines, and to the Australian government. I want to do what I can to assure we can continue the lease and management contract to keep Air Siam flying.

"The Australian embassy will soon see the investigators' reports and the passengers' statements, and they will discover what we have already been told by our own friends within the police force. There is evidence that the hijacker was not acting alone. I don't believe his co-conspirators to be members of any radical Chinese political group, even though that is the official view that our prime minister wishes the public to hear right now. I don't believe the Australian authorities will calmly accept the official story either."

"You are certainly right there, Father," said Thanakit. "What do you plan to tell them at this point?"

"I want the Australian government to get the facts first from me and to know that I fully support a full investigation into who is behind the hijacking attempt. I do not believe the Thai and Hong Kong intelligence services will find evidence pointing to the hijacker's accomplices, but they will certainly uncover more than we care to share about the operations in which Air Siam was engaged in that night. And by that I mean the plane's passenger manifest."

"Father, I do not believe either that this was an attempted hijacking by political radicals. Still, for respect to our family, I will not utter what I fear you do not want me to say. We both can be silent till we have more evidence about whom we each believe is behind this. I hold no ambitions other than to see Heron Holdings become a legitimate and profitable undertaking. I know you feel me naïve to think that we can profit as an honest company. But you did give me the chance to get the training I need to give it a try."

"I do not find you naïve, son. You are courageous, and I want you to succeed. If anything, you are a bit impatient and unprepared for the forces that are arrayed against Heron Holdings. Your uncle continues to scorn you and what you are attempting to accomplish. We must someday come to terms with him. He is my younger brother. Your uncle and I share the same blood, but your grandfather could never reconcile us.

"When cholera took his life, we were both angry young men. Angry at the colonial powers and then at Japan for occupying our new nation and then at the communist government for subverting what had been one of the earliest free market economies in the world. So free and so productive that we supplied Europe with huge provisions of Oriental goods from silk to ivory to porcelain China for nearly two centuries. At the time of my grandfathers, China ran huge surpluses with Europe. And when Europe ran out of silver to pay us, the British and its East India Company paid us in opium.

"They addicted us to substances that our population was unprepared to handle. They nearly destroyed our culture. And like in its American colonies, the British tried to control our trade and impose taxes on our sales to Europe. What was once legitimate commerce, overnight became smuggling under new trade laws that the British tried to enforce with their gunboat diplomacy. Our Chinese traders came under attack. Opium wars ensued. But that only hardened our resolve. From that colonial control emerged the Chinese triads, the syndicate traders. They were welcomed by the Chinese populace as saviors because they broke the British blockades, smuggling rice up the Pearl river to Canton and saving the lives of tens of thousands of Chinese whom the British blockades attempted to starve into submission.

"After the world war and defeat of the Japanese occupiers, the syndicates attempted to return to legitimate trading along the coast. But Chairman Mao's Communist forces took control of the mainland. They had to flee downriver to Macao and Hong Kong.

"That's when my father took our mother and us two boys to a new life in Thailand. He helped me establish Heron Holdings and grow it from a small fish and rice wholesale business in Bangkok's Chinatown to one of Thailand's largest land development companies. Our family was never allowed to become part of Thai politics or accepted by Thai royalty for more than what we were, Chinese merchants. But we had the freedom to expand into commerce and industry, and we did. And when we made money, Thai officials were only too happy to take some of it in exchange for the freedom to make more money, of which they expected a future take as well. And as a prosperous young businessman, I had no trouble attracting a beautiful Thai lady to be my wife. If she only had not died giving birth to you…"

Patthana's voice trailed off. He had told the story of his Chinese heritage to Thanakit several times, but this was the first time he had expanded it to include his brother's Hong Kong syndicate life and just how ruthless his business practices were. With the events of the last two days, he felt it was time Thanakit became aware.

"My father and brother were too restless for life in what was still a very rural and backward Thailand in those days. They longed for the bustle of Hong Kong, and so when my brother became of age, my father took him to Hong Kong to set up a trading business there. But my brother was soon attracted into the ranks of the illicit syndicate traders. He quickly moved up their ranks to become one of their senior lieutenants in charge of their human trafficking and prostitution operations across east Asia.

"Your grandfather disowned him. But he was my brother, and I could not bring myself to do that. I guess I somewhat admired him for his bravado. I also hoped I could rescue him from the criminal underworld by holding out the opportunity to become a legitimate partner in Heron Holdings. He now is a major financial lifeline for Heron Holdings through the Hong Kong banking system the syndicates have penetrated. In that regard, he has been my savior. But he never would agree to abandon his syndicate life. So I never allowed him to become a partner despite his efforts to subvert me. Now it's a game, a very cutthroat game, we play with each other, and he has never ceased his efforts to gain total control of Heron Holdings. So you do not need to speak the words of whom you think was behind the scheme to bring down that Siam Air flight.

"Still, my son, we must find a way to work with your uncle at least until Heron Holdings is solvent enough to stand on its own financial feet. Your uncle holds a lot of influence over our company's global network outside of Thailand, particularly in east Asia. Most critically, he continues to wear the mantle of the crime syndicates that make up our ancestral heritage. Do not forget your heritage in all of this, Thanakit. It is more powerful than any coat of armor you could hope to wear or any Western concept of business ethics in which you could wrap yourself."

"My uncle is a common criminal, Father. He has turned his back on his family heritage and taken his triad name,

Huan Lin, Jimmy, Golden Dragon Tooth. I doubt he is likely to change now. Yes, you may have chosen to channel illegal money from his syndicate operations into more legitimate operations here in Thailand. But he wants to use Heron Holdings as a front for expanding his syndicate's human trafficking and prostitution operations all over Asia. He's using you."

The older man recognized that his son was demonstrating far more rage than he had been assuming. He tried to soothe him. "Your uncle's wings will be clipped soon. He must abandon his Hong Kong base of operations very shortly. In two weeks the British will transfer administration of the Hong Kong territories back to mainland China. Macao is not a realistic option for him because mainland China also takes over that territory at the end of the year.

"The PRC has never considered Hong Kong to be a British colony. In its eyes, Hong Kong has always been Chinese territory under lease to the British. Most likely, the PRC has been waiting for this moment of administrative turnover to eliminate the remaining syndicate leadership.

"Your uncle today carries a British Commonwealth passport. He could freely move to England if he wanted or to any other member country of the British Commonwealth, if they would have him. But he would no longer be allowed to conduct syndicate business. To continue to operate in Hong Kong under Chinese administration, he must apply for a visa from the PRC like any foreign resident. It is unlikely that the PRC will grant any sort of visa to your uncle and his Chinese syndicate associates. The PRC simply does not recognize your uncle as a member of the British Commonwealth. I suspect it also wants to end—or more correctly control—the lucrative illicit trafficking businesses that the syndicates have operated since they fled the communist mainland two generations ago."

Patthana paused to allow his son to absorb the import of what he was saying. He got up slowly and walked over to the bar to pour himself another glass of scotch. He too, he confessed to himself, was not quite sure of how events would unfold over the next two weeks. The attempted hijacking of Siam Air was a more serious omen than he wished to consider. Back with his son, he continued.

"What all this means, my son, is that your uncle needs a more welcoming country to continue his syndicate operations. Under British administration, he has had a wide degree of freedom to operate within a certain set of, shall we say, unspoken norms in Hong Kong. In exchange for staying away from smuggling guns and drugs, the British have turned a blind eye to underworld gambling and the very lucrative trafficking in humans. The rules were strict but at least transparent, and he could easily operate outwardly legitimate fronts for his syndicate. He turned out to be very shrewd among the syndicates in building from his commercial trading roots. And the British were content because the syndicates kept the underground economy under control.

"But your uncle's reputation in Hong Kong is also well-known. The PRC is aware of his underworld connections and the wealth he has accumulated. I am sure the PRC has plans for getting its hands on as much of that wealth as possible. It is also unlikely that your uncle or his associates will be granted PRC citizen status or given a Chinese passport. Just like they were pushed out of mainland China a generation ago, they will again be forced to move on to another base of operation.

"If your uncle tries to stay in Hong Kong, he knows that the mainland Chinese will be much more arbitrary and harsher than the British in dealing with his operations. He will certainly be a target for confiscation of much of the wealth he has amassed in real estate, banking, and other business operations in Hong Kong. On July 1, 1997, the skyline of Hong Kong will look the same, but its ownership will have changed dramatically.

"What the PRC does not realize is that its reclaiming of Hong Kong will be ashes in their mouths. All the Heron Holdings properties in Hong Kong have been heavily mortgaged, far beyond their market value and much of that money transferred into Hong Kong banks where associates beholden to your uncle sit on their boards. What the mainland Chinese will inherit when they begin to administer Hong Kong are properties with massive amounts of real estate debt to pay off. The new mainland Chinese administrators will find that they are stuck with tens of billions of dollars of liabilities owed to international banks and overseas investment houses that have placed their money in emerging market funds that underwrote the loans that used those Hong Kong properties as collateral, sometimes many times over."

"Ashes in the mouths of the victors!" said Thanakit. "So my uncle's Hong Kong properties are so heavily leveraged that the PRC will acquire a lot of debts to foreign banks when they take over the territory?"

"Precisely!" said the older man. "Your uncle has been liquidating property and transferring his assets out of Hong Kong before they can be monitored and controlled by the PRC. He started months ago to look for a new base of operations."

"Father, are you telling me that my uncle is attempting to relocate here in Thailand?"

"Yes, Son. He believes the business climate is far more welcoming here. And he is correct. He knows the Thai authorities are easy to buy off. With money distributed in the right places, he can expand his lucrative trafficking operations without worry of exposure or threat. He has already amassed huge investments from money he has skimmed off the Hong Kong properties he has used as collateral for loans. He has been slowly transferring that money from Hong Kong financial institutions to banks here in Thailand. In two weeks, the only thing he will have left to get out of Hong Kong will be himself."

Thanakit stared in disbelief at his father. "How long have you been aware of his plans? Have you been letting this happen to keep Heron Holdings afloat?"

"Have I had a choice? I surmised this time would come for some years. Only recently have I had to turn to him for financing, but so far I have successfully rejected his control."

"What I hear you telling me, Father, is that Heron Holdings is already pretty much under my uncle's control. You have already sold the soul of the company to the devil. All my uncle needs to do now is collect on what we owe, which amounts to most of our Thai assets after we repay our other debts. It would appear to be too late to do anything at this point. We have already lost the control of the company!"

"You have lived in Asia long enough, my son, to know that it is not who you are but what people think you are that matters. And right now, Heron Holdings is still perceived to be a corporate showpiece of the Thai economy, a company built on sound financial footing and independent of foreign influence. We cannot afford to lose that positive public perception of the company. If we do, we are lost. Remember, under our system of Asian capitalism, we can take positive perceptions of our company to the bank, and that is all we need for collateral to borrow against. We can use investor confidence to attract funds that generate more investor confidence."

"So those perceptions would likely have changed, Father, had Air Siam disappeared over the ocean three days ago!"

"It would have been enough to expose our financial vulnerability. In which case you would be sitting here on the Blue Heron talking to your uncle in less than two weeks' time. The Americans have bought us some time, but not much.

"Your uncle is now even more pressured to capture control of Heron Holdings and use it as his base in Thailand. He has had Thai visas in his British Commonwealth passport for some time. He can conduct business or purchase property here like any foreigner. There will be resistance from those in the Thai government who know his record of illicit operations in Asia. But they too can be purchased. He has the money already here now to begin to do so. And he will try.

"Right now, Heron Holdings has the public respectability and presumed resources to command support from the Thai authorities, the politicians and military alike. Should they find out that we are not what they perceive, then we have no hope for the future."

"What you are asking of me, Father, is to get into bed with the devil. To make an accommodation with my uncle in order to save Heron Holdings. But what would I be saving? A company different than what we want it to be. It is not my intent to give my uncle's syndicate a new base of operations here in Thailand. To conduct his trafficking operations under our corporate skirts."

"For the sake of your family heritage, my son, I am asking you to apply all the skills you have gained in business school to keep Heron Holdings out of the hands of your uncle. You must realize, though, that we have only a few short days to head off any further attacks on the company from your uncle. We don't know what those attacks will be or when they will come. But they will come."

Patthana could see the beads of perspiration build on his son's forehead and cheeks. The old man held his silence while his son mentally processed what he'd been told. When Thanakit spoke, however, he did so with a tone of confidence in his voice that surprised the old man and gave him hope.

"Father, there is one course of action we can take to solve this problem. It is what in America they call fighting fire with fire. It is risky. It is disruptive. It will involve trading even more heavily on perceptions of Heron Holdings' key stake in the Thai economy. I don't know if it will work. But I don't see any other options."

"Tell me your plan, Son. But be aware. This is not a business school case study. This is not a theoretical college exercise. This is real life. This is survival."

CHAPTER 7

Sirima lifted and returned the phone receiver to its cradle several times before she found the resolve to dial the phone number passed along to her by an acquaintance who worked in the American embassy consular section.

Paul's message to call him on his vacation trip to Thailand did not surprise her. The circumstances surrounding his return visit certainly did dismay her, however. She speculated that it was unlikely that he understood what was unfolding around him and his companions. She wondered, when they spoke, how much she should tell him of what she knew and, if she did, if she would be able to disguise the anger it produced inside her.

The Ban Khao Resort receptionist asked Sirima to hold while she transferred her call. A minute passed before a voice answered, "Hello. This is Paul Ellis."

"Hello, Paul Ellis. This is Sirima."

"Sirima! It's great to hear your voice again! I'm so happy the US consul in Bangkok was able to get my message and phone number to you. I hope you are well. I also hope I can see you while we're here. I want to invite you to lunch or dinner. I want to catch up on what all has happened in your life over these nearly twenty years since we worked together."

"I am doing well, Paul Ellis. Thank you for inquiring. I would love to see you as well. I went back over your family cards and letters after I learned from the press you were in

Thailand and the adventure you had getting here. I hoped you might find a way to communicate with me while you are here. How are you recovering from your ordeal?"

"We're recovering fine and in fact enjoying VIP treatment as the airline owner's guests. We had a very unique arrival in Thailand, but I'm bouncing back well. I'll tell you more about that when we meet. Perhaps you would like to visit us here in Ban Khao. It's really a beautiful resort. I can arrange for a car and driver to come and pick you up and return you home afterwards. I won't take no for an answer! I may no longer be your boss, but I can still be very insistent."

"Your invitation is very kind, Paul Ellis." Sirima hesitated and then added, "But I just cannot come to Ban Khao Resort to dine with you there. Perhaps instead I could propose a Thai dinner and folk music program for you and your companions here in Bangkok. I understand from the newspapers that you're all celebrities right now, so it would be an honor if you could find the time to come."

"Of course, I can arrange the time to come into Bangkok," said Paul. "We may be popular in the press, but the Thai government is holding us hostage here in the country as material witnesses until it concludes its preliminary investigations of the attempted hijacking incident. Not that I want to leave anytime soon, particularly given how royally we're being treated. Where do you suggest we go for dinner in Bangkok? Just name the place!"

"You were never a person to sit idle for long, Paul Ellis," said Sirima. "Thai dinner at the Orient Hotel overlooking the Chao Phraya River should fit well with your hero status, I would think."

"As much prisoners here as heroes at the moment," Paul attempted to correct. "So a brief venture out to see some of Bangkok is a welcome if short reprieve. The Orient Hotel it is. What a classic place that hotel is! It's perfect for a reunion together. Would tomorrow evening be good for you?"

"Indeed, it would. I suggest we meet in the hotel lobby at about seven o'clock, if that is suitable for you. But start out from Ban Khao with plenty of time. Bangkok traffic is far worse today than when you worked at the embassy two decades ago."

"Seven o'clock in the hotel lobby sounds good," said Paul. "I'll talk to my two travel companions about coming as well, but I can't promise. So there may be just the two of us, or you may have the luxury of two or three gentlemen escorts. I'll have the resort receptionist book a table reservation when I know how many of us there'll be. Thanks for the traffic advisory. I'm looking forward to seeing you again, Sirima."

"And I look forward to our visit together as well." Sirima concluded their call with the traditional "*Kop Khun Ka!*" Thai thank-you.

As she signed off, Sirima hoped that Paul would bring along at least one companion. Not that Sirima would have been unhappy to dine alone with him. However, a Thai woman meeting a foreigner, a *farang*, in the lobby of a hotel in Bangkok invited only one conclusion from observers. She resented that in the Thai culture a simple dinner between male and female friends always engendered unseemly suspicions. She struggled much of her life to be independent and self-reliant so that her friendships with men could be one of equals in a culture that she knew had a long way yet to go before accepting such practices without judgement.

*****

Sirima arrived at the Orient Hotel a half hour before their scheduled dinnertime. Her office was on the other side of Bangkok, and one could never accurately estimate how much time it would take to negotiate Bangkok's always congested streets. Bangkok, the Venice of the Orient, was a tapestry of woven streets and *klong* water canals. The few bridges that crossed the *klongs* were major choke points that greatly obstructed traffic flows.

She came by taxi, a taxi driven by one of her cousins. Her work placed her in such controversial situations, often making the Thai national press, that she no longer entrusted herself to any taxi driver. Because she suspected her movements were sometimes being tracked, she now preferred to move about Bangkok in a taxi driven by a relative who would not be bribed to reveal her movements. Fighting for women's rights in Thailand was not without its dangers she had learned.

Her cousin dropped off Sirima early at the Orient Hotel and headed off to pick up other taxi passengers. She would use her idle half hour to compose herself after her cross-Bangkok trip. Taller than most Thai women and very slim, Sirima still was swallowed up in one of the high-backed large peacock chairs where she chose to sit in the hotel's lobby lounge. From there she had a view of the hotel entrance and could easily spot Paul when he arrived.

The Orient Hotel lobby atrium was more like a botanical garden with its floor-to-ceiling glass walls that on one side opened out onto a patio restaurant beside Thailand's longest river, the Chao Phraya River. Across the Chao Phraya rose the golden spires of some of Bangkok's most revered Buddhist temples. With the foliage dangling down from enormous pots hung from the ribs of the glass domed atrium ceiling, it was hard to recognize that it was a hotel lobby at all. One had to look carefully to find the registration desk and concierge office amongst the full size potted palms that dotted the floor.

She allowed the noble historic hotel's elegant and soothing surroundings, with its Thai orchid-draped floral displays and flowing lobby fountains, to work on her. Bangkok life with its interminable traffic congestion was stressful enough. Add to that the struggles of the average Thai to make a living, even in the city's boomtown environment of the mid-1990s. Sirima worried about where the country was heading. So anxious were the Thais to import Western culture that they were allowing the country's renowned values of simple, gracious, and sublime living to slowly drain from their daily lives.

It seemed ironic to Sirima that Westerners would come halfway around the world to experience a way of life on which more and more Thais were turning their backs. How unfortunate that modern generation Thais were so quick to discard traditional values for Western materialism. The Western designer jeans so sought after by young Thai women were far less comfortable, or sensual, than the Thai silk dresses their mothers wore against the country's oppressive hot and humid climate. Their craving for fast cars also made no sense in Bangkok's choked-up streets, where traffic moved at a snail's pace.

Western firms had been very effective at convincing Thais that there was something missing in their lives and that American clothes, cosmetics, and cars could somehow make up for it. Yes, Sirima recognized there was something missing in Thailand, but Western consumer products were not the answer. They only added debt to Thai consumers' pocketbooks and pollution to the air they breathed. Sirima feared the importance that Thais placed on appearances had led to a self-deception that was corroding the country's culture.

In the commercial section of the American embassy where she had worked with Paul Ellis, she had played a role in advancing this Americanization of Thai culture. She shuddered with the guilt she now felt from that experience. Still, she could thank the American embassy and its personnel system for how it changed her life and set her on a course to battle for the rights of women in a rapidly changing Thai economy and society. She was not naïve about the challenges she faced, the risks she took, and the compromises she made to help her Thai sisters.

Among those compromises, the largest that loomed for her as she moved into midlife was the sacrifice of no family of her own, no husband who could come up to the standards she set for a Thai man as a life's partner. She constantly struggled with herself over whether her personal sacrifices would ever bear fruit. Her limited but meaningful successes at rescuing young women from the sex trade were rewarding to Sirima, but the population of vulnerable girls was huge, and she knew she needed to find ways to attack the causes of sex trafficking, not just address the effects it had on the lives of the victims. She was hungry to help them. It drove her. As frustrating as the struggle was, it was what got her out into Bangkok's clogged streets every morning.

Sirima would never submit to the male-dominated Thai system of work and wage discrimination. She was not trained for that. Her father, a diplomat who twenty years earlier worked at the Thai embassy in the United States, took Sirima along with him and put her through college in America. "You need an education," he had declared. "Your two older brothers will take over operating the family businesses and managing our lands. An education will complement your beauty and make you a very attractive prize for some lucky man!"

"A lucky man" was not what Sirima ever had in mind, a secret she kept from her father. She made the most of her college years and graduated with a degree in economics that she felt would serve her well back home. During college, she was also an avid observer of the civil rights movement that was spreading across the American landscape in the 1970s. She returned from the United States motivated and equipped to fight for women's rights in Thailand.

Sirima looked up to catch sight of Paul entering the hotel lobby accompanied by a companion. Sirima realized that in the flowery Thai dress she wore, she blended in so well with the lobby lounge's indoor floral arrangements and water garden that, from a distance, Paul most likely could not readily pick her out. She used that brief moment to observe the two men as the hotel's doorman escorted them inside. She watched Paul halt almost immediately after entering the hotel to take in the lobby's sumptuous surroundings. He had aged to the point where the tight and intense physique of the young Foreign Service officer she knew had given way to the softer lines and more relaxed appearance of a middle-aged man. Still he was unmistakable as the tall and gaunt Paul Ellis she had known, and she smiled to herself at the flirtatious feelings she remembered experiencing the first time they were introduced. But he was married and her boss. Sirima knew such feelings had to be buried way down inside her, and never once during the three years they worked together did she even think to exhume them.

Sirima saw that Paul's equally tall and fit companion was much more selective in his gaze around the Orient Hotel lobby. Almost immediately he focused in on her in a manner that was discreet but penetrating. Even at a distance she felt his stare. She shifted awkwardly and feared that he might have noticed the discomfort he caused in her. She sensed he might be speculating she was their dinner companion because in the next moment he subtly elbowed Paul and murmured something to cause him to look her way as well. Paul broke into a wide grin and guided the two of them toward her.

"Sawadee, Sirima! Greetings!" said Paul.

Sirima stood to greet them. "Sawadee, Khun Paul! Welcome back to Thailand!" Sirima gently bent her right knee slightly forward and bowed her head toward him, hands flat together in the traditional Thai *wai* greeting. Then a bit surprised at herself, after all the years since she had last seen and worked with him, she found herself extending her hand to accept his and shake in the typical Western-style greeting so common among their former American embassy work companions.

"You're every bit as beautiful as when I last saw you so many years ago!"

"And you are always the diplomat, Paul Ellis." Sirima smiled, relaxed now to be talking to him again in person after so many years. "And if I may say, with all diplomacy aside, the years have been very good to you. I'm pleased that you have chosen to return to Bangkok and with friends as well, I understand."

"Oh yes!" Paul caught himself. "Let me introduce Dan Spencer. It's thanks to him that we arrived at all."

Sirima shifted her gaze from Paul and for an instant looked up into the eyes of the man whose gaze she sensed had never left her since the pair entered the hotel lobby. "Welcome also to Thailand, Dan Spencer! Sawadee!" This time Sirima repeated her wai with a respectful nod of her head forward and down in an effort to break the looks that locked them together. "Your name and picture have been in the local press and on television almost daily since you made your most heroic arrival here. I feel a special honor meeting you in person."

"Thank you for your welcome," Dan replied with his gaze still on Sirima. "But I must admit that I was acting less as a hero than I was as someone wishing to save his own life. Paul coaxed me to come to Thailand for a vacation, not to be a news celebrity or to do anything more heroic than get to know a bit about this paradise you call a country."

Sirima was struck by Dan's self-effacing words and engaging demeanor. She had not expected such from the man she had learned from the news was a decorated navy fighter pilot. "A country to you but a kingdom to us Thais," Sirima said more to inform than to correct him. "Our open system of constitutional monarchy has kept us from ever falling under colonial rule. Thailand means 'free land' in our language, and we have lived that way for so long because we have found ways to be good neighbors."

"That speaks volumes about which culture and society, yours or ours, has best mastered diplomacy," said Dan. "I wager America could learn a lot from Thailand about how you do it."

"I suggest we put diplomacy and politics aside for now," said Paul. "Sirima, we put ourselves in your delicate hands this evening. Lead us to dinner and walk us through the Thai menu! Dan boasted to me on the way here that he can take on the spiciest food that the Orient Hotel has to offer. I wagered him that Thailand would win that contest. So please put him to the taste test tonight!"

Through the dinner, Sirima listened as Paul recounted their experiences aboard the Air Siam flight to Thailand. Then through the *tom yam* chicken soup and the *pad thai* shrimp course, Sirima listened to him share highlights from his diplomatic work and travels since departing Thailand. He was an easy person then and now, Sirima, recognized, to draw out with a few simple questions about his work and family.

Sirima worked to keep the conversation focused on her two dinner companions, but she found it much more challenging to encourage Dan to share the highlights of his life. *Was it the hot and spicy Thai pork rolls she had ordered for them, or was there something else that was holding him back?* she wondered. After she exhausted her capacity to keep the conversation focused on her two dinner companions, she finally acceded to Paul turning the spotlight on her.

"I want you to know, Dan, that you are in the presence of a very influential Thai woman. A woman who—"

Sirima raised her hand to cut off Paul. She was certain he would overly embellish her work and accomplishments. She wanted to control the narrative.

"Please, Paul Ellis, allow me to tell my story!

"Over the last two decades since Paul left Thailand, Dan Spencer, I have had little contact with our former colleagues at the American embassy. A few Thai friends would call me from time to time with words of support, particularly when my name appeared in the local newspapers. Otherwise all have moved on. All, that is, except your friend Paul Ellis and his lovely family. Their annual holiday greeting cards and newsletters have been one of the few constants in my life.

"You see, Paul Ellis befriended me during a difficult period in my American Embassy job. He supported my efforts at forming a Thai employees association even as the other American staff dismissed my efforts.

"'Not necessary! A distraction!' The embassy's American personnel officer told me. 'The US Embassy complies with all Thai labor laws. Organizing Thai staff to advocate for what they already have is pointless,' he kept saying.

"'Yes,' I said. 'The US embassy complies with all Thai labor laws but still expects its Thai employees to make commitments that are hardships particularly for the women employees. Bangkok time is exactly twelve hours ahead of Washington, DC, time. Our American supervisors regularly stay at their desks into the evening here in Bangkok so they can have an hour or two of overlap to speak with their State Department counterparts who are just arriving at their Washington, DC, offices in the morning.'

"Our American bosses often request us to be on hand as well, I explained. They ask us to stay late to send out last-minute reporting cables or compose memos of conversation in response to their calls to the United States. That is fine for most of our male Thai employees at the embassy, but we Thai women employees often find that the late evening hours conflict with family commitments. Some of us live in areas of the city where getting home alone at night is not safe.

"My colleagues, particularly those with families, were too timid to speak up. Too afraid of losing their jobs. We frequently complained to each other about our work and family conflicts at lunch in the embassy cafeteria. 'It's time,' I argued, 'that we collectively petition the ambassador to authorize transport from the motor pool or allowances to pay for shuttle or taxi services to take us to our homes on evenings we are required to work late.'

"I did not get much support from my Thai work colleagues at first. 'We'll find ourselves out on the streets if we complain!' was their reaction. 'Working for the American Embassy is a plum job,' they reminded me.

"They were correct, of course. There were fifty others waiting in line for each of our positions. The US Embassy had done a lot to set an example of increasing the share of its

Thai employees who are women. But we all worried that if we pushed too hard, we could lose the gains we'd made.

"Still, I challenged them. 'What would you lose? You would lose the risk that your husbands will go off with another woman because you are seldom home in time to greet them or to sit down with them and your kids at dinner. You will lose the fear of being robbed on the way home from work late at night. What we are asking for is reasonable, and it's nothing the embassy can't afford to do.'

"So I assembled a list of concerns from the embassy's female Thai staff and collected signatures to support it. To my surprise, the ambassador responded promptly and favorably, instructing the personnel office to work with us to address our concerns. From that experience, we formed a US-Thai embassy employees' benefit association. They selected me to serve as its president, and when necessary, as its negotiator.

"But it was a short-lived victory. The embassy personnel officer was not pleased that we had gone directly to the ambassador with our grievances. New female hires became rare, and my employee association officers and I were passed over for promotions and annual performance bonuses. Paul Ellis had fought hard in my defense. He wrote glowing performance reports and recommendations for job advancement and salary bonuses with only limited success. I saw that I had become a pariah in the embassy personnel system. I stayed with the embassy, but only out of loyalty to Paul and appreciation for his support. Then, within a month after he ended his tour in Thailand and departed post, I submitted my resignation."

"That's awful," declared Dan. "I'm embarrassed to learn about that kind of treatment from the embassy of the country that purports to be a world leader for human justice!"

"All was not wasted I assure you, Dan Spencer," Sirima continued. "My American embassy experience was just the start of my career in fighting for the rights of Thai women. After leaving the American embassy, I campaigned for women's causes and became one of the first female ministers in the Royal Thai Parliament. But the political processes moved too slowly for me, so I decided that after I finished my term in Parliament, I would form a women's rights organization. As its leader, I've worked to raise funds to support myself and to conduct programs rescuing women from exploitive and dangerous work conditions, particularly the sex trade for which Thailand is notorious."

A Thai dessert of sweet lichee nuts arrived accompanied by a brief program of Thai dancing and folk music to entertain them. After the dancers and musicians withdrew, their conversation turned to events of the week that Paul and Dan had spent since they arrived in Thailand. Sirima was not comfortable when her dinner companions began to describe the luxurious resort surroundings and sumptuous lodging that the airline's owner had extended to them while they were in Thailand.

"I want you both to know that few things in Thailand are what they seem to be," Sirima began. "We Thais whom you credit with being masters of diplomacy, Dan Spencer, are also capable of great deceit. I regret to say that your host, Khun Patthana, is one to watch most closely."

It was Dan who jumped in to respond. "Watch for what?"

Sirima was silent for a moment, not sure how to begin and, more concerning, where to end. When she spoke, it was first to Paul. "Paul Ellis, when you invited me to be your dinner guest at Ban Khao and I told you I had to decline, I apologize for the inconvenience of your long drive into

Bangkok for dinner this evening. It was not for any disrespect to you that I declined your invitation to visit you at Ban Khao. It's just that Ban Khao's owner represents everything against which I have been fighting in Thailand during the years since you left Bangkok.

"It is never easy for us Thais to speak of our country's shortcomings, and it is always delicate to criticize one's own compatriots, but when offenses against the innocent are so grave, I have learned that discretion must end."

"Aha!" said Paul. "I suspect you are about to tell us that there's drug money behind our resort host. That when we saved his plane, we helped save a business a lot less legitimate than his airline and his resort. We actually have some suspicions of our own about him."

"I wish the situation were, as you Americans say, that black-and-white," said Sirima. "If drug trafficking were at the heart of it, Patthana's business operations would never have been allowed to grow to be the corporate empire it is today. Khun Patthana has been too smart to allow himself to become involved in the heavily sanctioned drug trade. One either ends up in jail or in sharing a major share of the wealth with the network of government enforcement agents who allow the drug dealers to operate.

"No, his business empire is built on something more sinister than dealing in drugs." Sirima paused for a minute to gauge her listeners' attention and openness to what she was saying. She also needed to assess how far she wanted the conversation to go now that she had opened the subject. The evening had been truly enjoyable. Paul and Dan were both gracious dinner hosts. She admitted to herself that it had been some time since she had felt so relaxed around men who were not part of her immediate family. And men who treated her as an equal. She was reluctant to break the enchantment of the moment, but she could not put out of her mind the thousands of women, young girls, even children who, that same night, who every night, lived lives of repeated sexual brutality by men of morals far different from those of her dinner companions. At the very least she owed it to those women and girls to make Paul and Dan aware of their plight and of the predatory role played in their lives by their host, Khun Patthana, and his Heron Holdings enterprises.

"Paul Ellis, I am sure you remember from your work in Thailand some years ago the challenges that our Asian form of Confucian capitalism presented to the American embassy and to American investors seeking to conduct business here. Your Western values of openness and independence clashed with the values of loyalty, privacy, and reputation that are central to how Asian commerce is conducted."

Sirima paused while the waiter cleared away their dinner plates and made space for Thai tea. Then she commenced to give her companions a short history lesson and some background about their Ban Khao Resort host.

"Khun Patthana came to Thailand with his parents from China after the Second World War. His family was poor in cash but rich in connections with Thailand's Chinese merchant community here and in Hong Kong. His family was associated as well with the Chinese syndicates or triads, the equivalents of your European and American Mafias. Such syndicates have for centuries controlled much of Mainland China's commercial trade and illegal smuggling. When the communist Chinese came to power, the syndicates moved their base of smuggling and gambling operations from the mainland to Hong Kong and Macao. But even those locations are temporary. Hong Kong reverts from the British back to the Chinese administration in less than two weeks.

"Patthana has a Hong Kong brother who is among the shrewdest and most brutal among the syndicate triad leaders. His syndicate has based its operations on gambling and human trafficking mostly for prostitution. The British Hong Kong administration is more concerned about drug smuggling. With his brother operating out of Hong Kong, Patthana set up his base of operations here in Thailand. The two brothers do not get along. But they are still brothers, so they have at least found a way to work together when money is to be made.

"Unlike Indonesia, Singapore, Malaysia, and Korea, Thailand has always been a more hospitable home to the overseas Chinese. They have settled here and intermarried into our culture and society since the beginnings of our kingdom. We have a saying here that 'if you scratch a Thai, Chinese blood will flow.'

"The Chinese merchants, and there are many honest ones, remain the backbone of Thai commerce even today. The Thai political system has confined its Chinese population until very recently to trade and commerce and kept them out of government and politics. But those connected with the syndicates, well…if they could not become government officials or politicians, they learned they could buy them!

"Khun Patthana has built a business empire that started from money lent him by his brother from his Hong Kong syndicate's Asian sex trafficking. That trafficking continues today. It's a billion-dollar-a-year business. The revenues from their human trafficking operations they use to finance legitimate operations and also, to bribe public officials who arrange for them lucrative government contracts and easy loans from government banks. Ban Khao Resort is one of those operations. Air Siam is another. And there are many more.

"Khun Patthana has invested heavily in Thailand, and behind his company's façades he continues to raise money through their lucrative trafficking in humans, mostly young women, for the sex trade. For more than two decades, Asian, European, and American businessmen have been coming to Thailand for golf and sex vacations. Now Patthana discreetly sends plane loads of girls to his customers in countries that range from Korea to the Middle East."

Sirima was about to continue when Dan interrupted. "So that's why the coach class section of our Air Siam flight was filled with row after row of young girls. They were being trafficked, literally, right behind our backs on that flight!"

"And remember, Dan," Paul injected, "how Ben translated the hijacker's last words?" He cried out that he was there to rescue all the slaves from the nasty capitalists. He must have been referring to the Thai girls in the back of the plane. He must have hoped that by landing the plane and its passengers in Thailand, he would be revealing the purpose behind the airline and its owner."

Sirima saw that they both were quick to grasp her point. "Yes, Dan Spencer, this is going on right behind your backs. And yes, Paul Ellis, your flight was being used to traffic young girls. Through Patthana's trafficking network and the Thai political connections he has, he easily arranges false work and travel papers for the girls. Many believe that they are going abroad to work as household servants or factory workers to earn money to send home to their families. When they arrive, they find out the truth, but it is too late. Patthana's clients hold on to their passports and identity cards. If they try to flee, they are arrested and essentially stateless with little in the way of help to get them back to their homes. Most of them become sex slaves. That is until they are worn-out, used up, and sent back to their families as impoverished as when they started out.

"Today there is an endless flow of these girls from rural areas where there is no work. They are drawn to the city by promises of jobs in restaurants and bars. Some young girls are actually sold by their parents to pay off family debts. Asian men pay a premium for younger girls, particularly for virgins. A brothel owner will pay ten thousand American dollars for a twelve-year-old virgin as well as a commission on her earnings."

Sirima paused and remembered from their earlier dinner conversations that Paul had young daughters back home. She sensed the feelings of disgust that he and Dan felt toward traffickers who exploited young girls. She struggled to soften her words a bit as she continued.

"Khun Patthana, I must admit, is far less ruthless than his brother in Hong Kong. The girls last only a few years in the sex trade. They lose their attractiveness, become pregnant, or contract diseases. Patthana's Hong Kong brother throws them into the streets. Patthana, at least, finds work for some of them in his factories or businesses. At Ban Khao, they clean your rooms and carry your golf bags. Patthana offers cradle-to-grave security in exchange for their total submission and loyalty."

"But there are laws. Human trafficking is a crime, as much as trafficking in drugs," said Dan. "Isn't there enforcement of international protocols against trafficking?"

"Yes, Dan Spencer." Sirima looked at him with a mildly reproachful glance. "But Patthana owns the law. So many of our esteemed members of the Thai government are on his unofficial payroll or serving on boards of directors of his enterprises that we joke he could hold his own Thai cabinet-level meetings. Your host runs many outwardly respectful businesses in Thailand, and he is a darling of your American embassy. His son, Thanakit, heads the Thai-American Chamber of Commerce and is held up as an example of the new generation of Thai businessmen. But his father, Patthana, continues to finance and operate many of his businesses with illicit cash."

"So what is being done to fight him? To rescue and protect the women?" said Dan. "Even with money and the law on his side, he must have weaknesses somewhere."

"In truth, we have many ideas but no effective strategy we can say that works. Suppressing trafficking is hopeless as long as there is so much money to be made and law enforcement authorities look the other way because of bribes or because they are directly involved in trafficking itself. When forced to act, the police and military usually arrest and punish the girls, not those who prey on them.

"Our efforts concentrate on educating girls and their families against the dangers they face in accepting job offers from agents who promise them the glamour of travel and easy money. We are also working from within Heron Holdings itself. Khun Patthana is an old man, but his son, Thanakit, with his American education, wants to make his enterprises profitable without the need of buying votes or influencing government contracting. And he believes that to be sustainable in the long run, Heron Holdings needs to become totally legitimate. But he is not yet in charge of the company."

"Well, then," Paul jumped in, "Thanakit may be a place to start. He welcomed us to Ban Khao and got us settled in. He shared with us that he is a US business school graduate. We joined him and his father, Patthana, for dinner two days ago. We sensed that he is not at all like his father when we observed the two of them briefly discussing the future of their family business."

"Educated and socially responsible younger business leaders like Thanakit are one of our few hopes in Thailand. But at the moment, that is all that Thanakit is. A hope. We cannot wait idly by for him eventually to take over and make over Heron Holdings. The lives of young girls continue to be destroyed daily.

"At present we are working to dry up the supply of girls by finding them good-paying jobs in legitimate businesses. But we are not so innocent as to think we can totally stamp out sex trafficking by trying to compete against it. This is about changing the culture of human exploitation, about treating women as humans, not as commodities.

"Thailand's sex trade is part of a larger problem. It is part of the darker side of what you Americans promote as 'globalization' and free access to world markets. Tear down the barriers to movement of people and goods and one unfortunate outcome is that it facilitates human trafficking."

Sirima felt she was getting too close to unleashing the frustrations that she struggled to contain that evening. It was disrespectful of her, she knew, to make her dinner hosts uncomfortable. She could sense she had already provoked a sense of anger in both men. She felt a bit awkward for making her dinner hosts sit through a shorter version of the lecture she had delivered many times to the Thai Parliament and press. She also realized the evening was growing late. She sought now to end their discussion.

"But enough of this talk, Paul Ellis and Dan Spencer! You both have a long drive back to Ban Khao, and I shouldn't detain my American hosts further. Not after the memorable evening to which you have treated me."

She anticipated and headed off their next question.

"My cousin drives a taxi, and I arranged with him to take me home. It's the ten o'clock hour when we agreed he would wait for me at the hotel's taxi park. My drive is a lot shorter than yours. You have a much longer way to go. At least there's less congestion on the road for you at this hour." She paused for an instant. "Thank you both for an unforgettable evening."

"Sirima, it's we who should thank you for arranging such a delightful evening of Thai food and folk dancing," said Paul. "You have also given us food for thought as well. We need to talk together, we three Americans. You've helped us learn a lot about our Ban Khao Resort host. You have given us some homework to do. I want to explore with my friends how we might do something for you and your women's causes! I hope we can see you again before we leave Thailand."

"I hope we meet again during your stay as well," Sirima said. "Just take care of yourself, Paul Ellis! And you also, Dan Spencer! Your Ban Khao Resort host circulates with some rough company. I guess you know that now from your experience getting here. That should be an even more compelling warning than mine."

Dan walked beside Sirima as they accompanied her to the taxi stand. "You're an enchanting woman, Sirima. Thoughts about you and your work will be on my mind long after the powerful taste of our spicy Thai dinner has disappeared from my mouth."

"The sweet lichee dessert and Thai tea should quickly take care of the spicy food, Dan Spencer. So I guess I will be out of your mind before you even arrive back at your resort tonight." Sirima displayed a coy smile on her face as she looked directly at him one more time.

"I'm not at all likely to forget this evening with you that quickly, Sirima. For the first time tonight, you are wrong," said Dan. "I've always felt more comfortable viewing the world from thirty thousand feet. But you've revealed that there is a lot for me to discover here on the ground in Thailand. Thank you for the close-up look tonight."

Sirima hung on Dan's last words as she drove away. He could be referring to her description of their Ban Khao Resort host, Khun Patthana. But she felt as if he might have been inferring something about her as well.

CHAPTER 8

Ben slapped their Thai limo chauffeur lightly on the man's shoulder as he and Paul climbed into their resort limo. "The Doll House! Take us to the Doll House in Pattaya!" Paul saw the burly limo driver and his equally husky Thai companion in the front passenger seat give each other knowing glances as the four of them headed off along Thailand's eastern coastal road. They were headed to Pattaya City, one of the best-known adult entertainment meccas of East Asia, forty minutes away.

Earlier that hot balmy afternoon, Paul had convinced Ben to play one more round of golf with the promise to accompany him to wherever Ben chose to go that evening.

"Pattaya!" Ben declared, and without hesitation, he called the resort desk to arrange for a car and driver before Paul had a chance to object. "If you can take Dan to a fancy hotel restaurant in Bangkok, you gotta take me somewhere so I have my own story to tell!"

"And what sorta story do ya wanna tell?" For Paul, sitting with a good book on the outdoor restaurant terrace served equally well after a day of chasing a little white ball. He knew Ben would seek more stimulation. After all, he was still on the mend from their long and stressful flight and far from restoring his golf handicap. Paul tried to convince himself that a night out on the town would indeed benefit Ben.

Dan declined to join them. He had done the Pattaya scene many times in his earlier life as a navy stick jockey flying in for some R and R time on the beach and in the bars after long dull days patrolling with his reconnaissance squadron up and down the East Asian coast. Pattaya was a pretty wild scene then, he told Paul and Ben. He expected that by now with most American troops withdrawn from the region, Pattaya would only be a shell of its former self.

Always the organizer, Paul attempted to structure their Pattaya visit. They would have a couple of drinks, they agreed, then have dinner and take in an evening show. The raunchier the better Ben had insisted. Fortunately, they had their Ban Khao driver and his companion to get them back to the resort. They could afford to drink a little. To live a little.

Ben looked across at Paul from their limo seats. "Pattaya City was the R and R landing zone for American troops during the Vietnam war days."

"I know. I know, Ben!" said Paul. "Remember, I lived and worked in Thailand toward the end of that war. The Thai government feared Pattaya would dry up when it ended. So it focused on replacing American troops with international tourists. You'll see signs in Pattaya now not only in English and Thai but also Japanese, Korean, Arabic, German, and French. The big petroleum companies fly in planeloads of oil rig workers from the Middle East to pass their vacation time at Pattaya. Dan's got it wrong. If anything, the city has flourished, not shriveled up."

"Well, whatever. I have it on reliable authority that for a good time, Pattaya is still the city to visit, and the Doll House is the place to be. It has some of the best-looking and friendliest ladies in Thailand, I'm told."

"Your authority being?"

"My computer students back at the Ban Khao Resort conference center," said Ben. "Several of them had hostess jobs at Pattaya watering holes before coming to Ban Khao

Resort to work. The day after we arrived at Ban Khao, I went searching for a computer to check my email messages and news from the US. I discovered a bevy of young Thai girls sitting around the resort's convention center business office with nothing to do. When I announced what I wanted, they were all over me to help.

"It turned out, though, that their computer skills were uniformly mediocre, so I ended up instructing all of them on how to use software applications and conduct internet searches. Word must have spread quickly because the next day, after our round of golf, I was giving a computer class to more than twenty of them. They're all eager to learn about computers, and the resort has state-of-the-art equipment I can use to teach them. I want them to learn everything I know."

"So you show them how to use the resort's computers to do Internet searches for porn sites. Is that it?"

"Well…kinda like that. You can't imagine the looks of surprise on their faces when we came across a Swedish porn site. They could not believe the size of the breasts on those blond European babes. I had the full attention of everyone in my class! Good teachers choose topics that stimulate their students, so they want to learn more!"

The smirk on Ben's face belied the seriousness with which he attempted to deliver his lecture.

"Oh! You make me feel so stimulated as well!" said Paul.

"Shudup!" said Ben and he settled into his corner of the limo and closed his eyes.

Paul knew Ben was all bark and no bite. He was someone who enjoyed the chase whether he was after elusive and obscure intelligence information or his next female companion. It was the love of the pursuit, not the pursuit of love that framed Ben's life of two short marriages and a series of shorter relationships. Paul speculated that Ben's current live-in companion back in the United States—as close to a wife as Ben now cared to get—would not hold much attraction for him after returning from their Asian adventure.

Despite Ben's wandering eyes, Paul found it hard not to like him. He had been a part of his family's life since they moved in next door to him in the Washington, DC suburbs ten years earlier. Only a few hours after the moving trucks pulled away, there was a knock on the door of their new home. Paul remembered when his wife, Sarah, answered, Ben was standing there with a plate full of freshly made chocolate chip cookies.

"Oh, how wonderful of your wife to send you over with welcome cookies!" Sarah had exclaimed.

Ben was crestfallen. "I baked 'em myself. All my wife knows how to do is fu…" And his voice trailed off.

Embarrassed at her misplaced assumption, Sarah recovered quickly and invited him in to get acquainted. Since that day, Ben had been a fixture in the Ellis household. Through their years as neighbors, Ben had been a regular at Paul's side, helping in the yard, lending tools and himself for fix-up projects, and preparing countless cookouts as their family barbecue chef.

Watching him doze off reminded Paul of the Christmas Eve a few years back when he called Ben, who was between female friends at that point, to come over to have some hot rum toddies and help him assemble his girls' Christmas gifts, two bicycles. The bicycles were to "buy off" his girls, who had been lobbying for a dog. An animal just did not work out for a family like theirs that traveled and lived internationally.

It was well into the evening after the girls had gone to bed, and Paul and Ben had finished assembling the bikes. Ben, with several hot rum toddies under his belt, stretched out on the family room floor to rest a moment before heading home next door. When Paul and Sarah were ready to retire, they realized that Ben had fallen into a deep slumber. They agreed it would be cruel to wake the peacefully sleeping Ben and send him back to his place to be alone on Christmas Day. So they covered him with a blanket and let him sleep off the evening in front of the warm fireplace next to the Christmas tree and bicycles.

With the first morning rays of light, Paul and Sarah were shaken awake by two excited little girls. Their daughters had been downstairs already and taken in the Christmas scene. "Whose Christmas gift is Ben?" their daughters asked in unison.

"He's mine!" shouted one of them. "I saw him first under the tree!"

The spirited tug-of-war over Ben continued with laughter and joking through gift giving and Christmas Day meals the five of them shared together. Ben loved it. They all did. Ben became their "Saint Benard" puppy that day, and all talk of wanting a real dog ceased.

"Ben's almost part of the family," Paul remembered Sarah telling him. "He loves to romp with the girls in the yard and tag along with you on your chores. I only wish he could find it in himself to settle down and be loyal to one woman. He would be a wonderful catch. This commitment phobia he seems to have just doesn't help him any."

"Ben tries hard to please everyone," was Paul's armchair analysis. "He feels there are so many lonely women in the world, and he was put on this earth to befriend as many of them as he can."

*****

Mulling over those thoughts made Paul a bit nervous about taking Ben to Pattaya. Ben had spent much of his career studying political and economic developments in China from the remoteness of a computer screen buried in the windowless bowels of the Central Intelligence Agency. He became the agency's leading Chinese linguist translating and analyzing mainland Chinese radio broadcasts and news reports using and polishing the Mandarin and Cantonese Chinese he learned in army language school before he joined the agency.

At the agency he had several intel scoops to his credit. Anticipating the Tiananmen Square demonstrations weeks before they happened had been one. However, except for a few short weeks that Ben had served in Saigon in the Army at the tail end of the Vietnam War and before he started at the agency, this visit to Thailand was his first exposure to Asia in the flesh. From what Paul had seen, Ben was taking the "in the flesh" part with too much gusto.

In his corner of the limo, Ben began to come back to life. He continued their conversation as if there had been no thirty-minute lapse while he was dozing. "I want you to know that I never make a move without conducting a thorough intelligence analysis. Pattaya included. Most of my girls—my students, that is—know the Pattaya scene very well. They gave me tips on the dos and don'ts. You're in good hands, my boy. And before the evening is out, I at least expect to be in some warm and inviting hands myself!"

Paul gave Ben a sarcastic smirk.

Evening was coming on as they approached the outskirts of Pattaya. The setting sun across the bay was yielding to the necklace of neon lights that began to illuminate the city's bars and eateries strung out along the crescent-shaped beachfront. Obese, lobster-red foreign tourists were abandoning the surf and sand and heading back to their hotels to nurse their sunburned bodies before venturing out into the awakening bar and night club scene.

The whirl of Pattaya nightlife hit both Paul and Ben as soon as they descended from their vehicle. While their limo drivers waited, they began the evening with a stroll along the strip of outdoor eateries, taking in the large signs and loud hawkers announcing each bar's specialties.

"Asian Women Escort Services!"

"Full Body Massage!"

"Great Drinks! Great Women!"

"24-Hour Topless Shows!"

"Liquor and Lap Dancing."

"No-hands dining!"

They had arrived at Asia's ground zero for the adult entertainment industry.

Paul saw quickly that Ben was not prepared for the commercial sex banquet that Pattaya spread out before them. Ben had to peek into every door and down every alley from which strident music and strobe lights assaulted him. Through each of the bar doors, they could catch enticing glimpses of exotic young female bodies gyrating to the music or sitting on barstools bent over drinks and chatting together while waiting for the evening's customers to arrive.

Paul had urged dinner before bar hopping to give them more endurance to get through an evening of drinking. "You're too goddamned practical, Paul," Ben had lectured him. "I want a drink before dinner, a drink during dinner, and a drink after dinner. Preferably with more companionship than just you! Besides, we can scope out the Doll House before it gets crowded, maybe line up some cuties for when we come back after eating."

The last point, Paul recognized, was Ben's poorly veiled attempt to appeal to Paul's practical side. Still, he had no credible reason for challenging his friend. So into the Doll House they went, Ben in the lead. As if preassigned, two young girls approached, flanked them on each side, and escorted them over to a cushioned sofa in one corner of a dimly lit cavernous room with small, dinner-plate-sized round tables with chairs around them scattered about. A long thin bar, with brass poles connected every six feet or so from its surface to the ceiling, ran the length of the mirrored back wall of the room. Above the bar, rotating lights played their beams down on the near-naked bodies of dancers who gyrated around each of the poles while the go-go music did its best to drown out street noise.

As the foursome sat down, a waiter came and stood opposite the low coffee table in front of them. Ben was already into ogling his female companion to see how anatomically correct she was. He was warned by his students at the Ban Khao business center that young boys often dressed up to look every bit as sexy as the girls. Ben wanted none of that. He had his standards.

He looked over briefly at Paul. "Order me a beer. And for our new friends here, whatever they want. The bill's on me!"

"Sounds good to me." Paul looked up at the waiter, raised two fingers, and shouted over the music, "Two Singha beers!" Then he gestured at the young ladies between them with an open hand to indicate they were invited to ask the waiter to bring them what they wished. "I suspect the girls will order some weak tea dressed up in cocktail glasses to look like theater-stage whiskey, Ben. After all, they're at work and have a long night ahead of them."

Ben was already lost in the deep dark eyes of his Doll House companion. "That's okay. Weak tea at whiskey prices is no big deal!"

"I agree," replied Paul. "It's worth the entertainment value of watching you carry on."

The girls exchanged brief words in Thai with the waiter, who hurried off to fill their orders. Paul was pleased to see that this little amount of communication was sufficient for the waiter to spring into action. In a moment he returned with a tray containing two tall glasses of beer and a bottle of Johnny Walker black label which he very dexterously opened with one hand to pour part of its contents into two smaller whiskey glasses on his tray. Paul realized instantly he should have insisted on opening the bottle himself and testing its contents before the waiter poured the young ladies' drinks. But he recognized that such a gesture would not have set well with their companions or the waiter. Best to let events flow as they may.

After an hour of small talk, with little communication beyond flirtatious smiles, Paul wasn't getting any more accustomed to the music, and the strobe lights were bringing on a headache. He was discovering that at his age, he no longer had as high a threshold for such sensations. "Time to dine! You got her name, Ben? You can tell her you'll come back later to see her. She'll be happy to see you again in a couple of hours, I'm sure. But without me. I plan to eat and stroll the strip while you stroke the merchandise."

"You're such a puritan!" said Ben. "And just where is your Christian charity? These young ladies need the work and the income. And you're just gonna walk around with your hands in your pockets, one holding onto your wallet and the other holding onto your dick! Why can't you rise to the occasion and pump something into the local economy?"

"And take home a little present to the Missus when I return? Not my idea of a fun vacation. Come on, you dirty old man! Let's eat!"

"You really know how to deflate a guy!" Ben untangled himself from his couch companion and signaled the waiter for the bill.

"Three hundred!" said the waiter.

"Three hundred Thai baht?" Ben did a quick currency conversion in his head. "Let's see, that's about sixty dollars. That's not bad."

"No," said the waiter. "Is three hundred American dollar."

"What?" Ben had a look of disbelief on his face.

The waiter was clearly prepared for his reaction. "Six beer, ten dollar each. Whiskey, two hundred dollar for bottle. Rest for cover charge."

"Outrageous!" said Ben. "I do not plan to pay anything like three hundred dollars for a bottle of scotch and a few beers. I want to speak to your manager."

"Manager coming," said the waiter, and almost on cue, a short, heavyset Thai emerged from behind the bar.

As he approached, Ben and Paul both rose to their feet, which the waiter must have immediately taken as the first sign of fight or flight. He quickly cleared the glasses and bottle from the table, set them down nearby on the bar, and walked over and stood feet spread, blocking the bar's entry door.

The manager was no more disposed to discuss Ben's complaint nor more fluent in his ability to communicate beyond what his waiter had told them. He stood about as tall as Ben's short frame, but his solid build left little doubt in either Ben or Paul that he was capable and willing to resolve the dispute physically.

Paul spoke in an effort to defuse the situation. "Look, my friend, we came to your establishment because it was

highly recommended to us. I am sure you want to maintain
your reputation and not be branded as a clip-joint."

"Many American come here. All have good time. All
pay bills, not cheat me like you want to do. You want to go?
You pay first. Three hundred American dollar."

Paul was not quick enough to stop Ben, who pointed
his finger at the manager and bellowed, "We didn't come in
here to cheat. We came to—" But before Ben could finish, he
found himself facedown on the table with the manager pin-
ning his outstretched arm behind him. The waiter moved in
quickly to restrain Paul with a block that took the air out of
him and sent him flying back into the sofa from which their
two female drinking companions fled.

Ben forced himself to his feet with his free hand, only
to feel the waiter's fist in his stomach. Paul lunged toward
the manager before he could land another blow at Ben. They
both went down on the barroom floor, but the manager was
back on his feet before Paul could raise himself to his knees.
The waiter's kick to Paul's side took his wind away again and
left him sprawled out on his stomach. "Hold off! This is not
necessary!" Paul attempted to get out, but he found himself
lifted up by the waiter and flung back into the sofa.

What happened then at first relieved and then terri-
fied Paul and Ben. Through the bar's open doorway came
their limo driver and his companion. No one moved as they
approached the four men frozen in their fight positions.

From the corner of his eye, Paul glimpsed a sliver of
light off a knife blade in the waiter's hand. Their chauffeur
must have seen it too, because he slowly walked over to the
waiter and stopped about three feet away. The waiter slowly
raised the knife blade, but Paul suspected he did so not to
attack their chauffeur but to defend himself.

Paul was correct. Even with the knife, the waiter was no match for their chauffeur. In an instant, the chauffeur's leg and foot struck out and crashed into the waiter's leg. With a yell, the waiter collapsed on the floor in agony.

Paul saw that the Doll House manager now sought some way to end the dispute. But the chauffeur and his companion were just beginning. They swiftly lifted the manager off his feet and threw him across the bar into a stack of liquor bottles behind it. Screams from the girls now drowned out the music. The strobe lights caught a surrealist ballet of flying bodies and debris as the chauffeur and his companion grabbed the waiter and sent him flying after the manager. Then they sent chairs and tables over the bar and into a pile where they'd flung the manager and waiter.

When there was nothing left to trash, the two men looked at each other and smiled. Then they reached down to Ben on the floor and to Paul on the sofa and pulled them to their feet. "We go to Ban Khao now! Party over!" said the chauffeur and led them out into the night air and straight to their limo.

Not a word passed between Ben and Paul during the hour trip back to Ban Khao. They sat leaning back in opposite corners of the limo's back seat rubbing their aching bodies.

As they got out of the car at the resort, it was Paul who broke the silence. "In the morning. We should talk. All three of us."

Ben nodded in agreement but said nothing as they headed to their rooms to recover from the evening. A week had passed since they arrived in Thailand, but to Paul, it now seemed more like a month.

CHAPTER 9

Paul was the first to arrive for morning breakfast on the hotel's oceanfront veranda. He chose a somewhat secluded table away from other guests where he, Dan, and Ben could talk freely. For a moment he allowed himself to be soothed by the gentle rushing of the ocean's breaking waves and the rustling leaves in the tall arching acacias that shaded the restaurant tables from the rising sun.

Ben and Dan appeared on the veranda, and Paul motioned them over. They exchanged good-morning nods with Paul without saying a word, and for a long silent moment, the three of them took in the sights of the day unfolding around them. Along the beach to their right, the early sunbathers were already filling the neatly arranged lounge chairs under large pastel-colored beach umbrellas. Small sailboats and wind surfers punctuated the bay as they slipped out from the marina.

Just down the beach to their left, tin-roof houses of the neighboring Ban Khao fishing village extended down to the water, where small outboard motorboats were lined up following a night of fishing. They could see the villagers now unloading and weighing the fish catch before dividing it up between the refrigerated dollies from the resort's restaurant and the pickup trucks of the merchants from nearby city markets.

Neither the colorful scene of the beachgoers nor the quaint setting of the fishing village captured the attention of Paul and his companions that morning. Paul was not in a pleasant mood. He was edgy. After menus were brought and the threesome selected their breakfast choices, he began to speak.

"I'm thinking we should move out of here. Soon. We should go back to Bangkok and get a hotel there until the hijacking investigation is over. Then we can fly back to the US. Or maybe there's still space available at the golf resort where I had originally booked us."

"Whatever for?" said Ben. "I'm beginning to feel right at home here. And I have some responsibilities now. My computer training classes are expanding with each session I teach."

Dan quickly jumped into the conversation. "From what we've learned about Patthana, your computer classes are with young girls who have aged out of the sex trade, Ben. Sure, they can use the training, but you're just enabling a very bad practice of debt servitude. Paul's friend Sirima tells us that by the time they're used up in the sex trade, they have accumulated huge debts to repay. Patthana apparently assumes their debts, puts them to work at Ban Khao and other places he operates, and takes a large part of their salaries to pay down their debts. Sure he provides housing and food, but it still takes years before they are debt-free. Do you want to be part of that system?"

Paul interjected, "That's my point. We're all aware that our host has a rather unseemly background and employs some rather brutal thugs. The glitter of this idyllic resort can't hide that from any of us any longer. That's why I think we should part company with him."

Ben continued to push back. "And how do you know that the resort where you originally booked us is not built on the same unseemly business, Paul? Maybe Patthana owns that resort as well. And if things are as bad as you paint them, why not try to expose them while you have this unique opportunity? To do that, though, you need to be here, in the belly of the beast, giving it ulcers and indigestion. You won't accomplish much hunkered down in a hotel in Bangkok."

Paul looked at Ben. He was surprised. Ben, the happy-go-lucky guy, was suddenly revealing a social justice crusader side of himself that Paul hadn't witnessed before. Maybe being slapped around in a Pattaya bar was precipitating his new outlook on the world.

"Well," Paul continued. "I'd like to learn more about how Patthana operates. Several things here do not compute for me. The resort and club facilities appear far too opulent and expansive for the limited number of local and foreign tourists we've seen during our week's stay. There's far too much common area for the number of villas, condo units, and hotel rooms sprinkled about the property. Even if the facilities are maxed out with visitors attending the half dozen golf tournaments that the resort hosts each year, revenues appear to fall far short of his operating costs, at least here at Ban Khao Resort."

"Paul, you know resorts host such events to get visibility, not always to make a profit directly," said Dan. "The benefits come later from increased patronage that the prestige of holding those events creates."

"Well," Paul said, "so far I see little evidence that Ban Khao is anywhere close to becoming a major tourist draw. In the week we've been enjoying Ban Khao's amenities, we've all been pleased with how few weekday golfers we've seen on the course. We can get just about any tee time we want even putting aside our VIP status here. We're here in Thailand's high tourism season, but even last weekend I saw no surge in city visitors. It passed like all the other days of the week.

"Then there's the resort staff and employees, our villa attendants, the groundskeepers, and food service crews. On a typical day, I see at least ten employees for every client staying here. Our villa pool attendant comes hourly to fish out an errant bug or leaf that has fallen into the water. The cabana staff rake the club's white coral sand daily to remove any flotsam washed up by the ocean and footprints left by guests strolling the beach the day before."

Paul paused while their table waiter approached to top off the water glass from which he had just taken a small sip.

"Granted, labor is cheap in Thailand, but the staff overhead at Ban Khao Village Resort seems far out of line with the facility's operating and maintenance requirements. Hell!" Paul complained. "I can't set anything down without the villa staff retrieving and washing it and returning it to my suite. It's all I can do to keep them from touching my Orioles baseball hat. I've practically got to sleep with it on my head to keep them from running it through the club's laundry. I'm not the type that wants or needs such pampering, particularly if it is at the expense of staff who have no choice but to work here."

Dan spoke up. "I suggest a compromise between you two guys that keeps us here at least until we can better consider all our options. Why don't you each invest some time in learning more about Mr. Patthana? I sense there's a whole lot we don't know about our host or about what the hijacking investigation is turning up."

The group fell silent. Paul sensed he had cracked open a door that they were becoming increasingly tempted to enter. At the moment, there seemed no end in sight to their stay in Thailand. Inspector Sittichai had been the only Thai official to come out to Ban Khao to speak with them. But he provided little information about when they were free to leave the country if they wished. All three, Paul felt, were becoming a bit bored and irritable by their nominal house arrest. Even the television media, based on the local cable channel programming they had watched, had moved on from carrying news about the attempted hijacking.

"And just what do you want us to find out, Dan?" said Ben finally.

"Well, Mr. Computer Wizard, I'm sure you are up to using your online investigative talents to discover more about how many and what types of businesses Mr. Patthana is into. Who are his associates, particularly in China, where this attempt on Air Siam Flight 224 likely began? Who are our host's big competitors, his enemies, and ones who might want to do him harm by crashing one of his planes into the ocean?"

Paul could sense where Dan was going. "From what Sittichai has chosen to share with us, it seems fairly certain at this point that someone set up the hijacker to unwittingly cause a fatal plane crash. We messed up those plans apparently when we were booked at the last minute onto that flight. That means that others were involved besides the dead hijacker."

"Well," said Dan, "don't we deserve to know who is behind the attempted hijacking? And if the Thai authorities don't tell us, shouldn't we try to find it out ourselves? If we can agree on that, then where we're staying now is about as good a place as any to do that. To me, that's a pretty good justification for staying around here a bit longer."

"I'm also troubled," Ben said, "by some of the information about the attempted hijacking that the investigators were beginning to release to the press this last week. Like in that local English language newspaper, the *Bangkok Post* article about the .76 mm Russian mouser that the hijacker used to kill the pilots and then himself.

"I'm familiar with that weapon from some of the Chinese news coverage I've read and translated at the CIA. It's a preferred weapon of the Chinese criminal underworld. It's not a weapon you would expect to see in the hands of a lone Chinese political radical. The press is reporting that shell casings from the weapon are identical to those found at syndicate murder scenes in Hong Kong. The hijacker's weapon apparently has a rather colorful crime history of its own."

"What galls me," said Dan, "is that the press is making a big deal about the two sets of fingerprints that were found on the weapon, the hijacker's and mine. About that, there was no debate. But the press is speculating that what might have taken place on that flight, is not what we told the police. To sell their papers, they're even suggesting that we might have been part of a botched hijacking and then tried to cover it up by eliminating our Chinese partner with his own weapon. That story seems to fit with the strange coincidence that a commercial pilot happened to be on board the flight, with an American friend who just happens to be fluent in Chinese, as one of their editorialists has put out there."

"The problem is, there's no other testimony to support our version of events," said Paul. "Inspector Sittichai told us that all the other first-class passengers on that flight refused to be drawn into the investigation. According to Sittichai, several of them left Thailand before police could question them further. Those that could be located uniformly refused to provide any specifics. Which tells me that for some reason, they're afraid."

"No surprise there," said Ben. "From my exposure to Asia, the other passengers were well aware of how the culture dictates against being too visible and against standing out in a crowd. There is no reason that any of the Asian passengers would want to be identified as witnesses to such an attempted hijacking, particularly when it took place on a plane of one of the richest and most powerful men in Thailand."

"I'm pissed to read that the press is proposing other stories about what happened aboard that Air Siam flight," said Dan. "It's not enough that I flew the plane to safety. The press is raising doubts about what we said happened on that flight."

Paul sought to take control of the conversation. He looked directly at Ben. "We've got one of the most seasoned China and Far East snoops right here in our midst. And someone whose job it was to learn and report the inner workings of Asian militaries, governments, and businesses. Ben, you've collected and analyzed all sorts of intelligence crap for most of your career. Maybe you can do a bit of intelligence gathering for us? We might just help get ourselves out of here and back home. I don't know about the rest of you, but I don't enjoy sitting around here like I was under house arrest."

Paul continued in a more serious tone. "Look, I'd planned to go into Bangkok during our visit here to pay a visit to my former US Embassy Commercial Service Center office. I think I'll do more than just visit the office and greet people. I'm gonna see what their records reveal about our host, Mr. Patthana. If it's anything like it was when I was running it, the office should have a file on his operations and some references to contact for information on his background. It collects that information to share with our US firms seeking to find a reliable Thai business partner for sales transactions or joint investment ventures."

Paul sensed that Ben was warming to the intelligence-gathering challenge that they were laying out for him. Ben rose to the bait.

"You're not likely to find anything very current poking around in musty embassy files. The Internet is going to give you a lot more recent stuff. The Internet has the most up-to-date records and the tools to analyze the data. Do you want to know whose money is behind Patthana? Then we should look into Chinese press releases on recent mergers and acquisitions, new partnerships, and commercial transactions. That information is now in electronic formats which can be easily accessed from anywhere there's a computer, including right here at Ban Khao.

"The fun begins when you sit down and see what patterns emerge from all that information. Let's say most of Patthana's firms are publicly held and traded companies. If so, Mr. Patthana must file reports with the local equities exchanges, and that will include the members of his boards of directors. Also, he probably sits on boards of other firms himself. And each one of those board memberships has a purpose beyond the prestige and fancy dinners it offers, certainly in Asia it does. That information reveals with whom he transacts business and what kind of deals those are.

"All that information is out there for the taking with the touch of a few computer keys, maybe not accessible to any of you 'cause much of it may only be in Thai or Chinese but still out there. If I can't translate the Thai, I have a class full of students who can help me!"

"You're not going to find *all* the good stuff surfing the web," said Paul. "In Asia, to conduct due diligence, you also need to contact people, lots of people. In this part of the world, contracts and partnerships are often arranged with a shake of the hand, not with signatures on a piece of paper or registries with the government."

"Talk to whom you want, Paul," said Ben. "But I can promise you a pretty good picture of Mr. Patthana and his associates within twenty-four hours. I defy you to top that. My fingers are far more agile than your legs and mouth in running around interviewing sources to gather that kind of information."

"You're on!" replied Paul. "Twenty-four hours! By the end of the day tomorrow to be a bit more generous."

"Why not start by asking the resort manager for a list of members and villa owners? Probably some good information right there," said Dan.

"Not a bad idea," said Paul. "Something to cross-check against names we come up with. I'll see if I can get the manager to provide a resort-members list."

"Don't waste your time or take a risk by asking! Don't be so stupid as to alert anyone like the resort manager to what we're doing," said Ben. "Don't you know anything about snooping? Be discreet! I can get that information for you by just exploring all the resort's electronic entrails from the comfort of its computer center and with the companionship of some of my brightest students. Patthana's computer systems are pathetically vulnerable to hacking! I was playing around doing that between my class sessions yesterday. I accessed the resort's financial records in less than five minutes. And those records reveal just what Paul is speculating. This resort is heavily in the red. So I'm pretty sure that much of Patthana's Heron Holdings businesses are an open book for me. I've practically got my personal hacking and intelligence analysis team in place now! It's just that my computer students don't know it yet. And right under the nose of Mr. Patthana's resort manager, who is delighted with me teaching them!"

"You boast a lot, Ben," said Dan. "But this time you might just be able to deliver. I'm putting my money on you, risky as that bet may be. Don't let me down!

"I certainly can't win a race here on the ground against either of you," Dan continued. "Still, I'll try my luck by accepting Paul's challenge as well. But I'm thinking about talking maybe to only one person." Dan fell silent for a moment then added, "Paul, I guess you wouldn't mind if I called on your friend Sirima, would you?

"Why should I? She's your friend now as well as mine," said Paul.

"What do you wanna do?" injected Ben. "Pump her for information or just pump her?"

Dan's reply reflected that he found nothing amusing in Ben's snickers. "You're a horny bastard, Ben! I should have known not to bring up the name of a nice lady in your company."

"Call Sirima!" said Paul. "Say hello to her for me, and thank her again for showing us a great evening in Bangkok. You have my blessing."

"I'm heading into Bangkok this afternoon," Paul continued. "At dinner tomorrow let's see what kind of picture we're able to put together on Pattana's business empire. And importantly, where Patthana might be vulnerable enough to hostile competitors that they would pull a trick like crashing one of his planes to cripple him."

"I'm on it as soon as I leave the restaurant," said Ben.

"Just be discreet with the resort's computer system," Paul warned. "Remember last night at the Doll House! Patthana's guys don't mess around. They can do to us what they did to the bar's manager and waiter."

"Trust me," said Ben. "I'm the most subtle and secretive spook you've ever met! I'm still smarting from that bar brawl, not so much from the blows I took from the manager and waiter as I am from the humiliation of needing to be rescued by Patthana's goons!"

Paul stayed behind on the veranda, while Dan and Ben headed back to their villa. He used his cell phone to schedule a car and driver to take him into the city. Then he settled back with a final cup of coffee before he headed out to Bangkok. He allowed his gaze to wander in the direction of the fishing village, and when he did, he allowed his eye to focus on an elderly villager sitting on an overturned plastic bucket near the water's edge. At the old man's side was a small boy maybe five or six years old. Both were absorbed in examining together a small object the boy had picked up along the shore.

Such an uncomplicated life, thought Paul. He or any one of his golf companions could buy the old man's house, his boat, his livelihood several times over. But none of them could ever experience the simplicity of his life. Paul hoped he could age as gracefully as the old fisherman he saw by the sea.

At some point, he told himself, he needed to find the time to walk down the road to the fishing village and take some pictures to show Sarah and their daughters back home a more authentic view of what Thailand was really like.

CHAPTER 10

Tong watched his grandson play among the morning flotsam and debris that had washed up on the sandy beach the night before. Through the hazy fog of his aging eyes, he tried to discern what the youngster held that seemed to fascinate him so. Tong pointed to the object. "Bring that here!" he said. The small boy dutifully approached and deposited his discovery into the lap of his squatting grandfather. Turning it over in his calloused hands, Tong smiled as he saw what had captured his grandson's attention. It was a sad smile. A multicolored plastic sandal, most likely washed overboard from a passing party boat the day before, was all that the sea could offer his grandson this beautiful tropical morning.

Tong recalled that when he was the boy's age, he wandered these same beaches unblemished by trash and full of birds, turtles, and crabs that now had receded under the press of progress. Back then, he could look out at a tree-lined necklace of white sand coves teeming with all forms of sea life. Now the same coves were punctuated by breakwaters, docks, and moorages for power boats, and the beaches were dotted with umbrellas shading tourists at the neighboring resort.

As he watched his grandson, Tong perked up his ears, anticipating at any moment the distant drone of a boat engine breaking through the low muffled sound of the morning surf, the fishing boat of Tongsuk, his son and the boy's uncle. It was early morning, and most of the other fishermen had already arrived with their nightly catches. Another hot and sticky tropical day was starting, and the sooner they could prepare the fish for market the better. The fishermen's families were at work checking and storing the nets and removing the smaller fingerlings trapped by their gills in the mesh. These were for their home cooking pots. The shrimp were collected into large plastic tubs, and the larger fish they stacked like kindling wood among the blocks of ice and palm fronds in the backs of pickup trucks parked in the embracing shade of the acacia trees flanking the roadway down to the fishing cooperative's sorting sheds and the villagers' humble homes.

Tong finally detected the low labored-engine sound he sought. "Sweet music," he said aloud. "Finally!" Not that Tong was worried for his son's safety. He knew Tongsuk was a capable fisherman. Besides, such concerns were useless. Tongsuk always fished the waters farthest out and stayed away the longest as if to prove his greater stamina, something the other fishermen had long since ceded to him as leader of their village cooperative.

More on Tong's mind were the challenges that the Ban Khao fishermen faced in filling their boats each day with a catch sufficient to support their families and keep their cooperative afloat. He knew that the sounds of engines revealed their success the night before. A strained chugging motor signaled that the boat rode low in the water weighed down by a good night's catch. A high-pitched whining engine, a sound Tong had begun to hear all too often, revealed an unproductive night.

How his boyhood village had changed! Back then, Ban Khao was a random collection of thatch-roofed houses and hammocks strung among the trees. The women, after working in the terraced hillside rice paddies in the early morning, would come down to the village shore, sit in the shade, and engage in idle prattle while mending the hemp fishing nets for their men. Thatch had given way to tin laminate roofs, and stronger nylon nets had replaced the ones made of hemp. With few nets to mend, the women seldom gathered together. He missed the cadence of the conversations.

Tong recalled the younger fishermen arguing years back for the cooperative to invest in the nylon nets. "The nylon nets last many more days at sea," the younger fishermen argued. "And they release our women from the tasks of weaving and repairing the hemp nets that last us only one fishing season under the best of conditions."

"Maybe so," said Tong. "But you need to work more days to bring in enough fish to pay for the more expensive nylon nets. And what are you freeing the village women to do? Now, instead of working here in Ban Khao, our women and girls travel each day to the city to earn money toiling in dirty factories. Some maybe even work in the dirty factories that make those very expensive nylon nets you prize so much!" Tong liked to tease and challenge the younger fishermen that way. As Ban Khao's village leader, he could command respect, even as he knew they would most likely ignore his arguments in favor of what they saw as more modern improvements.

Tong's long life had been an ongoing struggle with the intrusions of the outside world. He had not opposed change but accepted it with the same caution that he would a distant relative coming to visit for a short while but then staying on forever. He recognized that fishing and farming could never provide sufficient livelihoods or satisfy the growing expectations of the younger generation of villagers. He welcomed new opportunities for them outside the village, but he recognized more than they the need to be prepared to participate in a world much harsher than his had been.

It was just twenty years earlier when they first came to his village, the men in shirts and ties from the capital city, Bangkok. "We are representatives of the Royal Thai Government," they informed Tong and the group of village elders who had assembled to greet them. "His Majesty is sending us out to all villages in the kingdom to learn how we can improve your lives. We have brought with us engineers and officials from the big banks that are supporting His Sovereign's programs to bring better lives to all corners of Thailand. We want you to tell us how we can help Ban Khao."

Tong sat attentively with the village elders, listening to the official visitors. When it was his time to speak as village leader, Tong expressed his gratitude to the visitors for having taken the time to walk the one kilometer of dirt path that connected Ban Khao village to the new asphalt highway that now ran the length of Thailand's eastern coast between Bangkok and the border with Cambodia. "The main highway has definitely made it easier for our village to get our rice and fish to city markets for sale," Tong reported. "We have built a small market stand and a prayer house where our village path meets the highway, and we have cleared away a spot where buses can pick up passengers and the trucks can load the rice we grow and the fish we catch for sale. We are happy.

"Still," Tong continued with a tone of concern, "when our younger villagers travel to the cities for work, they discover they must know how to read and write to find a good job so they can have a life better than the fishing and farming they want to leave behind. We have no school, so all they can find are low-paying jobs. They often return to the village with strange ailments picked up from working in the factories and construction sites. Our village medications that have cured us before have no effect against some of the diseases they bring from the cities.

"I want my son and the child my wife now carries to be healthy and to have the skills they need to find good work if they choose to leave our village. I speak for the elders around me when I say we are most grateful for the Royal Thai Government's desire to help Ban Khao."

His fellow elders nodded firmly in support.

"What we ask is for the King to send a teacher and a doctor to live and work here with us. We can build them places to live, and we'll set aside some of our common land where we can construct a clinic and a classroom building. We have plenty of food, and for a very modest sum, the village women could be hired to cook and clean. With a school, we can prepare our children to get better jobs in the city. With a clinic to give medicines, we can fight diseases that weaken our people." Tong concluded with a forward bow of his head.

Tong and the elders watched the visitors as they huddled and mumbled among themselves. One large pink-faced engineer seemed particularly agitated. From the moment he arrived at Ban Khao, this foreigner, this *farang*, was sweating profusely from moving his huge body over the dirt path from the highway. He was the only visitor who had refused the fresh coconut milk and sweet, sticky rice cakes the villagers had offered to their distinguished visitors.

"Don't these ignorant people understand that the road to a better life for their village is, duuh, a road?" Tong heard but did not understand a word of the language that the sweaty *farang* spoke. When he asked, the visibly uncomfortable Thai government translator attempted to explain that the official visitors had other plans for Ban Khao, and Tong and the elders should be respectful of their offers.

"We can offer you a doctor and a teacher, of course," the leader of the visitor delegation finally said. "But most villages have asked for roads to get their products to market more quickly and electricity to power lights at night and radios and televisions for their entertainment. Start first with a road and electric power! These will help you attract a good teacher and good doctor to Ban Khao."

But Tong had learned from neighboring villages that roads and electric power had other effects. His tone was doubtful when he replied. "The roads and electricity attract bars and gambling halls to the neighboring villages. Then the merchants come to sell televisions, refrigerators, and motorcycles. But no one has enough money to pay for them, so they must borrow from lenders who charge high fees."

Tong looked around at the other village elders and felt emboldened by the looks of agreement he detected on their faces.

"I do not understand much about money," he continued, "but I know that many of those villagers have debts far larger than they can now pay. They have to sell their rice paddies, and their wives have to find work in the factories and markets to make the payments. Their older children often abandon classes to care for their younger brothers and sisters while their mothers work. The teachers who come soon leave because there are few children to teach."

Tong prevailed that day against the government officials and foreign engineers who advocated for roads and electricity. And though the visitors promised to pass along to the proper government offices Ban Khao's request for a teacher and a doctor, Tong and the village elders sensed they went away dissatisfied that they could not take another construction project back to their ministries and banks.

Months passed, and nothing further was heard in the village about Ban Khao's request. The other village elders began to mutter against Tong. "We have been disrespectful to His Majesty the King by rejecting his officials' generous offer of a road and electricity," Tong could hear them say.

Then, one night Tong's wife went into labor with their second child. Two village midwives came to Tong's home to help with the delivery. But after a long period of listening to her wailing and to the attendants' strained voices, Tong sensed that something was wrong.

"It's a breech!" one of the women shouted from the doorway of his thatched house. "The baby's twisted sideways. We can't get it out. Your wife is starting to bleed badly. You must get her to a hospital, to a doctor who can cut her open to release the child."

In a hanging sling they quickly put together, Tong and three other village men carried his wife to the main road along the barely visible pathway that threaded its way through the forest and along the stream that irrigated Ban Khao's rice fields. He could see the first light of dawn as they reached the main highway and waited for a passing vehicle to carry them the remaining distance into nearby Rayong, the provincial capital, and its hospital.

Tong fought off fatigue from the sleepless night as he waited for the doctors to emerge from the operating room. He struggled to his feet to greet the approaching nurse with his newborn baby in her arms. "She is fine," said the nurse.

"She!" said Tong as he became aware that he had a new daughter. Jai—his wife wanted to name the child if it was a girl, Lek Jai, "Little Sweetheart." So it would be, he had agreed earlier with his wife. "And my wife? How is she?" said Tong, but the nurse hurried past him without answering.

Chill dry air hit Tong squarely as the doctor and two nurses emerged through the delivery room door that opened into the sweltering hallway. The doctor approached Tong, but the two nurses with him walked by with their eyes focused on the floor. Tong already saw in the doctor's face the message he was about to hear. "Your wife was too weak to recover from her bleeding. She held on to every bit of her remaining energy to deliver you a healthy daughter. But when we removed the child, she released her grip and was gone."

Tong sat for several hours outside the hospital waiting for his wife's body to be prepared to take back to the village. Then with his wife's shrouded corpse and his swaddled newborn daughter, Tong and his village companions retraced their route back to Ban Khao village.

The funeral was a solemn event. His wife's family came from their nearby village but stayed only long enough for the monk to utter his closing incantations. They left before the funeral pyre was lit, and Tong knew that with the extended family ties now broken, it was unlikely he would ever see them again or, if they crossed paths in the Rayong market, even extend a greeting.

Of course, as a village leader, Tong had support. The women looked after his young son, Tongsuk, and arranged among themselves to wet-nurse his newborn daughter. But the look on their faces when they greeted him sent a clear message. "You should recognize that your wife's death was a sign to all of us. With a road, Ban Khao villagers will not face the long trip to a hospital that cost your wife her life."

It was about a year later, on the first anniversary of his wife's death and his daughter's birth, that Tong went to Rayong accompanied by two village elders. They headed directly to the offices of the provincial government. There, they counted out ten one-baht coins and engaged the services of one of the ubiquitous scribes who sat cross-legged and bent over their ancient Remington typewriters on the floor of the outer hallways of the provincial building's offices. As Tong recited the message from the Ban Khao elders, the scribe laboriously tapped it out in smudged Thai letters on a long legal-sized piece of paper. The scribe then ceremoniously affixed the final version with stamps and seals above the village elders' thumb prints and delivered it to the provincial duty secretary.

The message declared simply:

> *The elders of Ban Khao Village humbly inform His Highness that they respectfully accept the Royal Thai Government's kind offer to build a road and supply electricity to our village. We gratefully thank His Highness for such a generous gift to his people.*

"We will give your letter to the regional engineer. He will pass it on to the authorities in Bangkok. They will see what can be done," was all that the duty secretary said.

As Tong watched his son play along the beach, he realized that more than twelve years had passed before he and the village leaders heard the first sound of the bulldozers eating their way through the forest alongside the silent stream that led down to the ocean and the Ban Khao fishing village. Still echoing in his head were the sounds of clanking of metal and the drone of engines from the construction equipment, like an approaching army about to occupy their land and impose a new order of life which Tong suspected then that few in Ban Khao village understood and for which he feared none were prepared. Now, five years since the road was completed and electric power introduced, Tong had begun to sense his own aging as his energies slowly leached from his body. And in those same years, the village life as he had always known it was dying with him.

*****

Tongsuk guided his boat around Ban Khao's point and headed into the village's protected cove and toward the two figures on the beach that he recognized as his old father and little nephew. His body ached from sitting hours immobile at the tiller. He was much happier under the strain of his nets. And that night had been full of strains, a welcome punishment following so many nights of idle stiffness. He had departed Ban Khao at sunset the night before and motored for over two hours before he arrived at the shrimp beds. Under lights powered by automobile batteries, he set out his nets to drift along the shallow ocean bottom three fathoms below. Soon the open sea appeared ringed with slowly circling lights from other launches that arrived to join his.

The glimmer of all the lights coaxed the shrimp to school together with small squid and an assortment of fish where they could be easily netted and deposited into the boats. In the past, Tongsuk's father threw the fingerlings back over the side to survive and grow for a future harvest. But in more recent years the scarcity of fish began to give even these small fingerlings a market price that made them worth saving for sale. The village fishermen now threw nothing back into the sea even at the risk of dwindling future populations. Their families had to be fed and their creditors paid. The sea would have to look after itself.

The finished road to Ban Khao enabled Tongsuk and his fishing cooperative to market their catch at much better prices than his father could expect in earlier times. Before the paved road, the markets of Bangkok and the growing urban centers in the interior of the country were beyond the fishing village's reach, and the prices they had to accept were those offered by the truckers who charged high prices to transport their produce to market. With its own truck, Ban Khao's fishing cooperative could take its daily catch directly to market. But Tongsuk discovered also that from the start of its construction, the road to Ban Khao had changed the villagers' and his family's lives in other not-so-pleasing ways.

Tongsuk became aware of his emerging manhood about the time the noise from construction crews could first be heard in the forest and across the adjoining rice paddies. To Tongsuk the sound of the road equipment was at first a siren's call. The construction firms were hiring locals, and although he had not yet completed his schooling, Tongsuk pressed his father for the chance to apply, to earn real money. Tong would hear nothing of it. It appeared to Tongsuk that his father feared his socializing with the construction workers. So during the week, Tong sent Tongsuk away to the provincial high school in Rayong.

Unlike most of the other youth in Ban Khao, Tongsuk completed his schooling and worked as his father's apprentice on the boats that fished the shrimp beds. He saw now, as president of the Ban Khao fishermen's cooperative, the value of that education and training in leading his fellow fishermen through the challenges of making a living in the rapidly changing world around them.

But as a schoolboy, Tongsuk was drawn to the boisterous life of the outside world that emanated from the nearby road construction activity. At home from school on weekends and festival days, Tongsuk snuck away at night with his friends to roam among the rustic gaming stalls, bars, and brothels that clustered at the edge of the construction crew encampment at the road head. He delighted in gaming at cards, and when he came out ahead, he would quickly exhaust his winnings on drink.

As his father had warned, Tongsuk soon saw the road, and the electric power that came after, as a false prosperity. No sooner was the road completed and the village electrified than the vendors arrived. Their offers of motorcycles, televisions, and refrigerators—sold on credit because most villagers had little cash savings—were too attractive for many to resist. To help their families cope with rising debts, many of Tongsuk's Ban Khao friends began to abandon school to work in the factories and construction projects that sprang up along the country's booming eastern industrial and tourism corridor. Those few who stayed behind to fish and farm began to see village life as tedious and laborious compared to the stories they heard from their city relatives and friends.

Still Tongsuk remained loyal to the sea, his powerful, if arbitrary, ally against the troubling changes he could not control or fully understand. He struggled to keep his fisherman's life intact and his village's fishing cooperative solvent. But it seemed to Tongsuk that not a month went by when there was not one fewer fisherman or family in the village. Nearly half of the cooperative's forty fishing boats now sat along the beach with their hulls skyward as silent testaments to the fishermen who had left the village in search of an elusive better life. Family rice lands were abandoned also, sold to keep creditors at bay or simply forfeited in lieu of payments on debts that seemed to grow for Ban Khao households. Slowly the traditional economic and social life blood of Ban Khao was being drained away.

From the sea, as he approached Ban Khao each day, Tongsuk could see an entirely different sight than what he remembered when, as a young boy, he first fished off the shores of Ban Khao with his father. Then, the green and gently terraced rice paddies on the sloping hillsides around his village were dotted with Ban Khao families who worked shoulder-to-shoulder transplanting, weeding, or harvesting. Now those same fields were replaced by rolling fairways of the neighboring resort's golf course, where he could catch sight of maybe one or two of his former village classmates, holding bags for vacationing businessmen hitting little white balls across green carpets of grass.

Tongsuk recalled how men in suits from the city came again to Ban Khao not long after the road was completed. This time they were businessmen who informed the Ban Khao elders and the fishermen of offers for new jobs. "We are offering jobs, first as construction workers and then as waiters, maids, cleaning, and grounds crews for the Ban Khao Village Resort that we are building on the land we bought from Ban Kao families who moved to the city to live. The resort will provide many more jobs than the rice paddies ever had," they assured.

"Our resort will not harm the village," they also promised. "The Thai government would not allow it. Ban Khao village is on ancestral and public lands along the sea, and we will respect your rights of free access to the ocean. In fact, our resort will be a blessing to Ban Khao! The resort restaurant will buy much of what the Ban Khao fishermen catch from the sea, and we will train and employ anyone from the village who wants to work in our hotel, restaurants, and recreation services."

When Tongsuk gave them a skeptical look, they hastened to respond.

"Your village can continue its fishing tradition. The tourists who will stay at our resort like to see that. You are an attraction! We want Ban Khao village to be just like it always was."

Their words now echoed hollow in Tongsuk's ears. He could see that Ban Khao already was not the village it once was. And the road had brought heartache to his own family and to many others around him.

Still, Tongsuk battled to hold his declining fishing cooperative together. He was successful in getting the resort owners to cosign a line of bank credits that the Ban Khao fisherman's cooperative needed to purchase and repair its members' boats and nets. And the resort did employ many of the villagers and purchased much of Ban Khao's daily catch of fish and shrimp, just as the businessmen had promised.

But Tongsuk's village had also experienced the impact from the political disturbances that just two years earlier in Bangkok led the Royal Thai Army to intervene to control looting mobs but also drove away many of the foreign tourists and their money. For months the resort had few tourists, and the impact on his fishing village and its cooperative was harsh. Few visitors meant much less demand for fresh seafood in the restaurant or for work around the resort.

"We have no fear of the sea and can survive through the good fishing seasons and the bad," Tongsuk told his father. "Before we could use the rice paddy land to produce enough food to supply our households even in the leanest fishing season. Now, with no land to farm and with demand for what we catch uncertain, we face forces from beyond our village that we cannot control or even anticipate."

"You will find a way," his father would always say. "I trust you will find a way."

Tongsuk was not so confident. While many of his generation chose to leave, he had stayed in Ban Khao out of respect for his father's wishes that he take up the struggle to defend Ban Khao from the outside world. But Tongsuk continued to harbor a rage within himself over how the resort was dominating his village and how the road had harmed his family.

The thud of his launch coming to a halt that morning on Ban Khao's coral sand beach after a long night at sea woke again in Tongsuk a sense of despair. How could he help Ban Khao secure its existence and preserve even a small part of its way of life? He knew he would soon enter the ranks of village elders and likely assume the role of village leader that his father and the others expected of him. But that role filled Tongsuk with trepidation more than with pride. The better life that modern change was supposed to bring to Ban Khao seemed more elusive than ever.

*****

Jai liked to clean and prepare the upper floors on the east wing of the Ban Khao Village Resort hotel building. The rooms in that wing offered striking views of the ocean and had beds and furniture that most certainly had been designed and built with the hope that members of the royal family might one day choose to visit.

But it was not the ocean or the furnishings that appealed to Jai. Rather, from the windows she could, in moments when she was alone, catch a glimpse of her father and her son together by the ocean shore just where Ban Khao village abutted the resort. And if the timing was right, she could see Tongsuk's launch come into view and glide onto the beach where she soon would be preparing lunch for her three men—father, brother, and son.

This day Jai had a free moment as she waited for her floor supervisor to complete checking the rooms she had serviced for the day. As she looked down, she could see her father and her son intently examining something they held together in their hands. They were so many years apart in age yet got along so well. Even from her windowed hotel perch so high above them, she could feel the love and devotion of her father for her son. And the reverence of her young son for his grandfather.

Jai had traveled down some perilous roads before she fully discovered that sense of love her family shared for her. She shuddered to think that once she tried so hard to flee her father and brother, burdened by the shame she felt as a daughter and sister who had been defiled because of her own carelessness.

As Tongsuk's sister, Jai grew up trying to do everything she could to keep up with her older brother. She was thrilled that Tongsuk and his village companions often accepted her company. With her brother and his friends, she could go places a young girl could not go alone. But that did not guarantee her safety.

One late afternoon she had accompanied them to a street fair by the main road at the edge of the road construction crew's encampment. Toward evening Tongsuk and his friends became caught up in drinking and betting contests that left them nearly senseless. Unable to get them to break away, Jai, in disgust, left them to suffer the consequences of their own doing and headed back to the village alone.

She had just skirted around the construction camp and started down the unfinished village road when she heard approaching steps behind her and felt a heavy hand lock onto her bare shoulder. She turned to look at the toothless grin of a large, heavy construction worker. At thirteen, Jai was already conditioned to know that the smell of beer and whiskey on a man's breath meant he was seldom open to reason.

Tongsuk, when drunk, was uncontrollable, but she knew her brother would never harm her.

Now Jai faced a more sinister side of drunkenness. Her efforts to pull free only resulted in a painful tightening of the vicious grip. Her heart sank when two other workers joined their companion, blocking her path ahead. With false joviality, they walked her along with them behind a storage building and sat her atop a fifty-gallon oil drum. She a felt pair of coarse hands grasp her thighs.

"Please don't!" Jai said. "I'm still..." She stopped. Jai quickly realized what she had revealed. Tongsuk and his friends had filled her with horror stories about men who paid high prices for a night with a virgin. She recoiled as the three men chuckled over their good fortune, and she sat paralyzed while an argument ensued over who deserved "the pleasure." The debate grew heated until finally the larger toothless man lifted her up by the waist and with a burst of profanity kicked the oil drum on its side and sprawled her face down over it. She felt her clothing being ripped from her body and then a sharp pain shoot up through her as a sweaty stomach pressed hard against her buttocks.

Dizziness overcame her as she came in and out of consciousness during what appeared to be an endless drunken orgy. When the men had staggered off, Jai held tightly onto the oil drum as if she were bobbing wildly in a violent ocean. She could not remember how long she stayed that way or how she eventually rolled off the drum, dragged herself to her feet, and found her way back to the village before collapsing in her bed.

The next morning, the look in Jai's eyes and the bruises on her arms and body betrayed what she tried to conceal from her father and brother. "Please don't do anything!" she said. She pleaded with Tongsuk to control his rage and hunger for revenge. She beseeched her father to intercede.

"Tongsuk, you are only sixteen! You are no match for an older construction worker!" her father warned.

But father and daughter could detect they were no match for Tongsuk's determination. Jai collapsed into her father's arms as Tongsuk charged out toward the construction camp. Gone overnight was the freshness that Jai had felt on the threshold of young womanhood. What broke to the surface was a sense of worthlessness and guilt. She could no longer smother the feeling that somehow, slowly, she was destroying her family, first being the cause of her mother's death, then by exposing herself to her crude defiling. She was responsible for her brother going off likely to be killed. She fled her house and village in shame.

Jai later learned from her father and brother what had happened that morning. The awakening construction workers were not at all bashful about their exploits when confronted by the son of the village elder. They taunted him with boasts about how much they had enjoyed his sister.

Tongsuk picked out his toothless target for revenge and the two confronted each other at knifepoint while the rest of the encampment crew enclosed them in a circle.

The much larger man at first contented himself with feigned parries and boisterous laughter at Tongsuk's futile attempts to close in on him. Tongsuk made several unsuccessful lunges toward his adversary but would not give up. It soon became clear to everyone that one of the pair was not going to walk away from this fight. The crowd fell silent when a thrust too close for comfort from Tongsuk made the older man realize it was time to bring the skirmish to an end. Sidestepping one more time, he tripped up Tongsuk, who fell flat on his back in the dirt. With one foot the older man pinned Tongsuk's knife hand to the ground, used the knee of his other leg to pin down his other arm, then sat on his chest. Tongsuk struggled as the man raised his knife and prepared to pass it across his throat. Then Tonsguk's ears were deafened by two rapid carbine volleys, as the man convulsed backward and slid off him to the ground. Tongsuk looked up to see the construction foreman, an armed camp guard and his father emerge out of the scattering crowd. As the guard carted off the body, Tongsuk held onto his father for support. Then they walked slowly back to the village down the same unfinished road where his sister had fled the horrors of the night before.

When they arrived, they found that Jai was gone. In the weeks that followed, all their efforts to find her beyond Ban Khao failed.

Jai had sought refuge far from Ban Khao in a brothel, selling herself for food and shelter. As she began to show her pregnancy and all her attempts to abort failed, she resigned herself to the child that had been so savagely seeded within her. When she was cast out of the wretched brothel with her newborn because she could no longer pay her keep, Jai had little choice but to return to her village and to her family. After what she learned had been a frantic and fruitless search beyond Ban Khao by her father and brother, Jai was relieved that they welcomed her return with forgiving support. And Jai in turn vowed to dedicate herself to her family and to fill as best she could the role of the mother who had died in giving her life.

For all that had happened to her, her family, and Ban Khao, Jai still considered herself to be a lucky one. Along with the other village girls, she rose before dawn to work. But while the others boarded buses that took them to the factories in Rayong, Jai had only to cross the road to the neighboring resort hotel where she had been given work cleaning rooms. Her shift from early morning shift freed her in time to prepare the day's traditional noontime family meal of fish and rice.

And each afternoon, while Tongsuk slept off his night of fishing in a hammock nearby, she joined her son and father on the beach in the shade of the acacia trees, breathing in the salty smell of the sea, while tourists from the neighboring Ban Khao Resort strolled down the village road to take their pictures.

CHAPTER 11

Thanakit made his way through the resort's open-air dining room area toward the kitchen in the rear, leaving in his wake the entire wait staff bowing, hands together, in deferential wai greetings to the owner's son. On his way, he paused at the table of the three American guests, whom he could see were just concluding a late-morning brunch together.

"Good morning to you all!" he said. "Are there any special requests you have that I can address while I'm here at Ban Khao this morning?"

They indicated that all was well with them at the moment, but Thanakit sensed an undercurrent of discomfort and reserve in the looks and responses of the three. Perhaps, he thought, it was the outcome of the evening that Mr. Paul Ellis and Mr. Ben Morgan had spent in Pattaya that was affecting them. Thanakit quickly went back over the reports that their limo driver had given him earlier that morning about the altercation in which they intervened at a Pattaya disco bar. He searched for a way to cheer them up.

"I understand that the Thai authorities are progressing toward conclusion of their investigation into the attempted hijacking. I expect you all will be notified soon that you are free to return home. Of course," he added, "my father and I hope you will stay on at the resort a while longer, in fact, as long as you wish." Then after a round of well wishes for the day, Thanakit excused himself and headed toward the restaurant kitchen.

As he passed the bar, he stopped and opened the cooler to take out four bottles of Singha beer, slipping their necks between the large fingers of his left hand. He passed through the kitchen galley to the rear loading entrance, then walked down the back stairs to the roadway that led to Ban Khao fishing village.

It was an hour before noon. Thanakit knew he would find his friend Tongsuk settling down for his one big meal of the day after a long night trawling the shrimp beds. He had known Tongsuk since childhood. As they grew, their worlds diverged dramatically, but they still retained a brotherly friendship. And above all, Thanakit reminded himself, it was Tongsuk who once saved his life.

*****

They first met about twenty-five years earlier when Thanakit had accompanied his father to the site where Patthana's construction company was surveying the route to build an access road from the main highway down to the coastal fishing village of Ban Khao. While his father was busy mapping out the future road, Thanakit wandered off to explore the area, crisscrossing along the raised and narrow dirt paths that demarcated the villagers' terraced rice paddies. It was harvest season. The village farmers had already drained the water from the paddies, and the rice stalks stood tall and golden against the rich dark-brown clay earth beneath them. Off to one side, the villagers lined up to form a human combine and worked their way across the rice paddies, cutting the stalks of grain and pitching them into windrows that appeared to mimic the ocean breakers in the distance.

When Thanakit approached the river where the dirt path formed a T branching to the right and left, he took the right branch and began to follow it toward the fishing village. He had only taken a few steps when he was startled by loud snorting and movement on the path just ahead of him. Then he saw it, a large wild boar staring menacingly at him. Thanakit's interest in the village vanished in the awareness that the creature blocking his path was more than twice his size. He turned to make a hasty retreat back along the path only to hear more rustling on the other branch of the T. Then he saw several small piglets stumble up onto the pathway blocking his escape.

Thanakit had come to the T in the paddy path at a most inopportune moment. He now separated the mama boar on one side of him from her piglets on the other. He could see that the boar was not at all happy to have a human between her and her offspring. With a shriek, the boar charged. With a yell, Thanakit turned and ran ahead of her, scattering the squealing piglets out ahead of him. He quickly realized he could not maneuver around or ahead of the randomly scampering piglets. To his left was the rice paddy about a half meter below, but Thanakit feared that the boar could easily overtake him in the sea of dense grain stalks. And to his right lay the river, about ten meters below him down a steep muddy embankment. He quickly saw that the river was his only escape, and in one giant leap, he found himself sliding down the slippery hillside to the muddy waters below.

The boar in mindless pursuit of the intruding boy had too much momentum to come to a halt. It lost its footing and tumbled down the side of the embankment, coming to rest about a meter from Thanakit. They had both landed in the soft ooze of the river's muddy shallows a meter from the slippery shore. The mud began to tighten its grip as they each struggled to stay above water and gain the shore. Thanakit felt himself settle deeper into the mud as the deceptively shallow water rose above his waist. His only consolation was to realize that the boar was equally incapacitated with only its back and head visible above the water. Once perceived enemies, now they were united together in a struggle to survive. As he sank to where the water was nearly to his chest Thanakit realized his likely fate, an untimely death by drowning and an unceremonious interment with a pig! His cries for help mixed with the high-pitched squeals of the boar seemed to be smothered by the vegetation along the high embankment flanking the river. He began to lose hope.

Then he caught sight of a scrawny boy, not much older than he was it seemed, staring down at them from the embankment edge above. The boy took in the scene and then disappeared from Thanakit's sight. After a long moment the boy was back, this time standing erect on the edge of the embankment gripping in one hand a small curved scythe-like knife that, Thanakit recognized, was what Ban Khao farmers used to harvest rice. He had often seen them in the fields grab a cluster of rice stalks in one hand, and with the other hand cradling the knife, deftly cut it away about a hand-width above the ground. The knife was small enough to be nearly invisible in a farmer's hand, and as it was Thai tradition to respect every living thing, including a rice plant, the knife could cut down a rice stalk without the plant so much as being aware of its fate.

But in the hand of the boy above him, Thanakit could see that the harvest knife had become a weapon. Hesitating for only a moment to fit the knife tightly in one hand, the boy launched himself down the muddy embankment following the rut that Thanakit and the tumbling boar had created.

As the boy reached the bottom of the embankment he leaped forward out onto the back of the struggling boar.

No sooner had the boy landed than he reached down around the boar's neck with the knife and, in one sweeping movement of his arm, ran the blade across the beast's throat. The boar let out a terrifying squeal and nearly bucked the boy into the water.

Thanakit saw blood billow up around the boar and heard the creature wheezing as its life flowed from it. Then the boy stretched out his hand to Thanakit. He reached out his and grasped the boy's. Struggling together, they slowly worked him free from the clinging mud. Exhausted, Thanakit pulled himself up onto the dying boar's back behind the boy.

Finally, Thanakit heard voices shouting from above them on the embankment and looked up to see several faces staring down and pointing at them as they bobbed about in the river's bloody porcine stew. With poles and ropes, they helped Thanakit and his savior make their way to the shore and up the embankment. Three stronger men attached ropes around the boar and pulled it up behind the boys.

All the while the growing crowd of villagers cheered them as heroes. Wild boars, he later learned, were a constant problem for the villagers, uprooting vegetable gardens, breaching the irrigation canals, and trampling the rice fields. This boar had a particularly nasty reputation in Ban Khao and had evaded the efforts of many of the older men of the village to track it down. And now it had met its fate at the hands of two scrawny boys. Or so the villagers were to believe. Tongsuk never related the true sequence of events. Without protest, he allowed Thanakit to share in the glory of the moment. He made no mention of rescuing him.

"Why did you never explain to the others?" Thanakit asked his friend years later.

"It was for you to say, not me," was all that Tongsuk said.

That evening the village prepared a large feast with the barbecued boar as its main feature. Thanakit convinced his father to attend, and as they sat with the village elders, their fathers, Tong and Patthana, fell into animated conversation.

"Your lives are not going to be the same," Thanakit recalled his father saying. "You may lose the quiet of the village, but the doors of a better life will begin to open wide for you."

"I fear the life you describe will be one that few here in Ban Khao are prepared to live," Tongsuk's father had replied.

"For the older generation of villagers, you may be right. But for the younger villagers who have trouble finding work now, there will be new jobs the road and electricity will create. Jobs that pay more in a week than a rice farmer or fisherman can earn in a year," Thanakit remembered his father promising.

When not in school, Thanakit pressed his father to take him along on his trips to oversee the many construction projects his growing company had under contract. It was Ban Khao village and its new road, though, that Thanakit most liked to visit. On each of his trips there, Thanakit sought out his Ban Khao friend, Tongsuk. They would go off to explore the woods and beaches together or drift along the ocean's shoreline in a small boat watching the wildlife. Those images stayed with him as he grew up and the friends grew apart.

*****

The incident of the wild boar had become a bond between them and a life's debt for Thanakit. It had cemented a friendship that lasted into their young adult lives despite tensions that arose between their two families and their two ways of life. After the rape of his sister by a group of Patthana's road construction workers, Tongsuk vowed to Thanakit a sworn revenge on Patthana and warned him never to let his father return to Ban Khao alone or unprotected. Thanakit acceded in the hope that he, if not his father, could prove that the road his father built would bring a better life to Tongsuk and to all the Ban Khao villagers.

As they grew into young men, Thanakit and Tongsuk gradually parted company as their lives pulled them in different directions. Thanakit followed news of Tongsuk as his friend struggled to keep his fisherman's way of life intact. He never found a village girl to take as a wife. Thanakit suspected that memories of his mother's death and his sister's violation seemed to have robbed him of the desire to start a family of his own. Instead, as his father aged, Tongsuk took over leadership of the village fishing cooperative and responsibility for supporting his father, sister, and her child.

Thanakit finished his economics studies at Thammasat University and left Thailand to study for a business administration degree in the United States. When he returned, he took up command, alongside his father, of what was emerging as one of Thailand's leading construction and transportation empires.

It was on a weekend visit to Ban Khao village shortly after his return from the United States that Thanakit hatched his plan. He had learned from Tongsuk about the Ban Khao villagers' accumulating debts and saw an opportunity to apply the skills of his recently minted MBA.

"I need 100 million *baht* and your prayers," Thanakit told his father. "In five years' time, Heron Holdings will double its return on that investment."

Thanakit spread out a topographic map of the Ban Khao village area from the beach back to the main highway. He then laid over the map a plastic transparent sheet with some building designs sketched out on it. "Look, Father. Here is Ban Khao Village Resort." They looked down together at drawings of a beach resort and golf complex that surrounded the fishing village.

The father and son each saw in the drawings their own distinct visions. To the elder Patthana, the resort was a logical extension of his construction and transportation empire. The traditional golf and sex-tour meccas around Pattaya City down the coast had become overrun and seedy. Ban Khao offered potential to be a new tourism destination, for a more discreet and discriminating clientele. Ban Khao would be the first tourist beachhead for Heron Holdings along a stretch of Thailand's still pristine and unblemished shores.

To Thanakit, Ban Khao offered the opportunity for creating the good-paying jobs his father had promised Tongsuk's father. Jobs a lot better paying and healthier than working in Thailand's sooty and demeaning sweatshop factories. He felt confident that tourism would help preserve some of Thailand's traditional farming and fishing communities and do so at a profit. The villagers would supply fresh food and steady labor for the resort, and the resort would pay good prices and decent wages in return from the revenues generated from its tourist clientele. A win-win for the Ban Khao villagers and for the Heron Holdings investors. A social capitalism model right out of some of his US business school training.

Thanakit was determined to make his venture work. He had no trouble buying up rice lands surrounding Ban Khao village by paying off the lenders that had taken them over when the villagers could not pay off their debts. Work soon began on the resort complex itself, and before long many of the Ban Khao villagers returned to the community to work on resort construction and later in its operations. A lesson learned, Thanakit kept the gaming and drinking establishments far from the property and hired selectively to assure employment for and loyalty from all Ban Khao villagers.

He also engaged Thammasat University business administration students to help the Ban Khao fishermen organize a cooperative, pool their loans together, and refinance their cooperative's debts at manageable bank rates. In a short three years, Ban Khao Village Resort was ready for its grand opening.

His Ban Khao Village Resort venture was really two investment projects joined at the hip under the umbrella of Patthana's company, Heron Holdings. The resort itself encompassed two eighteen-hole championship golf courses. An expansive garden hotel and clubhouse all faced out on one of the beach coves. Nestled around one of the golf course's fairways were several private villas. This part of the resort provided a refuge for a select number of club members and families. As a major drawing point, however, this part of the resort played host to government and business VIPs who arrived with their "special female companions" to share the intimacy of the club's private and discreet accommodations.

Flanking the resort property along the cove to the east was Ban Khao village with its access road along the Ban Khao River and connector road and path to the resort service areas and restaurants. On the other side of the resort to the west was a block of high-rise condos with their separate recreation areas and access to the second golf course and beachfront looking out over an adjoining cove. It all looked idyllic. The only risk was that of a financial tsunami that Thanakit worried might soon hit Thailand, Heron Holdings, and Ban Khao village along with it.

The fishing cooperative depended on Heron Holdings to underwrite its operations. When it needed to replace its older fishing boats or upgrade its fish sorting and cleaning facilities, Heron Holdings extended to the cooperative the needed cash or guaranteed its loans. Over the years, the cooperative had come to depend on Heron Holdings for this financial support.

Now Tongsuk had approached Thanakit with plans for a more ambitious project, a larger and faster fleet of fishing boats that could go farther out to sea. The cooperative needed several million Thai baht for this venture. A large amount of debt for the cooperative but essential to its members' survival. Fish stocks close to shore were now nearly depleted. Larger, faster, and more powerful trawlers were needed to reach the more distant fishing beds along the edges of Thailand's Siam Bay continental shelf. Thanakit looked at the costs and financial projections and found them reasonable.

The problem was that Heron Holdings now had no liquidity. Its ventures into constructing office towers and high-rise apartment buildings around Bangkok had required tremendous cash outlays that left it overly extended with its Hong Kong underwriters. Many buildings were still under construction, and many of its completed structures had plenty of space yet to be leased and to begin generating income. Heron Holdings was short on cash. Moreover, the fishing cooperative still had outstanding loans on Heron Holdings' books. Thanakit fought against its board of directors when it pressed him to accelerate the cooperative's repayments.

Also worrisome, there was a buyer with lots of ready cash in the wings for Ban Khao Village Resort itself. A new buyer most likely would not feel the same sense of commitment to the welfare of Ban Khao village as Thanakit had. Patthana was finding it increasingly difficult to resist pressures to sell the jewel in his real estate empire as one of the few avenues to get out from under one of his financial liabilities. The sale of Ban Khao Village Resort would be a ready source of cash in a moment of serious financial stress.

*****

Thanakit approached Tongsuk alone on the beach and offered him one of the cold Singha beers.

"You look tired, my friend!"

"Not any more tired I suspect than you, my brother," was Tongsuk's quick reply. "You have a worried look on your face. You were never able to hide your feelings very well. I sense something is on your mind today."

Tongsuk had given Thanakit his opening. "Yes, a lot is on my mind, but nothing that my father and I can't handle. And I assure you that the cooperative will not be affected as long as you have trust in Heron Holdings."

Tongsuk took a long swig from the chilled beer bottle before he spoke. "Here in Ban Khao we trust only the sea. We know how capricious the sea can be. Still, the sea has been at Ban Khao's side a lot longer than your resort. We only ask that you and your father be as open and clear with us as has been the sea."

Thanakit looked away from his friend toward the open water that stretched out in front of them. He could not look his friend in the eye. "Tongsuk, you need to know that Heron Holdings is about to engage in some major financial negotiations with its investors and lenders. We see no reason you or the Ban Khao Village fishing cooperative should be affected. But for our plans to succeed, I must delay our loan to the cooperative to buy the new fishing boats. Not for long, a few months at most, I suspect. But right now, Heron Holdings is not in a position to release more money to the cooperative until its financial negotiations are complete."

"That means we must start the new fishing season with our old, worn-out boats and nets, am I right, Khun Thanakit?" Tongsuk always used the formal Khun with Thanakit when their closeness as friends gave way to addressing the harsh realities of the world around them.

"I think you are being too gentle with me, Khun Thanakit," continued Tongsuk. "I think what you say is more serious than what you care to share with me. My sister, Jai, reports to me that when any member of the hotel cleaning staff leaves, no one is hired as a replacement. She says her hotel room service supervisor has begun to introduce rules to save on everything from soap to towels. That has never before happened she tells me."

Thanakit was not aware that such measures had been introduced by his resort managers. He made a mental note to talk to them to find out who had given such orders and why. "Sensible economic measures are always important, my friend. Even at a luxury resort like Ban Khao."

Tongsuk was quick to reply. "But why put the burden on the cooperative by denying us our loan. We have nothing to do with making Ban Khao Resort more efficient. Your father could run his luxury yacht a few days less instead of making cuts in staff and delaying funds for the cooperative. You know how I feel about your father, Khun Thanakit. It is more than my sister's rape that I lay at his feet but also the destruction of our village life. And now it appears that jobs at the resort and financing for the cooperative are added blows against Ban Khao villagers."

Thanakit had no ready response. He sat in silence next to Tongsuk as they looked together out over the ocean. "Those new boats will be yours within a month's time. I give you my personal word. And those jobs will be returning to Ban Khao Resort as well. I will also see to that."

Tongsuk turned to face his friend. "With or without the boats and jobs, we will outlast Ban Khao Resort. Of that I am sure."

Thanakit looked deep into his friend's eyes. He saw clearly the intensity of concern that Tongsuk conveyed and felt his determination to fight for his village's survival. He was fearful that his own eyes did not communicate the same sense of confidence about Ban Khao village and the resort. He certainly was aware that he needed to overcome his own feelings of self-doubt if he was going to be able to save them both.

CHAPTER 12

Paul arrived at the US Embassy Commercial Center in Bangkok a couple of hours before noon. To accommodate its walk-in customers, the embassy operated its Commercial Center in an office building separate from the embassy, on one of the upper floors of the Diethelm Towers office building across Wireless Road from the main chancery. Being in a separate location, he knew, meant that the Commercial Center did not need to follow many of the embassy's security procedures. That made the Commercial Center a more inviting location for Thais seeking information about doing business with American companies.

Like its embassy equivalents around the world, the US Commercial Center promoted the sale of US products and services to Thailand. A second order of priority was to assist US individuals or firms wanting to buy from or invest in Thailand. For its US customers, the center conducted research and maintained records on prominent Thai business owners. That was the help that Paul was seeking.

He passed a lone Thai security guard, who conducted a disinterested examination of the small tote bag with papers and pens that he carried. Then he entered the Commercial Center's greeting area and headed into the main reference room. He was immediately struck by how similar the setting was to what he remembered from nearly twenty years earlier. The card catalogues had been replaced by computer terminals, but the room still housed the same floor-to-ceiling shelving and rows of grey metal file cabinets containing business references and records on US commercial laws and regulations and materials that profiled American and Thai corporations which were prominent in US-Thai trade and joint investment ventures.

Paul gazed off to the side of the greeting room at the office where he once sat. It was still outfitted with what could be the same wood laminate desk, book shelves and small meeting table he had once used. His old office was vacant at the moment, its current commercial attaché occupant most likely at a meeting in the embassy across the street. Next to that office were the four cubicles where the center's Thai business analysts worked. Paul smiled when he thought about how fortunate he had been to start his career in Bangkok with what was then a very competent and reliable staff of trade and investment analysts like Sirima. He wondered what the present commercial office staff was like. Well, he would soon find out.

He signed the visitor register, noting that he was "gathering information on a Thai company for a client considering possible investment opportunities in Thailand." Paul admitted to himself that, while not entirely accurate, his request would lead to help from the center's business analysts in locating records and reports they had compiled and collected on Heron Holdings operations.

Only one Thai Commercial Center analyst was on duty. She was assisting a young Thai visitor sitting with open volumes of reference books scattered in front of him at the center's long reference table in the middle of the room. At the sight of Paul, the Thai analyst turned from the young visitor and approached with an offer to assist. Paul felt awkward that he was the cause of the earlier visitor being abandoned and protested that he was prepared to wait.

"Oh, that is not a problem," said the Thai commercial analyst. "He is just a Chula student. Many like him come here for help on class research projects. We try to serve them all, but our time is limited. He is looking over materials I have set out for him at the moment. So I am free to help you now."

The "Chula student," Paul speculated, was from the business and economics program at Chulalongkorn University, the country's most prestigious private institution of higher learning. A student today, he thought, but a potential Thai business leader in a few years. The embassy commercial section would do well for the interests of the United States if it cultivated these future entrepreneurs with as much support as possible.

Paul explained his request. "I'm doing some due diligence for a private client on a Thai entrepreneur, Khun Patthana, and his firm, Heron Holdings. I came to look at whatever financial and trade reports the Commercial Center has on Heron Holdings."

A quick cross-check of the center's records sent the analyst over to the industry sector shelves from which she began to pull reports from the boxes under "banking," "construction," "transportation," and "tourism."

She handed the stack of materials to Paul with the standard disclaimer. "You must know that Heron Holdings and its affiliate firms are publicly traded companies on several Asian exchanges and are required to file disclosures with them. The Embassy of the United States does not retain those disclosures and cannot take responsibility for the accuracy of any of the reports I am sharing with you. The US Embassy also does not endorse any firm or investment."

"I understand," said Paul. "Perfectly. I'm interested in learning about the firms and its investment partners here in Thailand and elsewhere in Asia, particularly Hong Kong. I am just starting my research."

He sat down at the table opposite the Chulalongkorn University student and began to go through the pile of reports he had been given. It was a quick read for him. Nearly half the materials were in Thai, which he set aside. If he later felt he had the time, he could ask the center analyst for the names of Thai technical translators. The center always used to maintain such lists. Most of the English language materials were typical annual reports, corporate press releases, and PR stuff with little specifics and none more recent than a year old. Still, the reports did boast of Heron Holdings' participation in a range of emerging market country stock portfolios held by some of the best-known American, Asian, and European investment houses and mutual fund groups. After less than a half hour looking through the materials, Paul saw an apparent pattern of relationships with big American and Hong Kong investment houses.

That interested Paul. It meant that others likely had done more recent checks into Patthana's business operations and found them acceptable. He took notes enough to send email queries later that day to some investment analysts he knew back in the United States. He could count on getting a quick turnaround, given his closeness to several investment portfolio managers he had helped as a commercial attaché overseas in the past. *Time to cash in on some of the business favors I accumulated,* thought Paul. *If I get faxes and emails off by evening time, I can get friends to work on this while I'm asleep tonight. That will give me some leads to follow up on tomorrow while I am still in Bangkok and still meet my reporting deadline to Ben and Dan at dinner tomorrow evening.*

As Paul concluded his research, he glanced up to discover the young Thai student discreetly gazing at him. He smiled when he caught the student's eye and was surprised when the student uncharacteristically put aside his Thai timidity to speak. "Could I respectfully ask the American a question?" said the student.

"Of course," said Paul. "I'm happy to help you if I can."

The Thai student's face brightened noticeably. "Sir, do you know of any recent international corporate mergers involving American companies? Do you know how such international mergers are approved in the United States? Can such international mergers be challenged under American antitrust laws?" the student inquired in surprisingly good English.

"Why, yes," Paul replied. "There are some very good examples, some currently in anti-trust litigation, in fact."

"Litigation?"

"Yes. Judicial review or arbitration," Paul clarified. "Look, a good place to find that information is not in the Commercial Center files but on the website of the United States Securities and Exchange Commission and the US Department of Commerce. From those sites you can get both a summary and the majority and dissenting opinions in antitrust cases."

The student took this all in with increasing excitement. "Would it be so much trouble to guide me to that source?"

"Not a problem! Let's see what we can find right here using one of the Commercial Center's computer terminals!" Paul thought back to how his arrival had left the student slighted by the embassy commercial analyst, and he was relieved to have the opportunity to be of help. It was almost like being back in his old job!

"And those materials in front of you, can I be of some service to you as well?" The student was now pointing to the stack of Thai language reports that Paul had set aside for lack of ability to read them.

"Perhaps." He nodded. "Can you give them a quick look and tell me what you find? I am looking for information about a Thai company, Heron Holdings. I did not expect that so much of what I asked for would be in Thai."

For the rest of the morning the two partnered to assist each other in their respective investigations. The student, who introduced himself as Sentthap, told Paul he was in his final year of study at Chulalongkorn's Business and Economics School, much as Paul had earlier surmised. Sentthap was quick to pick up on what Paul was looking for and in no time had helped assemble a list of individuals and firms as well as major contracts and construction ventures in which Patthana's Heron Holdings was involved both in and outside Thailand. In return, Paul unearthed some dynamite information sources over which Sentthap salivated as perfect for the case study paper he and some of his classmates were preparing together on US international corporate mergers and acquisitions. Paul took a moment to send off email requests to his contacts back in the United States for additional background information on both their needs.

"We could have an answer as early as tomorrow morning from my friends back in the United States," said Paul "Remember, they work while we are sleeping and vice versa."

"Vice versa?" asked Sentthap.

Paul smiled. As they concluded their work, he looked at his new investment research partner. "Let's go for some lunch. My treat, or do you have a class to rush off to?"

"No more classes today. My classes were early this morning. There is a noodle shop on the corner. Good Thai food. Student prices. I think you will like it."

"Excellent. You lead the way," said Paul.

Sentthap had helped him assemble some intriguing information about Heron Holdings' associations though he had yet to make much sense of it all. "This report shows that Heron Holdings includes investments in firms that have minority ownership interest held by the Thai military," Sentthap said as he pointed to one Thai trade magazine. "This newspaper article reports on an agreement Heron Holdings recently signed with a major Hong Kong bank for an open line of credit. It is interesting to me that some of Heron Holdings' shareholders are on the board of that bank."

"It's very interesting that it would be lending to firms in which it holds a position," responded Paul. "I wonder how common that practice is in Asia?"

"Oh, so, so common here in Asia, I think," said Sentthap. "You seem very interested in Mr. Patthana and in Heron Holdings. You should know that my international business professor does research and writes books and newspaper articles about many of the large Thai enterprises and their influence on the country's economy and its politics. He's the professor that I'm preparing my research paper for but, in my case, on American firms. I think you should meet with him about your questions. He has mentioned Heron Holdings in his lectures with us."

"I'd be delighted," said Paul. "Do you think he would be available today? I plan to return tomorrow afternoon to a resort near Rayong where I am staying while I'm here in Thailand. I have all of today and all tomorrow morning here in Bangkok."

"He is a very easy man to see. He holds office hours for students in the afternoons. I do not see why we cannot visit him when we finish lunch. The campus is an easy walk from here, and I am going that way to meet with my classmates anyhow. Can I take you?"

"Of course. I need to take a break from all the information we've been looking over together. The walk and exercise will do me good. I also need to work off that big bowl of Thai shrimp and noodles. How delicious. *Arroy mac!* I think you say if I can still remember a few words of my spoken Thai."

The Chulalongkorn professor was in his office, and yes, he would be delighted to see Sentthap and meet the former American embassy official. Paul was ushered into his office, where he reached over a desk strewn with papers and books to shake hands with Professor Songkhram, a short, paunchy man he took to be about his own age. From where he stood, Paul could see displayed above the desk on the wall behind the professor a framed PhD diploma in economics from the University of Chicago issued 1977, twenty years back and about the time Paul was stationed in Bangkok.

Professor Songkhram opened their discussions with descriptions of his university years in the United States during the time of the country's savings and loan scandal and how that drew him to focus his studies on business ethics and corporate accountability. "I was fascinated," indicated Professor Songkhram, "by the open and transparent manner with which your savings and loan crisis was managed without causing more serious financial chaos."

"I want to bring the US model of accountability to Thailand's corporate environment," the professor continued. "To start, I am making business ethics a part of every Chulalongkorn business student's study program. That is why I send my students out into the Thai business community to research corporate practices, good and bad, in just about every corner of our national economy."

"Professor Songkhram has written several books about corporate abuses in Thailand," Sentthap broke in. "He also writes editorial columns in Thai and English-language newspapers."

"Which does not make me very popular in Thailand's business world," the professor added with a smile.

Paul sensed that his queries about Patthana and Heron Holdings resonated strongly with the professor.

"I am pleased to see that my class assignment has led one of my students to meet an American with a similar interest. I probably do not need to lecture you, Mr. Paul Ellis, about the practice of what we call Confucian capitalism in our part of the world. I am sure your diplomatic duties here exposed you to how Asians do business with the shake of a hand. For centuries it has been based on individual and family honor, not formal and legally binding contracts and agreements.

"Your American administrations have vigorously promoted globalization, a world with low tariffs on goods and free movement of money and people. It was on everyone's lips when I was attending graduate school in your country, and it continues to be at the center of all international trade agreements your government negotiates. That along with your advances in communications technology make the world a smaller, more connected place.

"More and freer trade benefits all participants, your American trade economists argue. A rising tide raises all boats, they always claim."

The raised ridges of the professor's welcoming smile that Paul noticed when he arrived now gave way to more serious lines in his face.

"At one level that may be true. But only if the norms of fair trade are followed. Listen, as a typical American, you have a retirement savings account, am I correct?" Paul nodded yes. "And in that investment account, you most likely hold mutual fund shares. Am I right?" Again, Paul nodded in agreement.

"Your mutual funds, if they are balanced, most likely hold shares in companies in emerging market countries. Right now, for example, Hong Kong is the darling among international emerging markets, and your American mutual fund managers are climbing all over each other to place some of your investment money in companies there. They do their due diligence research on those companies and find that they have strong balance sheets, they are in growth sectors, they have outwardly solid management structures.

"Those American mutual fund managers seldom look beyond the fundamentals to the families, the strong ancestral families that have controlling interests in those companies and often use those companies as a means to legitimize illegal activities. So let's say your mutual fund holds stocks in an outwardly reputable Hong Kong bank with a strong balance sheet and solid low-risk loan portfolio in local real estate. What your mutual fund managers seldom check is who the borrowers against those real estate assets really are.

"In fact, those banks are strong because they are capitalized with revenues earned in some of Asia's biggest commercial sectors—illicit human trafficking, drugs, and gambling. Where do you think illicit revenues end up?" Professor Songkhram continued, answering his own question. "The Chinese syndicates use those illicit earnings to capitalize the very banks that American investment managers unwittingly help legitimize with their clients' money. Bad money gets in bed with good money.

"It's much harder to fight this illicit trade in drugs and humans as long as it appears to be overlooked by foreign investors ignorant of the Asia businesses and banks in which they hold a financial position."

The professor paused, and Paul took the opportunity to jump in.

"Your student Sentthap over lunch earlier today hinted at what you are telling me. He acquainted me with your research. I applaud your determination to bring change to a system that is very vulnerable in today's changing global economy."

"It's not me who will face the challenges or make the changes, Mr. Paul Ellis. It is young men like Sentthap here. It is to them we must entrust the task. My goal is a simple one. I want to give his generation the best set of skills possible to succeed in meeting the challenges that come with those changes. I also want his generation to discover they can benefit from practicing corporate ethics. Or as you in America say, 'Doing well by doing good.'"

Paul looked at Sentthap and saw the wisdom in the professor's observation. "I sense the current generation of young Thais is very conflicted between traditional Eastern and modern Western ways. Your Confucian capitalism is based on the same set of core values of education, work, merit, and frugality as our open-market Western capitalism. Those values have served each of our cultures well. What is humbling for us Westerners is that Confucius set forth those values over 2,500 years ago. We in the West discovered their value only a few hundred years ago, and we are struggling now to sustain them as part of our Western culture and economy."

Paul continued. "I have returned to Thailand after working here two decades ago. I see today a country that is attempting to embrace the principles of Western corporate accountability but is strongly tempted by Western consumerism. I'm concerned that Thailand may not always be adopting the best of what we Westerners have to offer."

Paul could sense that Professor Songkhram was now studying him closely. Gone from the professor's face was the smile that he had sustained since greeting them in his office. "In Thailand, Mr. Paul Ellis, there are those who conduct some of these more sinister business operations behind the curtain of legitimate foreign investment. Heron Holdings is one of the most troubling," said the professor. "To understand what I am saying, you must look beyond Heron Holdings. Look at the company it keeps. Heron Holdings is an international corporation that has grown beyond its capacity to govern itself. Its president, Khun Patthana, may have tried to turn away from some of the criminal undertakings for which his Chinese ancestral family was notorious. But he is too entangled in that family history to extricate himself completely, I suspect. He has been grooming his son, Thanakit, to continue the makeover of his corporate empire, but I see little evidence of change so far.

"The financial house of Heron Holdings is so large and so much a part of the Thai economy today that it has many corporate windows through which clever criminals can creep and do real damage to our Thai economy. And that is the real fear that I have.

"So, Mr. Paul Ellis, from where you are sitting today inside Khun Patthana's most treasured Ban Khao Resort home, I suggest you look closely at some of those business affiliates that Heron Holdings has. Look into the makeup and motivations of those firms and individuals with which Khun Patthana is partnered. I know how you and your American companions arrived in Thailand some ten days ago. That arrival was most fortuitous for your host, Khun Patthana."

Professor Songkhram shifted his glance from Paul to Sentthap. "Here is a special assignment and extra credit for you and your classmates, Sentthap. Pull out the Heron Holdings corporate filings from the Thai, Hong Kong, and Tokyo exchanges and assemble for Mr. Paul Ellis and me a list of corporate officers and board members of each. Use the university business school computers to get that information from the internet if necessary. You young computer wizards should be able to collect and assemble that information in a day's time.

"Look for patterns of ownership by sector and industry linkage and then report to Mr. Paul Ellis and to me what you find. Rank the frequency with which certain names appear and then do a key word search on those names from the Bangkok and Hong Kong press over the last year or so. Count for me the number of articles published about those corporate leaders' names and group the articles by type. I mean not by type of industry but by the type of news. I am particularly interested in names that appear under key words like *crime, fraud, smuggling,* and *human trafficking.*"

As they left the professor's office, Paul turned apologetically to Sentthap. "It looks like I've created some extra homework for you today. I'm sorry."

"Please! No!" Sentthap countered strongly. "This is exciting. Professor Songkhram does not assign research tasks lightly. He demands the greatest accuracy and the strongest evidence. It is a special privilege to know he trusts us enough for such an assignment."

"But not at the expense of your other studies, Sentthap!" said Paul.

"Of course not," said Sentthap. "I promise! I must go now to meet with my classmates. We have a lot of work to do before we are ready to meet again with you. Professor

Songkhram will want to see how quickly we can complete our investigations. I'll get their help this afternoon. Where are you staying the night in Bangkok? If you like, we could stop by your hotel this evening to discuss what we have found so far."

Paul hesitated. "I'm staying the night, I must confess, at the Royal Orchid, one of the Patthana Enterprises' hotels. Rather than you come into that lion's den, let me treat you and your friends to dinner at a nice restaurant nearby. You name the place. I'll meet you there. It will be a small way of repaying you for your help."

"That really won't be necessary. We should be the ones showing you the scenes of Bangkok. Perhaps the way we students know it. It's not anything like what the tourists see."

"Well, okay. I accept your offer of a street tour tonight, but all food and drinks are on me. Let's get in both some working and relaxing together. Just tell me where and when to meet up with you. I'm sure my driver can get me there."

*****

Paul called his limo driver and arranged to be picked up at the edge of the university campus. He went directly to his hotel. After a short nap and a shower, he changed from his more formal slacks and dress shirt into jeans, a polo shirt, and his Orioles baseball hat. Then he had his driver drop him off in a boisterous part of the city filled with open-air markets and eateries. "Pick me up right here in three hours," he told the driver and dived into the river of humanity flowing among the vendors' stalls.

Sentthap must have spotted him immediately. Along with three of his Chula classmates, he emerged out of the crowd and escorted Paul to a small bar on the edge of

Bangkok's famous and raunchy Pat Pong street. "This way!" Sentthap shouted. "There's a quieter place where we can eat and talk."

The evening was one of the most enjoyable that Paul had experienced in some time. He was amazed at how warmly he was accepted among the Thai students and how intensely they grilled him about America and Americans. Their youthful energy and spunkiness were contagious, and he found himself engaged in a couple of drinking games that ended up with him betting, and losing, his Orioles baseball hat to Sentthap, who, Paul was aware, had been coveting it all evening.

Oh well, Paul mused, *the hat I can easily replace at home, but not the rambunctious moments together with these enthusiastic and energetic young men.*

Already Paul had taken to Sentthap like the son he had hoped to have had. He and Sarah had been blessed with two wonderful daughters. He had no regrets. Still, these moments with Sentthap and his friends were something that he realized he missed in life. Well, he could live them now, at least for one evening. *Top that, Ben,* he thought. *Getting information this way is a hell of a lot better than sitting in front of a computer screen and breaking into private databanks. I think these young guys and their professor will come up with a lot more interesting stuff about our host than you can dredge up working from a Ban Khao Resort computer.*

CHAPTER 13

Sirima half expected and more than half hoped for the early
morning call that she received from Dan Spencer. He had
phoned to say his companions had abandoned him to other
pursuits, which gave him the opportunity to invite her out
for an evening, this time just the two of them. Since their
dinner together with Paul three nights earlier, she had speculated she might need to be ready for the moment when he
did call. She wanted to be in control.

Dan proposed dinner aboard one of the floating restaurant ships that cruised up and down the Chao Phaya River,
taking in the sights of the Royal Palace and the myriad golden
dome-spiked Buddhist temples. He could arrange to come in
one of the Ban Khao Resort's chauffeured limousines to pick
her up and drop her off.

Sirima countered with a suggestion of her own. The
hordes of tourists and the loud music played aboard those
boats made the dinner cruises poorly suited for conversation.
Instead, she proposed that they dine at an oceanfront seafood
restaurant just a short walk down the beach from her family's
vacation condo, where she now liked to live and work. Since
her condo was near Rayong, midway between Bangkok and
where he and his friends were staying in Ban Khao, it seemed
a more practical alternative to a longer drive into the capital
city. Although the restaurant served simple fare, the food was

delicious, and the atmosphere was much more conducive to conversation.

She was pleased that Dan readily consented to her suggestion. He should call her when he started out, Sirima told him, and she would give his driver directions for finding her condo.

"If you can come about 7:00 p.m., we can stroll along the beach to the restaurant. The sky is clear this time of year, and we should be able to watch the sunset as we walk."

Sirima did not need to convince Dan further. "Sounds like a plan. I look forward to seeing you again. I'll arrange to be there at seven."

"You can dress casual," replied Sirima. "This is a very humble Thai family restaurant where I will take you."

"I like that even more. I love to go native. See you soon!"

"Sawadee! Goodbye until then." Sirima signed off with a smile, knowing that Dan would be surprised if he knew what "going native" really meant in Thailand.

Sirima was pleased that she was able to dictate dining arrangements more suitable than the touristy venue that Paul had suggested. She was dismayed with herself, however, that since Dan called that morning, she could not get him out of her mind. Nor could she push back the memories of her first exposure some years back to American men. Those experiences kept flooding her mind and distracting her from the list of tasks she had assigned herself for the day. Normally she could turn off her personal world when work deadlines loomed. But not this time, she discovered.

The memories she had found herself revisiting all that day were those of the young American boy with whom she shared a first infatuation and physical love together. She had met him at a fraternity party during her third college year in America. Her father had warned her to beware of such events, and she was naturally cautious and reserved, particularly since she needed to project the Asian distance and poise of a Thai diplomat's daughter. Her sorority sisters saw no need for any of that. Sirima would listen intently to their discussions in the evenings over their adventures and misadventures into the loss of virginity and then the sexual privileges they used to manipulate their fellow classmen. She had nothing she could contribute to those conversations and used her silent demeanor to deflect questions her dormmate sisters directed to her about the sexual mores and morals of Asian women. Mostly she would blush and brush aside their inquiries until they finally left her alone.

When the time came to confront the reality of a young man with whom she had begun to build an attraction, she was amazed when they finally found themselves alone. He did not have the experience to match how ardently aroused he claimed she made him feel. More accurately, he was shy and timid about leading where she told him she was now prepared to go. Nudity, which Sirima found natural, he seemed to approach with shame. All lights were out at his, not her, request. It was she who had to guide his groping hands as he struggled to remove her clothing. It was she who had to guide him through the motions of lovemaking. It seemed as if he was the virgin, not her. And when he discovered he was indeed her first sexual partner, she was amazed at how guilty and apologetic he felt for robbing her of something she had been seeking to give up for some time, but not just with anyone.

For a year and a half till they completed their college programs, they continued a close but awkward love life. And while he made all sorts of pledges to come to Thailand someday to find and marry her, she well understood how unlikely that would be.

Her return to Thailand did not staunch her budding sexual yearnings. Still, Sirima never adjusted to the much more dominate and driven nature of Asian men she encountered who pressed her with their overtures of romance. After a while she concluded that she could never adapt to the submissive role Asian men expected of their women in life as well as love. With that, her sex life pretty much dried up. Sirima's encounter with Dan was the first time in several years she found herself fanaticizing again about those past moments of sexual intimacy.

Sirima glanced out her second-floor window and across the courtyard toward the gate that the condo security guard was opening for Dan. She would only have a moment to study him unobserved as he approached her unit. Intrigued by this man she had just recently met, she looked for subtle movements in his pace and stride that might give her more hints of what he was like. She suspected it would be the only time she would have a chance to do so without his penetrating and disarming eyes on her. She was sure that once his eyes did lock onto her, she would again need to struggle to fight the feeling of vulnerability she had experienced at their first meeting three nights before over dinner with Paul.

Opening the condo door, she welcomed him with a proper prayerlike, hands-together Thai *wai* greeting. The sun was setting toward the horizon at the edge of the Bay of Siam, so she suggested they start off directly down the beach toward the cluster of restaurant and bar lights that were starting to puncture the evening landscape.

They began to walk in awkward silence. It was Dan who finally spoke first. "We learned today that the Thai authorities are concluding their investigation, at least the part of the investigation that involves us. Most likely we'll be free to return to the US within a few days if we wish."

Sirima couldn't resist teasing him a bit. "Do you wish? Are you ready to return home, Dan Spencer? Haven't you enjoyed your stay with us here in Thailand?"

"Sirima, it's been a week since we landed in Thailand. After that hijacking attempt, I was ready to get on the next plane, or boat, back to the US...or bus if that was the only way to leave! I can't explain how drained I was after getting that plane and its passengers back on the ground. I was not happy at all to hear the Thai authorities ordered us to remain in Thailand as material witnesses until they concluded their investigations."

Sirima saw she had struck a raw nerve but was not sure what to say, so she let him continue.

"We've been treated royally by our host at Ban Khao. I've learned a lot about Thailand, particularly from you. That dinner together with Paul is the highlight of my visit. But you also revealed some very troubling things about our host and started Paul, Ben, and me talking together about what more may have been behind the hijacking. All three of us have begun to think less about returning immediately to the US and more about discovering what's going on around us. Besides, this waiting for the Thai investigations to conclude has confronted me with the reality that I have very little to return to in the US right now."

"Nothing to return to, Dan Spencer?"

"Nothing really...That's not important."

Sirima sensed that Dan had just exposed a wound he might have preferred not to reveal. She wanted to press him further but feared he might withdraw. Why would he want to share more about himself with her anyway? They still were practically strangers. Perhaps, she thought, a different tack would enable her to learn more about him.

"Well then, Mr. Pilot Hero, if you go, you should go knowing that I will be here to welcome you back. Since I left the American Embassy, I've had few opportunities to continue to cultivate the American side of me. Some of the best days of my life, Dan Spencer, were in your country as a college student when my father worked at the Thai Embassy in Washington, DC."

Sirima now saw herself opening up to Dan instead of coaxing Dan to open up to her. She tried to regain control but found it hard.

"You and Paul helped me recall some of those memories of my time in your country. I'd forgotten and, yes, perhaps rejected those American ways when I left my job at the American Embassy here in Thailand. Freeing our Thai women from all forms of modern slavery that still exist in my country today has been my life's work since then. Do you have any idea how much Thailand needs the values of equality among the sexes like you have in America?"

"I'm just beginning to understand, Sirima." Dan now leaned forward toward her as if to say something private, but clearly it was obvious no one was anywhere close to be able to hear or understand him over the gentle rush of the wind and surf. "Paul went to Bangkok today to gather what information he can on Patthana Enterprises. We've heard some troubling stories during our meetings with the investigators. You mentioned some things also at our dinner together."

They walked on in silence for a moment. Then, as Sirima hoped, Dan continued.

"I did not tell you the other night that after I boarded that Air Siam flight in Hong Kong, I walked back to the coach-class section of the plane and saw rows and rows of young Asian girls seated there. We later learned from the hijacking investigators that those girls were being trafficked.

I asked if our host, Patthana, was behind that. They wouldn't give me a direct answer. From our dinner together with Paul, you pretty much confirmed that for us. It's true, right? Patthana is a trafficker."

Sirima paused. They had arrived at the entrance to her favorite seafood restaurant. The briny aroma of boiling seafood pots filled the air. "I know the family who owns and operates this restaurant. I asked them to reserve my favorite table, the one over there next to the railing where we can look out at the ocean. It's quiet there, and we can talk about this more. I have not had the chance to come back here for some months. My work. You, Dan Spencer, are responsible for getting me out again."

"Guilty as charged! You can punish me with some more of that hot and spicy Thai food!"

"Let's see if you like the punishment of cooking your own Thai dinner from raw ingredients!" Sirima flashed Dan a mischievous and taunting look.

"Whoa! There couldn't be a worse punishment! I've seldom stepped into a kitchen in my life, and that was mostly to ask, 'What's for dinner?'"

"Then we'll see if you have any hidden cooking talents tonight, Dan Spencer! Or you starve!" At that, the waitress arrived, and Sirima rattled off in Thai their dinner order. In only a few moments, she returned with a large platter stacked high with raw seafood of every type and ringed by fresh uncooked vegetables. In the center of the table and to the side of them, the waitress placed a small round charcoal-fired grill and on it placed a pot of bubbling broth that had already been heated to a boil in the kitchen.

"Now you can follow my lead, Dan Spencer!" From the implements in front of them, Sirima picked up with one hand a set of tongs and with the other a wooden-handled wire mesh basket, no bigger than a small teacup. With the tongs she selected some raw seafood and vegetables from the platter and plopped them into the wire basket. She then placed the basket and its contents into the boiling broth. "Now, Dan Spencer, it is your turn!"

She watched as Dan struggled to grab the slippery shrimp and squid with the tongs and coax the pieces into his wire basket. He was clumsy but determined. Still his efforts with the tongs proved futile. She looked on amused as he improvised by putting the wire basket close to the seafood platter and then swept some shrimp, fish, and squid pieces into it. Clever, she thought.

When Sirima judged that the boiling broth had done its job, she retrieved her basket and signaled Dan to do the same and then to dump the cooked contents onto the plates in front of them. She saw Dan's relief and delight as they now used their forks to dip the cooked pieces into one of the array of spicy sauces that the restaurant had arranged in dobs around the outer rings of their plates. Sirima was pleased to see how Dan absorbed himself in trying the variety of spices and seafood. He appeared proud of having cooked for himself. She liked his adventuresome spirit.

After a while Sirima gave Dan a more serious look. "You asked me earlier about Khun Patthana. I can tell you that a major part of his business empire has been supported by revenue that comes from sex trafficking. Air Siam is a part of those operations. He uses his airline to fly his human cargo around Asia because he pays immigration authorities and local police to look the other way. Sex trade revenue in Thailand alone is in the hundreds of millions of American dollars each year. Globally, sex trafficking is a billion-dollar business. Patthana and his partners are more clever than most traffickers. They wash their sex trade money through Hong

Kong bank accounts where the money is used to finance outwardly legitimate construction and transportation industries. Because those businesses employ lots of people, Patthana is praised at the highest levels of our government for his businesses' contributions to the national economy."

"Maybe here in Thailand," said Dan, "but what about the British authorities in Hong Kong? I'm not sure they are so easily corrupted. Am I right?"

"You are correct, Dan Spencer. As long as Hong Kong is under British management, crime and corruption are, shall we say, regulated, but it is not eliminated. Too many people stand to lose if they are shut down entirely. The British authorities have focused on eliminating drug trafficking more than human and sex trafficking or gambling. The British only have so much law enforcement power in the few remaining colonies and territories they administer today. What worries me is that soon the British are leaving, and what little protection they have given to trafficked girls may end. And more critically, when mainland China takes over Hong Kong administration, they will certainly look closely at where the human trafficking money is going...if they have not begun to do so already. I am sure that China will allow sex trafficking to continue if it can divert some of that money for its own use."

"What does all that mean for what you're trying to do to protect young girls and stop sex trafficking here in Thailand?"

Sirima could see that Dan was beginning to grasp the immensity of human trafficking operations in Asia. But he still did not seem to understand how deeply it was being felt locally.

"What really concerns us here in Thailand is the amount of Hong Kong money coming into the country right now. We suspect much of it is from revenues held in Hong

Kong banks by the crime syndicates that control the trafficking operations. They get their money out of Hong Kong by investing it in construction and land development projects in countries like Thailand. Just look at the number of buildings under construction in Bangkok. The city is crowded with cranes putting up far more buildings than the economy can justify. I suspect the Chinese syndicates see Thailand as a new safe haven after the British turn over Hong Kong administration to the government of mainland China at the end of this month. That is very soon. The syndicates will find the Thai government and military much easier to buy off, to manipulate, than the mainland Chinese regime when it takes control of Hong Kong."

Dan held up his hand as if to ask Sirima to slow down. "So let me put some military experience to work on what you're describing, Sirima. If the Chinese syndicates take control of a large enterprise like Patthana's Heron Holdings, they will have a beachhead in Thailand. The country's dependence on foreign investment money will make it hard to dislodge the Hong Kong syndicate bosses who are sitting on piles of that illicit cash, particularly when they can use some of that cash to bribe Thai authorities to allow them to conduct their operations here."

"My fear, Dan Spencer, is that they already are very close to establishing that beachhead, as you call it, and that Patthana and Thanakit, his son, are targets for takeover. There never was to be a hijacking, I believe. The syndicates are ruthless enough to crash a plane in order to bring down Patthana's business empire with it."

"Do you think our host, Patthana, is aware of this? Or his son, Thanakit? When Paul, Ben, and I met Patthana aboard his yacht, the Blue Heron, he told us of his efforts to distance himself from his Hong Kong partners and their business operations."

"I am concerned, Dan Spencer, that Khun Patthana might already be too weak to do that. My friends in the government tell me that he has become more and more dependent on borrowing from Hong Kong banks to keep his operations going. They say those banks have been very willing to lend to him, but those loans have conditions. And those conditions include Heron Holdings' involvement in the Hong Kong syndicates' sex trafficking operations."

"Sirima, I don't know much at all about doing business in Asia. And I know even less about illicit businesses like human trafficking. What I suspect is that illicit activity cannot be permanently stopped by more laws and more armed forces alone. The only forces that illicit traffickers respond to are market forces. If demand is strong and a profit can be made, markets will dictate that people will be trafficked, that drugs will be trafficked, or guns or exotic animals for that matter. Take away the profits and you take away what drives their business. It will all dry up. If you can reduce demand and cut profits, you have a much better chance of stopping trade in humans or anything else.

"I guess then, Dan Spencer, I should abandon my work to convince our Thai government and military to enforce the laws we already have against sex trafficking. I have been working so hard at that through the relationships I have been building with military officers and immigration authorities. You're telling me I need to follow both the money as well as the trafficking trails to discover who is making the profits and focus my energies on exposing that?"

"I believe it would be a more promising approach, Sirima."

They fell silent and finished cooking their seafood dinner together. As Sirima finished a second tall Mai Tai drink—she almost never had a second such powerful drink—and Dan downed the last of his bottle of Singha beer, she realized that they'd been eating, drinking, and talking for so long that they were the only patrons left in the restaurant.

"Look at the hour!" Sirima finally said. "Well, if you have nothing waiting for you in America, Dan Spencer, you can think about staying here in Thailand and helping us solve our problems. There are a lot more girls than just one plane load to rescue! But you have made a good start."

"They are still out there, Sirima. I may have rescued them from falling into the sea, but my guess is they still fell into the wrong hands after we landed. I can't really take credit for much."

Sirima was not sure she should have returned to the topic of Dan's indifference to returning to the United States. Still, she realized she had monopolized the evening with concerns over her world and not succeeded in pressing Dan to tell her more about his life. She was sure that the life of an American fighter pilot had to be an exciting one, and she regretted not probing deeper into his personal history, as uncharacteristic as such inquiries were in Thai culture. But then, since she never really considered herself all Thai, she could rationalize digressing from her cultural norms.

She heard Dan take a deep breath. "I never like to run from a good fight, Sirima. I thought the fight was over when I landed that plane in Bangkok, but you've shown me there are other battles going on here in Thailand. I've had my head in the clouds for too long. You've helped me recognize that there's a lot going on down here on the ground that I should be more aware of…and perhaps more involved in."

Sirima was startled when Dan let out an audible groan.

"I feel sick. No, not to my stomach. The food was great. No, I feel sick because you have helped me realize that saving that plane may have led to me saving the business empire of the very sex trafficker you're fighting. I've been of no help to you. In fact, I most likely have set back your organization's efforts to rescue women from the sex trade. I don't like being on the wrong side of that battle. I feel I need to make amends, to Thailand, to you. I just don't know how."

Sirima heard Dan let his voice die off before finishing his last thought. She sought to bring him back to it. "Being involved can mean many things, Dan Spencer."

Dan did not respond. He did not need to. The deflated look on his face spoke for him.

They began their stroll back toward Sirima's condo along the beach shore. The beach was now entirely deserted. Almost no pale-skinned *farang* tourists gathered on this section of Thailand's beaches, and most of the local Thais had retired to their homes after a long day of work.

They walked in silence for several minutes. Sirima thought about what she had revealed to Dan and wondered what his reaction might be to all she had shared. Then he spoke slowly and deliberately. "What if I were to extend my stay in Thailand?"

As a Thai whose language is filled with subtle intonations that can dramatically change the meaning of a word, Sirima was at a loss for how to sense what Dan was saying. Was it a question or just an idle speculation? Was he trying to draw out supportive encouragement from Sirima to help him decide to stay, or was his mind already made up? And if so, to stay or to go?

They walked on a bit, and as they did, she noticed that the full moon behind them now cast clear shadows of their bodies on the sandy surface ahead of them. Shadows of the palm trees that lined the beach looked like they were etched into the white coral sand. Sirima glanced down the row of tree shadows and then focused in on their two shadows side by side moving ahead of them. As she looked, she saw Dan's shadow extend its arm and hand out toward hers. As if she were guiding a shadow puppet, she saw her shadow's hand reach out and meet his.

Now she felt as well as saw the shadows of their hands together. His large hand engulfed hers, and while the pressure of his fingers pained her a bit, she pressed slightly to assure him she did not want him to let go.

Sirima was captivated by their blended shadows floating just ahead of them, hand in hand. Each step she took in the soft powdery coral sand as she followed their shadows made her feel like she was both floating and sinking. She did all she could to avoid Dan's glance, his eyes. She knew she would falter if she looked up at him. Then Dan stopped. They had reached the short path up from the beach to her condo. Now she could see his shadow bend over into hers as he drew her closer to him in a firm embrace.

After a moment he raised their hands together and gently placed her fingers against his cheek. The prickly stubble of his evening beard sent what felt like a thousand electrifying jolts through her body. She craved more and cupped her hand against his cheek and chin to take in as much as she could, fantasizing momentarily what that same feeling would be on her breasts, her thighs. She struggled to regain composure only to lose herself once more as he lifted her chin so that she could not escape gazing into his eyes. Composure now was totally beyond her grasp. She did all she could to just stay standing.

Dan must have sensed her wobble. With his free hand, he pulled her close to him. She leaned into him for support as much as for yearning. He had taken her prisoner; she was under his control, not in a confining way, not in any constraining way, but more the way an orbiting sphere is drawn toward the body around which it spins. She emitted a feeble moan, not in protest against Dan for his boldness, but in a self-rebuke for the feelings she could no longer hold back. Then she relaxed into Dan's arms completely. Sirima only half restored her senses at the sound of the closing patio door as Dan guided them toward her condo apartment.

Now they stood together, he behind her, looking out her condo window at the incandescent ocean surf lapping at the moonlit sandy beach. In silence, she reached behind her for Dan's hands and placed them on her hips. He guided them up to cup her breasts. She inclined her head backward onto his chest in a sign of resignation she felt sure he would not mistake. She wanted him to bring her down from orbit, to plunge her toward the warmth of his body.

Dan's hands slipped from her breasts and worked their way down her blouse, unfastening the buttons as they descended. At her waist, both his hands worked together to release her belt and unzip her skirt. As her clothes slipped to the floor, his hands rose to her shoulders then moved down her arms until again their hands came together. She clasped her hands tightly in his. Then releasing his grip, he guided the tips of his fingers across the outlines of her eyes then down to her mouth, where they gently pried apart her lips to find the wetness of her tongue. She gently began to suck the tips of his fingers.

Dan paused. He made no effort to force his way toward the union she now desired. A moment passed, and she regrouped her energy and regained her balance. Then in one slow deliberate move, she guided his hands up toward the clasp of her bra. And as if recreating the memories of her introduction to intimacy with a bungling college boy, she helped him remove the rest of her clothing.

Now totally naked, she felt exposed but protected in the warmth of his body. She turned to face him, her hands now moving swiftly to pull the polo shirt free from his trousers. She extended her arms as high as she could to pull it off his six-foot frame. They giggled at her awkward attempts to lift it off above his head. Her nipples brushed his chest as she tried to reach higher until her legs almost collapsed from under her. He caught her around the waist and lifted her. In an instant she was airborne with his shirt free in her hands as he held her up to where their lips met. The strength and firmness of his arms amazed and comforted her.

She now looked directly into the eyes that had penetrated her soul the night she first caught sight of him. So far away then, so close now. The same look, the same effect. This time she did not feel uncomfortable but welcomed the submission his eyes provoked. The intimacy of the moment suddenly flooded her consciousness, and she pulled herself toward him and clung tightly to his body, her arms around his neck and her legs around his waist.

"That way." She nodded toward the bedroom with her head. She slid forward into the cradle of his arms and buried her head under his chin, this time placing her lips on the softness of his neck. His neck muscles went taut as she gently kissed him from shoulder to ear.

As he held her in his arms and moved slowly toward her bed, she sought with equal passion to experience the moment as well as the anticipation of what lay ahead. When Dan lay her down across the bed, she refused to release her grip but pulled him down on top of her, cradling him with her body. She spread her legs under him, inviting him to enter her. Instead she felt him gradually slide down to where his wide torso wedged her legs even more open. His lips arrived at her breasts, and the moisture of his mouth at once warmed and chilled the sensitive tissue of her nipples. She writhed with languid pleasure as he gently brushed his lips, cheek, and chin across her chest.

Then she realized the wetness was no longer coming from his mouth alone but also from his eyes. Tears!

He tried to look away, but she grasped his head and lifted it up to hers as she strained to confirm what she felt. Reluctantly, he rose up like a shy child to reveal a tear-streaked face. She gazed with questioning eyes, not certain how to judge or interpret what she saw.

He moved the length of his body to lay against her side. At her hips she could feel that he had gone soft where moments earlier when they had disrobed each other he had been firm and erect. Sirima quickly ran through a mental list of ways to restore his vigor but failed to arrive at a choice she felt would not be mechanical or manipulative. She felt it better to let him be in control. She wanted him to know that. It was the only way, she felt.

Still, she wondered, was this failing that he was now experiencing part of the mystery about Dan that she now so ardently wanted to understand? She damped the fires of her own passion and sought contentment in the warm embers of their tight embrace and open intimacy, if yet unfulfilled desire.

"Daniel Spencer," she finally said. "I feel very protected with you close to me. You have come into my life in the strangest of ways at the most stressful of times. You are good for me in a way you cannot imagine. Even if you go away tomorrow and I never see you again, you are now a part of me that no one can take away. I don't care if you return to your friends and brag about how you got this Thai woman into bed with you. Make up whatever story you want about this evening together. It is a small price for being so close to someone to whom I could open my thoughts. You have given me strength even as you count me as your conquest."

Dan looked over at her. "You're already so strong, Sirima! You don't need any help from this aging American flyboy. You've accomplished so much already."

"It's not just your help or protection, Dan Spencer, it's your understanding that I value. You listen to me and respect my thoughts. That's more important than pleasing me physically."

Dan interrupted. "That's not the situation."

Dan lay silent, leaving Sirima to ponder the meaning of his words. She gazed at him in the dimness of the evening moonlight.

Finally, he continued. "Look. We've spent six, maybe eight hours together talking, if you count today and our dinner the other night. Well, in those few hours you've shared more of yourself and your work with me than my wife shared during our twenty years of marriage."

"Your wife?" Sirima stiffened and withdrew slightly.

"Yes, my wife, my deceased wife."

"Oh, I'm sorry to hear…" Sirima felt foolish. To compensate, she nuzzled up close to him again.

"Don't be sorry! We married the year I got my wings. But the dashing pilot turned out to be less of a hero and more of a detached and distant figure to her. She never adjusted to the long separations of military life. Daily grinds of policing the air lanes along the China Coast eroded my own sensitivities, I guess. I'd come home to bed down with her, but she wanted to be out and be seen. She still craved the excitement, the parties and fun that accompanied our courting and flight school living. Most of our marriage we spent in our separate worlds…mine at thirty thousand feet and she, finally, I began to learn, three feet off the ground in a bed with I'm not sure how many others.

"I saw it coming every time I came back home on leave. But I did nothing. At first it was drink and then it was medications. Drugs. Antidepressants, she said. Then the stronger stuff. It started out, apparently, as a weekend thing, she once confessed to me. That was on one of my last home leaves with her. At first for the thrill of it, she said, but soon that too was not enough to satisfy her. 'If I do one more line, then I'll get back to feeling good,' she said to a friend the night she died. Well, she chased that one more line till it took her over the edge.

"I should have been more of a man to her, but I finally resigned myself to the fact that I had lost her long before she ended her life with an overdose. Her death ended a separation that I had already allowed to happen. It just made the separation permanent, irrevocable. I simply never realized it until it was too late."

Dan turned toward her, and Sirima saw now a set of eyes that were more liquid than penetrating. "Sirima, holding you, touching you, caressing you tonight left me spinning out of control. I got very good at maneuvering a five-ton pressurized metal tube with wings through the air at supersonic speeds. But on the ground, I can't seem to keep up a pound of human flesh."

They both smiled at his self-deprecation, but Sirima sensed that he was hurting. She sensed he felt he was failing her just as he was beginning to know her. She worried he would give up before they had a chance to begin. She did not want that and determined not to let it happen.

"Well, you're on the ground now, Dan Spencer. You made a very smooth landing here with me. And tonight, you are mine, and you are in my control."

They drifted off to sleep in each other's embrace. Sirima slept lightly but forced herself not to move for fear Dan would awake and release the unconscious hold of his arms around her body. She needed that closeness. At dawn when he did stir and as he rolled over on his back, she began to caress him with her tongue and fingers. She stroked gently until he began to restore the vigor he had briefly attained the evening before. Then, as Dan began to gain full consciousness, she rose astride his hips and eased him gently into her. She undulated slowly and felt him grow even larger. She smiled inwardly and said to Dan without speaking, *Now, Dan Spencer, for once release yourself to someone else and wake up a part of you that you forgot you had.*

And responding as if he had heard what she was thinking, he did, rising and releasing himself to her and to the moment.

CHAPTER 14

Paul sat opposite Inspector Sittichai's desk, waiting. The inspector had greeted him at the Thai Police headquarters entrance and personally escorted him to his office. Then, most apologetically, he excused himself for what he promised would only be a moment to attend to his superior's unexpected request for some information related to a different investigation he was also handling. Paul was to feel at home in the inspector's office while he waited.

As Paul looked around the room, he stared at the wall across the desk between the two towering piles of what he assumed were case folders, each one about two inches thick, each wrapped tightly with a red cloth ribbon. On the wall hung a picture of the King of Thailand dressed in royal garb. The photo was flanked on one side by an image of the Thai national flag and on the other by a shield-shaped plaque which Paul took to be a certificate of service below the insignia of the Royal Thai Police.

Four chairs were huddled around a small round pedestal table in one corner of the small musty office. Each of the chairs and the table also served to store additional piles of similar file folders. No working or meeting space beyond the two empty chairs and a couple square feet of desktop, thought Paul. Not a conducive work environment. More like the office of someone mostly out and on the move elsewhere.

*****

Inspector Sittichai had called Paul early that morning and in a deferential but unequivocally official tone requested that Paul see him in his office. The perfunctory tone of the call implied that Paul should take the request seriously. Could Mr. Paul Ellis arrive in about two hours? Yes, Paul said he could. Could he arrive with his personal identification? Yes, of course he would do so, as he had been instructed to do so on each of the several other visits to the police headquarters that he and his companions had been asked to make in the ten days since their arrival in Thailand. "Good!" said the inspector. "I have already dispatched a police vehicle to collect you."

Paul dressed quickly and headed for the Ban Khao restaurant to fortify himself with a quick breakfast before his trip into Bangkok. He had hardly finished a first cup of coffee and a piece of toast when a waiter came over to his table to announce that a car had arrived for him. Paul went out to greet two uniformed Thai police officers standing by their patrol car. One held a piece of paper with his name spelled out in English on it. Paul hesitated before getting in the vehicle. He wanted a newspaper to read on the trip into town as he suspected neither of the officers would know enough English to engage with him in a conversation. He pointed to the villa and headed that way, attempting to indicate with hand gestures that he would return immediately. He was somewhat surprised to see one of the officers shadow him there and then back to the police vehicle.

Paul realized he should have left a note for his companions but recognized that neither Dan nor Ben would notice he was gone for the day. Each had found their own way of escaping what was now becoming a pampered but dreary daily routine of golfing and eating. For all three of them, it seemed to Paul, much of the gleam of their luxury stay and celebrity status in Thailand was giving way to the more doleful discovery of a troubling side of Thai life.

On the trip into town, Paul gave the newspaper a quick and distracted read before his thoughts drifted to Sentthap and his business school classmates. Three days had passed since he had first met them on his trip into Bangkok to learn more about their resort host's business empire. That visit had produced a reservoir of information both from Sentthap's university professor and from discoveries that Sentthap and his friends made as they practiced their due-diligence skills in what became a business school project for them and a trip behind the curtain of the Patthana business empire for Paul.

Paul realized he was now going into Bangkok almost daily since that first overnight visit with Sentthap and his friends. Each of those days Paul had met with these very bright, young, and energetic university business majors as together they delved more deeply into the past and present operations of their subject, Khun Patthana and his Heron Holdings business empire. All the while Paul experienced again a taste of student campus life albeit with a Thai flavor. Paul's Chulalongkorn University research team had constructed a very detailed picture of a huge Thai business empire so heavily burdened with debt and uncontrolled spending that it appeared to sustain itself only on the financial ties and personal connections Patthana had cultivated with powerful Thai political and military clients.

Dan, for his part, had followed his first evening and night out with Sirima with two subsequent dinner evenings together, returning midmorning the following day to be greeted by raised eyebrows from his companions. "Well," Dan protested at the looks of his companions, "Sirima is a fine lady with a huge challenge rescuing young girls from lives of exploitation. And by golly, maybe, just maybe, there's something that I, Dan Spencer, can do to help her." And what he also had come to learn from Sirima, reported Dan, was that staying at Patthana's resort was like living in the belly of the beast. He'd move out tomorrow, Dan had declared, except for his two companions and the intel they were gathering on Patthana. Dan openly speculated that their intel just might become a tool to loosen the grip that Patthana held on the illicit Asian trade in humans that they had stumbled onto when they boarded that Air Siam flight in Hong Kong.

As for Ben, Paul was surprised to learn that he had used the Ban Khao business center facilities and staff to operate his own unofficial CIA listening post into what Patthana and his Chinese partners were up to. Ben had connected to some of the key Chinese-language websites he had been following during his CIA career at Langley. He also began using other open-source commercial and financial websites to track monetary transactions and money flows between Hong Kong and Bangkok.

Paul could see that Ben was again as happy as a pig in slop with all the outpouring of cryptic Chinese characters that he could read and analyze. And decipher them he did. His deciphering seemed to unveil a network of incestuous investment ties between members of boards of some of Hong Kong's biggest banks and some of its most active crime syndicates. Following that money trail so excited Ben that he worked around the clock, taking time only for short naps and to conduct computer training classes for the bevy of eager young Thai business center staff who in return pampered him with all sorts of sweet Thai delicacies that drew him away from his American hamburger dependency. No small accomplishment, knowing Ben as Paul did. Ben had begun to declare that he actually liked Thailand and Thai food. To which Paul and Dan mockingly declared they were "shocked"!

Paul was also making progress using information compiled by his student researchers to bring into better focus the scope of Patthana's Heron Holdings operations. Collectively Paul and his research team constructed a flow chart of the money pipelines that Heron Holdings used to blend together illicit funds collected from human trafficking with cash from legitimate Asian and American investment firms. These were the same American investment firms that promoted balanced mutual funds that included Hong Kong banks and real estate as safe third-world assets to help diversify their clients' equity portfolios.

So even his personal retirement accounts, Paul discovered, held stocks and bonds in Hong Kong firms that were part of the network of enterprises making money in part from human trafficking in the region. What also dismayed Paul was how the financial flows from Hong Kong to Thailand over the last six months had ballooned in such overwhelming proportions with almost all going to Heron Holdings, a financially vulnerable Thai business empire.

Paul was still grappling with that finding when the police vehicle delivered him to the entrance of the Bangkok Central Headquarters of the Thai police. He followed his escorts into the building and the main reception lobby and paused while the officers signed him in.

He looked with wry humor at the colored lines radiating out on the floor of the police headquarters reception area. Above him on the wall in Thai and English were color-coded interpretations of the lines. The yellow line led to the section for reporting lost and stolen passports and personal property. The green line took the visitor in the direction of traffic violations. The well-worn red floor line directed mostly friends and families toward the detainees' holding area for those tourists arrested for minor drunkenness and similar noncriminal offences. The brown line led to the administrative offices and the department of international criminal affairs.

Inspector Sittichai arrived at reception and directed Paul along the brown floor ribbons up two flights of stairs and down a narrow hallway past the now familiar meeting room where the three companions had last gathered a few days earlier to read and sign the statements they had made to police the morning of their arrival. Dan and Ben, Paul recalled, had read the drafts and made only minor notations and corrections, which they initialed in the margins. Paul had been more meticulous, correcting grammatical errors and passive sentences that, left unchanged, could be subject to more than one interpretation.

Now Paul was back again at Thai police headquarters, this time alone. He expected that as payback for parsing his statement so diligently, he had been called into Bangkok to review and sign a new version, this time cleaned up and more readable.

On this visit to Inspector Sittichai's headquarters office, Paul sensed some subtle changes in what had come to be routines in his investigation visits. Before, Paul had been invited into Bangkok with one or both of his traveling companions. This time he was asked to come into Bangkok alone. Before, he had met with the inspector and his team in a formal conference room, been offered tea and introduced to one of several young Thai translators whom he was told would help him in responding to questions from non-English-speaking Thai members of the inspector's investigative team. This time there was none of that.

Paul could hear the drone of conversations that wafted over the glass partition walls that rose to within two feet of the ceiling and separated the inspector's cubicle office from what he suspected were probably many like it on this top floor of the Royal Thai Police Headquarters, International Affairs Division. It was now a little past noon, and the pungent smells of fat fried pork and steamed fish rising from the noodle stands on the street below entered the small square window above the office and penetrated Paul's nostrils. The odors reminded Paul that he had not eaten since early morning and then had only the time to down a cup of coffee and a slice of toast. His stomach began to grumble. He was getting impatient. As he waited, he sensed that he was being watched through the glass wall partition behind him. Why he felt that way he was not sure, but he determined not to turn around to look.

He was still only half awake as he sat in the inspector's office. He had been up late the night before going over the information that Sentthap and his friends had assembled and presented to him earlier that day. He had also not rested much the night before pondering what he had learned and anxious to share what he discovered with his companions when they had the next opportunity to meet together. Now that would need to wait till the evening at least.

What Sentthap had assembled for him corroborated Ben's suspicions. There appeared to be growing Chinese crime syndicate involvement in the Thai economy. So deeply involved were the Chinese syndicates that their leaders served on and often ran the boards of directors of all the major financial institutions save the Thai Military Bank and the Bank of Thailand, the nation's central bank. Equally revealing, the same syndicate family names emerged across a spectrum of publicly traded Hong Kong companies, many with high rankings given by Wall Street emerging market rating firms.

The office door opened, and Inspector Sittichai entered with another police inspector whom Paul had not met before. Inspector Sittichai stood for a moment looking at Paul then extended his hand to shake his hand in a Western-style greeting. Paul smiled at the inspector, who then turned to introduce the other officer with him, Inspector Noi from the Bangkok District Criminal Investigations Office. Inspector Noi did not extend a hand but instead gave Paul a very brisk Thai *wai* greeting.

Sittichai motioned Paul to sit again in the seat from which he had risen. The other officer came forward to sit next to Paul, while Sittichai went around behind his desk to sink into a chair that left his head lower than the stacks of files around him. To Paul it was as if Inspector Sittichai were peering out from behind a paper bunker. As they sat, Paul noticed the other officer take something tucked under his arm and place it in his lap. It was a clear plastic bag tied shut at one end. Inside the bag Paul could see an orange-and-black object. It was his Baltimore Orioles hat, the one he had given Sentthap four days earlier. For an instant he did not move his gaze from the plastic bag and hat, and when he did lift them, he discovered both Sittichai and the other officer looking intently at him.

Inspector Sittichai was the first to speak. "I received a phone call very early this morning from Inspector Noi's office. One of his night-duty officers found a young man badly beaten and unconscious in an alley off Soi Convent street near the university. The young man was taken to the police hospital, where physicians tried to save his life. However, he died shortly after.

"There was no evidence the young man was robbed," Sittichai went on. "He had money and his papers on him. Those papers helped us contact his family immediately. They informed us that he had shared with them that you were a recent acquaintance. The young man was named Sentthap. Is it correct that you knew him?"

Paul had been following Sittichai's words with increasing disbelief, half hearing them and half wishing he did not. At the mention of Sentthap's name, however, Paul could no longer contain his composure.

"But how? How did this happen? What makes you sure that Sentthap was his name?"

"Our efforts here now are to collect the facts, Mr. Ellis, and what we know only is that the young man whom his parents have identified as Sentthap was beaten to death last night. Can I ask you again, Mr. Paul Ellis, have you ever met a young man by the name of Sentthap?"

"Yes!" said Paul almost automatically. He now wanted that question behind him so he could learn where the inspector's inquiry was leading. "Yes, I met him four days ago."

"My colleague, Inspector Noi, has reason to believe that you were with this young man Sentthap as recently as last night. Inspector Noi has already located two of the young man's acquaintances who have stated this. Is that also correct?"

"Yes. That is correct also." Paul knew he should decline to answer any further questions without legal counsel present. Still, he felt a deep sorrow for the young man he had befriended, more concern than he felt for himself.

"I treated Sentthap and two of his university classmates to dinner at a restaurant near Chulalongkorn University last night. I wanted to show them my appreciation for help they were giving me in getting some information and for showing me some of the sights of Bangkok." Now Paul had opened up a new line of inquiry by volunteering information about what he had been doing in Bangkok over the last few days. It was time for him to stop, he determined. Perhaps Sittichai recognized the same because Paul saw him return to the topic at hand.

"Mr. Paul Ellis, at this point we just want to obtain some basic facts. You are welcome to obtain counsel from your embassy if you wish before we continue. But please understand we are not accusing you of any crime at this point. You are, what you say in America, a person of interest. We must investigate all possible explanations for this unfortunate incident. Are you willing to cooperate with us in this investigation?"

"Yes," said Paul. "Of course. I want to know how this happened and why. If this is truly the Sentthap that I met and worked with these last few days, this is a tremendous loss of a very promising young man. A needless loss."

"Very well." Sittichai pointed to his colleague sitting next to Paul. "Deputy Inspector Noi is from our Bangkok district homicide division. His office is investigating the victim's death. He has asked for my cooperation because of one piece of evidence found at the scene of the killing. Also, two of the victim's student acquaintances who came to the hospital this morning mentioned you by name as his American friend. Please take a close look at the plastic bag that Inspector Noi is holding in his lap and tell me what you see."

Paul looked down again at the plastic bag and somewhat mechanically reached out for it. Inspector Noi looked first at Inspector Sittichai, who nodded slightly and then passed the bag to Paul.

Paul cradled his old Orioles hat in his hands and then saw it slip out of focus, and tears welled up in his eyes. "I see the hat that I gave to Sentthap, no, that I lost to Sentthap in a friendly wager three nights ago and that he had been wearing every time I saw him since." Paul wiped his eyes with the sleeve of his shirt as he gently handed the plastic bag and its hat back to Inspector Noi.

"Mr. Paul Ellis," Inspector Sittichai continued. "Inspector Noi has just a few more questions he would like me to ask you. His English is not good, so if you don't mind, I will translate."

"Of course not!"

"Very well! Can you please describe your evening with the victim last night. In as much detail as you can. Please take your time."

Paul could now see that Inspector Sittichai had a pen in one hand and a pad of yellow lined paper. Paul explained how he was working together with Sentthap and his friends on their business school project, their dinner together afterward, and then his departure around the ten o'clock hour in the Ban Khao limo back to the resort, leaving Sentthap's friends to scatter back to where they lived, while he gave Sentthap a ride in his limo to a point where he could be dropped off closer to his home some few streets away from Paul's route through Bangkok back to the Ban Khao Resort.

"Yes," Paul said, when the inspector asked if he went directly back to the resort after that, what time he arrived, and did his friends observe his arrival there. Paul responded but then reminded himself that when he arrived, Dan was out for the evening with Sirima, and Ben was camped out at the resort computer center. He had turned in for the night without seeing either of them and only caught a glimpse of the two in the morning when he rushed to get a bite of breakfast before being picked up by the car that Inspector Sittichai had sent for him. Paul realized he did not have much of an alibi.

As Paul concluded, an assistant came into the office and handed a folder to Inspector Noi, who read it over quickly and handed it to Inspector Sittichai. Another long minute of silence followed. Paul concluded it best not to add more without being asked.

"Very well, Mr. Paul Ellis. Thank you for responding to the questions that we have for you at this point. Because you and your companions have been so cooperative in our investigations of the attempted plane hijacking, I want to be as open with you as I can." Sittichai was looking down at the folder. "I have been handed the victim's initial autopsy report. Of course, we are waiting for laboratory tests of substances in the victim's blood and evidence of what might have contributed to his death. I can share this with you, however. The victim is a young Thai male, twenty-three years of age, weight approximately 130 pounds. Death from internal bleeding caused by blunt force blows to the head and torso, resulting in broken ribs and punctured lung, possible concussion."

Paul suddenly felt very sick to his stomach. His thoughts immediately flashed back to the bar fight the night that he and Ben went out on the town in Pattaya. He recalled that he had shared with Inspector Sittichai that incident in one of their earlier meetings together. Sittichai at that time had admonished him and Ben for being such clueless tourists and wandering into one of Pattaya's notorious tourist traps. Paul now recalled Sittichai telling them that Khun Patthana's drivers also served as his bodyguards, and they were lucky at that time they had their backs. Still Patthana's drivers were not the kind of people you wanted to cross; Sittichai had confided.

Now Paul was silent, thinking how reckless he had been to depend on Patthana's henchmen for limo service each time into the city. Of course, they would be watching him and whom he met during those visits, perhaps reporting back to their boss if they suspected anything troubling. And hadn't Paul been doing just that, investigating their boss, the head of Heron Holdings and a man they would protect at all costs? Could those same henchmen have used their Bangkok underworld network to track down Sentthap and threaten him if he continued to help Paul? But why would they kill Sentthap? Or were they just trying to rough him up and went too far? After all, Sentthap was young and slim, almost delicate in stature, certainly no match for Patthana's driver henchmen. Paul still shuddered when he thought how those two had savagely beaten the bartender and bouncer they confronted in rescuing Ben and him.

Finally, Inspector Sittichai broke the silence. "I want you to understand, Paul Ellis, that our investigation into this event is just beginning. The Thai police have many persons to talk to yet. We have much more evidence to collect. I am hopeful you will also cooperate with us in this new development in which you are involved."

Paul nodded.

"Yesterday afternoon I received approval from our Foreign Ministry for you and your companions to return to America. We have full and complete statements from you and your companions about the attempted hijacking. We appreciate your help and cooperation. You all were free to leave Thailand today. However, this new development requires me to cancel that order, in your case indefinitely and in the case of your companions until Inspector Noi can obtain statements from them. This Sentthap killing appears to be a local incident with no apparent international connections, so it falls outside the scope of my international crime division. Inspector Noi will lead the investigation. If you see any connection, however, between this incident, the attempted plane hijacking, and any other purpose you have here in Thailand, please tell me."

Paul again nodded his understanding.

"I regret that I must instruct you to remain in Thailand and to notify Inspector Noi at all times of where you are in the country. Inspector Noi asked me to encourage you to consider moving from Ban Khao Resort to a hotel here in Bangkok, but that is entirely your choice, as is your decision to seek guidance from your American consulate on retaining legal counsel, even though, as I say, you are only considered by Inspector Noi's office as a person of interest.

"I will do my best to support Inspector Noi in his investigations and in helping him identify suspects in this apparent killing. And of course, if I can be of any further assistance to you in my capacity—"

Paul interrupted, "I think right now I need to return to my companions. I need to inform them of what has happened. Can you or Inspector Noi arrange transportation for me back to Ban Khao?"

"Of course. Inspector Noi will call now for a car to take you back to Ban Khao. I am sure the inspector will be contacting you again soon. In the meantime, I can be reached at the numbers I have given you earlier. If you have more information you can share with Inspector Noi, I can relay your messages to him. We have worked many years together."

As Paul rose from his chair, he realized how unstable he felt, how fatigued he had suddenly become. He noticed that each of the inspectors detected his exhaustion as well.

*****

Sittichai peered over his stacks of file dossiers at Paul and Inspector Noi as they left his office. He sat down again to a moment alone in his paper bunker and allowed himself an unguarded moment to speculate about the likely outcome of Inspector Noi's investigation of the Sentthap killing. Paul Ellis was innocent of the crime; Sittichai was confident. If the killing was not a random nighttime attack, several of which occurred every twenty-four hours in a city of two million people like Bangkok, then he suspected that the attacker or attackers were likely to be Patthana's overzealous henchmen. If that were the case, then there was very little likelihood that Inspector Noi would get a conviction or that Patthana's drivers would even be charged. Khun Patthana was simply too powerful and had too many friends in the Thai government and security forces to allow that to happen. But Sittichai did not want to see the American take the fall for this murder, if indeed he was innocent. And Sittichai believed him so.

Still, he was sympathetic to the American's plight. He realized just how naïve Paul and his companions had been when they launched their own investigation into Patthana's past. At first news that the Americans were poking around in Patthana's affairs, he, Sittichai, should have worked to get them on a plane back to the United States. It was too late for that now. Sittichai had another death, of another young man, to complicate his investigations into what was behind the attempted plane hijacking that had brought these three Americans to Thailand and pulled them into the orbit of Asia's shadowy criminal underworld. He laughed to himself over what, if anything, the Americans could do in a few weeks' time to affect Patthana's world, given that he, Sittichai, had been working years to do so without much progress.

Sittichai did see one opportunity emerge from the Sentthap murder. With Paul Ellis implicated, he could make the case to keep open his investigation into what was behind the attempted plane hijacking given one of the Americans onboard Air Siam was now a person of interest in another crime. Little evidence had emerged to support the case that more than a lone delusional hijacker was involved. Sittichai still held fast to his theory that behind the hijacking was a struggle between Patthana and his Hong Kong syndicate associates over control of his business empire.

CHAPTER 15

"Benjamin?" said the male voice on the other end of the midmorning phone call. "Benjamin Morgan?" Ben shifted immediately into a defensive, fight-or-flight mode. In high school when he found himself all too frequently in the vice principal's office because of his challenges to authority, his punishments always began with "Benjamin…" Since then, when he heard himself called by his full first name, Benjamin, the fear of trouble ahead always engulfed him.

"Yessss," Ben gave a drawn-out reply.

"Benjamin," the voice repeated after Ben's confirmation, "this is Pete Walters at the American embassy. The Deputy Chief of Mission asked me to call and invite you in for a visit. The Thai authorities are allowing you to go home soon, and there are a few procedures that you need to complete with the embassy before you depart. Can we send some transportation around for you at noon today?"

"I guess so," said Ben.

"Fine," the caller responded. "We're dispatching an embassy car right now. It will arrive in about an hour. You should be back at the resort in time for dinner and to check your evening email messages at the resort's business center. I look forward to meeting you shortly." Then the caller hung up without giving Ben a chance to respond.

Ben was amused by the caller's coyness. He knew immediately Walters was no regular embassy staffer. From his CIA career, Ben was keenly aware that American embassies in listening posts like Bangkok were staffed with both diplomatic and intelligence personnel. The diplomats did the standard reporting on political, economic, and military developments in the country and helped the ambassador press the host country's government to support US positions on votes that came up in United Nations and other treaty organizations in which both countries were cosignatory members.

But embassy staffs also included intelligence officers, mostly from the CIA, who were stationed overseas most often under the guise of diplomats. In the case of Thailand, a scattering of Defense Department, Justice Department, and Drug Enforcement Agency officials also sat in embassy offices, though the nature of their work with Thai law enforcement and investigation counterparts allowed them more transparency in their roles of building country capacity to enforce international criminal laws.

Ben knew that for many career ambassadors, CIA field offices colocated in an embassy facility was like a magpie's egg in a robin's nest. A CIA country station chief and staff did not report directly to the ambassador but still, for appearances sake, were considered part of the embassy's country team. CIA field agents also had their own budgets and operating procedures. Outwardly they tried to blend in with the diplomatic community, but they largely lived and worked in their separate worlds.

Ben felt certain that Walters was a standard CIA field officer. His reference to the DCM, the deputy chief of mission and the second in charge after the ambassador, signaled Ben that his embassy visit was to be discreet and low-key. An ambassador's calendar was largely representational in nature. Handshakes and press pictures with Ben, Paul, and Dan after their heroes' arrival in Bangkok were the extent to which the

American ambassador cared to become involved with them. The DCM's office had been much more on top of their daily activities and contacts with the Thai law enforcement officers who were investigating the attempted plane hijacking.

The caller's reference to his email messages from the Ban Khao business center was also not lost on Ben. Walters was letting him know that his electronic messaging, particularly his inquiries back to his former colleagues at the agency, had not gone unnoticed. *Probably Walters has copies of all the messages I sent back to the agency,* thought Ben. *Maybe he also has electronic copies of my agency personnel records as well, goddammit! In that case Walters will know about my Asia region political and language expertise and might be aware of some of the sensitive information on China I have unearthed, analyzed, and reported at the agency.*

The last giveaway Ben registered from the phone call was its abruptness and brevity. He had not clocked their conversation but estimated it had taken less than thirty seconds. Brevity in open line communication was a standard agency operating procedure, not like the more relaxed pace at which the embassy diplo-heads worked and talked. If anyone had time to monitor Walters's call, there would be very little information to raise suspicion and little time to lock in on and trace the communication. What concrete information was shared about Ben's email messaging, about the likelihood they would be headed back to the United States soon was clearly harmless enough that it did not matter if it were overheard by anyone monitoring the villa's phone lines.

Ben barely had time to wolf down an early lunch before a dark-blue sedan pulled up to the villa. A Toyota, Ben observed, with regular Thai plates. Ben knew that the US Congress's "Buy America" policy required the US Embassy to purchase American-made vehicles for use at overseas posts and identify them with diplomatic license plates. The CIA with its separate budgets and desire for blending in with the locals was under no such constraint. In Thailand, it bought Asian makes and models of the vehicles it used and registered them as civilian vehicles to blend in more with the locals. For Ben, however, the vehicle that picked him up was another clue about whom he would be dealing with on his arrival in Bangkok.

As the car transported him outside the serene setting of Ban Khao Resort, he began to feel anxious about the meeting that lay ahead. Ben, Dan, and Paul had talked into the late hours the night before. Paul's news that he was a person of interest in the death of a Thai university student was a shock, the more so because Paul felt responsible for exposing the young student to dangers that Paul now recognized were associated with investigating one of Thailand's most powerful business leaders and one that was also associated with international crime syndicates. Paul had declared that he'd had enough of their Ban Khao host's hospitality and swore he would not spend another night at the resort. They would camp out at a Bangkok hotel, Paul swore, until his name was cleared and hopefully those responsible for the student's death were in custody. Paul was convinced that the university student's murderer was one of Patthana's goons, most likely the very driver who had been assigned to serving—and observing—them since they arrived at Ban Khao resort.

Dan had called Sirima with the news and to cancel their dinner together that night. Ben cancelled his evening computer classes. They had worked most of the evening to calm and console Paul. But the nerves of all three were on edge. What had started as an idle pastime of investigating their host had become a more dangerous and costly venture that now placed Paul on the wrong side of the Thai law.

Sirima, Dan had declared, raised his awareness of how pervasive sex trafficking was in Asia and how corrosive were its effects on the fragile Thai culture. Paul had well-documented information from his university students' research about Patthana's dealings with the multi-billion-dollar-a-year sex trade industry.

And Ben, well he now realized he should have been more discrete in exploring links between their resort host and some of the very ruthless characters he had encountered in his career as a CIA China analyst. *Several times in my twenty years of CIA service, I have come across the same Chinese underworld characters,* thought Ben.

As the Thai countryside rolled by outside his car window, Ben sought to put himself at ease by reflecting back over how his life had followed a path from a teenage Vietnam army recruit to becoming one of the CIA's leading sinologists, only to turn his back on it all and opt for early retirement from the agency.

Despite his iconoclastic behavior in high school, Ben graduated as an honor student but with no interest in going to college. That immediately made him Selective Service System military draft material for a war that was underway in Southeast Asia. He was from a middle-class family and a bucolic Chicago northside neighborhood. At the time he graduated from high school in 1973, Ben remembered, each US congressional district had a quota of recruits to fill based on its proportion of the US population from the last national census. In Ben's congressional district, many of his classmates went to college with student deferrals from the draft until they left school or completed their degree programs. Ben's district was seldom able to meet its quota with volunteer enlistees because there were so many student deferrals. The solution for meeting quotas in districts like Ben's was a draft lottery with names drawn randomly each month from a list of remaining eligible selective service registrants. The only exceptions were men with mental or physical disabilities or strong pacifist beliefs. Ben could meet none of those disqualifications. He felt like cannon fodder!

Well, Ben remembered thinking at the time of his selective service registration and physical exam, *if I enlist voluntarily, I'll have a shot at what I want to do during my military service.* Wrong! He selected the signal corps when he signed up because it gave him the best chance of sitting behind the lines. Instead, he was assigned to a demining and demolition squad that would put him out in front of the infantrymen who carried the guns and sloshed through the rice paddies and dodged between Vietnam villagers' huts.

Ben's basic training was followed by special demining training, which concluded with certification tests before being assigned to a platoon and division. Ben's strategy, when he filed into the exam room with his forty classmates, was clear. He would flunk the test, fail to get the certification, be reassigned elsewhere. At that point he didn't care where or what. Anything would be better.

However, when Ben started to take the test, he was furious. The questions were so simple and the answers so obvious that clearly all the army wanted was to have the dumbest in its midst to clear the way with their blown-up bodies for the infantry fighters to follow. Ben looked around the room and saw how most of his classmates were agonizing over the test questions. And here he was, Ben, who could solve a Rubik's cube in a matter of minutes and clean out fellow players in only a few poker hands. He was ashamed as well as furious.

Ben took a deep breath, dived into the test, and handed it back in about twenty minutes while most of his companions were still struggling to complete the first page.

"You know, Private Morgan," said the sergeant proctoring the test, "there is no failing score!"

"I know," said Ben and he headed to the door.

It was a few days later when his platoon was preparing to deploy that Ben was asked to step forward during assembly. "Private Morgan, you are requested to report to your commanding officer. Immediately!"

"Yes, sir!"

"You are dismissed!"

His commanding officer was blunt. "Never before has any recruit completed demining certification with a perfect test score, and never has anyone completed the test in less than the full allotted hour," he told Ben. "You're either one smart-ass genius or one cheat'n SOB. I don't know which you are, and I don't care to find out. What I do know is that, either way, I don't want you in my unit. I've requested your reassignment, but at the moment there is no other deploying squad you have trained for, so you are being sent to the Army-Navy Defense Language Institute at the Monterey Presidio in California. So pack and go! You can pick up your transfer orders on your way out. Now leave!"

"Yes, *sir!*" exclaimed Ben.

Always the fan of solving puzzles, Ben approached language training as if he were solving another puzzle or cracking a code. He was happier than a pig in slop. Ben learned that the army and the military in general were in desperate need of language translators, particularly for Asian language specialists during the Vietnam war. For all its other limitations, the military had excellent foreign language training programs. Many argued it was better than language training provided by the vaunted State Department, which was mainly concerned that its diplomats had enough speaking and listening proficiency in the host country language to be able to conduct break-the-ice cocktail circuit conversations with their foreign counterparts. The Defense Department wanted much greater mastery of a foreign language to assure accurate and timely intelligence that potentially could save soldiers' lives.

Ben was happy to take on the challenges that the Defense Foreign Language Center gave him. He chose written and spoken Chinese as his language area because it was the most daunting and least attractive language for most military recruits and enlistees. Classes were intensive and for extended periods of time. Ben didn't care if the training never ended. He set records for the number of new Chinese characters he could master. He worked on Chinese phonetics, both Mandarin and Cantonese, with his instructors and with every Chinese restaurant worker he encountered as part of his total-immersion training program.

In a year, Ben was translating basic Chinese newspaper and broadcast communications and was reporting intelligence he gathered on the amount and types of war materials that Peking was shipping to Hanoi for supplying the Viet Cong. At the end of two years, he was ground truthing and testing the reliability of the Army's native Chinese staff intelligence reports out of Taiwan, Bangkok, and other listening posts and finding frequent flaws and misleading falsehoods in their information gathering and reporting.

By then, however, it was 1975, and the last American troops were shipping out of Vietnam and being discharged from duty. The Army's need for Chinese intelligence gathering also dropped off dramatically, and Ben found himself back home in the Chicago suburbs. Not for long, however.

Only a few weeks after his discharge, he received a call from a CIA recruiter with an invitation to visit Langley, Virginia, for an interview. A couple of weeks after that call, Ben was back at work, this time as a CIA intelligence analyst on the agency's China team.

During his twenty years with the CIA, Ben never stopped building his mastery of the Chinese language to cut through the subtle meanings of the language to ascertain the facts. He maneuvered a two-year stint with the agency at its Hong Kong listening post, and after work he would throw himself into total immersion Chinese conversation classes. Years later at the agency, when he was asked how best to learn a foreign language, Ben was ready with a reply. Three places he would always say. First in the classroom to learn the language structure, then in the streets to learn how it's really used and spoken and where those rules can be broken. But to really dominate the language, focus on intensive evening classes between the sheets with a native speaker! In Monterey and Hong Kong, he met a number of female Chinese exchange students who were attracted by his command of their language, as well as his performance in bed. He never hesitated to express his appreciation for their dedication to helping him accelerate his command of their language.

Ben quickly became proficient enough in the language to cause the Communist Chinese a few headaches. One of his crowning accomplishments was exhuming the Chinese character for *homosexual*, which was so perverse for the puritanical Chinese Communist party that it would not dignify the lifestyle in print. That is, until the CIA turned to Ben to plant it in news stories about one Chinese Communist Party member the agency wanted to disgrace and see removed from power. Sure enough, shortly after the party leader was exposed, disgraced, and dismissed for his alleged lifestyle,

Chinese Communist Party linguists adopted the character for *homosexual* that Ben had slyly reinserted into the official lexicon.

Ben's contributions to the intelligence world extended far beyond that, he knew, even though much of his intelligence findings were ignored. He had foreseen the coming events surrounding the June 1989 Tiananmen Square demonstrations months before they happened, but US policy makers at the time failed to take his agency assessment seriously, and the United States was caught by surprise and unprepared to respond.

Shortly after that, the world became distracted by the 1991 breakup of the Soviet Union, and US government interest in mainland Chinese developments waned. Ben soldiered on in his failed efforts to keep mainland Chinese issues on the US government's radar, but by 1995, when he reached his twenty-year mark with the agency, he'd had enough and opted for early retirement. The only lasting contribution with which he could content himself was the cadre of CIA sinologists he trained and equipped to continue after him. Ben sighed deeply and wished them well, but his expectations were not high.

*****

Two main gates separated access for visitors and for employees to the sprawling gardened American Embassy compound in central Bangkok, and the driver chauffeuring Ben chose the gate leading into the parking area reserved for American officers and staff. After being waved through by embassy security, the chauffeur drove behind the main chancery complex to an unimpressive two-story building that stood out only for the communications antennae that bristled from its roof. An American woman in army uniform had already been contacted by the guard at the gate and was waiting to greet him at the building entrance. She handed Ben a visitor's badge to wear and asked him to leave any cameras, phones, and recording devices he was carrying at the reception desk.

Peter Walters, Ben's caller that morning, promptly entered the reception area, shook Ben's hand, and introduced himself by name only, no title. Then with a "Let's meet in my office," he turned and headed down a partitioned hallway. Ben followed, and they entered a small office furnished only with a desk and a chair, bookshelves along two of the side walls, and a small round glass-topped meeting table and four chairs huddled in one corner. Ben noticed that despite the rows of bookshelves, they all stood empty. He saw that the desk was empty as well. The only visible paper of any kind was a yellow lined legal pad and three large manila envelopes next to a pen on the meeting table.

"You keep a very neat office," Ben said with a smirk.

"I travel a lot. I really don't have much time to consider myself at home anywhere. Some coffee or tea?" Walters motioned Ben to sit at the round meeting table.

"Water, if you have it bottled." Ben had no interest in subjecting his sensitive stomach to the strong local Thai tea.

"You got it! Just a moment." Walters stepped out of the office to pass along Ben's request to one of the unseen clerical staff around the corner. He returned and took one of the chairs at the table opposite Ben. They sat together, their heads scarcely three feet apart, as if at some small intimate French bistro table. All they needed, Ben thought, were two espresso coffees, a couple of croissants, and a surly waiter standing over them.

Walters began. "Now, Benjamin, I understand you and your two companions are anxious to put this very unfortunate vacation trip behind you and get back to the States. Investigations of this sort of international incident can be lengthy and cumbersome, particularly when they are led by local authorities in a country with a very formal and bureaucratic government like Thailand. To move things along as quickly as possible, our embassy has helped the Thai investigators identify the political dissident groups behind this attempted hijacking." Walters spoke in a tone that, to Ben at least, was troubling for how soothing he felt Walters was attempting it to be.

Walters continued, but now he was more pointed in his comments. "The DCM is concerned, however, about some personal, how shall we say, inquiries you are making during your stay here in Thailand. The point is your efforts are complicating the hijacking investigation for both the embassy and the Thai government. Benjamin, we are asking you to stop what you are doing before it lands you in more difficulties and in a place where the embassy will be unable to come to your assistance."

Ben chose to play innocent for the moment to see how much Walters would volunteer about how closely the CIA was tracking their activities. "I need some help here understanding what you're telling me. Just what have we done to get in the way of the Thai government's investigation of the attempted plane hijacking?"

"Look," Walters said. "It should be sufficient to say that we, that is you, your friends, and the US government, are on the same team. We have a very professional team on the ground here in Bangkok to deal with international incidents such as the one you were accidentally caught up in. You should also be aware that when you concluded your career with the agency, you agreed to step aside and let the next in line take on those responsibilities. I can understand your interest in wanting this attempted hijacking incident fully vetted. But as a private citizen, you no longer have the tools at hand to be as effective as you once were. Most important, you are forgetting that you no longer have access to agency resources and manpower."

So Ben realized Walters had learned about his reaching back to his former CIA colleagues for help. He shouldn't have been surprised, but Walters's little sermon was beginning to annoy him. No one in his entire career had faulted Ben for not turning out Sino-Asian intelligence reports that were unmatched in value to the agency and the USG offices it served.

Ben realized that even with the limited intelligence gathering tools he had at his disposal as a private citizen, he still had the skills for sniffing out and analyzing sensitive information. And he was sure Walters was aware that as a private citizen, he could gather information wherever he wanted. If the agency wouldn't listen to him, perhaps others would. Ben suspected that Walters was also aware of that and was seeking to persuade him that silence was the most expedient course for all of them if indeed they wanted to head back to the United States soon. But now, he felt that maybe he wasn't quite ready to head home.

Ben pushed back at Walters. "And you no longer have the authority to stop me as a private citizen from gathering information from where and from whom I choose."

"We'll do what we need to do to help you come to your senses," said Walters. "Personally, I don't give a damn about saving the skins of any of you. My job is to keep you from embarrassing the US government. Please, Benjamin, don't make our work hard for us!"

"Hard for you?" Ben said. "For most of my damned career I tried to help the agency get the best intel to the people in our government that needed it. But administration after administration blindly stumbled through one Asian crisis after another. Now it's happening again. And what's behind the attempted Air Siam hijacking is another clear manifestation of serious trouble ahead for the US and our Thai ally.

"US policy has focused on containing mainland Chinese communism until it collapses from its own bureaucratic weight and internal inconsistencies, just like the Soviet Union did a few years ago. But successive US administrations haven't been concerned about what might replace a communist regime in China. They have adopted the attitude that anything is better. But the communist revolution in China was rooted in efforts to overturn one of the most exploitive and oppressive empires in the world. The powerful syndicates that operated within China during that empire were not destroyed by the new Communist Chinese government under Mao. They were merely dispersed. Communism has not destroyed the feudal society that held the Chinese in its grip. It simply replaced it with a new authoritarian power structure.

"I informed the agency some time ago about the seriousness of these Asian crime syndicates. But all the US administrations I've worked under have viewed them as little more than minor annoyances and on occasion even ad hoc allies in keeping the Chinese regime off balance. Why, we have had US presidents who even had one of their associates sleeping at the White House! So the syndicates have been free to continue to expand their illicit activities. None of my reports were taken seriously, and past US administrations ended up being manipulated by these crime syndicates operating behind our Chinese friends."

Walters exhibited an immediate change in attitude in response to Ben's defiant tone. "Look! Here's the situation.

You guys have stirred up a bit of trouble for yourselves, and you're getting in deeper. Not a week after the three of you arrived in Thailand, you and Paul Ellis were involved in a brawl in Pattaya that destroyed a bar and landed its owner in the hospital. The owner's lawyer is claiming you and Mr. Ellis are responsible for the damages and has prepared criminal and civil suits against you. Go ahead, protest that it was Patthana's goons who did the damage. I believe you. The Thai authorities most likely will believe you as well, but I doubt a Thai court will rule in your favor. The bar owner certainly is not going after a man as powerful as Patthana and his goons who busted up the place. But the owner will not hesitate to take on the two of you for every US dollar he thinks he can wring out of you. You'll be tied up in Thai courts for months."

Ben knew this.

"Add to that your pal Paul Ellis has been encouraging a group of neophyte liberal Thai university students to sniff around where they shouldn't. It's resulted in a Thai student's murder and Ellis being implicated."

Ben knew this as well.

"And your ex-navy pilot buddy, Dan Spencer? It's bad enough that he has incriminating fingerprints on the gun used to kill the Aussie pilots. He's been cavorting with one of Thailand's most radical women's rights advocates who's crusading against the human trafficking operations of your resort host. It makes it look as if Mr. Spencer and Ms. Sirima were accomplices behind the attempted hijacking in order to call attention to Mr. Patthana's, shall we say, unique passenger manifest. Interesting twist to the 'American heroes' story, isn't it?"

Ben had not considered that interpretation of Dan's overnight dinners with Sirima. Still, he held off registering any surprise that Walters could detect.

"Are you beginning to see a pattern here, Ben? A pattern that suggests maybe you are not the 'golden boys' the press made you out to be?

"And what about you, Ben?" continued Walters. "Well, let's put aside the fact that you've compromised the careers of your own successors with your messages back to the agency. We're aware you've been collecting some rather sensitive information that would tarnish the dignity of your very powerful Thai host who cannot afford to have that happen right now. That puts a big round target on your back if word gets out. And in this city, that's likely to happen without you even being aware.

"If certain powerful elements in Thai military and political circles become aware of what you are up to now, your royal treatment as hijacker-foiling heroes will be over, maybe your lives with it. And you've accomplished all this mischief being in the country just ten goddamn days! Congratulations! I'm so amazed at what you've done."

Ben resented Walters's sarcasm but granted that indeed a very ungracious interpretation could be given to the actions of the three of them. Fortunately, Walters had to stop his lecture when the American woman in army dress entered the room and deposited two very welcome bottles of water in front of them. Ben grabbed his and drank over half in one gulp.

Walters continued once they were alone again. "The Thai government loves to make a show in the press that it can arrest and prosecute foreigners who disrupt the worlds of respected Thai businessmen, not to mention screw, beat up, and murder its citizens. Unfortunately for all of you, there's circumstantial evidence to question your motives here in Thailand."

Now Ben was furious. "And you'd be willing to help the Thais prosecute us, wouldn't you?"

"Look! We are prepared to do whatever it takes to persuade you against what you are doing. For your own best interests as well as for those of the US government, I don't want to see your names in the press on any of these issues. It does nobody any good. And this silly private investigation you're conducting, if it goes on any longer, it's going to get you into the kind of trouble that we can't and most likely won't want to get you out of. That's if we don't find you floating facedown in a Bangkok klong first!"

Walters opened one of the three large envelopes sitting in front of him, the one with Ben's name on it. He pulled out Ben's American passport, the passport that he hadn't seen since the day he arrived in Bangkok, and he, along with Dan and Paul, had temporarily relinquished to the Thai investigators questioning them.

"Ben, I hope I can persuade you and your friends to back off. Now! Here is your passport and the passports of your friends. You have no idea how hard it was to convince the Thai authorities to release Mr. Ellis's passport to the embassy and to allow him to leave the country. He's still implicated in a murder. It's only the ambassador's promise to honor our extradition treaty with Thailand that he can return to the US with you both. You can sign for all three of these passports right now, take them back to Ban Khao Resort, pack your suitcases, and leave the country tomorrow. Call the consulate when you're ready. Staff there will get you seats on the next available flight to the US."

Ben paused for a long moment then picked up his passport, held it, and looked at the receipt form in front of him.

He glanced at the envelopes with Dan's and Paul's names on them as well. He looked up at Walters, who must have registered his look as a plea, because he opened those envelopes as well and dumped out their contents on the table.

Ben picked up the pen from the table, signed the three receipt forms, collected the three passports, and put them in his inner jacket pocket.

"If you have nothing further to share with me, I want to go."

"Nothing more. But let me repeat, if you or any of your buddies consider staying on and continuing what you've been doing, you need to be aware that you can expect no further sympathy or support from the American Embassy."

Ben made one last attempt to reason with Walters. "So you are not willing to consider the possibility of Chinese syndicate subversion of the Thai economy? You are not prepared to warn the Thai government about how vulnerable the country is if it does not take steps to curb money flows from the Hong Kong syndicates. Is that it? Do I have it right?"

Walters, Ben felt, was dismissive but also more open. "The Thais have a way of working things out with their neighbors, and we have a way of persuading them on what steps to take when necessary. You, if anyone, Ben, should be aware of how effective the threat can be of sharing sensitive information about the financial manipulations of key government and private figures. It's a common agency tool. You were excellent during your CIA career at unearthing that information for us both in China and here in the rest of Asia where the Chinese have so much influence.

"And yes, to your surprise, the agency used much of it. What you gathered for us was very useful in gaining favors from Asian governments. I can personally thank you for sensitive personal information about the private lives and financial mischief of former prime ministers and their cabinet members here in Thailand. The subtle threat of making that information public secured some key votes in support of US resolutions. I bet you didn't know that. Talk about effective! Ya' know, a hundred million dollars in foreign aid couldn't have garnered the Asian governments' support for the United States the way some of the intelligence you gathered on the private lives of Asian leaders did, Ben! You were one of a kind among agency analysts. I'm just a little bit jealous of your reputation."

"Walters," said Ben. "You may choose to believe me or not, but I swear to you that we are on the same team. I have every bit as much interest as you in looking out for American interests over here. What's different is that the rules I can play by now are a lot different when I am outside the agency and outside the US. I still have access to much of the same electronic data, and my research skills are just as sharp today. Much of the information I gathered for the agency was from public sources—newspapers, media programming, and official government records. It's not what's in those public sources but how you read and analyze what's in them that tells the most interesting stories and reveals the most troubling intentions to cause trouble."

Ben continued. "Now I can make my own rules about what to do. If the CIA chooses not to listen, so be it. There are those in the press who will. And if they act, they can bring about changes that the agency in all its covert and overt efforts cannot."

Ben rose from his chair, turned around, and with both hands on the table bent over and looked directly at Walters still seated. "Do you think for one moment that the Thais are in control of this playground they call a country?

"The Chinese crime syndicates have significant assets in most Asian countries. They own and operate global corporate conglomerates of banks, transport, communications, construction, and manufacturing. The syndicates control much of the region's commodity trade. While they operate outside the city gates politically and economically, as they have for centuries, the overseas Chinese through their Asian family and corporate relationships control far more of the Thai economy than what they own outright.

"The PRC is moving to take over administrative control of Hong Kong from the British just days from now. Some of the most ruthless Chinese syndicates are looking for a new base from which to operate. They are already moving out of Hong Kong. And where, Walters, do you think they are planning to relocate? Well, the signs point to Thailand, and the evidence suggests that the syndicates have been building up to it for years. Look at your outstanding Thai businessman of the year, Mr. Patthana. Surely you are aware that his parentage goes back to leaders of some of the most powerful Chinese syndicates. Patthana, it seems, has been building an empire based on money from human trafficking.

"He's part of the Chinese syndicates that are establishing a financial beachhead here. And if you look at the flows of capital from Hong Kong, you will notice something else of interest. The syndicate-controlled banks have moved more money out of Hong Kong than they have on their balance sheets. Several times more. How? By heavily leveraging their Hong Kong investments. One of the first things the PRC will do is confiscate assets of the Hong Kong-based crime syndicates. It will deny syndicate members Chinese citizenship or even visas to remain in the Hong Kong territory. If they stay, they likely will end up in prison. The Brits won't save them.

They can't. Under their administrative agreement with the Chinese, Hong Kong is a leased territory, and its Chinese residents are considered Chinese, not British citizens.

"If you've read any of my reports, you'd have seen where I warned about how the crime syndicates have managed to borrow from their own financial holding companies several times over against the value of their real estate assets. Inflated land values allowed the syndicates' holding companies to leverage foreign emerging market investors funds and invest that money somewhere safer, in particular in Thailand, after July 1. That's what has been driving the construction and land development boom in this country. But with that Chinese syndicate money has come more influence in Thai politics.

"When the PRC assumes administrative control of Hong Kong and seeks to confiscate syndicate properties, it will be a hollow victory. What the PRC government will inherit is a host of heavily mortgaged real estate with liabilities far exceeding its value. In all likelihood, to avoid embarrassment the PRC will end up paying off the very capitalist investors they despise or face going to court, something the PRC does not want to do at a time it is seeking to encourage more Western trade and investment with the mainland."

Walters listened in silence. Ben sensed that he held little interest in the picture of imminent financial chaos he was painting. After all, Walters' job was to save the USG from embarrassment, not save foreign governments like Thailand's. And Ben realized that uppermost in Walters' mind was packing the three of them onto a plane bound for the States and as far away from Thailand as possible. Walters had made Ben and his companions an offer they were not expected to refuse: safe conduct out of the country under US diplomatic immunity before they found themselves in deep legal trouble with the Thai authorities.

Sure, he and his buddies could go home, and from the comfort of their suburban retirements they could read about Asia's slide toward lawless corruption and economic collapse while the rest of the world focused on the "opening" of mainland China. But Ben no longer was willing to accept the human toll in lost and exploited lives on which the Asian "miracle" had so far been based.

He foresaw only greater concentrations of poverty and riches if the current course of events played itself out, and he was determined not to let that happen. Since the US embassy was clearly disinterested, Ben decided that the only way to precipitate a change in the course of events was to get the world's attention where it hurt most, in the pocketbooks of the tens of thousands of Americans whose pension plans and retirement accounts held sway over the funds that had been channeled into the country.

From what he and Paul had ascertained, Ben was sure they could make a compelling case that would resonate through American financial circles. He felt confident they could pull it off and do so from a computer terminal back at the resort.

Ben now wanted to end their discussion and get on his way. "All right! I guess I should go back and tell the others to pack. Maybe one more round of golf tomorrow before we go?"

"Well, at most one more round of golf, but don't extend it beyond that!" Walters led Ben back down the cubicle-sided corridor and to the vehicle idling at the building entrance.

On his return trip back to Ban Khao Resort, Ben began to relax. His mind was far from thoughts of any more rounds of golf in Thailand. There was another game he wanted to play.

Ben fingered the three passports in his inner coat pocket. It was nice to have them back, but he didn't believe they were going to be used to leave Thailand as soon as Walters wished.

CHAPTER 16

Thanakit instructed his driver to head directly to the Ban Khao Resort wharf, where they pulled up alongside his father's limo. *Good!* thought Thanakit. *Father is already on board the Blue Heron.*

He exited the vehicle then turned and spoke to his driver through the open car window. "You can take the car and retire for the evening. I'll stay on board tonight. Come for me in the morning. About ten o'clock. I don't have anything on my schedule before a noontime lunch meeting in Bangkok."

He slowly headed up the Blue Heron gangplank. His steps were heavy. He did not hurry. He knew another confrontation with his father lay ahead. This time it was not about Heron Holdings' illicit business dealings, nor the financial vulnerability of his father's enterprises. This time it was about the death, most likely the murder at the hands of his father's bodyguards, of a university student.

His stomach had churned earlier in the day when his father's legal counsel called him with the news and to assure him that steps had already been taken so that the police would not take their investigation in his father's direction. Sufficiently generous payments would be made to senior Thai law enforcement heads to guarantee that. Besides, legal counsel had informed him, the police had another person of interest they were looking at as a possible suspect, an

American who apparently had been associating with the student in the days and hours leading up to his murder. What shocked Thanakit was the name of the American that his counsel was able to extract from the police: Paul Ellis, one of the three Americans who earlier had rescued their Air Siam passenger jet and helped avoid the financial collapse of Heron Holdings.

The rest of the day Thanakit had been absorbed in wondering what the connection was. How did Paul Ellis become involved in a murder? And how with the Chulalongkorn University student? Why would his father's henchmen be concerned enough to commit this murder, if as he suspected, they were the perpetrators of the crime? He had these and other questions to sort out with his father along with much more imminent concerns. Foremost among them was how Heron Holdings was going to free itself from the international crime syndicates descending on Thailand.

Thanakit found his father waiting for him on the aft deck, a glass of scotch in one hand and a tall glass of ice water in the other. That was his signature way to drink; Thanakit knew. His father was a firm believer that a good scotch should never be diluted with water or ice but enjoyed only in its pure state. The water and ice should serve to clear and refresh the palate before the next sip of the golden liquid.

Without speaking, Khun Patthana raised his scotch hand in extending a greeting toward his son and motioned with the ice water hand toward the bar. "You'll need to fix yourself your own drink, son. I've dismissed the staff for the evening. It's just you and me and my Chinese cook who can't understand a word we say."

Without his normal respectful greeting to his father, Thanakit popped the cap off a bottle of soda water and poured it over a glass of ice. To Thanakit, the effervescent liquid seemed to hit the ice with a sound many times louder than normal, almost like the surf as it broke against the nearby rocks of the Ban Khao harbor's breakwater reef.

His abrupt demeanor must have registered with his father, thought Thanakit, because a long silence followed before his father sat down in one of two large rattan peacock chairs and motioned to him to sit beside him in the other. They were just feet apart but settled far enough back in their chairs looking out toward the ocean that neither could peer into the other's face. They could just as well have been speaking over the phone, were it not for the delicacy of the topic. Thanakit speculated that was the way his father wanted it to be.

Not waiting for his elder to begin the conversation, Thanakit broke another Thai tradition and spoke first. "Our legal counsel called me today, I assume at your instruction, Father. He informed me about a university student's death. I was shocked to hear that the police are calling it a murder and that one of our American guests has been implicated in the crime. Father, tell me what you know about this! What's going on?"

Patthana began obliquely. "I instructed the drivers to support and protect our three American guests when they chauffeured them outside the resort. They did that, but they were also watchful of the Americans' movements. They shared with me that the Americans were asking a lot of questions about Heron Holdings, including the sex trafficking operations of our Hong Kong affiliates. Remember, we were able to keep from the press that Air Siam was transporting over 150 young girls, all of them sex workers, at the time of the attempted hijacking. The police were discreet, but apparently the Americans learned about some of our operations during their interrogations. This must have upset them enough to begin investigating on their own. That apparently led them to discover your uncle's syndicate involvement with Heron Holdings through the Hong Kong investment houses that have been financing much of our operations. This knowledge about Heron Holdings' ties to the crime world needs to be contained, particularly right now when we depend on Hong Kong bank capital to survive."

Patthana paused to take a slow deliberate sip of his scotch. Then in a more steady and deliberate tone he began again.

"Somehow the American Mr. Ellis found a contact at Chulalongkorn University, a professor who has been particularly troublesome for me because he has been investigating international monopolies operating in Thailand, including Heron Holdings. The professor has discovered some of our ties to the international organized crime syndicates, particularly the syndicate run by your uncle in Hong Kong. He assigned some of his students to help Mr. Ellis in his own investigations. One of those students was the boy who was killed."

"And?"

"I instructed the driver who had been chauffeuring Mr. Ellis around Bangkok to warn the student to stop collaborating with the American."

"Just that?"

"Well, to rough him up a bit, if necessary, to show I was serious. Evidently our driver was a bit too aggressive, and the boy a bit too frail."

Thanakit rose from his chair, walked to the nearby railing, and turned so he could look directly at his father. "And now we have a boy's life to account for. A young university student no less. A business student, a lot like me. I don't have the stomach for such actions by your goons. This is not the way I want to see Heron Holdings operate."

Patthana looked at his son standing at the railing with the ocean and shoreline behind him. Again, the white fluffy foam of the breakers gleamed in the moonlight behind his son, making him look as if angel wings had grown from his shoulders.

Thanakit could detect an apprehensive look on his father's face, but he could not discern why.

"I am not worried about the police," Patthana finally said. "The boy's body was found in an alley in an area of Bangkok filled with gay bars. The murder can be spun to look like it was a crime of passion. A news story with the slant that he got what he deserved for his lifestyle. The police will use his death as a pretext to crack down on the gays, which they love to do whenever they get the chance. And then after a while everyone will lose interest in the case. Attention will shift away from our American guests as well."

"Father, are you not at all distressed about the moral dilemma this puts us in?"

"Son, right now we are dealing with the survival of a business empire. The death of a Thai student is a price we have to accept!"

"I can't agree with you, Father. Heron Holdings has been operating for too long on the miseries of others. And now a murder! The driver responsible for this must be held accountable. Maybe not immediately, but as soon as we get past the financial threat that could be the end of us all. Promise me that."

"I can promise, but I am not sure the Americans will go along. They are wrapped up in this murder as well. I need you to talk to them. Tonight. You are the best person to assure them that we can help exonerate Mr. Ellis. Tell them that I will arrange with the Thai investigators so they all can return to their country. The police have reported to me that the hijacking investigation is close to concluding. With their investigations into Heron Holdings, the Americans have overstayed their welcome here at Ban Khao. It is time they find their way back to the United States.

"Go and talk with them! Express my regrets about Mr. Ellis' university student friend. Assure them that the student's killer will receive justice. Tell them we are working with the police so that justice happens soon. Tell them that in the morning I will call the superintendent of police, a close friend of mine, and insist the three of them be allowed to return to their homes. Any more information about the hijacking that they might provide can be collected from them in their country."

"I need to use your car. I dismissed my driver for the evening."

"Take it. Here are the keys. I don't want to involve my driver in this. He's asleep below deck by now anyway. Come back after you meet with the Americans and sleep here on the Blue Heron for the night. We still have much to discuss in the morning."

*****

Thanakit stopped his father's limo under the covered portico of the Americans' villa. He got out and knocked on the door. It was Paul who answered. From the American's disheveled appearance, Thanakit could see that he suffered from a lack of sleep. With a look of resignation, Paul motioned for him to come in. They walked out onto the veranda, where he found the other two Americans sitting around a table with plates of half-eaten food.

"I apologize if I am arriving during your dinner hour. I can arrange to come back later, but I do need to talk to you all at some point this evening. I hope you understand."

It was the American pilot who spoke first. "You're not interrupting dinner. We finished some time ago. It is just that none of us has much of an appetite right now. I imagine you can understand why."

"I can indeed. That is why my father sent me to meet with you tonight. You have been involved in some very unfortunate events during your stay here at Ban Khao. We, my father and I, want you to know we regret how you have been caused so much inconvenience. We want you to know what we are doing to help."

"We're not the ones who really need the help right now," Paul interjected. "Speak to the family and friends of the dead university student to learn what you can do to help them. Or to the families of all the young girls your father's associates have been trafficking. Start with the ones that were on the plane with us coming here.

"We're ashamed that we've been accepting generosity that has come at the expense of so many others. We have all agreed this evening that we can no longer accept your father's hospitality. We're preparing to leave in the morning. It's good you came so that you can inform him for us. This is goodbye. Please tell him that."

"I am not surprised by how you feel. From what I understand, you have learned a lot about my father's businesses. But you are looking back, not ahead. And looking ahead, you'll see that I am pushing my father to divest Heron Holdings from those illicit practices. That's why my father sent me to America to get the type of business administration training needed to lead Heron Holdings into the future as a responsible and wholly legitimate enterprise."

Now it was Ben, the man Thanakit recognized as the Chinese translator, who spoke. "It's not just what we have learned about Heron Holdings. It's what we've experienced particularly in the last two days about how your father operates. It's hard to believe what you say and even harder to believe you are able to make a difference when the lives of good people like the university student mean so little to you."

Thanakit tried to explain his father's commitment to seeing that those responsible for the student's murder were brought to justice. He could easily tell that the Americans clearly were not satisfied. He learned from them that earlier in the day their passports had been returned and that they had been encouraged by their embassy to leave the country as soon as they could pack. He was also surprised that, despite the urging of their embassy, none of the Americans planned to leave until they saw that justice was done to the killer of the student.

Thanakit recalled his earlier meeting with the Americans, the meeting in which they shared their speculation of a plot by Chinese syndicates to subvert the Thai economy and establish a new safe haven for their operations after administration of Hong Kong passed from the British to the mainland Chinese. He had suspected as much from his father's syndicate associates, but he was amazed at how quickly the Americans had come to the same conclusion during their brief stay in the country. It was also unsettling to hear the Americans report what they knew about the financial vulnerability of Heron Holdings.

It was Paul Ellis who spoke up again. "We need to be open and honest here if we're to get anywhere, Mr. Thanakit. We don't trust your father, and we don't see any evidence that he has the welfare of the Thais in mind. We also don't believe he is fully in control of his own enterprises. Heron

Holdings now appears to be at the mercy of its creditors, and those creditors are fronts for the Hong Kong Chinese crime syndicates. The next step for them is a simple one, call in their loans to Heron Holdings, loans that Heron Holdings can't repay right now. That will force you into bankruptcy. Then they can pick up the pieces for a fraction of their value using the assets they have been transferring from Hong Kong and converting into local *baht* currency accounts here in Thailand to take over Heron Holdings and relocate their criminal operations here."

"I am aware." Thanakit now began to open up with the Americans, more in a way that surprised himself.

"That is not why I came here tonight," Thanakit continued. "I came because I am fearful for your safety, and my father and I want to help you with the Thai authorities so that you can return to the United States. All of you."

Ben spoke this time. "The American embassy returned our passports and urged us to leave Thailand as soon as possible. Everyone seems concerned for our safety. Or is it their safety? Funny thing is, two days ago, before an innocent student was murdered, we were ready to get on a plane back to the United States. But this evening before you arrived, we decided we owed it to that student to stay until we see that justice is done for him. And perhaps more important, to see if we can help right some of the injustices that Paul and the student had uncovered. So we are going nowhere right now."

Paul spoke up to emphasize they were united behind what Ben had declared. "Look. We appreciate your aspirations for making Heron Holdings into a responsible enterprise that benefits Thailand. But I guess we've lost our innocence since learning about the legacy of corruption and exploitation that is behind your father's business empire and just how difficult it's going to be for you to change that. So maybe the question is not how you can help us but how we can help you. As Ben said, none of us plan to go anywhere now until we see some justice for the student who lost his life and for all those girls whose lives have been ruined by the commercial sex trafficking operations of your father and his associates."

Thanakit looked into the faces of each of the Americans and recognized the degree of determination in each. His mind was accelerating now. In Asian culture, it was never wise to admit one's weakness or vulnerability. Still Thanakit sensed he had no choice. He feared the Americans would go to the police or the press with what they knew unless he could offer them a better option. He had only one.

"I underestimated all of you when we first met," began Thanakit. "I also had no idea about the challenges I faced in attempting to bring change to Heron Holdings. Since returning to Thailand, I have learned that the ties my father's company has with his Chinese associates penetrate deep into Heron Holdings' corporate flesh like a cancer. I worry that to kill the cancer, I might kill the victim, to destroy all that my father created. But I abhor the way he went about building his business empire and the human toll it has taken. I think it is now time to act. But I cannot act alone. I need help."

Thanakit saw the confused and skeptical looks on the Americans' faces. But they appeared to be attentive to what he was saying.

"I have information about one vulnerability that our crime syndicate creditors have. And with your help, I can use it to make what you Americans say is a rear-guard attack on the syndicates. If that information is shared in international financial circles, it would immediately cause investors to pull back their participation in Hong Kong financial markets. That would have ripple effects on the value of major Asian currencies, particularly the Thai *baht*, and greatly weaken capacity of the international syndicates to secure a foothold in our firm and in our economy. My father's business operations would suffer, yes. I would be telling the world that Heron Holdings is so sick that anyone getting into bed with our company would contract the same disease. My father would consider me a traitor to the company, but his company has been conspiring against the interests of the Thai people. There is a greater good here to consider, and if Heron Holdings can survive in the end, so much the better. If not, better it should die and take its criminal heritage with it."

"Would you really do that?" said Paul. "You know you risk losing everything!"

"I am not comfortable with taking the reins of my father's enterprises just because I am his son. I want to earn that honor on my own. I feel even more strongly that I do not want to inherit business operations tied to underworld syndicates still engaged in illicit trafficking in humans and sustained by paying and subverting local authorities."

Ben was the first to pick up on what Thanakit was proposing. "We could easily prepare stories to run in the international financial press, stories that investment managers would see when they wake up in the morning US time. Planting stories in the press is part of International Espionage 101. It's one of the first tricks taught in spook school. And now with the internet, word spreads quickly. With even a moderately alarmist twist about financial market turbulence, money will immediately start moving out of Hong Kong banks or Thai securities and into more secure assets. Within a day we could shrink the value of all the financial assets that the Hong Kong syndicates have been covertly transferring into the Thai banking system. We'd be pulling the financial rug out from under them. Beautiful! I'm ready to begin!"

They all looked at each other. The Americans, Thanakit saw, were waiting for him to respond. But for Thanakit, it was not so much a reaction as an invitation to seize a moment he had realized would not come again. It was time for him to act.

"Yes!" said Thanakit. "Let's begin. Tell me what you need for a good story."

In the next hour Thanakit shared with the Americans the names of key Asian financial institutions which had disguised how highly leveraged they were in Thai firms they were preparing to take over. Ben added juicy morsels of information about the involvement of the outwardly legal Hong Kong firms that were investment darlings in the emerging markets portfolios of US mutual fund managers. What those US fund managers did not know and what the Americans and Thanakit were about to reveal was that those Hong Kong investments were in firms that had incestuously comingled Hong Kong bank boards of directors made up of some of the regions' most notorious international crime syndicates. Thanakit and Ben had the investment values and the syndicate bosses' names. Paul composed the narrative and internet-based contacts of the US financial news outlets. Within a few hours they were ready. When Ben hit Send from their villa computer, they paused to look around at each other. Would it work?

"Our message," said Ben, "is arriving in the early morning New York time. It will have a full day to circulate while we sleep on it. When we wake, we can see if we got the results we want."

Thanakit prepared to depart. "At this point I do not plan to share with my father what we have done here tonight. It is best that he wakes to the news in the morning with complete surprise. He can claim he had no idea how much the

Hong Kong banks had been penetrated and subverted by the Chinese syndicates. That will save him face. In the morning I will find out who in my father's employ was responsible for the student's death. It seems a small thing next to what we have just done to roil Asia's financial markets, but it is a place to start in righting the wrongs which Heron Holdings has caused. Thank you for your help."

Thanakit now looked at each of the Americans as he stood in their villa doorway preparing to leave. "Please do not plan to leave Thailand just yet!" he said. "My father may not know it, but I think we are going to need your help in the next few days. You all now know enough about Heron Holdings operations to help guide me in that process. I need you. This is not the type of golf vacation you had in mind, is it?"

With that Thanakit turned and bowed with a Thai *wai* of respect to the Americans then headed out the door to his father's car.

*****

Tongsuk had crept into the back seat of the large white limo and crouched down out of view on the floor between the seats. The covered area where the vehicle was parked at the entrance to the Americans' villa shut out what little light there was from the moonlit evening sky. It left his crouching figure all but invisible in the shadows. Only on very close examination was Tongsuk exposed by the glint of light from the long steel blade of a Chinese dagger he held in his hand.

He and the dagger had been companions now for several years, waiting for the right moment when they would finally and fatally work together. The dagger first came into Tongsuk's hands four years earlier. He had been shrimping far out into the Bay of Siam in an area often frequented by Chinese sea pirates notorious for descending on any lone Thai fisherman they could find. Any fisherman foolish enough to separate from his companions could find himself overtaken by the sea pirates, robbed of his catch and anything of value, his boat burned, and most likely himself floating dead in the water. The Chinese sea pirates were known to be vicious. Stories circulated that they would not only kill the fishermen they overtook and captured but that they would use their flesh as bait for shark fishing. Only by staying in groups large enough to fight off the sea pirates could the Thai shrimpers consider themselves safe from such a fate.

Given his penchant for fishing at a distance from his fellow fishermen, it was perhaps inevitable that one day Tongsuk would cross paths with the Chinese pirates that patrolled the outer ocean reaches and preyed on lone fishermen they came across. And that day came when first light of morning was finally emerging, and he was nudged from his semiconscious sleep to see a boat about twice the size of his glide up close. Before he could fully shake off his sleepiness, he realized one of the four Chinese pirates aboard the other boat had jumped into the far end of his and started to pull up his anchor rope to secure it to the larger pirates' launch.

Tongsuk was not one to surrender his boat and most likely his life to the pirates. He was prepared. Before his Chinese attacker could stabilize himself after jumping aboard, Tongsuk violently threw his body against one side of his boat, causing it to rock violently, almost tipping over. He swiftly threw his weight back to the other side to right his boat to cause the Chinese intruder to lose his footing and fall over the edge into the water. In an equally swift move, Tongsuk grabbed an oar from the bottom of his boat and brought it down on the neck of the intruder in the water with such force that the head nearly separated from the body.

The remaining three in the Chinese launch looked on, so shocked by the violent ending of their companion that they were not prepared for Tongsuk's next move. Quickly he pulled the starter cord on his small outboard motor, set it in reverse, and began to back away. But instead of attempting to flee his attackers, after he had backed off about one hundred feet, he shifted into forward gear and at full throttle aimed his boat like a torpedo toward the stern of their larger boat. The impact from the smaller boat was enough to sheer off the larger boat's rudder and swing it around so abruptly that two more of its occupants landed in the water, leaving the third to grab the useless tiller handle to avoid the same outcome.

Unconcerned about the sole Chinese pirate left in the attackers' boat, Tongsuk maneuvered quickly toward the two in the water, and in a fashion similar to the fate of the first, he dispatched them equally quickly with a vicious chop of his oar to each of their heads.

Now only one pirate remained. He had armed himself with a long Chinese dagger that magnified the glint of the morning sun off its thin steel blade. The dagger was no discouragement to Tongsuk in his smaller boat. He now motored around the disabled pirate boat and its remaining attacker, circling it much like a shark closing in on its prey. As he circled, he sat holding the tiller in one hand and his oar aloft in the other, much like a lance. The remaining attacker had to turn constantly and adjust his hold with his free hand to keep sight of the circling figure. Then he started making feint charges at the larger boat and its attacker, each time turning away just before colliding to produce a wake that began to rock the larger boat with increasing force. As the remaining attacker struggled for footing in the bobbing boat, Tongsuk, in a burst of speed, headed directly at his opponent and veered off, this time causing the two boats to collide at their sides hard enough to throw the attacker into Tongsuk's boat.

The attacker struggled to right himself from where he landed, but he was not quick enough to avoid the lethal oar that now came crashing down on his dagger arm. He rolled over in agony, now releasing the dagger, which Tongsuk quickly grabbed and used to dispatch the last attacker with a quick sweep across his throat.

Exhausted, Tongsuk lay next to his last victim until the sun was fully visible on the horizon. Then he pulled himself erect and, with his oar, rolled the fourth attacker into the ocean to bob up and down like a log alongside the bodies of his companions.

Except for the Chinese dagger, Tongsuk salvaged nothing from the Chinese pirates' boat that day. He allowed it to drift off as he headed to rejoin his fishermen companions already headed into shore after their night at sea.

He retained the memories of his encounter with the sea pirates down deep in his being. He never shared the story or revealed the Chinese dagger, which he had hidden under an oar lock, waiting for the time when he would have the opportunity to use it again to extract revenge. Revenge against the man whom Tongsuk knew was behind the defiling of his sister, the usurping of his village lands, and the destruction of his village's way of life.

That opportunity to settle accounts, it seemed, had now come. Tongsuk knew that Khun Patthana almost always traveled with a driver and a bodyguard. For some reason this evening, neither was in sight. Khun Patthana, it appeared to Tongsuk, had driven his limo alone to the foreigners' villa.

That provided an opportunity to act, to settle a debt for his family and his village.

As Tongsuk crouched down on the floor of the limo's back seat, he could hear the villa door open and some words exchanged. He next heard the car door open and the driver enter and insert the key into the ignition. As the vehicle moved off slowly along the winding villa road back toward the wharf, Tongsuk chose to act. Swiftly he rose and grabbed his victim's head, pulled it back and plunged the dagger into his chest. The limousine lurched forward and swerved into a ditch. Tongsuk forced open the limo door and prepared to flee into the night, but not before his victim slumped toward him to where he could see his face.

For an instant, Tongsuk froze. Then he fled into the night leaving the dagger where he had driven it, into the chest of Patthana's son and his friend, Thanakit.

CHAPTER 17

Sittichai shot upright from his desk at Thai police headquarters. He asked the caller to repeat the message. Had he heard it correctly? He was being summoned, the caller repeated, to participate in the investigation of a murder that had happened the night before, this time at the Ban Khao tourist resort near Rayong. What he wanted to confirm was the next part of the message. The resort owner's son, Thanakit, had been found murdered there. He apparently had been visiting three Americans at the resort the night before according to his father. Since the Americans were his "property" in the earlier hijacking investigation, Sittichai was now assigned to the murder investigation team to obtain statements from the three foreigners about their dealings with Thanakit that night.

He was to leave for the resort immediately, check in with the senior homicide investigator, and chief of police already on the scene. Sittichai did not take time to listen further. He stood up and spun around to grab his inspector's jacket on the back of the chair. As he put it on, he looked across the room from his desk at the clock on his office wall: 10:00 a.m. He would be there before noon. He was out his office door the next instant. He didn't take the time to requisition a police HQ car and driver but instead drove his own vehicle to the resort. On his way he called ahead, requesting more details. A resort groundskeeper had found Khun

Patthana's limo in a ditch with Thanakit's body in it during his early morning rounds and called the resort security officer, who immediately went to Patthana's yacht to notify him. Patthana's security service then called the Thai police and sealed off the resort. No one was allowed in or out. The police chief had radioed HQ with requests to contact the Thai army for a military helicopter to overfly the shoreline and the Royal Thai navy to assign a coast guard boat to patrol off the beach. The resort was in lockdown.

Perhaps on this visit to Ban Khao resort to question the Americans, he thought, he might meet in person the subject of his years of investigating international organized criminal operations in Thailand, the resort owner and head of Heron Holdings, Khun Patthana himself. Sittichai had yet to do so. Always in past investigations involving Heron Holdings—and there were several—it was one of the more senior police investigators who stepped in. Sittichai was passed over, he suspected, most likely because he had turned down numerous opportunities for an extra-official role as one of Khun Patthana's paid private police informers in exchange for sharing information about how investigations of Heron Holdings operations were unfolding and how embarrassing evidence in such cases might quietly vanish. And there was plenty Patthana did not want known that Sittichai had reported to his superiors but that never went beyond them, except to Patthana himself, Sittichai feared. File copies of those reports still lingered in Sittichai's office buried among the piles of paper reports that he had compiled to document his investigations into the illicit activities for which Khun Patthana and his syndicate-based business operations were notorious but never tried or convicted.

The inspector arrived at Ban Khao Resort and asked for directions to the resort lodge where, he was informed, the homicide investigation team had set up its headquarters. On his way, Sittichai drove past a white limo lodged in a ditch now with police crime tape surrounding it and armed police guards standing patrol. When he reached the resort lodge, he learned that Khun Patthana had arrived earlier to identify his son's body and to meet with the resort medical staff who confirmed Thanakit was dead. Afterward he retreated to his private yacht to await further reports from the police and coroner.

The police forensics team had already assembled a preliminary report. Sittichai reviewed the report and requisitioned one of the police force Thai-English transcribers on site to go with him to the Americans' villa to take their statements. His knock on the door was greeted by the villa houseboy. He and his transcriber were invited in to wait on the pool patio, while the houseboy went off to inform the three Americans.

The retired pilot, Dan Spencer, was the first to join him. Sittichai noticed his well-groomed appearance and alert nature. His air force culture and discipline, Sittichai surmised.

"Good afternoon, Inspector, this is somewhat of a surprise. Is there a reason you've come to Ban Khao today?"

"There is," replied Sittichai, "but I prefer to wait until your two companions can join us to explain."

"I understand. I'll go and make sure they're aware you're here."

"That is not necessary, Dan Spencer. Your houseboy should already have announced to each of you that we are here. Please stay with me right now." Sittichai spoke, addressing the pilot using the traditional Thai practice of using his full name, not so much out of respect, but more to establish a degree of distance and detachment.

"Of course," Dan replied, and he slowly took a seat a few feet from where the inspector and his transcriber remained standing.

Ben was the next to appear. "G'morning, Dan. Oh, hello, Inspector. The boy told us we had guests but didn't say who. If I had known, I would have taken a few minutes to make myself more presentable. We were all up kinda late last night, so we're just beginning to move this morning, that is, what's left of the morning."

Sittichai made a mental note of Ben's comment. "You are fine as you are, Benjamin Morgan." As he replied, Paul came out on the patio to join them. "Greetings again, Paul Ellis. Now if you all will please sit down. I must share some troubling news with you and ask you some questions."

As the three Americans followed his instruction, Sittichai sensed each revealed a certain awkward uneasiness. He allowed nearly a full minute of silence to follow before speaking again.

"I am here because of the very sad news that Khun Patthana's son, Thanakit, was found murdered this morning a few hundred yards down the road from your villa. I understand from his father that he had been meeting with you last night."

Sittichai looked on as the three Americans' faces dropped in the shock and disbelief he had seen so often in the faces of acquaintances of murder victims.

He could see that Paul Ellis was particularly troubled by the news. "Please, can you tell us—"

Sittichai raised his hand to cut him off. "Right now, I have no clear answers to questions about the unfortunate death of your host's son. I ask your patience. I came here because I need to solicit your cooperation as we investigate. First, I ask that you do not leave your villa until my colleagues and I talk to each of you and until we determine it is safe for you to move about the resort. Because you apparently are the ones who last saw Khun Thanakit alive, the Thai domestic crime homicide unit considers you all to be particularly important material witnesses. For that reason and for your own security, I am posting a police sentry at your villa. Please notify me if you need to go out. I'll arrange an escort, but you will need to report the purpose of your trip and what is your destination."

Dan jumped in. "We'll cooperate fully. Just tell us what more we can do. What do you need from us now?"

Sittichai continued, but rather than focus on any one of the Americans, he directed his gaze above and beyond their heads to the flowered wall and green vegetation surrounding the patio. "This murder is important for many reasons. There is some urgency right now to gathering information quickly, so I am choosing to interview you all together. My companion will transcribe your statements and prepare the written Thai report. Later I most likely will request you to submit more full individual reports as soon I can arrange for Thai-English translators. For now, let us begin. Please share with me information about discussions you had with the deceased last night as well as any other contacts you have had with him since your arrival at Ban Khao two weeks ago. Who would like to begin? The others of you can add details as you believe appropriate."

Sittichai waited while the three Americans looked at each other in a silent searching for who would take the lead. He was relieved when Paul Ellis offered to respond first. Sittichai had grown attached to the American who once worked in Thailand, understood much about the culture, and had been very articulate in responding to his earlier questions. He also empathized with the American over his involvement in the death of the Thai university student. At their last meeting, Sittichai recalled, Paul Ellis had shared the concerns of all of them about the nature of their host's business operations and underworld connections. Sittichai imagined he would hear more of that now from the three of them.

Over the next hour, Sittichai and his translator compiled detailed notes from the three Americans on each meeting they'd had with Thanakit back to their first evening with him when they all arrived at Ban Khao. What did not surprise Sittichai were the Americans' common observations about the conflicts over the future direction to take Heron Holdings that existed between Thanakit and his father. What was concerning to him was what the Americans had confirmed from Thanakit about the extent of Heron Holdings financial difficulties that left the firm highly vulnerable to takeover by its creditors.

The interviews were tense and exhausting for Sittichai, so he was relieved when a police courier arrived at the villa and asked for him. He was instructed to leave immediately for the resort lodge to meet with the chief homicide investigator. Sittichai turned to the Americans to excuse himself. "I am called away for a moment. I want to meet again later today. While I am absent, my only request is that you not share anything about what is happening here with either your friends or with the press. I'm sure I can count on your collaboration. Thank you."

On their way, the police courier indicated that when Khun Patthana learned Inspector Sittichai was at the resort, he asked that he come to meet with him on the Blue Heron before he departed at the end of the day. At the lodge, Sittichai met the chief homicide inspector in charge of the murder investigation, and the two drove down to Patthana's Blue Heron yacht at the Ban Khao harbor pier.

For his first meeting with Khun Patthana, Sittichai felt well prepared but still uncomfortably apprehensive. Over more than a decade, the inspector had been tracking the operations of Khun Patthana and his Heron Holdings. He had assembled information detailing a network of Asian crime syndicate associates within Thailand and elsewhere in Asia, particularly Hong Kong, where Khun Patthana had obtained much of the financial support he needed for building and operating his business empire. Sittichai sometimes had castigated himself for allowing Patthana and his corporate machinations to become such an all-consuming obsession. But a study of the darker side of this man, one of the wealthiest and most powerful corporate tycoons in Southeast Asia, was just too fascinating for Sittichai to resist. Patthana was his quarry, and obtaining a conviction for his human trafficking, fraud, and bribery activities was what drove much of Sittichai's investigative work. Still, as long as Patthana showered his largesse on political and law enforcement leaders, Sittichai considered that his chance of seeing justice delivered was remote.

In all those years of pursuing his quarry, Sittichai had never met Khun Patthana in person. He had never been afforded the opportunity to question him directly about the involvement of his business operations in several unsolved criminal activities involving his international associates. In most cases when Sittichai felt he had solid evidence of Khun Patthana's illicit Asian sex trafficking, he was instructed by his superiors to back off from pressing formal charges.

So why was Patthana asking to meet with him now? Sittichai could only speculate that Patthana feared he was partnering with the Americans to further complicate his life. He also anticipated that Patthana would want to know what he learned from the Americans about what his son, Thanakit, had discussed with them the night before he was murdered.

Sittichai would not be surprised if his quarry, Patthana, was attempting to conduct an investigation of his own into the death of his son. Well, he would soon find out.

Several of Patthana's security detail were milling around the pier next to the Blue Heron when Sittichai arrived. He was greeted with very stern faces and unfriendly stares as he passed through their gathering and up the gangplank behind the senior investigator. On board they were ushered into the inner office suite, where Patthana sat, head in hands, at the far end of a large flat glass-covered navigational chart table. The rustle of their arrival caused Patthana to look up, revealing a pale, grief-stricken face with shallow and clouded eyes. Sittichai stood transfixed by the shadow of the man he had hoped to meet someday. The senior homicide inspector took a step toward the table before Sittichai saw Patthana raise his hand to stop him.

Then with a wave toward the door they had just entered, Patthana spoke. "Please leave us. I want to meet alone with Inspector Sittichai."

Sittichai was surprised and embarrassed that his police comrade, the domestic homicide officer in charge of the investigation, was being dismissed and not allowed to be present. Still, his companion, with a respectful *wai*, bowed and backed away and out the door behind them. Sittichai and Patthana were now alone together.

A long moment of silence followed before Patthana spoke. "So finally, I meet the man who your colleagues tell me has been tracking and studying me for much of his Thai police force career. I imagine you know me well enough to write my biography."

"I sometimes feel like I know you like a brother!" Sittichai responded almost without thinking. He feared he sounded disrespectful with his comment. Still, he was being truthful, he knew, and he suspected Patthana understood as well.

Patthana showed no sign of offense. Instead he spoke with a degree of openness that surprised Sittichai. "Perhaps our lives would have been better if you were my brother, Inspector. Then, maybe…" Patthana let his voice trail off and fell silent again before continuing, "I would trade all that I have acquired if I could get my son back. His loss means that much to me. He was my hope for a new Heron Holdings and a better future for all Thais. I am still not able to accept that he is gone."

Another pause followed before Patthana continued. "You are aware I am sure, Inspector, that I do have a brother. He is a brother who is perhaps every bit as methodical as you but with very different motivations. He is unwavering in his belief in the traditions and principles of our Chinese syndicate heritage. He holds to those values as strongly as you uphold yours and your oath to the Kingdom of Thailand."

"If you mean he is true to your syndicate principles, I will agree with you. But I also have seen the effects of how ruthlessly your brother operates," replied Sittichai. "I have investigated how he bends the will of others in the direction his personal winds are blowing. I've read the international intelligence reports on his syndicate operations. It is clear from those reports that if others do not bend to his will, he does not hesitate to break them in half."

"What I have shared with my brother, and there is much that I did not, is that we both held respect for those who are true to their values, those who are incorruptible, like yourself, Inspector. I will not try to convince you of my brother's merits or his belief in the principles by which the syndicates operate. Neither do I need to recount the abuses we Chinese have suffered under our former colonial masters and current ideological leaders. These abuses have driven us to the margins of the law to survive and to retain a small sense of family pride. My family heritage is built from a long line of survivors who have proven resilient against all efforts to force our Chinese ancestors to bow to the will of foreign powers. The Chinese syndicate families have survived for so long because we hold family bonds sacred above all else. Now my brother has broken those bonds."

Inspector Sittichai felt more relaxed and began to fit into his investigative frame of mind.

"You believe he is guilty of arranging your son's murder? We are aware that your brother and his aides arrived in Thailand a few days ago. You can trust we will interrogate him thoroughly."

"And you will find he has a strong alibi, no doubt. A Chinese dagger is not strong enough evidence for you to connect him to my son's death, but for me it is a clear sign. It's a message that the bonds of family mean less to him than satiating his thirst for money and power."

Sittichai could see that some color had returned to Patthana's face. He wondered now what it was that Patthana wanted to share with him.

Patthana continued. "My son had been meeting with the Americans because, he told me just a day ago, they have compiled information that points to the Hong Kong syndicates' involvement in the international banking institutions and equity investment firms that are among Heron Holdings' major creditors. The Americans were preparing to take that information to the press. Some of that information apparently was gathered with the help of the university student who was murdered by one of the members of my security detail. I had instructed them only to warn off the student from his collaboration with the Americans, not end his life.

"I want you to know that I am turning that murderer over to you today. There was no need for that student to die. He was only a boy. Much like my own son. I can hardly expect you to find my son's killer when there is blood on my hands from the murder of another innocent young man. They both had good aspirations for Thailand. Neither deserved to die."

"But now both are dead!" Sittichai allowed his anger to surface briefly. "Perhaps now you can experience from your own son's death how the student's family and friends must feel about their loss. I must be fully honest with you. I appreciate your help in providing us with the student's killer, but if the killer is in your employ, we must consider it likely that what he did was under your orders. That makes you accountable for the student's death as well."

"You are very direct, Inspector Sittichai. I will not waste your time or mine in attempting to dissuade you with either threats or rewards for doing your job. I also know a little bit about you, and I know that my efforts to buy you will be useless. Instead, in addition to handing over the student's murderer, I will make you another offer. An offer that should reward your persistence in searching for illicit activities among Heron Holdings' operations."

Patthana paused as if to reflect on whether he should say what was on his mind and what would be the consequences if he did. "I am not proud of what I had to do, but I am a practical man, and I keep excellent records of all Heron Holdings' transactions, including the operating fees, shall we call them, that Thai government and military leaders require for me to conduct those operations without disruptions. Records of those unofficial payments are insurance for me against losing Heron Holdings. My goal has always been to keep ownership of Heron Holdings within my family. But now I have lost that family. My brother has betrayed me, and my son is no longer alive. I have been considering what to do with those records, particularly if something should happen to me. I am thinking about sharing those records with you."

Patthana rose from his seat at the end of the table opposite Sittichai. He walked slowly down to the end, where the inspector was sitting, and stood over him. A wry smile broke across Patthana's face. "Sharing those records with you is not an easy thing for me to do, I want you to know, Inspector. You of all people have caused me perhaps the most trouble and cost me the most money. I have never seen such rigorous and thorough investigative reports as yours. Yes, I said 'seen' because your superiors used them to extract even more money from me. I had to pay or your reports would be used against me and against Heron Holdings. Damn you!"

Patthana's face had turned red, and the inspector thought he saw him tremble. But Patthana continued on.

"Your superiors knew how to turn a profit from your work, Inspector. They saw you as a money pit, that's why you were always assured of having a job. Not only because you are good at your work, but because your work could be used to help them fund their retirement."

Sittichai took in Patthana's backhanded compliment with an audible grunt as Patthana continued.

"I will wager, Inspector, that your superiors did not share with you a single Thai baht of what I had to pay them to suppress those investigative reports of yours. I bet they didn't even do so much as buy you an evening with a girl. Or even treat you to lunch. Am I correct, Inspector? Yes, I can see from your face that I am." Patthana went back to his end of the table and collapsed back into his chair.

Sittichai looked at the obviously deflated financial titan sitting opposite him. He grappled with why Patthana would now share such records with him. If Patthana feared losing control of Heron Holdings, he certainly would not want to see it fall into his syndicate brother's hands. That was what the American Paul Ellis had shared with the inspector about his conversations with Patthana's son, Thanakit, the night before his death. But where would Patthana go? What would he do? Without his business empire and its financial muscle to protect him, vengeance from those he exposed would be quick and fatal if he no longer had incriminating evidence of their corruption to protect him.

Sittichai finally responded. "I am honored that you would consider sharing such sensitive information with me, but it's the Royal Thai Police anticorruption unit that you should approach."

Patthana quickly responded, "Never! Some of them are among the most frequent names in my records of payoffs. You are the only person on the Royal Thai Police force for whom I have any respect, any trust, any confidence, even though you have cost me a lot of money all this time! Do we have a bargain?"

"And what are you asking from my side of the bargain?" Sittichai responded.

"My brother, Jimmy, arrived in Thailand with his Hong Kong entourage but only on temporary visas. He is stateless now that he has left Hong Kong, where the British administration granted him Commonwealth resident status for as long as it administered the island. The Chinese government is aware of Jimmy's syndicate background and will arrest and jail him. Because of Jimmy's criminal reputation, the British won't allow him to settle in England, Canada, or anywhere else in its Commonwealth. So, he and his syndicate associates are preparing to reward Thai authorities handsomely if they grant him indefinite residency here. You must never let that happen.

"The names of those people who would grant him that status are in those records. The release of those names and the Thai banks in which they are involved would very quickly make my brother a political pariah and end any chances that he operates here. That would prevent him from making your job as international criminal investigator a whole lot more complicated and dangerous than I have made it for you!"

Sittichai looked up at Patthana and thought he detected a slight mischievous curl of a smile on his face. "So my side of the bargain is to make sure the records you provide me are seen by the right people in the government, Interpol, and if necessary the press or whomever has a say in decisions to provide your brother with a safe haven for his operation here, correct?"

"Use your judgement. My brother is not aware of those records or of the extent to which his name is associated with those we've bribed."

"And am I able to share the source of those records?"

"You will have no choice. My name is on many of the transactions that approved the bribery payments. As I said to you, I keep full and accurate records of important transactions. You cannot keep me out of it."

"But aren't you concerned about your own safety?"

Patthana, for the first time in their conversation, expressed a note of annoyance. "So now you're worried about me, after all these years of trying to take me down? I'm surprised at you, Inspector! Here I'm offering up on a silver platter the bare butts of some of the most corrupt senior political, military, and business leaders in the country, and you're concerned about my health? Why have you been tracking me for years if not to achieve this very moment of victory? Can't you see the irony here? I'm giving you the records that will condemn the very police superiors who I paid to block your efforts to prosecute me. Please don't try to talk me out of it. I'm making plans to take care of myself."

"Very well! We have an agreement." Sittichai spoke more softly now, both to calm himself as well as to reassure Patthana that he was okay with his proposition. "I imagine you need some time to recover from your son's murder. And there is work I need to do yet in questioning potential witnesses and in finding his murderer. I respect your need for privacy. How do you propose to transfer those records to me? When do you suggest we meet again?"

"You may come back to Ban Khao anytime you need to as part of your investigation, of course, but I do not think we will ever meet again. As for the Blue Heron files, let the Americans be the point of transfer. It was they who originally saved me and Heron Holdings from financial collapse two weeks ago. It was they who have exposed the financial threats to the survival of my enterprises. You have good working relations with them. They seem to be suitable intermediaries. Please tell them to expect some records from me in your name."

Patthana reached in his pocket for a pen and a pad of paper with Heron Holdings name and logo on the sheets. He wrote on one of the sheets and handed it to the inspector. "Here's a deposit toward our agreement, the name of the man you want for the student's murder. You should be able to take him into custody today. I instructed him along with each of my other staff to make himself available to your police investigators for questioning about the...the events of last night. You can detain him then."

Sittichai could see it was hard for Patthana to say the words "my son's murder." Together they rose slowly from the opposite ends of the table where they had been sitting. Sittichai came around to Patthana and took the sheet of paper from his hand. They faced each other, and for reasons that Sittichai did not fully understand but he sensed they both seemed to welcome, the two adversaries briefly embraced in a supportive hug. Then Sittichai, without a further word, turned and left Patthana sitting alone.

CHAPTER 18

While Inspector Sittichai was called away, Paul asked Ben to find the online English-language edition of the *Hong Kong Business Times* for July 2, 1997. He wanted to see if the most respected financial and commercial news outlet in Asia had picked up on the two news stories Thanakit had composed and Ben had planted with the wire services the night before.

As Paul and Ben scrolled through the electronic version of the HKBT newspaper, they found that the first four pages were dedicated to pictures and descriptions of the July 1 ceremonies surrounding Britain's turnover of Hong Kong administration to the Chinese the day before. There were dozens of pictures of dignitaries from around the world who had attended the Hong Kong transfer ceremonies. Included was a half-page photo of the American ambassador and his Chinese diplomatic counterparts in front of the US embassy now downgraded to consular status. Long articles lauded the peaceful transition of power. Demonstrations against the takeover, conducted mostly by progressive university student groups, had been small and muted. The HKBT also set aside space to recount the two centuries of colonial British and mainland Chinese conflict of which the territory of Hong Kong had been a part. The historical commentary went back as far as the opium wars and right up to the peaceful passage of Hong Kong control from a former colonial power to a communist regime. "A rare peaceful transition from colonial rule in the last century!" trumpeted the newspaper.

Paul noted another news article reporting that most of those who were eligible and wanted to leave Hong Kong had already done so, in most cases under British citizenship status to relocate to Great Britain or to any of the British Commonwealth countries where they would enjoy the full rights and privileges of British subjects. Those remaining in Hong Kong were granted residency status and given up to five years to apply for either British or Peoples Republic of China citizenship, the news articles reminded. After that and upon expiration of their residency status, those remaining in Hong Kong would automatically become PRC nationals.

"That confirms what Thanakit pointed out to us, remember?" said Paul. "Members of Hong Kong's crime syndicate would certainly be among those seeking to escape Chinese control. I can begin to appreciate how critical for the syndicates is finding a new base of operations."

It was the small single-column article back on page 6 of the online newspaper that caught Paul's eye next. "There it is," he said and called Dan to join them to look. Paul read out loud the headline: "Thai Property Developer Defaults." Ben began to read the entire article from where he was sitting at the computer.

Bangkok, July 1. Thailand's largest property developer, Heron Holdings, missed a June 30 deadline for interest and principal payments due on foreign currency loans from its Hong Kong creditors. For the first time in many years, a major Thai construction and transportation company is unable to meet its loan obligations.

A reliable source confirms that Heron Holdings is heavily leveraged at present and cannot meet its short-term financial obligations without major debt restructuring. With many of its land development projects still unfinished and unoccupied, including several Bangkok office and residential towers, Heron Holdings is unlikely anytime soon to increase net revenue flows from existing operations to have enough remaining funds for debt servicing.

This default will most likely increase pressures on the company's stock on the Hong Kong Asia-Pacific securities exchange. Major investment houses which earlier this year dropped their ratings of Heron Holdings (HHT) securities from "buy" to "hold" have for the first time changed their ratings to "sell."

"Well, that's one," said Paul. "Let's see if the HKBT picked up the other press services article that Ben planted for us. Keep scrolling down, Ben!"

"Look. We made it onto the following page as well. See! There, under the article heading, 'New Organized Crime Concerns Surface—Could Potentially Roil Asian Financial Markets.'" Ben read again.

Hong Kong, July 1: Regional intelligence analysts report significant capital movements in the last two weeks by two major Hong Kong

*banks with alleged connections to
Chinese organized crime syndicates.
Both unnamed banks have recently
transferred sizable holdings elsewhere
in Asia, most likely in anticipation
that they will face increased constraints
on their operations once the transfer
of Hong Kong from British to Peoples
Republic of China control is complete.*

*One country destination for much
of these funds, according to reliable
sources, is Thailand, where Chinese
syndicates have taken major positions
in several commercial investment banks
in addition to the powerful Royal Thai
Military Bank. From these new Thai
investments, it is speculated that the
Chinese syndicates will continue to
launder and manage funds from the Asian
trafficking and gambling enterprises they
allegedly operated from Hong Kong during
the colony's British administration.*

*Interpol and the American Central
Intelligence Agency would neither confirm
nor deny that any unexplained movement
of Chinese syndicate funds has taken
place, though recent quarterly financial
statements released by the destination
banks offer evidence of these transactions.
What is indisputable are the more reliable
international exchange balance sheets of
the Central Bank of Hong Kong, which
show mounting Thai foreign exchange*

*obligations that track closely with
international lending to that country.
Intelligence analysts point out that
Thailand now has international financial
obligations that exceed four times its foreign
exchange reserves, placing the country on
a very precarious financial footing. Any
drop in foreign exchange earnings from
Thailand's export-led economic growth
would leave the country unable to meet
its international obligations. With the
Thai baht pegged to the dollar, Thailand's
growing international debt obligations are
quickly becoming unsustainable as its foreign
exchange reserves continue to dwindle.*

"Okay," said Paul. "Let's look at the exchanges. Let's see what Heron Holdings stock valuations are now. Asian trading is most likely done for the day. I hope we have at least begun to move the needle."

Paul could see a skeptical look on Ben's face.

"It's doubtful you'll see anything yet," said Ben. "Hong Kong traders most likely will shake off the news as something they have already factored into their valuations. They're already aware that the Heron Holdings stock price has been soaring on unrealistic earnings expectations but don't want to see their trading commissions disappear.

"As for US traders, remember it's early yet. Six o'clock in the evening in Thailand is six in the morning, East Coast time in the US. It's too soon in the day for US financial analysts to pick up on the reports we sent out last night. Besides, they will certainly perform their due diligence first, check their sources, triangulate with other information, including,"

Ben added with a wry smile, "a close look at the two articles that we planted in the wire services which the HKBT published for us. Then they will act. But that won't happen until we here in Thailand are already asleep tonight. I expect you'll see some real changes by the time we have breakfast in the morning."

"You're right," said Paul. "There's a trading time-lag to deal with. I wager that after the New York analysts finish doing their homework, then the information we put out there will start moving US securities markets. Which means the earliest we can see an impact will be at some time during tomorrow's trading day."

Dan looked at Paul and Ben. "I still don't see how a couple of business news articles in an obscure Asian financial rag can produce much of an effect on the US stock market, let alone on global currencies like we're hoping to achieve. It seems pretty implausible."

Paul countered, "All it takes, Dan, is for one US investment analyst to send out a 'the sky is falling' alert in one of their daily letters to investors. Or it may be some analyst employed by one of the big mutual funds, like Fidelity, Schwab, or Vanguard, who picks up on it and decides it's risky for their individual and institutional investor clients to be in mutual funds holding stocks or bonds associated with any Asian corporation or bank with alleged organized crime connections. They may have innocently been doing it for years, unaware of the organized crime linkages to their investments, but now that the information is public, they will need to act. And that means distancing themselves from such investments as quickly as possible.

"The US Securities and Exchange Commission monitors American investment houses very closely to determine possible illicit financial transactions like money laundering and setting up safe haven accounts where crime syndicates can stash their cash. The European markets are also tightly monitored by their monetary authorities as well. There's much less oversight and regulation of Asian securities or money, however."

"Of course," Ben added, "as long as US investors are experiencing double-digit annual growth on Asian equities and bonds, they're happy to add them to the 'emerging markets' equity component of their diversified portfolios. But as soon as any reputable US stock or bond fund senses there is any chance of criminal involvement with overseas firms in their investment portfolios, it's going to move quickly to divest itself from those firms.

"And that's what starts a domino effect of one investment house after another selling off its troubled securities before the market value drops further. And the more investors who head for the doors, the faster stock values will fall, and that's what we're looking to see happen by early tomorrow."

"But won't that mean," asked Dan, "that if Heron Holdings stock values drop, it will be cheaper and easier for the Hong Kong syndicates to buy up those shares and gain control of the company? Isn't syndicate takeover of Heron Holdings what we're trying to avoid?"

"It is and it isn't," replied Paul. "Yes, Heron Holdings will be an easy takeover on the Bangkok stock exchange. That's exactly what Thanakit expected the Hong Kong syndicates wanted to do, at least since they set eyes on Thailand as their new base. Buy up and gain control of Heron Holdings. That's what appears to be behind their attempt to bring down our Air Siam flight. They wanted to make Heron Holdings so weak that its stock would drop in value to a level about equal to the assets they needed to transfer out of Hong Kong. But what the Hong Kong syndicate leaders apparently still believe is that Heron Holdings' financial underpinnings are strong. They do not yet know, and only Thanakit and his father knew until Thanakit confirmed what we found out with Sentthap and his Chulalongkorn University colleagues, is that Heron Holdings is so overleveraged with borrowing that what the Hong Kong syndicates will take on is a huge debt liability if they try to buy the company outright.

"Once the Hong Kong syndicates buy up Heron Holdings shares with the hard currency they have been transferring to Thailand, they will find themselves taking on all of the company's debt obligations, and much of those are denominated in hard currencies, US dollars, British pounds. The syndicates will find that it is too late for them to recoup those hard currency assets because Heron Holdings stock values will have declined, and it has no hard assets to cover them if investors decide to cash them out.

Heron Holdings will essentially be underwater. It'll owe much more than its assets are worth. Remember when a company gets into financial trouble, as in the case of Heron Holdings right now, it's the bank lenders who are first in line to collect on their loans. Only after that can the shareholders, now largely the syndicates, lay claim to any company assets—if there are any remaining assets after liquidating loans. It will wipe out the syndicate's assets and at the same time make syndicate members very unpopular here in Thailand because of the massive number of development projects that will all of a sudden stand idle and leave thousands of workers without jobs."

"So what do we do now?" asked Dan.

"Sit tight and hold our breath," replied Paul. "I wager we'll know in the next twenty-four hours if we've been successful in blocking Chinese syndicate efforts to move their base of operations to Thailand. It's kinda sad, I guess, to see the collapse of a large corporate enterprise like Heron Holdings. It will put lots of people out of work, and a lot of contractors won't get paid for the work they have already performed in building those towering office complexes that dot the Bangkok skyline. It'll certainly disrupt the lives of Heron Holdings investors as well."

"I can't get very concerned about Heron Holdings investors," countered Ben, "given what we've learned about the human trafficking Patthana built his corporate empire on and even now depends on as a source of operating capital. I can't cry over seeing all that come to an end. And I don't think Thanakit would have wanted it any other way. It is just a shame that he is not here to see it happen."

"And to support his father through it all," added Dan. "I imagine old Patthana must really be suffering the double loss of his son and now his company. I wonder..."

Dan was interrupted by a knock on their villa door. A moment later, their houseboy entered the patio area where the three Americans were gathered. He was accompanied by Inspector Sittichai.

"I came to continue our conversations of this morning," began Sittichai. "This time, however, I have come alone. My hope is that we can share information in confidence, things that we can keep amongst ourselves. Is this a good time? Can we begin?"

"Of course," said Paul. Dan and Ben nodded in agreement.

CHAPTER 19

Jai was pleased but apprehensive about the news she received from her Ban Khao Resort hotel supervisor. An important foreign visitor would be occupying the Royal Suite on the uppermost floor of the hotel. Her floor! In fact, the foreign visitor had reserved the entire floor for himself and for all those traveling with him.

For some time, Jai had been waiting for such an occasion. She had loyally serviced the upper floor rooms daily, but visitors to these more elegant and expensive units came only sporadically, and never had the royal suite been used. This would be a first for her and her coworkers.

Jai was understandably a bit nervous. Her floor supervisor told her that the occupant of the Royal Suite was a very demanding person and staying as the guest of the resort owner, Khun Patthana. Most likely he would expect special attention and services. So might the others who were traveling with him. "They are coming from Hong Kong, where the hotels are very fancy," her supervisor said. "You must be available and prepared, Jai, to respond to their requests courteously and promptly." Her supervisor did promise that, during her shift, Jai would be assisted by as many other resort hotel staff as she might need. Still, Jai would be in charge.

Jai welcomed the added responsibility but was not sure what to expect. The last two days had been unsettling for everyone since the death, or murder she soon learned, of the resort owner's son. First, dozens of Thai police arrived at the resort. That was followed by a lockdown of the facilities. No one could enter or leave the resort the day after the murder. She had to make special arrangements with the Ban Khao village women to cook dinner for her father, brother, and son that day because she was not sure when she would be allowed to cross the road and return to her family in the village.

During that day, everyone at the resort was questioned, including Jai and all the resort's hotel staff. The police asked about the occupants of rooms on the floor assigned to her. There were none, she had said. The police asked if she saw anyone suspicious in the hotel during her work hours. She replied she had seen nothing. They asked about when she had arrived for work and when she had returned to her home, and she said she had worked as normal that day from 5:30 a.m. until she finished her shift at 1:00 p.m.

She reported, when asked, that as far as she knew, all the Ban Khao fishermen were out at sea that night and did not return till early morning on the day the body of the owner's son was discovered. She remembered that her own brother, Tongsuk, had not come back with the other fishermen but arrived later, as was normal, quickly falling asleep in their house without even taking time to eat the rice and fish she had prepared and left for him on his return. Of that, Jai was not surprised, because Tongsuk must have been very troubled by the death of Thanakit, his friend since they were young boys.

After the questioning, the police ordered Jai and the other hotel staff to remain near their workstations at the hotel until they were notified that they could leave for their homes. The resort guests were also denied permission to leave the resort until later in the day. When given the option, most resort guests chose to check out early after news of the murder became more widely known and their activities constrained by the police investigation. Jai learned that the police also prohibited any new guests from checking in until their investigation at the resort was completed.

By noon of the next day, the resort became abandoned and empty of most hotel guests. Jai's supervisor informed her that the Hong Kong visitors would be among the first resort guests to check in since the murder.

The next morning, Jai was straightening up rooms when she heard the Hong Kong visitors leave the hotel elevator on her floor and make their way to their rooms. She caught only a brief glimpse of the man who would occupy the Royal Suite. He came up the hotel elevator an hour after the others had inspected each room, it seemed to Jai, to make sure it was suitable for him and his group. He then disappeared into the Royal Suite. It would be the only view Jai would have of him, a man of short stature, thin with a smile-less face of sharp-edged features, who looked somewhat like the hotel owner. She thought she might have another opportunity to see the man when she was called to deliver ice to the room, but when she knocked on the door, she was greeted by one of his staff, who took the ice bucket, gave her two more to fill, and closed the door behind him. That pattern continued until the end of her shift, as Jai saw a steady parade of restaurant waiters deliver food and bottles of liquor to the royal suite and to the men in the other rooms.

Then there were the girls. A steady stream of them began arriving later in the day, according to Jai's coworkers on the afternoon shift. The girls were from outside the resort; her coworkers reported. All were dressed in expensive clothes and were heavily made up. They entered not only the Royal Suite but also the rooms up and down the hallway occupied by the Hong Kong visitors. The parade of young girls in and out of the rooms continued into the late evening. The floor staff reported that the only exception was the Royal Suite from which the Hong Kong VIP visitor had left to have dinner aboard the resort owner's private yacht.

The resort hotel night staff reported an orgy of drinking and debauchery that they would recount for days on end. Early the morning when Jai arrived, the rooms and hallways were strewn with the men and their girls lying about naked in drunken stupors in a scene that defied description. It would take days for Jai and her coworkers to clean up the mess, they estimated. Then, suddenly around mid-day, all the Hong Kong group departed as quickly as they had arrived. All was quiet again.

*****

Patthana had planned meticulously for meeting his brother, Jimmy, on board the Blue Heron. He had made similar arrangements many times before when preparing to entertain influential Thai leaders and politicians whose endorsement and influence he sought for his investment operations. His resort staff and yacht crew knew exactly what food and drink to order and stow on board the ship.

Still, he had placed orders for some special deliveries that he chose to handle himself when they arrived. He took extra precautions to assure that none of his Blue Heron crew or resort staff were involved. He arranged to have the supplier's employees carry these deliveries on board the yacht and store them below deck under his personal guidance. Then Patthana returned to the yacht's aft deck, and with a cup of the strongest tea his chef could make, he sat down to look out toward the open ocean from the Blue Heron deck.

It was now two days since Thanakit had been murdered. With his closest staff, Patthana arranged his son's immediate Thai Buddhist cremation. His ashes already filled an urn on a table in the main entry room of Patthana's personal suite aboard the yacht. He would allow none of the traditional ceremonies to take place around the cremation. He wanted no public display of mourning. His son's spirit still resided over him and over Heron Holdings, and Patthana was not yet ready to let him go.

The Thai and international press had published reports of his son's murder, though because of the secrecy still enforced by the police investigation, they had few details to share about the nature of the killing and possible motives behind it. For Patthana, Ban Khao Resort was an ideal place to keep the press at arm's length, and though resort guests were aware the police had determined the death to be a murder, they were of limited help to the press in providing details of the circumstances. Patthana instructed the resort administrator to inform the press only that a police investigation was underway, and when completed, a statement would be issued.

Patthana realized how exhausted he was from the police investigations into his son's murder. The police had turned up no murder suspects. He was fine with that. He was content to have the police continue their investigations at their own pace but speculated they would find little additional evidence to connect his son's death to the person he felt certain had orchestrated it. He needed no more evidence to convince him who was responsible for murdering his son. His younger brother. He was about to entertain the person he believed was responsible for arranging his son's murder, his brother, Jimmy.

Patthana had been informed that since his arrival in Bangkok a few days earlier, Jimmy had been discreetly courting support, particularly from the Thai banks to which he had transferred his assets from Hong Kong. Patthana also knew that Jimmy was using all the cash he could borrow to scoop up Heron Holdings stocks at their depressed prices and that he had, on paper at least, majority control of the company. Still, Patthana believed in the strategy Thanakit had set in motion to thwart that control. He was proud of his son's instincts to put in place plans to undermine the efforts of Jimmy to acquire Heron Holdings as their front company for his syndicate operations in Thailand.

Patthana knew, however, that he had no time to mourn Thanakit's loss. He now needed to focus on adding his own personal touch to executing his son's plans for keeping the Hong Kong syndicates at bay. He resolved to fulfill Thanakit's goal of turning Heron Holdings totally away from its illicit involvement in Asian sex trafficking. He was prepared to pay whatever price necessary to do so. Thanakit's brutal murder, just as he was on the edge of saving Heron Holdings from bankruptcy, gave Patthana the fortitude to make whatever sacrifices were necessary.

By evening, Patthana had completed arrangements to receive his brother, Jimmy. All he needed to do now was wait.

*****

Jimmy instructed his driver to stop a short distance from the Ban Khao dock where his brother Patthana's yacht was moored. As he and his brother had agreed, Jimmy would walk the short distance to the Blue Heron with two of his bodyguards accompanying him, no one else. Except for Patthana, his two bodyguards, and the ship's captain, everyone else was to be off the yacht; they had agreed. Jimmy insisted his two bodyguards first verify that there were no weapons on their persons or on the ship. Then after the two brothers met, they would dismiss their bodyguards, who would leave the ship together. Those were the terms for the meeting of the two brothers, and Patthana indicated he would comply.

Jimmy sat in the back of his limo and waited while his men swept the yacht for weapons. He welcomed the moment to reflect on what lay ahead. He now owned half of all Heron Holdings' assets, including the Blue Heron. He was no longer a creditor or minor corporate shareholder. It had required Jimmy to liquidate almost all his syndicate bank assets to purchase Heron Holdings shares, but he had succeeded in gaining majority control with the drop in share prices and the flight of investors from their Heron Holdings stocks that had accelerated over the past few days. Jimmy prided himself on his cleverness. How easy it had been to gain control of his brother's outwardly powerful but inwardly vulnerable corporate empire!

Jimmy recalled that he had begun planning for this move to Thailand almost two years earlier when he realized that the Chinese takeover of Hong Kong administration would make it very difficult for his syndicate to continue its operations there. His brother, Patthana, firmly and consistently turned away all his overtures to transfer his operations to Bangkok in a joint venture that would allow them both to conduct business—legal and illegal—in a country with a government almost as permissive as the British had been in Hong Kong. The British said no to drug and arms trafficking and demonstrated their seriousness through multiple arrests and convictions of Jimmy's associates when they ignored those warnings. But the British simply winked and looked the other way as Jimmy's syndicate took over control of Asian sex trafficking that now made up much of the syndicate's lucrative operations.

Income from human trafficking was not enough for Jimmy, however. Hong Kong had another inviting market that he began to tap into very effectively. His syndicate was gradually moving away from shaking down street vendors, pimps, and whores and instead starting to manipulate stock markets and banks. It was easy to take revenue from his syndicate's human trafficking operations to purchase Hong Kong real estate that he could then use as collateral for borrowing additional funds and attracting new investors. And since Hong Kong had a global reputation as a rapidly growing emerging-market economy, individual and institutional investors, particularly in the United States, became what seemed to be a limitless source of funds for buying up land, putting up buildings, and starting new businesses. Using income from human trafficking to leverage legitimate investments and borrowing was where future money was at.

Over the last two years, Jimmy had been moving money into Thai banks and positioning those funds as ready capital for investment in the country's booming real estate and infrastructure sectors. His major Thai competitor, whom Jimmy felt should have been his partner, was his older brother. But Patthana blocked his efforts to pay off Thai government authorities for the approvals he needed to set up operations in Thailand. Older brother Patthana was too strong and too well-placed to work around and too principled to work with.

Jimmy's opening finally came when Heron Holdings went public to raise more funds to expand its land development business. Still, buying into Heron Holdings to gain control of its operations proved to be elusive. Thailand was experiencing a period of rapid and exuberant economic growth that boosted the value of Heron Holdings' equities, making brother Patthana the wealthiest land developer in Southeast Asia. Almost invincible, it seemed. Except, of course, for the financial obligations with foreign banks that Heron Holdings required to underwrite its operations.

Jimmy sat admiring the Ban Khao Resort facilities that now were more than half his. He had put nearly all the money he transferred from his Hong Kong operations into Bangkok banks and waited, hoping that Heron Holdings' stock price would drop to levels where he could purchase enough to gain full control of Patthana's business empire. What goes up must come down; he kept telling himself. He was convinced he would eventually gain control of his brother's construction and land development empire and do so in time to abandon Hong Kong before a new Chinese administration moved in and he had to move out.

His timing was perfect. Heron Holdings had been using short-term borrowing on international markets to finance major long-term land development schemes. The company was greatly overleveraged with only limited cash income to service its mounting financial debts. Jimmy's scheme to bring down one of its commercial airplanes would have worked to sabotage the company by pulling investor support out from under it.

Jimmy saw now, however, that just a little bad news in the financial press was enough to make major investors look closer at Heron Holdings and discover its vulnerabilities. Those investors had now started to head for the doors. In just two trading days after the release of news about Heron Holdings' debt exposure, followed by the shocking news of the death of its chief financial officer, Thanakit, its shares dropped to a fraction of their previous highs, bringing them well within reach of Jimmy's financial grasp. He gave his Bangkok securities broker his buy order that morning, and by lunchtime, he became Heron Holdings' principal share-holder. And recipient of a phone call from his brother.

It was now time to meet Patthana on Jimmy's terms. It no longer was a question of persuading his brother to part-ner with him. Jimmy was now in a position to instruct his minority owner brother on what to do. And the first thing was to have his brother tell his Thai political friends to keep their hands off Heron Holdings operations, whether legal or illicit. Jimmy's only reason for keeping his brother around was to ease the transition of control and continue to obtain favors from Thai government leaders. After that, well, as Patthana had said to him so many times in the past, neither Hong Kong nor Bangkok was big enough for them both. Eventually Jimmy would need to retire his brother for good.

What Jimmy still could not fathom was the death of Patthana's son. He certainly had not ordered the murder of his nephew. Information was spotty about how Thanakit's death had occurred, and the police had yet to make public any preliminary report with a suspect or motive. All Jimmy could surmise was that Thanakit had come across informa-tion that one of Patthana's enemies—and there were many in Thailand—did not want known. Jimmy was concerned and therefore cautious. He did not know how his brother was reacting to his son's murder and if, as was most likely, Patthana had concluded he, Jimmy, was behind it. He still needed Patthana's cooperation, even as a figurehead corpo-rate chief to assure him access to Thailand's powerful politi-cal leaders.

For that reason, Jimmy insisted on a meeting between just the two of them, to agree on how they would administer Heron Holdings together, at least in the near future. When Patthana suggested the Blue Heron as the place to meet, he had agreed.

Jimmy saw his men signal that they had concluded their sweep of the Blue Heron, and it was safe for him to board. Jimmy exited his limo and, flanked by his two bodyguards, headed toward the yacht. In procession they walked up the gangplank and onto the Blue Heron. Jimmy surmised that when he left the yacht later that evening, he would leave as the new CEO and chairman of the Heron Holdings' corporate board, with a majority of its voting members appointed by him, not his brother. Heron Holdings would officially be his.

*****

Patthana listened to his brother's steps on the yacht's gangplank but made no attempt to move from the large rattan peacock chair where he sat. He did not rise, even as his brother reached the deck and called his name.

"I am here, little brother," Patthana replied when Jimmy called out his name a second time. "Come sit in the chair beside me. It is the chair where my son sat only days ago. Forgive me if I am too weary at the moment to rise and greet you as you feel you deserve."

"You have no reason to ask my forgiveness for anything," Jimmy responded. "You have suffered greatly in the last few days."

Patthana ignored his brother's comment. "Dismiss them! My men will accompany them off the ship." Patthana waved his hand toward his two bodyguards, who stood erect at the railing, looking carefully at their boss as well as the three men who had come up on the deck.

Patthana waited until the shuffling of feet ended as the four bodyguards descended the gangplank to stand watch on shore. Then he signaled again with a sweep of his hand toward the back of the deck. "You may fix yourself whatever drink you want at the bar beside you."

Jimmy said nothing, but Patthana could hear ice cubes clink into a glass and the sound of water being added along with, most likely, the premium scotch from the yacht's bar. Then Jimmy came around and stood at the railing facing Patthana. For the first time since they were young men decades earlier, Patthana saw his brother again in the flesh. The occasional pictures of Jimmy at Hong Kong events had caught Patthana's attention over the years, but those photos were rare. Jimmy, like most syndicate leaders, was a very private person. So Patthana was a bit startled to see his brother looking at him from a distance of only three or so meters. What shocked Patthana was the appearance of a man who resembled a withered and aged image of his own son, Thanakit. How strong were the hereditary bonds that mirrored their family features! Patthana at first could not find the words, but he suspected that his brother sensed his uneasiness.

"You look tired and drawn, big brother," said Jimmy.

"You should not be surprised at that. You have put me through a lot in the past few weeks, from a near airplane disaster to—"

Jimmy cut him off. "That's all behind us now. Just some necessary jousting between brothers who never got along so well even when we were young and growing up. You have earned a rest. I am impressed with what you have accomplished here in Thailand, so impressed that I pledge to keep Heron Holdings under our family's control. And I will do that, I assure you. From where I sit now as the Heron Holdings majority shareholder, I can rescue you with enough money to keep our corporate operations afloat and assure that the company continues to be Thailand's leading business empire."

"You are too kind, little brother," injected Patthana with a note of evident sarcasm in his voice. "Yes, it is ironic that going our own ways after Father died, we find ourselves needing each other so many years later. I will grant you that. But times change, little brother. My son, even during his short term on earth, has shown me that. The days of the syndicate control over Asia's markets are gone. Our former colonial masters have been banished. The days when we were the people's heroes because we stood up to and maneuvered around the world's colonial powers have ended."

Patthana took a moment to spread his arms wide, his ice water in one hand and his scotch in the other. Then he continued before his brother could interrupt.

"The colonial powers criminalized the legitimate commerce in which our Chinese ancestors had engaged for centuries, only to take over those markets for themselves. But we have outlasted them and regained control of our economies. Thanakit has shown me that we can compete effectively within this new world order we are experiencing. And do it legally. That is the tide of history, and we, even small economies like Thailand's, can ride it to success."

Patthana was surprised at how forceful he must have sounded, given how physically drained he felt. He had not intended to engage his estranged brother in an intellectual debate when there was so much tension between them. But then Patthana conjectured that maybe that might be a good place to begin. And his brother seemed to recognize that too.

"You have always been the optimist in the family, big brother. You have let yourself believe that because the waters appear calm on the surface, there are no longer turbulent currents below." Jimmy took a long sip from his glass and continued. "Our ancestors have always been tradesmen. We continue to be tradesmen even today. Around the world, we Chinese show our commercial skills even when governments may declare what is legal trade today is illegal tomorrow. When the British outlawed our families from their traditional trade in grains, tea, fine linens, porcelain, and precious metals, overnight they made us illicit smugglers. But we carried on as traders to survive.

"Today China may have restored control of its markets for our traditional commodities, but you know as well as I that those same former colonial powers, along with the Americans, continue to exercise controls over us. Only now it's through financial markets. It's through the flow of money instead of commodities. And money can move a lot more quickly than commodities in this modern age. That's where our struggle now resides with the West."

Patthana had no quick response to his brother's assertions. He felt he needn't offer one. They had different outlooks on how to survive in the future. He, Patthana, by decriminalizing his operations and cutting loose from the human trafficking business; his brother, by modernizing the syndicates' operations to be able to tap into financial markets and bend them to his will, by falsely and fraudulently representing businesses he operated, not as what they were, but as what investors thought them to be.

Patthana turned to look directly at his brother. "It's time we talk business. To do that, I want even more confidentiality than what we have tied up here at the dock." With that, he instructed his captain to cast off the ship's lines and to motor out into the Ban Khao Bay. "I want you to see what a gem Ban Khao Resort is, little brother, and to do that, we must go out beyond the harbor and look back at what Heron Holdings has accomplished here."

For the next hour, as the darkness of the evening began to settle over the bay and the stars and moon assumed their nighttime duties from the sun, Patthana continued to engage his brother in talk about the different turns in life that each had taken.

"You know, Jimmy," said Patthana at one point, "our father's money got us going, you in Hong Kong and me here in Thailand, but going in two very different directions. In the long run, I don't think the path you are on has a happy ending for you. If it did, you would still be in Hong Kong and not here meeting with me now."

Jimmy's reply was quick. "I'm meeting with you here precisely because it is your operations that don't appear to be headed toward a promising outcome. You have been too busy building your corporate empire to realize that your syndicate financiers in Hong Kong have some time ago expanded beyond managing street walkers to manipulating stock markets. The sex trade is a continuing and stable source of income, but if you really want to grow that income, you need to leverage it with the wealth of foreign investors who are too lazy or too avaricious to look closely at what you are doing with their money.

"You were happy to have my syndicate money fund Heron Holdings operations, and I have no doubt you had the best of intentions to return it with all interest and fees that are coming due. But your son discovered for you what I have known for some time in Hong Kong. You are in no position at present to meet those financial obligations. And that is what has led to the drop in Heron Holdings' stock prices. They fell in today's trading markets to the point where they became very attractive to be picked up by someone wanting to gain control of your operations. And that someone is your little brother."

Patthana smiled. His little brother had stepped directly into the financial trap that Thanakit and the Americans had set. It would be so simple right now to pull the cord and close the trap that would leave his brother with only ashes in his hands, with so much Heron Holdings debt that Jimmy would accomplish little more than transfer those debt obligations from his shoulders to Jimmy's. But for Patthana, that was not a sufficient punishment for Jimmy taking his son from him.

The Blue Heron had now reached open waters about a kilometer off the coast. Patthana commanded his captain to idle the yacht's motors and allow them to drift in silence. Patthana looked out over the deck railing as the lights of Ban Khao Resort faded into the night and the pearl sand beaches disappeared on the horizon.

"I guess it is time for the business you came here to conduct with me. While you get out your papers, let me pour us each a final drink as adversaries."

With that, Patthana rose from his chair and went over to the bar. From the cabinet he extracted his prized bottle of scotch whiskey and poured two tall glasses of the amber liquid and handed one to his brother.

"Oh yes," said Patthana. "As I remember, one thing we share in common is that we both like to drink our scotch straight with a glass of ice water at the side."

Patthana headed back to the bar for water, but this time he opened a small cabinet door at the back and without looking, reached in to where his hand felt a small black switch. Then he turned and raised the other hand with his glass of scotch toward Jimmy. "To you, little brother!" he said. Patthana took a long swallow from his glass and savored the burning liquid as it tumbled down his throat. Then he raised his glass again toward his brother and threw the switch.

*****

It was midmorning when the first fishermen from the Ban Khao village cooperative landed their boats on the shore with their catch from another night of fishing the shrimp beds. This morning, however, they were surprised to find a group of Thai police officers waiting for them at the water's edge. The police had questions for the fishermen.

Where had they been fishing the night before? The fishermen pointed out beyond the horizon to where the shrimp beds lay.

Did they see or hear anything while they were out on the water? All shook their heads to say, "No."

Except for one fisherman who remarked that he looked up at one point—it was when the moon had risen to its zenith in the night sky, he remembered—to see a sudden bright flash of light near the horizon. That was followed by the boom sound of a thunderclap. It happened so quickly and ended without any further disturbance, the fisherman said, so he gave it no further thought. That is, until he was motoring into the village beach that morning. There were no clouds in the sky that night; the fisherman recalled. Yet there was what looked like a flash of lightning and the sound of thunder.

After the fisherman had mentioned the strange light and sound, others indicated that they too had seen a light or heard a sound but hadn't given it much thought because it appeared so distant.

After their questioning, the Thai police officers withdrew toward the resort without any comment. It would not be until later that day that word would reach the Ban Khao village fishermen that the light some had seen and the sound some had heard were from a massive explosion aboard the Ban Khao Resort owner's yacht. The police reported finding only fragments of the Blue Heron floating on the water surrounded by a multicolored halo of an oil slick. Those searching later for evidence about what happened found no signs of survivors.

CHAPTER 20

Paul caught sight of Sirima as she walked toward him down the road to Ban Khao Village. He raised himself from where he had been squatting and taking pictures of the village fishermen stowing their nets. He waved her over to him. The tropical morning breeze off the ocean caused Sirima's flowing emerald-green cape to billow up around her long, tightly wrapped traditional Thai sarong, making her appear to float along the road.

From the time that Paul was first posted to Thailand, he had marveled at how elegantly the local women moved, whether they were just strolling on the streets of Bangkok or sitting and eating at one of the outdoor food stalls in Thailand's small rural towns. Thai women stood out among their sisters from around the world, it seemed to him, for the way they managed to add effortless grace to the most mundane of everyday tasks. Even the village women working around him now to sort their husbands' and sons' fish catches moved about their chores with a certain poetic charm.

"Sawadee, Paul! Greetings," said Sirima, her soft voice never rising to the level of a shout but still clearly audible above the rustling of the palm fronds and lapping of the waves against the shore.

"Sawadee, Sirima!" Paul gave Serina a clumsy *wai* greeting with his hands in response to hers. "Stop right there! Move just a bit to your right so I can get you in a picture of the fishing co-op office building behind you. I want to include you in some of my photos as well."

"I hardly add any realism to your shots of local life, Paul." Sirima gracefully raised her arm and pointed beyond his shoulder. "If you want that, you should be photographing the villagers working in the fish sorting sheds."

"Oh, I've taken several photos over there already. In fact, I've been here since shortly after breakfast, when the shrimp boats started arriving with their night's catches. If you remember how we worked together back in our US embassy days, I always worked best when I was up against deadlines. I'm about to get on a plane home to the US this evening, and here I am, at the last minute, taking photos to share with Sarah and the girls."

"Oh yes, Paul, I certainly do remember how you worked hardest on the nights before you had a presentation to make or a report to submit the following morning. You often dragged me into it at the last minute to assemble copies of handouts for the attendees. Sometimes you had me working right up to when they started sitting down to meet with you. You don't need to remind me." Sirima laughed in a lightly scolding tone.

"You can see that I haven't changed much since then, Sirima. I promised myself when we first arrived here at Ban Khao that I would walk across the road to the fishing village to take pictures to share with my family, and as always, I'm doing it at the last possible moment."

"You still have an hour before we all meet for your farewell lunch, Paul. I drove in earlier with Dan, and he and Ben have been showing me around the resort complex. I feel more comfortable coming to see Ban Khao Resort now that the Thai government has taken it over from the man who built it with human trafficking money. I can wait for you back at the resort restaurant, if you need more time."

"No, Sirima. I'm done with the picture taking, but I can use your help talking to some of the fishing cooperative members gathered over by the co-op office. They appear troubled by all that has happened at the resort. Several tried in very broken English to ask me what will happen to their cooperative now that Thanakit and his father are both dead. They sound very worried about what that means for their future. Ban Khao Resort is one of their principal seafood customers. It also provides jobs for many of the villagers. I've tried to respond to some of their questions, but my Thai is nonexistent."

"Of course, Paul, but I'm not sure what is the best way to calm their concerns. We both know that the future of Ban Khao Resort is not very bright right now. You told me that it has never generated income that came anywhere near what is needed to cover its operating costs. I suspect the resort may get shut down."

"Well, Sirima, that's what they need to hear, I guess."

Sirima nodded and the two of them headed to the co-op offices. After twenty minutes of discussion in animated Thai with the co-op members, Sirima turned to Paul.

"They understand better now that they must fall back on their own resources and search for other markets and jobs, at least for a time and until the resort's future is clear. They do have one question that I think you need to help me answer. I'll translate for you, but here's the question: they are asking me to whom to return the loan money that Thanakit had arranged for them to repair and replace their fishing boats. They say the money arrived last week in the co-op's bank account. They feel responsible for returning it. They are telling me that perhaps returning the loan will help keep the resort open, so they can continue to sell it seafood and to work there."

Paul thought for a moment. In the scheme of things, the amount of the co-op's loan from Heron Holdings was probably so insignificant that most likely the debt would be overlooked in the process of liquidating assets by creditor banks and investors. The co-op might never be asked to return the money. What amazed him, though, was the simple sense of honesty and responsibility that the Ban Khao village co-op members demonstrated in their offer to restore to Heron Holdings its loan in full. Naïve as they were that repaying the loan would have any effect at all on Heron Holdings' huge indebtedness to its creditors, they wanted to reach out to help in what they saw as the resort's time of need.

Paul lamented that Thanakit's hopes for turning his father's firm away from its corrupt and exploitative operations were over. Thanakit was gone now and with him, it seemed to Paul, that chance for change. It was humbling to hear an offer to help rescue Heron Holdings and its resort operations come from the struggling fishermen's co-op. Paul mused how the values of economic frugality and financial responsibility were still alive in Thailand's small village communities. But for how much longer, he wondered. He feared that the very survival of Thailand's village culture was threatened by powerful market forces at play in the world's expanding global economy.

"Tell the co-op members to keep the loan money in their bank account for now, Sirima," Paul finally said. "I'm pretty sure it's an interest-free loan, so no harm doing that for a while. Tell them I will personally intervene with the resort's creditors to request the loan be excused so the co-op members will be free to use the money to buy their boats."

Paul realized he was getting a bit over his head financially with such a promise, but he had developed a feeling of empathy toward the co-op following Thanakit's death. Someone else needed to care now that he was gone. By golly, he told himself, he would find a way to get the Ban Khao village fishing cooperative the financial support it needed to stay afloat, even if Ban Khao Resort might sink under the weight of Heron Holdings' overzealous borrowing and investing. He swore to himself that he would keep Ban Khao Resort from dragging down the fishing co-op with it, even if he had to mortgage his own home back in the United States to get money to repair the coop's boats!

*****

When Paul and Sirima arrived at the resort terrace restaurant, waiting for them in addition to Dan and Ben were Police Inspector Sittichai and Chulalongkorn University Professor Songkhram, who had driven out together from Bangkok.

Paul smiled widely and spread out his arms. A Thai *wai* greeting was just too confining for how pleased he felt. "I'm so happy to see you both again before I return to the US. Thank you for accepting my invitation to lunch. I owe both of you so much for your support and trust. Professor, I spoke with my wife, Sarah, by phone yesterday. We are arranging to contribute some money to your business ethics training and research center. Both our daughters are completing college, and we recognize that with one of them on a full tuition scholarship and the other attending an inexpensive local state university, much of our college savings are still in place. We want to use some of those savings to fund a scholarship at the Chulalongkorn Business School in memory of Sentthap."

"I thank you very much for your kind offer," said the professor. "Sentthap was an inspiration to his classmates. We all miss him. A scholarship in his name sends a special message that ethical practices are a worthy set of values for guiding business decisions."

As Paul was discussing funding arrangements with Professor Songkhram, he saw a wry smile cross Inspector Sittichai's face.

"Professor, once you and Paul have your Sentthap scholarship fund set up, please let me know personally," said Sittichai. "I think I can convince some very well-placed Thai bankers to make financial contributions as well. I wager I can even secure funding for a full professorship chair in business ethics in your department."

Paul wasn't exactly sure what Sittichai had in mind until he remembered the three file boxes of Thai financial records and reports that Khun Patthana had arranged to be delivered to his villa for Inspector Sittichai. Though the inspector was reserved about what the files contained, Paul understood that some included compromising information about questionable Heron Holdings' operations in which Thai political and business leaders had likely been involved. Inspector Sittichai had made it clear that he now had material evidence to convict several influential Thai political leaders and government office holders of fraud and abuse, including some of his own superiors in the Royal Thai Police Force. Sittichai had indicated to Paul that he was prepared to make sure they paid heavily with imprisonment, public humiliation, or just plain cash to worthy causes for their abuse of public trust.

As the restaurant staff seated the six of them at a round table in the otherwise empty resort terrace restaurant, their conversations ranged widely. What struck Paul was how warmly and openly his recent Thai acquaintances now shared their thoughts.

Sittichai spoke as he sat down next to Paul. "You are not aware, Paul Ellis, but I was very close to turning in my police badge when you three Americans made your rather dramatic arrival in Thailand. When trouble started following you everywhere as you began to poke around in the shadows of this deceptive Ban Khao Resort paradise, I realized just what a gift you were to me. After so many frustrating years of following and gathering evidence on the illegal business practices of one of Thailand's most powerful business tycoons, you helped me close my case even at your own personal peril! You helped cap my career as an investigator. I owe you a huge debt of gratitude. And all this happened because of a missed flight connection in Hong Kong!"

Paul felt overwhelmed and at a loss for words to respond to Sittichai. Fortunately, Dan and Ben came to his rescue with a change of topics.

Dan spoke first. "Ben and I will follow you back to the US in a few weeks, Paul. We both have a lot of stuff going on here for us in Thailand now. I'm going back only to close out my rental apartment and put into storage what I don't want to ship out here, because I'm coming back to Thailand. My military pension and some savings I've accumulated are enough to live on quite easily here, particularly with Sirima at my side to bargain when we go food shopping in the local Thai markets."

Paul could see a blush in Sirima's cheeks, but she quickly brought it into check. "I am not giving up on my fight for the freedom of Thai women and girls. I'm pleased you are willing to enlist in that struggle as well, Dan. But there will be no easy retirement for you, you old American flyboy!"

"I'm your willing enlistee, Captain Sirima! And I'm good at following orders!" Dan gave her a half salute and a wink.

Paul could see a brightening in both their eyes as Dan put into words what he had been holding back in private until this moment. Sirima turned her head and took a sip of water from her glass, Paul suspected, to hide her embarrassment from all the men around the table gazing at her.

Dan continued in a more serious tone. "Sirima's well on the road to making a difference in the lives of a lot of exploited women and girls in this country. I know I can support her in that, if only to be there for her when she needs a shoulder to lean on. I guess what I mean to say is that our Early Out Club is now defunct since I'm reassigning myself to Thailand under a new commander in chief. It's not that I'm giving up anything back home, since that all has mostly slipped through my hands. It's just that golf and fishing trips are no longer how I want to fill up my retirement days. With Sirima, I've got a new mission. I'm back in the air again because Sirima's brought me down to earth, as crazy as that sounds."

Ben snickered. "You're too damned mushy, Dan! That's what it sounds like. It's been a long time since I've seen such a lovesick puppy as you are right now. I want to think that our Early Out Club is not defunct at all. Instead, it's gone international. Paul will be on the other side of the ocean, but that doesn't mean we're gonna let him forget us here in Thailand. And we are sure not going to forget him for all the trouble he has gotten us into by planning this trip. Besides, I think we'll need him to provide us with field support from back in the US."

Paul's eyebrows went up. "I'll do my best to help you if I can," said Paul. "But remember, any trouble you get into from now on will be of your making, not mine."

"Fair enough," said Ben.

"What worries me," continued Paul, "is that there are still a lot of very bad guys out there that will not be happy to see Dan and Sirima team up to take away their illicit income from exploiting women and girls. I'm sure the bad guys have no problem with the three of you picking up a few starfish that have washed up on the beach and throwing them back into the ocean to give them a second lease on life. After all, the beach is strewn with tens of thousands of such starfish. It's clear to me now that there is an unlimited supply of young Asian girls to exploit as long as poverty prevails in Thailand. Sure, Dan and Sirima can begin to make a difference in the lives of a few. But if they start really increasing the number of trafficked women they rescue, that's gonna face pushback from some rather rough characters who won't like them taking away their sources of income."

Paul could see that Ben was beginning to wind up for a hardball reply.

"That's why you shouldn't be the only ones on the beach pitching starfish back into the ocean," Ben said to Dan and Sirima. "That's why you need me and Paul as well. You need sage voices like ours to protect you! These abused young women and girls whom you rescue need someone to equip them to survive on their own when they are thrown back into life's ocean so they don't get washed up into the hands of human traffickers again. And we can work together at that!"

Paul could see that Ben had picked up on the skeptical look in his eye, and he would not release his control of the conversation. Ben barreled on.

"In the last couple of weeks I've seen how capable and smart are the girls that Mr. Patthana 'used up' in his illicit commercial sex operations but kept on in other jobs around the resort. My computer classes here are filled with these eager young ladies. They're climbing all over me to learn. So let's not look at just rescuing these girls from traffickers but also retraining them so that they have new skills and can survive on their own in that big cruel world out there. Why, until the management throws me out or the banks close down this place, I'm going to continue teaching computer classes to anyone who comes in the resort's business center doors. I'm going to have my students get out the word and recruit their friends, then I'm going to start working with the best and brightest in my classes to become teachers of the others. This thing can snowball, even in a developing country like Thailand and a tropical paradise like Ban Khao!"

"Dreamer!" replied Dan. "I'm sure you can build up your computer classes, Ben. No doubt about that, but you're not a Thai. How are you going to shake the donor trees till some real money starts to fall in your lap so you can purchase equipment and classroom space and pay your instructors?"

Paul caught an excited look on the face of Professor Songkhram and put up his hands to halt the debate between his two buddies so that the Professor could jump in.

"I have been reading about a special type of enterprise that is beginning to catch on in America," began the Professor. I want to assign some of my students to look into it more closely, perhaps even to try their hands at a pilot startup as part of their MBA programs. It is a business model that you Americans call a social enterprise, and its goal is not only to produce a profit for its investors but also to generate benefits for American workers and communities where it operates. Most of these social enterprises in America apparently have focused on construction and operation of affordable housing or setting up community banks to lend to minority entrepreneurs who want to start up and operate small businesses."

The group leaned in. The Professor now looked at Ben. "Mr. Ben Morgan is very correct that it is not enough just to rescue exploited girls from being trafficked for sex or from the debt bondage in which they have been entrapped. You must also equip these girls with skills they can use to earn a living so they are never forced back into that desperate way of surviving. Social enterprises hold promise for mobilizing private capital when government agencies lack the resources and don't have enough money to scale up their own social services. And the shortage of government funds is likely to get worse if Thailand continues to drift into a recession as it is doing right now. That will create an even greater demand for programs that the Thai government is not equipped to run."

Paul felt he needed to introduce a note of caution.

"Look, let's get real. We know the demand is out there in the numbers of young girls who need help. We know the Thai government has neither the money nor the political will to make more than a token response. We know we don't have that kind of money among us that can make up for that. Where does that leave us? With lots of warm and fuzzy ideas but no rock-solid financing for putting them into practice."

"Not so fast!" said Ben. "While Dan and I were showing Sirima around the resort this morning, I noticed how she seemed to be scoping out this place. She dropped a hint at one point that Ban Khao Resort could be repurposed as a great location for her organization to run its rescue and rehabilitation programs for trafficked girls. Let's make that happen. Let's buy Ban Khao Resort and help Sirima's organization run it!"

Ben's declaration brought the table conversation to an immediate halt. A long silence followed.

Paul gazed around the table at his lunch companions. He began to reflect on the range of backgrounds each of them had. None had much in common with the others in personal lives and careers. Yet he recognized that collectively they had a huge reservoir of human talent and experience as well as key connections. Ben sounded like he was coming from way out in right field, but the surreal series of events that had enveloped the three of them since arriving in Thailand made Ben's cavalier declaration almost seem credible.

Still, what were they thinking? At this point in their lives, he, Dan, and Ben had been looking, Paul always assumed, for some idle relaxation swinging a golf club or holding a fishing pole. The compelling plight of so many exploited Asian girls had clearly reached down deeply into their inner beings. Their innocence was gone. A growing sense of commitment was taking its place.

As good as they were, their Thai companions—one university professor, one police inspector, and a women's social justice advocate—could use every bit of support that three privileged American retirees could throw behind them to battle sex trafficking in Thailand. Paul realized now that it was not possible for him to go back to the States with the same view of Thailand that he had when he left as a young foreign service officer some two decades earlier. And clearly, both Dan and Ben were now so committed that they were preparing to leave their American comforts and safety behind and take on one of Asia's most insidious social problems. Who was he, Paul, to declare that his friend Ben was insane in making such a proposal? Crazy as Ben sounded, their whole visit to Thailand bordered on the unbelievable. But the unbelievable had been happening around them almost daily over the last three weeks.

Inspector Sittichai was the first to break the silence. In slow, deliberate statements, he responded to what Ben was advocating.

"Ban Khao Resort and all its assets are now in the hands of a government-appointed receivership formed at the instruction of the Thai Courts," Sittichai pointed out. "Because there is strong evidence to support the charge that some of the funds for building and maintaining Ban Khao Resort were obtained from illicit operations conducted by Heron Holdings, it is most likely that all its assets, including Ban Khao Resort, will be confiscated by the Thai Ministry of Interior. After the value of Ban Khao Resort is determined by external auditors, and if there is no objection or an alternative ruling from the Thai Parliament, Ban Khao Resort, along with other Heron Holdings properties against which there are no claims, will be sold at auction to the highest bidder."

Inspector Sittichai paused as he appeared to contemplate what would next take place. That gave Dan the opportunity to interject. "And just how long will that process play out? When would Ban Khao Resort be up for auction?"

"That is hard for me to tell you, Dan Spencer, because normally these procedures take months, sometimes years, while potential purchasers jockey for favored positions in acquiring government assets. In the case of Ban Khao Resort, however, I do not think it will be very long. The resort will be making very little money while in receivership but will continue to have major operating expenses that the Ministry of Interior must pay from its very limited budget. Ban Khao is not like a drug dealer's confiscated car, boat, or airplane that can be parked somewhere until it is sold at auction. Ban

Khao is an operating business but, at the moment, a money-losing one."

The group paused while waiters took their lunch orders and refilled their water glasses. Paul looked around the empty restaurant. Except for the lack of customers, the resort looked as peaceful and idyllic as it was the day they arrived. It manifested no signs of the turbulent events for which it had been a setting over the last few days.

"The good news," Inspector Sittichai continued, "is that if you are serious about acquiring Ban Khao Resort, most likely there will be very few bidders willing to purchase a money-losing enterprise and certainly an enterprise with a dark history and cloudy future. The resort will probably sell at auction for a fraction of its value. But then, of course, the buyer must immediately take on all of the resort's operating expenses and any debts accumulated while in receivership."

"That's assuming Ban Khao is operated as a resort as it has been until now," said Sirima. "My organization has no interest in running a resort, certainly not a money-losing one. But we can use the facilities to support our programs. We could use some of the resort hotel rooms as dormitories for our program beneficiaries and the restaurant as a cafeteria for their meals. The rest of the hotel and the restaurants could be operated as concessions for a fee paid to the organization once we can draw back vacationers. We could close down the golf links to save money and use the villas for staff and for conducting training classes.

"I doubt that there will be any problem convincing many of the Ban Khao villa owners to exchange their deeds for suspension of their jail time given that they received those property deeds in payment for supporting some of Heron Holdings' illicit operations," added Sittichai. "So that is not likely to be a problem for you. Again, I suspect that I can find a few donors among the records in Patthana's file boxes. Don't forget also that as a nonprofit, you would not have tax liabilities. That will help reduce your operating costs."

Paul saw a wide smile cross Sirima's face. "We might just make it work, Dan!" she said.

"I see some real positive opportunities for your rescue and rehabilitation programs here at Ban Khao," Professor Songkhram suggested to her. "You could also use the hotel and restaurant as training facilities for your program participants so that they could find jobs in Thailand's exploding hospitality industry. To attract vacationers again, you could offer special lodging rates as incentives to come and stay as real-time customers for your student trainees. I'd be happy to task some of my business students to work with you in developing a business plan to raise financing and run your operations."

Ben piled on, "I think there also may be opportunities to obtain training grants or contracts from private businesses for computer classes given the growing demand in Thailand for workers with data processing and digital skills."

"So all we need to do is raise how many millions to buy Ban Khao?" asked Paul.

Again, silence followed until Professor Songkhram broke in. "I estimate that the market value of the entire resort facility, including land, buildings, road network, harbor moorage, power plant, water system, and other infrastructure must be close to 30 million American dollars, but that is a very crude calculation. It may be more. It may be less if Inspector Sittichai is correct on the limited number of buyers likely interested in acquiring a debt-burdened resort, I anticipate that you must raise about $10 to $15 million to outbid the few who might be interested."

Inspector Sittichai nodded in agreement.

Again, silence followed. Paul realized that the professor's estimate even on the low end was a sobering figure.

Unfazed, Ben turned to Sittichai and asked, "How soon do you think, Inspector, that Sirima's organization needs to demonstrate it has that kind of money in its account to qualify as a participant in the bidding?"

"It would be necessary to have the money or formal underwriter commitments within a month, I think," said the inspector.

"Our current organization's cash balance is less than 100,000 in US dollars at the moment," said Sirima. "I guess we have a long way to go and not much time to get there. Right now, I am not sure where I can borrow that kind of money."

"We will make it happen," offered Ben in a voice that was uncharacteristically soft but firm. He was staring directly at Paul.

Paul and the others all looked toward Ben. He sensed that none seemed willing to ask Ben how he planned to make it happen. Paul certainly did not want to deflate the moment by asking. He suspected none of the others did either. He also suspected that they all just wanted to believe that it was possible but, like him, were not at all hopeful it would happen. "Ben, we need to talk," said Paul. "Maybe on the way to the airport. Just you and me."

*****

Lunch concluded, Paul turned to look at Dan and Ben. "I'll miss you guys very much when I get back home and discover that my companions are now half a world away."

His gaze now shifted toward Sirima. "Whatever happens here at Ban Khao, I am so happy that you and Dan have teamed up together. He's had such a cheery look in his eyes these last two weeks, and he's behaved like a human being instead of a cocky ex-pilot since you came into his life. I can thank you especially for that!

"Professor," Paul continued. "My wife and I will contact you after I am back in the US. Regardless of what the future holds for Ban Khao, I promise you that Chulalongkorn will have funds for a business ethics program in memory of Sentthap."

Paul stood now and turned to look at Sittichai. "Inspector," he said, "I have put you through a lot over the last three weeks. You have a difficult job, and we three Americans have not made it any easier for you by stumbling into Thailand the way we did and then getting into so much mischief sniffing around where we shouldn't have. I hope you can forgive us. Our intentions were good, even if our investigative skills were sloppy and downright unorthodox. I think your patience and perseverance in pursuing Patthana and his illicit operations have been rewarded, now that you have ended what we understand was one of your longest-running investigative cases. Thailand will come out the winner for all your efforts at exposing those who have done so much to help themselves at the expense of others."

"Well then, Paul Ellis, I guess I can also think seriously about retiring." The inspector let out an audible sigh. "It is time to turn over Thailand's future to the kind of students that Professor Songkhram and his colleagues are training. Or maybe I'll teach also. I've been offered a position at the Royal National Police Academy. Maybe I can train a new generation of honest police."

"They will shape Thailand's future all right," said Paul. "I fear though that the deaths of Sentthap and Thanakit foretell that the next generation of Thais will still face a real struggle in making Thailand a more equitable society. They'll need all the preparation that you and Professor Songkhram can give them."

*****

An hour later, one of the resort's limos came to a halt at the villa entrance with Ben at the wheel. "I gotta learn to drive on the wrong side of the road sometime," Ben declared as Paul heaved his luggage into the back and climbed in beside Ben. "I figured taking you to the airport through Bangkok traffic would be the acid test."

"Oh, wonderful!" said Paul. "Looks like my departure from Thailand could turn out as dramatic as our arrival. Do I really want to experience this?"

"You don't have much choice, my boy. But look, we've plenty of time before your flight to get lost on the way and still make it to the airport. You're in good hands."

"Ya, sure," said Paul with a tone of resignation in his voice. "Don't I remember you saying those same words on our memorable outing to Pattaya a couple weeks back? Let's not forget how that turned out?"

They pulled out of the resort and onto the main coastal road toward Bangkok and Don Mueang airport north of the city. Paul was thankful that it was midday on a weekday, and beach traffic was light. A long silence followed them down the highway until Paul spoke up.

"Ben, is there something you should tell me? I have an idea about what's on your mind, and it worries me. You've seen how these Asian crime syndicates work, and it's not pretty when they get mad at someone. If you have plans, as I suspect you do, to hack into one of their bank accounts and steal enough money to buy Ban Khao Resort, you better be aware of what might happen to you, as well as to Sirima and Dan if they figure you out."

"They won't," said Ben.

"So that is indeed the plan you have in mind?"

"Something like that. It's still a work in progress at this point. What I do know is that I gotta move fast. Things are still unsettled since Hong Kong administration was turned over to mainland China. The collapse of the Thai *baht* currency and implosion of Asia's securities markets these last few days have added to the confusion. From what I see right now from the online news reporting, money is flying all over the place, much of it fleeing from the region to other parts of the world. It's the best time to tap into some of that money without people noticing. While you're winging your way across the Pacific this evening, that's when I need to make things happen. Tonight!"

"And what exactly do you hope to make happen?" asked Paul.

"Ya see, for some time the CIA has been setting up and funding blind accounts in Swiss banks as conduits for money to pay informants around the world, including much of Asia, where they have even paid well-placed assets, spies that is, to collect information and cause mischief through their connections inside China. I know a lot about those Swiss accounts and how they work from my years with the agency."

"So you're going to break into some of those CIA accounts and borrow some agency money to buy Ban Khao Resort, is that it?"

"Oh, no!" protested Ben. "I would never touch one of my former employer's accounts. That would be unethical. Besides, they have too many safeguards built in and too many ways to trace who is attempting to hack into them. I know, because I set up some of those accounts for the agency's Chinese informants. No. Those accounts are off-limits. My plan is to set up an entirely new blind Swiss bank account and help some Chinese crime syndicate money find its way into it while so much money is searching right now for safe havens away from PRC control."

"So where are you going to find this money to fund the account once you set it up?"

"Don't know yet. But I don't think it's going to be hard. I just need to go phishing."

"Fishing?"

"No, *phishing!* With a P-H not an F!"

"What's that?"

"Well it's a new internet term for an old con artist practice of baiting and manipulating innocent, or not-so-innocent, victims into turning over their money. The practice has been around for centuries. Only recently it's started to make its way onto the Internet. It's mostly an attempt to get gullible folks to share their private bank account information like IDs and passwords so perpetrators can go into those accounts and clear them out. Can't tell you much more than that at this point, Paul, or I'd have to kill ya," Ben said with a sly smile. "Besides, I just don't know yet who and what is out there to bait and phish for right now. Or how I'm gonna work it. But I will."

Ben was silent for a while. When Ben spoke again, Paul sensed his determination.

"What I know now," Ben volunteered, "is that I think I can find a way to stick it to some of those crime syndicate traffickers who have generated so much money from young girls they drew into the sex trade. It will be poetic justice, don't you think, to scam their money and put it into a place like Ban Khao School for Women and Girls, where it can go to work rescuing girls who they have been trafficking and preventing girls and women in the future from being caught up in such exploitation!"

"Yes, Ben, I agree with you there. But remember, the guys you are hoping to hack play rough. Anyone who would attempt to crash a planeload of innocent people, well…" Paul let his voice trail off for a moment, recognizing he was about to get on a plane again. He wanted to keep such thoughts far from his mind. "Promise you won't do anything that will get you, Dan, or Sirima into danger!"

"You have my word, Paul."

Paul did not feel relieved.

*****

After Ben dropped him off at Don Mueang airport, Paul headed directly to the United Airlines check-in counter. As he did, he passed the airport's flight schedule board that listed all departing flights, their destinations, and boarding times. He noticed that all the Air Siam flights were listed as "Canceled." He suspected that most people at the airport were unaware of what was behind the grounding of all of Air Siam's planes.

An hour later, as he strapped himself into his seat and prepared for takeoff, Paul felt a conflicting sense of remorse and relief come over him. If not for Sarah and the girls, he would have happily joined Dan and Ben in their partnership with Sirima to help Thailand's most needy and vulnerable. Relieved, Paul thought how fortunate it was that his family did not live where such human tragedies like sex trafficking still exist. As the plane lifted off and headed out over the Bay of Siam, Paul felt the exhausting stress of the last three weeks in Thailand catch up with him. He slipped quickly into a deep sleep that would last him nearly the entire flight across the Pacific.

EPILOGUE

Three years later

Paul looked out over the throng of Thai faces as he, Sarah, and their two girls exited Bangkok's Don Mueang airport customs area. The sight brought back to him memories of the hordes of excited family members, anxious friends, and aggressive tourist touts who were always present no matter the time of day to descend upon arriving passengers from the international flights arriving in Bangkok.

After a few minutes of scanning the crowd, he heard a screech from his girls. "Saint Benardo!" yelled the oldest. "Over there by the taxi stand! See him?"

Paul and Sarah looked, and sure enough, floating above the crowd in front of them was a poster sign with the image of the head of a floppy-eared Saint Bernard dog. Photoshopped onto it was a picture of Ben's face. Paul smiled as he followed the handle of the poster down to see the face of the real Ben beaming back at him. Beside Ben, he saw three attractive young Thai girls beautifully dressed and each holding an orchid lei. Paul's four family members and the four members of their greeting party swam toward each other through the sea of people until they met. Immediately the young Thai girls flung the leis over the heads of Sarah and the girls. Then with heads bowed down to meet their hands pressed together and pointed toward their chins in the Thai *wai* greeting, they exclaimed together, "Sawadee! Welcome!"

He saw Sarah and his daughters all raise their hands to their lips, then wipe away tears of joy from their eyes before each took the hands of one of the Thai girls between theirs and, in their best practiced Thai, replied, "*Sawadee! Kop khun ka.* Greetings! Thank you!"

Then they headed with their luggage toward the nearby VIP zone and the shuttle van with Ban Khao Training Center painted on its side. With the six ladies in the back, Ben at the wheel, and Paul beside him in the front, they headed out of the airport toward Ban Khao. In the back of the shuttle, the Thai girls carried on a conversation in amazingly good English with their three American guests as they asked non-stop questions about America and what it was like for girls to grow up there. Paul listened for a while as each of the Thai girls then shared her story, her dreams, and her plans.

"We are all Ban Khao Training Center participants," one of them said. "We are completing our programs as tour guides and hope to get our official certifications so we can start working. There are sixty students in our class who are graduating this year. Our center director, Khun Sirima, selected us as greeters for you special American guests because we received the highest marks in our English classes."

Once out on the coast highway, Ben glanced at Paul and spoke over the din of nonstop chatter in the rear of the shuttle.

"So you're finally back with us, Paul. It took three years to get you to return. Dan, Sirima, and I had to appeal to your ego to make it happen. So welcome, Mr. Distinguished Commencement Speaker, to the first ever Ban Khao Training Center graduation for the class of 2000! You'd better give a good rousing speech for all these young people going out into the real world with real skills to earn an honest living! We've built you up as someone important."

"I'll give it my best, Ben. I've never had such an honor before. I don't think there's a more worthy group of graduates than the ones you've been training. I'm just amazed by the reports of progress the three of you have made in getting the Ban Khao Training Center up and running in these last three years. In fact, as much as anything, I came to see for myself if it's all true. You know I've always suspected your hyperbole and your tendency to embellish the facts."

"Oh, it's all true, Paul, and then some. As our US-based training center board member, you've read the annual reports and conference-called into our board meetings, so you know a lot already. But I've only shared a part of what's been going on in my messages and phone calls with you since you left Thailand three years ago. Of course, Sirima and Dan, and yes, the inspector and professor deserve most of the credit for what you're going to see. All I did was shake some Asian money trees. I couldn't exactly put down in messages to you how I did that stuff, if ya know what I mean."

"I can only imagine, Ben. I want to hear about that in detail now that I'm here. I'm overwhelmed that you found the cash to buy Ban Khao and fund its operations. You've kept me awake at night wondering from whom out there you, let's say, acquired the money."

"I promise to give you a full accounting, Paul. Perhaps we'll go for a walk and talk on the beach out of earshot of everyone, and I mean everyone."

Paul looked over at Ben and was amazed at how he had learned to navigate Thai traffic with such ease. What other maneuverings Ben had been involved in, he could only wonder.

"Above all, I want you to assure me that you're keeping yourself and everyone else out of danger, Ben. You and I both know that there are some very nasty characters out there that wouldn't hesitate to do you harm if they figured out that you had scammed them for their money."

Ben took a few minutes to answer, and Paul wondered if he'd been a bit too harsh too soon. He recognized that his own role over the last three years from back in the United States had been limited to supporting Ban Khao Training Center as its US board member, doing little more than helping find some American funding sources and providing some of his own money to fund scholarships for Ban Khao program participants and Chulalongkorn University business students.

When Ben finally responded, his tone was more serious. "I owe you the full story, Paul, and you'll get it. Then you can judge. Now, let me give you a heads-up on some of the changes you're about to experience at Ban Khao."

"I'm more than ready."

"First, what's familiar. You, Sarah, and the girls are staying in the same villa where we three guys stayed three years ago. It hasn't changed at all except the staff now are hospitality trainees, as they're called in the business. Dan and Sirima are housed in the center director's villa next to yours. I'm just down the road from all of you at the chief financial officer's home. Two of the other villas have been assigned to our full-time center program director and center administrator and their families. They're both Thais."

"And all those other villas scattered around the Ban Khao hillsides?" asked Paul.

"Some of those villas are being used as short-term accommodations for special guests and consultants who the center hosts from time to time. Like right now, we have a marine park specialist who's working with the center and the Ban Khao fishing village to stabilize the Ban Khao River estuary as a breeding ground to restore the shrimp population. He's a Filipino, the same as his two assistants. They're training some of the fishermen to scuba dive and become certified as marine park wardens and underwater tour guides. Marine eco-tourism is a big draw here in Thailand and attracts lots of people, so it's gonna be a moneymaker for the center, what with all the facilities at the former resort's marina. We've also got a great group of young boys we're training for that alongside some of the seasoned fishermen from the village.

"But you'll need to talk to our marine biology consultant to learn more about that. Diving in marine parks is not my thing. You won't get me into anything deeper than a tall cold glass of beer!"

"I saw mention of the Ban Khao marine park program in the center's last annual report," said Paul. "I was somewhat surprised because I expected the focus to be solely on rescuing young girls."

"You've got a bit of learning ahead of you, Paul, as I did as well in these last few years. The Asian sex trade, particularly here in Thailand, is not just made up of young women and girls, I'm sad to report. Enough said about that right now. I gotta fill you in on the other changes at the resort, I mean, center."

Paul gazed out the shuttle window at the rolling rice fields glistening in the morning sun. Their emerald-green tones were every bit as bold as the shimmering green color in a Thai woman's silk sarong. He wondered if perhaps the colors of Thai clothing were an unconscious effort to mimic the colors of nature around them. "Update me on the golf course, Ben," he finally said.

"Sure. At the moment, Dan and Sirima have decided to keep intact eighteen of the thirty-six holes of the golf course. But that may change. Those two are the silliest of lovebirds. I can't believe it. But when it came to what to do with the golf course, they've been on opposite sides of some heated debates. Sirima was all for ripping up all the fairways and tees, restoring the whole thing to rice paddies that we learned from the villagers were originally their lands sold to pay off debts. Philosophically, I guess, Sirima is very much opposed to catering to the idle rich in Thailand, and they still exist, mind you. Many wealthy Thais rode out the financial storms that hit the region after you left to go back to the US. Some even came out ahead of the game, richer than they were before. The very rich seem to come out okay everywhere.

"Anyway, Dan argues that some of those rich folks are also politically powerful, and Ban Khao should massage them a bit to gain their support and squeeze some money from them to pay a share of the center's operating costs. Sirima says she'll go along with what Dan proposes for the moment. His strategy is to attract them to Ban Khao for weekends of golfing or business conference cum golf visits and then expose them to a new—what the heck does the Chulalongkorn University professor call it...a new pair a' dimes here at Ban Khao."

"Paradigm," corrected Paul, though he knew Ben was joking. "I can imagine their golf course debate has been lively. As for myself, I'm concerned that you all are trying to take on too much too fast. Sounds like cutting the golf course in half is a good compromise."

"Dan or Sirima can tell you more about that. Me, I don't have a dog in that fight, so I stay out of it. Anyway, not many golfers so far, but what is working is the half of the golf course converted back into irrigated rice and vegetable fields. Sirima and the professor talked with one of his college classmates who is now an instructor at another Thai university, Thammasat, which is kinda like Thailand's agriculture college. The Thammasat professor came up with some research and training grant money to support a few aggie graduate students in a project to introduce modern farming techniques that are environmentally friendly. You know, farming with no chemical fertilizers and bug killers or stuff like that. I hope you get a chance to meet some of those graduate students. They're real smart kids. They have the place kinda torn up now digging irrigation canals, but they're putting a lot of the villagers to work again, and everyone's pretty happy, it seems."

Paul thought back over the last few years for a moment. He had been correct that the former resort's loan to the fishing village was simply lost in the whole process of selling off Heron Holdings assets at auction. The loan was just one more of its accounts receivable that the new owner, now the training center, would be responsible for collecting. And the training center had no intention of collecting those funds anyway, as the center's board of directors had decided at its first official meeting.

"Tell me, Ben, any news on how the Ban Khao Village fishermen's co-op is doing?"

"Not anything new or unusual that I am aware of," said Ben. "Seems to be doing okay with their seafood sales. I'm sure you'll want to talk more to Sirima about that when you get a chance."

It seemed to Paul that he and Ben were only beginning to get started on all the recent news from Ban Khao when they arrived at the center's gate and road heading down to what had been the resort's facilities. Paul was flooded with memories and emotions from their three-week stay three years earlier. He wondered if he could ever appreciate the full drama and tragedy in the lives of those wrapped up in the history of Ban Khao Resort, from the owner to all those entrapped in sex trafficking. He began to doubt that he was capable of speaking to Ban Khao's first graduation class without being overwhelmed by the knowledge of what each of the graduates had already gone through in their lives and the emotional scars they carried from being trafficked. He understood that however much Ban Khao Training Center was able to equip them for better lives, those scars would remain.

*****

Sirima and Dan were waiting at the training center's open-air restaurant when Paul and his family, refreshed and recovered a bit from their long trans-Pacific flight, arrived for an early dinner the evening of their arrival in Thailand. Formal Thai greetings followed by warm American hugs were shared all around as they prepared to sit down to eat.

Almost immediately, Paul noticed what he would not expect the rest of his family to detect. The faces of both Dan and Sirima exhibited visible signs of exhaustion and strain and even a bit of aging since he had said goodbye to them three years earlier. Damn, he thought to himself, there had been some costs to getting the Ban Khao Training Center off the ground that he had not anticipated. Still, outwardly at least, neither Dan nor Sirima showed any signs of abated energy or enthusiasm.

Dinner conversation was light and jovial with Dan, Sirima, and Ben indicating that it should be an early night for the Paul Ellis family so that they could catch up on their sleep and adjust to the time zone change. While Sarah and the girls showed no sign of waning enthusiasm, Paul recognized that they would all hit an exhaustion wall very soon.

After dinner, Dan and Sirima suggested they stroll back up the road from the restaurant to their villas. With Ben, Sarah, and his daughters leading the parade, Paul was able to follow along behind and engage both Dan and Sirima in a more personal discussion.

Paul did not pull his punches. "You both look exhausted! If I had any idea what I sense Ban Khao must be costing you physically and emotionally, I probably would have told Sarah and the girls I needed to get back out here to help much earlier than now. I feel awful. I feel I've let you down."

Sirima looked at Paul and, uncharacteristically for a Thai woman, took his arm in hers at the same time she took Dan's walking on her other side. They walked on a few moments in silence, until Sirima spoke.

"You may not remember, Paul Ellis, about our farewell lunch before you left us three years ago when you talked about picking up the starfish that had washed up on the beach and throwing them back into the ocean to give them a new chance to survive. Even if one or two survived, you argued, we would have made a worthy effort."

"Of course, I remember," replied Paul. "I still worry that the numbers of starfish on the beach continue to multiply and you don't. It's a task far beyond anyone's capacities."

"There's even more to it than that, Paul," said Sirima. "Many of those starfish on the beach are accompanied by little starfish. By the time we can rescue and offer a safe haven to trafficked girls, they often come to us pregnant or with one or more children. When we began our rescue programs here at Ban Khao, right off we had to provide for their children as well. That meant to offer the girls training, we needed to provide day care and kindergarten facilities and recreation programs for their children. That led to involving the government health and education services and regulators.

"We wanted to involve our students in the care of their children, so we set up a childcare cooperative. On a rotating basis our student mothers take care of each other's kids while the rest work in one of the center's job training programs. While they spend a half day performing their childcare duties, they also receive training from government hygienists, nutritionists, and early childhood development specialists to improve the chances their children will get a good start in school. Our center's childcare programs are great training opportunities as well. Some of the girls even want to go on and get formal training as nurses and teachers."

Dan interjected, "Starting up the childcare program for these young mothers rescued from trafficking has taken Sirima and her staff a huge amount of time and has greatly limited the number of trafficked girls and young mothers we can reach. Yes, we are a bit exhausted. Still, I firmly believe Sirima has a workable plan for rescuing and rehabilitating trafficked girls. But we don't yet see how to scale up our operations to reach so many more in need."

"We need to find ways to set up similar programs back in the villages from which girls are attracted into the sex trade," added Sirima. "We need to start running prevention as well as rescue programs if we are to make a difference."

Paul was silent, but he recognized that what he was hearing from Dan and Sirima would most likely keep him up all night, even recognizing how exhausted he was from their long flight from the States. "Sirima, you and Dan have what appears to me to be a technically sound and financially viable rescue and rehab program. I'm sure it can prove itself self-sustaining under the right set of conditions. Please recognize that it still needs time to mature. I worry you want to move too fast."

They had reached the villa where Paul and his family were staying. Ben had already said good night to Sarah and the girls and was waiting outside, as Paul, Dan, and Sirima approached.

"You're going to hate me forever, Paul, when I tell you what Sarah and your daughters shared with me," said Ben. He took a deep breath, looking at Sirima and Dan before turning again to Paul. "They told me they are so happy already with what they've heard about Ban Khao and seen in the faces of the students they've met that they don't want to go back to the US anytime soon. I told them there were plenty of opportunities for them to volunteer as English teachers and trainers. They want to work with Sirima wherever she can use them. They think they can really help make a difference."

Paul was not surprised but feigned annoyance at Ben's pronouncement. "Thanks, Ben, you are a true friend! You knew this was going to happen, didn't you? You maybe even planned it, you scoundrel! Now in the morning I'm going to have to talk some sense into them. It won't be the first time I've had to save them from some of the crazy schemes you planted in their heads when they were younger."

"May I remind you, my good friend," replied Ben in what Paul recognized as his humorous and blustery way, "that you are no longer the master of a household with a wife and two children! You all are now a family of four adults. Both your daughters are college grads now, and they have dreams and plans of their own. Not even I have much influence over them now," Ben added with a chuckle. "You certainly don't have the control you think you have. It's just that you're not ready yet to recognize it. Go ahead, work on them in the morning, but I will put down some good beer money that there will be fewer than four of you flying back to the US next week, or at least flying back to stay. Maybe, with a little more time, Dan, Sirima, and I can even hook Sarah. You may end up flying home alone. Or maybe staying on longer yourself. What do you think of that?"

"I'm thinking I need some sleep right now, Ben. If I can sleep at all. The three of you have a real Asian tiger by the tail here in Ban Khao. I grant you that under the best of conditions, you need all the help you can get. It's just that…"

Paul saw that he had reached the end of his capacity to think or reason for the night. He sensed his companions recognized that as well because it was Dan who came to his rescue.

"Ben, you're beating up on Paul when he's too exhausted to push back," said Dan. "You two will have ample time over the next few days to get into those verbal fistfights you used to have together. Just remember, it's real people we are trying to help here.

"Paul, before you go in, you should know that Sirima has arranged for some of the center's students to take Sarah and the girls on a tour of the Ban Khao Center and Village in the morning. While they're doing that, the four of us should meet and look over some of the center's financials. After that you better sit down with Sirima and go over arrangements for the graduation ceremony and reception. That's only two days away. So for now, good night. Get some rest. You'll need it."

Sirima helped conclude the conversation. "We want to make a big show of the graduation of our first class of students this week, Paul. We are so happy you agreed to be part of it. Our other graduation ceremony guests will include some very influential political and business leaders and maybe even a member of the Royal Thai family," she beamed. "We need to show all of them that what we are doing is worthy of support to help us grow. And we have some wonderful success stories to share. Like Jai, a young girl from the fishing village next to us. She has been one of our most promising and dedicated students. You will meet her also tomorrow because she is our graduating class valedictorian."

"Sounds perfect," said Paul. And as if by some unspoken signal, the four came together in a group hug before departing. Maybe he could fall asleep after all; he thought. And yes, he confessed silently to himself, he was aware of the temptations he was putting out there to his two daughters by bringing them along on his return visit to Thailand. Still, he felt compelled to share the excitement of the Ban Khao Training Center and the dreams of its students regardless of what impact it might have on his family.

*****

Jai could not contain her excitement at the news when she heard it. A member of the Royal Thai family, one of the princesses, was coming to Ban Khao to attend the center's graduation ceremony. This was very good news, she learned, because it meant that the royal family knew about the work that the Ban Khao Training Center was doing and was happy to recognize it by making an official public visit.

Best of all, thought Jai, the princess and her entourage would be occupying the Ban Khao hotel's royal suite, where she had worked for so many years hoping that one day a visit from the royal family would occur. Jai also felt more confident than ever that she could handle the royal visit. In the last three years, the Ban Khao Center directors and staff had discovered the work skills and dedication she brought to the hotel operations. They first promoted her from cleaning staff to floor supervisor and then gave her opportunities to take some hotel management classes and supervise some of the trainees. She began to think she could amount to something.

She was also happy that her young son was able to attend the small primary school that the center convinced the government to open in Ban Khao village both for children of the village families as well as for the children of some of the young mothers participating in the Ban Khao Center's training programs. She happily put in her time as a teacher's aide on the rotation days she was assigned to assist in her son's primary school. She was learning so much on how to raise and prepare her young son for the schooling she never had a chance to complete. In fact, soon she would graduate with her own primary school certificate, perhaps right alongside her son thanks to the Ban Khao Center's accelerated learning program for her and its other participants who had not had the opportunity to complete their basic education.

Jai's one regret was that her father and brother would not see how she performed her new duties and was now able to support her young son on her own.

First, she lost her brother. Shortly after the death of his childhood friend Thanakit, the son of the Ban Khao Resort owner, her brother, Tongsuk, had gone out to sea one evening with the other boats as was normal. But he did not return with them the next morning or the next. She had watched her father sitting at the ocean's edge listening day after day for the sound of her brother's boat that he told her was sure to return.

But as days turned into weeks, her father began to waste away until one day, when she returned to the village after work and classes at the center, she was met by a group of the fishermen at the edge of the road. She could see on their faces what she did not need them to tell her. Her father was gone.

All that remained of her family now was Jai and her son. She would have felt helpless had it not been for the training center. She knew she was not alone. She was part of a new and bigger family, each member with her own stories of challenges like hers. They all had a chance to plan and work for their futures, not just to survive, but to grow.

Now Jai was about to realize a dream she had held close to her heart for so long. The dream of serving a member of the Royal Thai family. Realizing her dream made her feel she could imagine even bigger things for herself and could achieve those as well.

*****

"Awesome talk you gave at the graduation ceremony, Paul," said Ben. They were strolling together just the two of them along the Ban Khao beach, each holding a bottle of Singha beer. They could hear in the distance the commingled voices of the ceremony guests and center graduates on the restaurant terrace above them. They were alone on the beach and for the first time felt relaxed and more at peace.

"Thanks, Ben" said Paul. "They were just words, you know. What counts is the effort you all have put into this, particularly your center participants."

"By the way," Ben continued, "I asked the center's business office to reschedule your return flight reservations, you and Sarah early next week and your daughters open ended at the moment. I guess that means I've won myself some beer money."

"Gladly paid," said Paul. "Add it to my Board Member expense account. I'm sure you can find some creative way of vouchering it, right?"

"Can't do that, Paul," said Ben in an officious tone that was half scolding and half in jest. "We have some very high ethical standards here at Ban Khao Training Center. If we are to avoid negative audits, we need to account for every US dollar and every Thai *baht* we bring in and we spend."

"Well, fine. It's on me then," said Paul. "Which brings us to the subject we agreed to discuss when we were alone together. What sort of financial alchemy did you perform to get your hands on the money to buy and operate Ban Khao Resort? Can we talk about that now?"

Ben looked out over the former resort's harbor and beyond it toward Ban Khao Bay. "Well, first," he began, "the Thai government's court-appointed receivers assessed the market value of all the Ban Khao Resort's assets and came up with a number to be about what the professor had estimated for us, 20 million or so in US dollars. Then the resort's creditors started piling on, and when all their claims were totaled up, it appeared that there was in excess of $50 million in liabilities against those assets. Everyone from builders to the suppliers of those cute little drink umbrellas had claims they wanted settled once the resort was sold. The Thai courts did not want to bother with dividing up the assets to auction individually, a limo here or a villa there. That didn't make any sense. So as I wrote you when you were back in the States, the whole resort came up for auction in one package a couple of months after you left for home."

"Yes," Paul said. "And you told me you purchased it not for pennies on the dollar, but for pennies! How in the world did you manage that?"

"First, there weren't many bidders because whoever acquired it would also acquire those debts. In fact, there was only one bidder. Us. That was Sirima's trafficked-women's rescue organization. We got the whole damned property by paying only some legal bills and the auction fees. Maybe a couple hundred thousand, max. Sirima's organization was able to cover that without a problem. All legit! All witnessed and recorded. Her organization became the sole owner of Ban Khao without any protest."

"Along with all those outstanding debts as well, correct?" said Paul.

"Yes, all those debts as well," replied Ben. "But here's where the poetic justice of it all kicks in. Much of that debt was not owed to legitimate creditors or investors. It was in-kind gifts, shall we say, that Patthana granted to the politicians or military types whom he needed to cultivate. In exchange, Heron Holdings granted them multi-year leases to villa properties or shares in the resort corporation. However, for them to cash in on those credits would be to acknowledge the bribes they had received in exchange for construction contracts, real estate deals, and stuff that Heron Holdings needed to do business. Some did come forward, stupid as they were, and for some reason known only to Inspector Sittichai, information about the favors they showered on Heron Holdings began to appear in the Thai press followed by corruption charges against them shortly after that. When all this became known publicly, the rest of the creditors ran for the hills and disclaimed any and all debts owed them by Heron Holdings."

Paul looked disbelieving at Ben. "There had to be some legitimate creditors in all that. Did they get screwed too?"

"Absolutely not," said Ben. "All the resort staff got their full salaries and all the suppliers, including the guys that made those little drink umbrellas and stuff, were paid in full. We made sure of it. We wanted no disgruntled creditors if we were to build support for the center's programs. Altogether, legitimate debts totaled, maybe, to one million bucks. I can't remember the figures exactly now."

"Soooo?" said Paul. "Where did that money come from? Also, what about the money that's keeping the Ban Khao Training Center operating and paying for all the renovations that Dan and Sirima are making to convert the resort into a training center?"

"From a Swiss endowment fund bank account," said Ben.

"An endowment?" asked Paul. He looked straight at Ben, who had a mischievous smirk on his face. "Or is that a question I shouldn't be asking you?"

"No," said Ben. "It's a perfectly legitimate question. I can write it down for you." Ben picked up a small stick that had washed up on the shore, squatted down, and wrote three Chinese characters in the sand.

Ben stood up. "There! That's the name of the benefactor who donated $100 million to the training center's endowment fund. Dividend and interest earnings from the account last year generated enough income to cover almost 90 percent of the center's operating costs and most likely will continue to do so into the indefinite future, or certainly until the training center can begin to generate more revenue from some of its hotel and concession operations."

Paul looked down at Ben's Chinese scribbles in the hard sand. He could not make any more sense of them than he could of Ben's explanation so far about how $100 million fell into the training center's pockets.

"That's fine," said Paul. "Now, can you tell me where your benefactor found $100 million to bestow upon Sirima's organization?"

"That really is the fun part of the story, Paul. I told you the CIA has set up Swiss bank accounts to channel funds to a number of its overseas field agents and assets, as the CIA calls its informants. I was involved in overseeing some of the Swiss accounts that funded those Asian assets while I worked for the agency. So I knew how to set up an account in the name of Ban Khao's benefactor.

"Getting $100 million into that account was also easy. Remember how money was fleeing Hong Kong after British administration ended three years ago? Remember the meltdown of the Thai *baht* along with the Indonesian, Malaysian, Philippines, and Singaporean currencies that started with the Asian financial crisis just before you left us? It was a wonderfully turbulent time to stick it to the Asian crime syndicates that were making their money off human trafficking and the sex trade.

"As the Chinese syndicates all over Asia began to move their money into safe havens, including Swiss banks, it was a simple matter to insert into their transfer orders the destination Swiss bank account that I set up for Ban Khao's benefactor. Not directly, of course, but as part of multiple payments to and from the bank accounts they were using. In less than two days, our benefactor's account was overflowing. I turned off the spigot within forty-eight hours when the account passed 100 million US dollars. Quick enough so that no one really had time to notice. Then as an added precaution, I moved that money into the Ban Khao Training Center's endowment fund account and closed the mystery donor's bank account, all behind the curtain of Swiss financial confidentiality.

"I had time to do one more thing to distract everyone from what I was up to. When I hacked the crime syndicate's bank records, I also moved around some account numbers, this time to give the appearance that one syndicate was milking the funds from another. I left a trail of account numbers that any fool could follow to banks where, say, the drug syndicates in Malaysia or the gambling syndicates in Macao stashed their cash. I kinda started a little trade war between some of the syndicates. They got so absorbed in settling scores with those they believed had bilked them out of their money they never noticed the missing $100 million.

"If you'd been reading the Asian press, you would have picked up on some of the international stories about the dustups between the crime syndicates that came out of that. Remember we were worried that Thailand would become a destination for Hong Kong syndicate trafficking money and the base for their future trafficking operations. Fortunately, when the value of the Thai baht collapsed, the syndicates had to scramble to find somewhere else to stash money. Thanks to you, Dan, and me, that safe haven won't be in Thailand!"

"So," said Paul, "Ban Khao has its steady flow of investment income from the assets donated by its Chinese benefactor, but the cash flows are modest enough by Swiss standards that they don't raise the suspicions of international financial regulators."

"Yes. The Center now enjoys the financial security that Sirima needs to operate and expand her rescue and rehab programs," Ben added with a clear note of pride in his voice.

"And the Chinese characters in the sand?" Paul finally asked.

"Well, to satisfy the Swiss banking authorities, I had to set up an account using English letters for the Chinese characters that spell the name of our benefactor. They needed to investigate our benefactor to determine if the money came from somewhere legitimate. That required a bit of creativity. I made a quick trip to Hong Kong, and as our mysterious and reclusive benefactor's personal representative, I purchased the services of a local lawyer, essentially to create a legitimate life for him, stuff like purchasing an inconspicuous condo unit and setting up a bank account. I described our benefactor as a trade representative for children's toy manufacturers in China. Stuff like that. Our benefactor became just one more obscure name on a list of tens of thousands of trade representatives registered in Hong Kong."

"And the Chinese characters?" said Paul.

"They spell the name of Ban Khao's very generous but reclusive Chinese benefactor, which you must never divulge, Paul!" Ben looked down at the three characters he had drawn in the sand and pointed. "It's time you learn a bit of Chinese, my man. Here's your first lesson. He began at the bottom and worked up. "The first character is the Chinese word for 'Foo.' Say it!"

"Foo," responded Paul.

"The second character is for 'Ling.' Say it!"

"Ling," said Paul.

"The third character is for the Chinese sound 'Yu.'"

"Yu," said Paul, this time without being told.

"Now put them together."

"Foo Ling Yu," Paul said.

"Yes, Paul! Very good! Your Chinese pronunciation is very good."

"Ya' know, Paul." Ben looked at him with a slight grin. "There are very few benefactors in the world today as generous as Foo Ling Yu. Now let's head back up and join the party!"

Paul took a few steps before it fully hit him what Ben had done. "You clever bastard!" he said and broad smiles broke out on both of their faces.

As they walked back up toward the sound of the training center graduation party, behind them the gentle ocean waves lapped up onto the beach and washed away the Chinese characters that Ben had drawn in the sand.